SI FANTASY WORLD AND NOW ALL THE MEN WANT ME

VOLUME 1

JACLYN OSBORN

Sent To a Fantasy World and Now All the Men Want Me

Published by Jaclyn Osborn
Cover Illustration by Artly Inspired
Cover Typography by Sleepy Fox Studio
Edited by One Love Editing

Table of Contents

Note to Reader

First of all, thank you so much for grabbing a copy of this story! This book was a joy to write, and I hope that love shines through the pages.

No relationship is the same. Love comes in all forms. *Sent To a Fantasy World and Now All the Men Want Me* is a "why choose" romance; meaning, Evan, the main character, will have multiple men over the course of the series who will all love him fiercely. His men will form close bonds with each other but won't necessarily be together romantically. All will be devoted to Evan.

This isn't cheating.

They are aware Evan is with the others and are accepting of it. All will be happy, I promise.

I hope you enjoy this low-angst, fun, and swoon-filled romance featuring an adorable bookworm who's transported to another world and finds the kind of happiness he's only ever dreamed of.

Happy reading,
Jaclyn

Chapter One
Don't Trust Strangers… Even If He's Hot

"Have you ever had two dicks in you at once?"

I nearly choked on my ramen. "What?"

Jonah stood beside my chair, sleeves pushed to his elbows and blond hair casually messy. His expression was what got me. He was way too serious. "Two dicks. At the same time."

"I…" I wiped at my mouth. "I just want to eat my lunch, Jonah." And preferably not wear it as well.

"Hang on." He scrolled through his phone before holding it out to me. "Check them out."

I took the phone and saw a photo of two shirtless guys on a boat, arms around each other. Both were hot as hell, with bulging pecs, tanned skin, and sporting washboard abs. "Okay?"

"They're a married couple," Jonah said. "And they're looking for a fun time with a third. They DM'd me a few days ago and asked to meet up. I'm totally down for it, but I've never had a threesome with two dudes before. Have you?"

"No. Can't say that I have." More than one guy would have to actually be interested in me for that to happen. "But I downloaded an awesome mod for Sims 4 the other day that lets your Sim have wild sex. Like super graphic, nothing blurred. Orgies too."

"No shit?"

"Yep. My Sim also opened his own strip club and fucked a guy in the bathroom."

Jonah blinked at me. "You can have a strip club in Sims? How did I not know this?"

I shoveled more noodles into my mouth. "Guess you're not one of the chosen ones."

He grinned before putting his hands together and bowing his head. "Teach me your ways, oh great master."

"I accept offerings of books, muffins, and iced coffee. Only then will I reveal the answers you seek."

Jonah stole an egg roll from my takeout box and bit into it. "My presence should be payment enough."

I eyed the egg roll. "That's my last one, you jerk."

"Oh? Your last one?" Jonah slowly waved it around before taking another bite. "So good."

"I hate you."

"I think I'm gonna do it with those guys. I'll let you know how it goes." He winked before shoving the rest of the egg roll into his mouth and leaving the breakroom.

Jonah was a college student working part-time with me at the café. I'd first met him about six months ago when he'd rushed in from the street to get out of the heavy rain. Typical meet-cute for a romance, right? Soaking wet hottie and the coffee-addicted bookworm who came to his rescue. But not really. After setting his backpack at a table and asking for a job application, he had then ordered a hot chocolate to warm up. One flash of his pretty smile and I'd promptly spilled said hot drink all over him.

We laughed about it now, but it was still mortifying. We weren't exactly besties, but I enjoyed working with him. He was the typical popular guy, and I was the nerdy type who mostly kept to myself.

After finishing my lunch, I cleaned up before returning to the front counter and checking the dessert in the glass case. The café served a small variety of sandwiches and salads but was known for its coffee and pastries. My favorite was the banana nut muffin. Not to brag, but I made some amazing ones.

I dreamed of opening my own café someday. A safe place for people to relax with a delicious coffee and sweet treat while escaping into the pages of a book. A dream was probably all it would ever be.

The front door swung open as two girls walked inside. A spring breeze blew in behind them, rustling the napkins on the counter. One ordered a nonfat vanilla latte, and the other wanted an iced mocha with oat milk.

"Are you going to the festival tonight?" Vanilla asked as they waited.

"Marcus wants to go," Oat Milk responded. "But I don't know yet. Isn't it more for kids?"

Fully aware I was eavesdropping but not caring, I listened as I worked on their drinks. I vaguely recalled hearing something about a spring festival downtown. It had started earlier that day and would go into the night.

"There will be rides, food, and all that good stuff." Vanilla whipped out her phone, and her fingers moved at lightning speed as she texted. "For kids or not, I don't care. I want a funnel cake."

Funnel cake did give a huge incentive to go. But then I thought about the crowds of people and noise and promptly changed my mind. Besides, I had a hot date that night with a sword-wielding ex-soldier turned assassin named Ayden. Canceling on him was out of the question.

"Is Ayden a book character?" Jonah asked later that afternoon after I told him about my Saturday night plans. He was wiping down tables while I restocked the desserts.

"Maybe."

He laughed. "I think it's cute how you're such a book-obsessed shut-in, but don't you want to get out sometimes and live a little?"

"Reading *is* living," I said. "Ayden and I are about to enter the demon lord's kingdom together. And the other day, we sailed with pirates before overthrowing the captain and commandeering the ship. Tell me where you can find an adventure like that in the real world."

"You got me there. But your precious Ayden can't touch you like a real man can. He's just ink on a page."

"I already bought all my snacks for a whole night on the couch with my Kindle."

He picked up a straw wrapper and a few napkins customers had left on a table and tossed it in the trash. "You can eat them after finding a guy to suck your dick."

"You say that like I have men lined up around the block."

"Well, maybe you *would* have a bunch of dudes if you got out of the house long enough to meet them."

"Why would I leave my house? Everything I love is there."

"Well, if your plans fall through with your precious Ayden"—Jonah rolled his eyes—"let me know. I can give you my buddy's number. He's not a demon-fighting assassin with sexy rippling abs, but you may have some fun with him anyway." The last was added with a wink.

"Yeah. I'll think about it," I said, knowing damn well I wouldn't.

Jonah smiled, but his eyes told me he knew I was full of shit. It never stopped him from trying though.

Truth was, I wanted a connection with someone real. Fear held me back. I had very little dating experience, and the few guys I *had* dated turned out to be total dicks. I was afraid to put myself out there again. I preferred to stay in my own bubble with nothing but books to keep me company, escaping into other worlds instead of living in the one I was in.

It was easier that way.

As five o'clock rolled around and the baristas working the evening shift clocked in, I wished Jonah luck on his two-dick special for later that night and left. I only lived five minutes from the café, so when the weather was nice, I walked to and from work.

As I walked past a dogwood tree in full bloom, covered in pink flowers, I breathed in a lungful of air… and immediately had a sneezing fit.

I liked spring. But spring didn't like me.

Once home, I opened the windows in my cramped little apartment to let in fresh air while I debated on dinner. Heaviness pressed down on my chest as I grabbed my phone and saw an email from my favorite pizza place.

"Happy Birthday! Thank you for being a valued customer. Have a one-topping pizza on us."

How sad that they were the only ones to wish me a happy birthday. Not that I'd told anyone else, not even Jonah. Birthdays had never really been a big thing for me growing up and still weren't. It was just another day.

After gorging myself on pepperoni pizza—the food of champions—I showered, changed into boxers and a baggy tee, and settled in for a night of uninterrupted reading.

My e-reader had a different plan.

Ayden and I had just reached the demon lord's kingdom and were fighting our way through a demon horde when my Kindle froze. I tapped the screen, and nothing happened. Cursing—because I had very little patience when it came to technology—I turned the device off, gave it a few seconds, then turned it back on. But tragedy struck. The screen did a little fizzle and went dark.

"No, no, no," I said after doing everything I could think of to turn it back on. Admitting defeat, I set it on the cushion beside me. "Thanks for all the good times, little buddy."

After hanging on to dear life for the past four years, my Kindle finally joined its fallen brethren in Bookhalla—like Valhalla but for beloved e-readers that had met their fateful ends.

I ate a handful of gummy bears as I debated what to do. I still had my computer games and my hoard—er, collection of physical books I still hadn't read, but nothing called to me. I felt too restless. After an hour of moping around aimlessly, unable to decide what I wanted to do, I dragged my feet to the bathroom.

Studying my reflection in the mirror, I crinkled my nose and turned my head from side to side. A mop of dirty-blond hair, green eyes, and a dusting of light freckles on my nose. Average build that leaned more toward thin. I stood at a whopping five foot seven.

"Happy birthday, Evan." I lightly bumped the glass with my fist. "Here's to another year of being… me."

My restlessness from earlier skyrocketed. Suddenly feeling like the walls of my apartment were closing in around me, I dug through my closet for a clean shirt, hoodie, and jeans, and then put on my Vans and left.

Going out would be good for me. Jonah would be proud.

The sun hadn't fully set yet, leaving some areas of the sky dark. Orange, red, and streaks of dark purple washed across the horizon. I moved down the sidewalk, hands shoved in the front pocket of my hoodie. Cars drove past blaring music, the bass thumping heavily and rattling the windows. Smells wafted in the air, coming from the different restaurants.

In the distance, flashing lights bled through the darkening sky.

The festival.

My feet carried me that way. I didn't have anything better to do. Might as well stop in for a funnel cake or hot dog. Or both because I was grieving the death of a dear friend and deserved to eat everything in sight to help soothe my broken heart.

Main Street had been roped off for the event, and I entered the fray of people. The free admission was a nice perk.

The church parking lot at the corner had been transformed into a sort of fairground with a few rides. Lights blinked on a Ferris Wheel, the carts of people rocking a bit too much for my liking as the ride moved in circles. Screams came from the evil monstrosity known as the Zipper. Trapped in a rotating metal cage while being spun in the air? Yeah, no, thanks. Hard pass.

As I stood in place, debating which direction to go, a little girl bumped into me. Slammed was more like it. Pretty sure if she didn't have a future career lined up, she'd make a great linebacker.

"Say you're sorry, sweetie," the woman with her said before giving me an apologetic smile.

The girl ignored her—and me—and instead pointed up at the Zipper. "Momma, I wanna ride that!"

"Oh, I don't know about that one." The mother grabbed her hand. "Let's find something else that won't scare you."

"Only babies would be scared of that." The little girl rolled her eyes before the two continued walking.

"Thanks, kid," I muttered under my breath. I guess I was a baby now.

I continued down the street, heading away from the rides. It was my twenty-third birthday, and I wanted to live to twenty-four, thank you very freaking much. Vendors sold jewelry, clothing, and wind chimes, and others offered services like face painting and henna tattoos. Kids crowded around the petting zoo off to one side, squealing so loud they could probably be heard from Mars. Those poor animals.

People gathered in front of the lit-up food stalls, and I scanned the menu items on the front of each one before committing to one of the long lines. Snow cones, hot dogs, burgers, funnel cakes, and popcorn.

"Jesus," I muttered. Seven bucks for a corn dog? What a rip-off. Now the free admission made sense. Everything was grossly overpriced.

Deciding on popcorn—because the line was shorter—I bought a bag and munched on it as I strolled along, checking out the festival. Overpriced games to win crappy stuffed animals, creaking rides I was fairly sure would break down any minute, and massive crowds of people? Why did I ever leave my apartment? The overly salted bag of popcorn wasn't worth this level of torment.

"Do you believe in magic?"

I turned and came face-to-face with the hottest guy I'd ever seen in my entire life. He had a dark complexion, shaggy brown hair, and big brown eyes.

"Uh. Magic?"

He smiled and motioned to the store behind him. "Adventure awaits inside."

The storefront had been vacant the last time I'd visited the downtown area. Now, an antiquated sign hung above the entrance, reading: *Lupin's Mystical Emporium.* The window was dark, as if covered by some type of curtain, preventing me from seeing inside the shop from the outside.

"Why do I feel like if I go inside, someone will hit me over the head, and then I'll wake up with one of my kidneys missing?"

"Such a wild imagination," he said with an amused look in his eyes. "Rest assured we have no interest in your organs."

"Only in my money? How rude."

That amusement in his eyes dropped down to the dimple in his cheek as he smiled.

I glanced at the sign again. "Are you Lupin?"

"No," he responded. "He's my husband. My name is Saint."

Husband. The ease with which he admitted it to a total stranger—especially there in the freaking asshole of the South—surprised me. It also made me happy.

"Cool name." I'd never met anyone else who had it. "I'm Evan. Is Lupin like a fortune teller or something?"

"Oh, he's much more than that. Those who enter Lupin's domain always leave changed in some way. But one must have an open mind and open heart, or the magic will pass them by."

"Seriously though... what is this? A magic shop?"

He waved a hand toward the entrance. "Step through the doorway and find out."

I looked at the shop again. No way to see inside. "No offense, but this is the part in a horror movie where I start yelling at the character to stop being stupid and run away."

"Could it not also be one of those movies where the main character nearly turns down the chance of a lifetime? Where they nearly miss out on a great adventure?"

"Adventure... in a magic shop."

"Come inside or don't," he said. "The choice is yours."

Damn curiosity. It would be the death of me one day. If I turned away now, I'd spend the rest of the night—and probably periodically for the rest of my life—wondering what would've happened.

"Fine," I said. "But I'm taking my popcorn with me. Even if it is super salty."

Saint chuckled under his breath as I walked past him.

The bell above the door gave a musical little jingle as I stepped inside the shop. Incense burned on a nearby table, smelling woodsy with sweet notes. Crystals and colorful stones were arranged on a round display with decorative bags you could buy to keep them in. Books and leather journals lined a

16

shelf. Wooden figurines sat along another shelf, one of a tree with a face in the center—not creepy at all—and another of a woman with flowers in her long, flowing curls and a peaceful expression.

Stepping farther inside, I scanned a collection of astrology books, rings, and bracelets with symbols etched along the bands. Someone then bumped into me.

"Oh, I'm sorry," a woman said, taking a step backward. Her mousy brown hair was pulled back in a low bun, and dark circles rested under her eyes, as if she hadn't gotten a good night's sleep in weeks.

"No worries," I told her. "It's easy to get turned around in here. So much to see."

"Yes." She flitted a wary gaze throughout the room.

"Are you worried about your kidneys too?"

"What?" Her eyes flashed to me, a bit of alarm in them now.

"Sorry. Poor attempt at a joke." My cheeks heated. *And this is why I don't talk to people.* "You just seem nervous, so I was tryin' to lighten the mood. Our organs being sold on the black market probably wasn't the direction to go. I see that now."

"Oh." She smiled, but the skin at the edge of her eyes remained tight. "Mystic shops aren't really my thing. I don't know why I came here. I just got off work and was on my way home when I stopped on a whim."

"And then you were drawn in by the pretty face outside? Yeah, he suckered me in too."

That time when she smiled, it was less tense. "I'm Victoria."

"Evan. Nice to meet you." I held my bag toward her. "Want some popcorn? It's saltier than a little old lady gossiping about her husband-stealing friend Janice, but it's oddly addicting."

"No, thank you," she said with a laugh.

A jingle came from the entrance as someone else walked inside. His expression hovered between curiosity and nervousness. Moments later, another person came in. I swept another look around, noting the handful of customers browsing the items. Something strange? Every person had come alone. Like only the loners of the festival were drawn to the little shop of (possible) horrors.

I should leave.

"Good evening," a smooth voice said from behind me, and I turned. The man's medium-length hair had various shades of blond, both light and dark, and he wore a white suit that hugged him in all the right places, emphasizing his slender frame while also complementing the strong set of his shoulders. A dark purple shirt was beneath his jacket. "My name is Lupin. Welcome to my shop."

***

Charismatic, friendly, and certainly easy on the eyes, Lupin drew in those around him. He moved around the shop, chatting with customers. Some bought gemstones; others browsed the selection of books before choosing one to purchase.

Victoria found a necklace with a moon charm and clutched it in her hand like it was the answer to all her problems. Lupin chatted with her as they walked toward the counter to check out. As she left, she seemed so much lighter than when I'd first seen her.

A floral fragrance filled the air, coming from a doorway with a thin green-and-gold curtain. Saint moved aside the curtain and disappeared into the room before exiting a while later, holding a tray with a teapot and two smaller bowls. He placed the tray on a table against the wall and filled teacups before offering them to the customers, free of charge.

A weird little curiosities shop appearing out of nowhere and then offering free tea? Laced with some type of drug, perhaps?

Murder husbands.

"Well, that's not sketchy at all," I mumbled to myself.

"Sketchy?" Lupin appeared at my side. "We think of it as being kind to our guests. Tea soothes the soul."

"Sorry," I said, cheeks heating. "I didn't mean to offend you."

"None taken." He smiled. "I understand your wariness. Many who come to the Emporium feel the same as you. That's why they come. Life has beaten them down, and they're desperate for something... more."

"I came because my e-reader died. Tragic, I know."

"Can you download a reading app to your phone?"

"Too small. I like a bigger screen when I read. My phone is for my games." No reason to tell him what type of games I played... definitely not the dating simulation ones where you could romance several hotties at the same time before choosing one of them. Nope.

"Perhaps it was a blessing in disguise," he said. "It led you here."

Saint approached with a steaming cup of tea and handed it to Lupin. "Here you are, love."

"Thank you." Lupin accepted the cup. With his free hand, he pulled Saint toward him and pressed a kiss to his temple. "What would I ever do without you?"

"Forget to eat, stay hydrated, and a dozen other things." Saint's eyes crinkled as he leaned into Lupin.

My heart thrummed a little. I was no expert on the matter—clearly—but their tender gazes radiated love. The kind of love I'd only read about.

A jingle came from the door as someone exited the shop. The shuffles from the other customers had gone quiet. Looking around, I noticed I was the only one left.

"Oh." How long had I been in there? It felt like only minutes. "Guess I'll get out of your hair."

"Please don't leave yet," Lupin said, tone friendly. "You haven't found what you came in here for."

"I didn't come in here for anything. Your hubby suckered me in at the door."

"Ah, yes. He does have a certain allure that charms those he meets." Lupin smirked at Saint, who offered him a shy smile in return. His gray eyes then shifted back to me. "However, you didn't happen upon my shop by chance. Fate guided you to me."

"Fate? I wouldn't go that far. I mean, this place is awesome if you're into the whole witchy and mystics thing, but it's not really my style. Well, apart from the books. They're kinda cool."

"And yet, you've been here for a while. Searching for something."

I looked between them. "Let me guess. You're about to tell me you have all the answers I seek, and for the limited-time offer of *only* two hundred bucks, you'll give me those answers? Plus tax, of course."

"You resort to sarcasm and jokes when you're nervous," Lupin said. "Yet, deep down, your heart is crying out for someone to listen. I read people. More so, I can hear the cries of their hearts. And yours, Evan, is drowning so far in the depths the screams won't stop ringing in my ears. That's why you were drawn here. It's why you haven't even stepped toward that door since you've come inside."

"Yeah? And why is that?"

"Because the Emporium only makes itself known to the souls who need it most." Lupin walked over to the nearest display and touched one of the necklaces. "The woman, Victoria. She's been swamped at work on top of dealing with the stresses of a messy divorce. It's affected her sleep and taken a toll on her health. The item she purchased tonight will allow her to have the best night of sleep she's had in months. Isaac, a man who was in here earlier, just lost his job and is at the end of his rope. The charm he found will give him clarity and open up more opportunities."

The more he spoke, the more *something* clawed in my chest. A desperation that had my feet planted in place despite the logical side of my brain telling me to get out of there. Lupin seemed genuine, but I didn't trust him as far as I could throw him. Which wasn't far at all, seeing as to how I could barely lift a 24-pack of soda without struggling.

"I feel like y'all are about to scam me," I said. "To spare you some disappointment, I want you to know I live paycheck to paycheck, and what little money I have left over after bills, I blow on books and junk food. So you won't get a big payout by conning a sucker like me. You'll get like forty bucks, a mountain of credit card debt, and a gift card to Applebee's."

Lupin's mouth skewed up in a half-smile. "Tell me something. Do you enjoy your life?"

"What kind of question is that?"

"An honest one."

"Okay…" I stared at my half-eaten bag of popcorn before crinkling the top to close it. "My life is fine. I get by."

"You *get by*. Interesting. What brings you joy?"

"Reading, mostly," I answered. "I also like my job at the café. Making coffee and pastries is fun."

"Walk with me." Lupin motioned with his head for me to follow. My legs moved on impulse. So much for not trusting him. Dumb body. He led me over to the register before he went behind it and grabbed something from the glass case. He slid the item toward me over the counter. "Here."

"A rock?" I picked it up. It had a flat, smooth surface and was emerald green with thin streaks of other colors: dark blue, yellow, red, purple, and mixed shades of pale green and brown.

"It's a wishing stone," Lupin said, leaning against the counter. "It knows the deepest desires of your heart. So allow me to ask you… what do you wish for the most?"

"Being in bed with a bunch of hot dudes wouldn't be too bad."

His lips twitched.

Saint sighed.

"Hey, you asked." I shrugged and set the stone back down. My fingers wouldn't release it though. Instead, I played with it by slowly spinning it on the countertop. "Being an omnipotent badass would suffice too. Like an overpowered main character who can just snap his fingers and demolish an enemy army. Hero of the kingdom of Lustville. Heartthrob for all the pretty boys to swoon over."

Saint pinched the bridge of his nose. "Must we continue this, Lupin? He clearly isn't taking this seriously."

Lupin, however, was amused. "Would any of that truly make you happy?"

"Sure. Why not?" No sense in telling him about my crappy dating history. The only time men swooned over me was when I took too much melatonin before bed and had wild sex dreams where all the dudes wanted my dick. One time, it was like King Midas with his golden touch, but the shiny treasure was in my pants.

"Power, money, and sex," Lupin said. "These are what most people first wish for, thinking it will bring them happiness and fill some void inside them. For some, it does make them happy. Yet, I feel like your desire runs deeper. What is it *you* truly want?"

A sarcastic reply was on the tip of my tongue, but someplace inside of me responded to his words. I squeezed the stone. "To feel like I belong."

"You don't feel that way now?"

"No." My throat threatened to close up, and I swallowed a few times. "I never have." I slid the stone back toward him.

He shook his head. "The stone chose you. Keep it."

"Huh?" I withdrew my hand, leaving the stone on the counter. "Look, I'm sure you think you're helping or whatever, but I really don't have the money. I could barely afford the bag of popcorn. It's a pretty rock, but I'm going to have to pass."

"No money required. Consider this as my gift to you." A smile shone in his eyes, shadowed by something much more mysterious. "For your birthday."

"How did you know it's my birthday? Did you swipe my ID or something?" I checked my pockets, finding my wallet right where I left it. This night was getting weirder and weirder.

24

Lupin pushed back his sleeve to glance at his watch. "Perfect timing." Some kind of tattoo, like black symbols, disappeared up his sleeve. "The shop is now closed. Be safe walking home, Evan."

And then, I was standing on the sidewalk in front of the building.

How the hell did I get out there so fast? I turned to look at the shop. My confusion only deepened. The sign was gone.

For Lease was written on the storefront window.

I stumbled backward, anxiety prickling at my chest and pulse pounding. Around me, the food trucks and vendors were packing up. Some had already left. The sun had long since set, and the moon hung in the sky. I must've been in there for hours, but it felt like only minutes. With my thoughts spiraling, I stepped off the curb and into the street. The lights from the rides turned off, and men worked on taking them down.

Trying and failing to come up with a reasonable explanation for it all, I left Main Street and returned home. Once there, I collapsed on my bed, not even bothering to take off my shoes. I pulled the blanket over my head and tried to forget about my confusing night.

Something jabbed me in the belly, and I wiggled around before pulling the stone from my hoodie pocket. I had left it on the countertop. So how did it get in my pocket?

"Curious and curiouser." I glided my thumb along the smooth surface. A wishing stone, Lupin had called it. A chance to have my heart's deepest desire granted.

"So allow me to ask you... what do you wish for the most?"

"I wish I could go somewhere else," I whispered, my eyes stinging as I clutched the stone in my hand. "A world like I've only seen in my dreams. Somewhere I can call home and feel like I belong. I want to love and be loved for who I am, not who others want me to be."

But nothing in life was ever achieved by wishing for it. As awesome as it would be for Lupin to be some wish-granting wizard, things like that didn't exist in real life.

Only in books.

Tomorrow was a new day.

But I knew I'd still be the same me when I woke, stuck in the same old life.

Chapter Two
Evan in Hottie Land

"Boy," a deep voice said before something nudged my leg. "Wake up."

I opened my eyes to a bright, sunny sky and groaned at the assault on my poor retinas. I rolled over and closed them again, resting my cheek on the soft grass.

Wait. Grass?

I flung upward and smacked my head into something hard.

"What the fuck?" I rubbed at my forehead and cracked open my eyelids. A dark shape hovered in front of me. As the sleepy haze cleared from my vision, I made out a pair of broad shoulders and something shiny covering them, like metal. Well, that was the culprit. The metal had made a little *ding* sound as my head banged right into it.

"You don't look to be bleeding," that same deep voice said before he touched my head. His face then came into view, and I forgot all about my aching noggin. He had a sharp jawline and blue eyes surrounded by long, dark lashes. Short black hair was swept back, though a strand of his bangs fell forward. "Who are you?"

"I was about to ask you that same question."

His brow tapered. "I'm Maddox, captain of the Second Order of Knights. Now, state your name."

Captain of the knights? I tore my gaze from him and checked out my surroundings. I was in a grassy field with a forest to one side of me and a dirt road on the other. In the distance, smoke spilled out from the chimneys of small wooden houses— some made of stone—with a backdrop of rolling hills.

What the hell was this, some kind of LARPing retreat? It was a form of live-action role-playing where you dressed up in full costume and gear and went on quests, usually with a group of friends. The events sometimes took place in the countryside to add to that medieval-fantasy atmosphere.

I'd never been to one but had, secretly, wanted to.

"Look, Mr. Captain of the Knights, I have no idea where I am right now. Mind breaking character for a moment to tell me how I got here?"

Last thing I remembered was leaving the festival and going home. How did I go from being a blanket burrito in my bed to lying in a field in the middle of freaking nowhere?

"Breaking character?" he asked, hand moving to rest on the hilt of his sword. Damn. This guy was the real deal. I'd handled enough cosplay weapons in my life to know the real thing when I saw it. He must've spent a small fortune on his costume. "You are on the outskirts of Bremloc. You're fortunate you weren't attacked in the dead of night being this close to the dark wood."

"The dark wood?" I glanced at the forest. "Ah, are you on a quest to vanquish the dense fog of miasma poisoning the people of, what did you call

28

it, Bremloc? Do demons live inside the forest and attack anyone who enters? I'm not sure what the rules are for this role-play."

"Role-play? You say such strange things. Yet, you have yet to tell me your name. I suggest you do so now."

"I'm Evan. Lord of the Muffins."

"Lord of the... Muffins? I am unfamiliar with this title."

"It's new."

His gaze moved down my body in a way that made my face hot. "Why do you dress this way?"

"What way?" I glanced at my hoodie and jeans. "Oh. I'm not in costume."

He touched my hoodie sleeve. "Is this how people dress where you're from? How strange."

"Stop calling me strange," I said. "You're the one weighed down with chainmail."

"Captain!" another guy called from the edge of the field as he hopped over the small fence and approached. He wore armor as well, sword sheathed at his side, but as he reached us, his floppy brown hair and big eyes took away any of that intimidation factor. Cinnamon roll would suit him better. "Is he injured?"

"Only from where his head bumped my shoulder." Maddox rose from his crouched position. "Otherwise, he is unharmed. Though, I question his mind."

"My mind is fine," I mumbled.

I would say this was a very vivid dream, but the ache in my head was too real for that. Which only left two other possibilities: I had memory loss and didn't remember joining the group of nerds on their LARPing adventure, or I had been kidnapped.

But who'd want to kidnap a twenty-three-year-old bookworm whose only social skills involved taking people's coffee orders?

Maddox's gaze lowered to mine. I'd never had someone stare at me so intensely before. "Tell me why you're here, Muffin Lord."

I burst out laughing. "Dude. You can't say something like that with such a straight face. You're going to make me piss myself."

"What kingdom are you from?"

What would it take to break this guy's composure? If he was a paid actor for the event, he should get a raise.

"All joking aside, I really don't know who you are or how I got here. Last thing I remember is being nice and warm in my bed. Then, I woke up here to your bright and smiling face."

Said "bright and smiling face" continued to glare at me.

"Perhaps he's a spy?" Sir Cinnamon Roll suggested. "Or a bandit. Our scouts reported a gang of them passing through a village to the east two days ago."

Maddox's expression turned lethal. "Is that it, then? You're one of the bandits?"

In their little game, the bandits were clearly the bad guys. "I've never stolen a thing in my life. I'm not really the plundering type."

"Take him to the castle," Maddox said. "I'll question him when I return at midday."

"Yes, sir." The other man bowed his head before grabbing me by the arm and lifting me from the grass. With an arched brow, he gently squeezed my bicep. "If he *is* a bandit, he's not very strong, at least. Very thin."

"Hey, that was a low blow. It's not my fault I eat all the time and never gain weight." I yanked from his hold and lost my balance.

Maddox caught me against his—very strong and muscled—chest. "Thin and clumsy-footed as well." He passed me back over to the other cosplayer. "Bind him if you must. Just ensure he doesn't escape."

"Escape to where?" I asked. "I don't even know where I am."

The knight captain merely stared at me. "You may gag him too."

"Rude."

"Also, have Briar examine him."

"Who's Briar?" I asked.

Maddox turned away without another word and walked across the field to where a black horse waited. He swung up into the saddle and guided the stallion toward the road. And I'd be lying if I said I wasn't checking out his, uh, smooth handling skills.

My stomach growled. The only thing capable of deterring my gaze from the eye candy in armor was my empty belly. "Got any food around here? I'm starving."

"I'll fetch your morning meal once we arrive at the castle. But only if you cooperate." Sir Cinnamon Roll led me over to a brown horse. "Hop on."

"Um." I stared at the stirrup. "I've never ridden a horse before." Read a ton of books where characters rode horses? Sure. But not in real life.

"I'll help you. Grab here." He placed my hand on the saddle before taking hold of my waist. "Place your foot in the stirrup and pull yourself up."

The first attempt was an epic fail. I stepped into the stirrup, my muscles shook, and I fell backward into him. If there was ever a time when I realized I was out of shape, that was it. "They make it look so easy in the movies."

"Movies?" He blinked at me before focusing back on the horse. "Try again."

Three tries later, I finally managed to pull myself up and swing my leg over—not so gracefully. I wobbled at first but then found my balance. The ground looked too far away. "It's so high up here."

"Your personality amuses me." After making sure I wouldn't fall to my death, he grabbed the reins and walked beside the horse, leading me down the dirt road.

"What's your name?" I asked.

"Callum. And yours?"

"Evan."

"Well, Evan, I hope for your sake you are no spy." Callum offered me a weak smile. "Or this horse ride might be your first *and* your last."

The sinking feeling in my gut had nothing to do with my roaring hunger. Sure, I'd dialed up my sarcasm and played along with their little charade, but the truth was, this whole situation was freaking me out.

And that feeling only got worse.

A short while later, the quaint countryside faded and gave way to more houses and people. The dirt road transitioned to stone as we entered some kind of marketplace. Buildings stretched on both sides of us, and crowds visited the various vendors selling food, jewelry, leatherware, and other goods along the bustling street. Smells of cooking meat and baked treats mingled in the air. There wasn't a single person in modern clothing. No one broke character.

I definitely stood out in my blue hoodie, jeans, and Vans.

"This is kind of elaborate for a LARPing retreat," I said. "Or is it a Renaissance festival?" I'd been to a few of them before, and it had looked a lot like this. However, this was the biggest and by far the best I'd ever seen.

"I do not know those words," Callum answered. "What is a Renaissance festival? Is it like the Festival of Lights?"

"What's that?"

He spoke over the noise of the surrounding market. "A festival held each year as we welcome summer. There's music, dancing, and merchants who travel in from other kingdoms. When the sun sets, we then light lanterns and release them into the air with our wishes for the coming season. You've never attended one before?"

"Can't say I have." The rocking motion of the horse was becoming a bit uncomfortable. My ass would be so sore later. Also, in fear that I'd fall off, I kept squeezing with my legs and gripping the saddle tighter. My whole body was tensed up. "I'd kill for a dip in a hot tub right about now."

"Hot tub?" Callum asked. "We have a hot spring. Perhaps you can visit later."

"Later. You mean after Captain Ice grills me?"

"Captain Maddox does what's necessary to keep our people safe. He's dedicated his entire life to the kingdom. It's quite admirable."

"Well, he could learn how to smile every once in a while." Callum almost had me believing this shit was real. Why would anyone go to such lengths to trick a nobody like me? "How long are you guys going to keep this act going? I think I've been pretty patient, considering how nuts all of this is."

Callum offered me a thin smile before facing ahead. He wasn't going to respond? Fine. I'd play along for a little longer, but once I got off this damn horse, I wouldn't rest until someone gave me real answers.

We continued along the street, leaving the busy marketplace.

"No fucking way," I muttered as a castle came into view. It wasn't some building that had been thrown together for a retreat or festival. The thing was an honest-to-god medieval castle with all the bells and whistles. White stone turrets and probably a hundred rooms. The gates opened as we approached.

"Sir Callum," a man in a guard's uniform said with a curt bow of his head. His dark eyes trailed to me before moving back to the knight. "What business does the boy have here?"

"Captain Maddox ordered me to bring him in for questioning," Callum responded.

The guard nodded and allowed us to pass, but not without giving me another wary glance.

Callum led us to a grassy area where other men were gathered, most of them shirtless. Some sat beside a firepit and ate from wooden bowls, while others carried supplies to and from a small shed. Horses neighed from a fenced-in pasture to the left, and a few men brushed their coats.

"Do you need me to help you dismount?" Callum asked.

Not wanting to fall flat on my face in front of all those muscled studs, I swallowed my pride and took his hand. "Thanks." Once on my own two feet again, I walked beside him. "Where are we going?"

"I'm taking you to Briar," Callum responded. "He's the chief herbalist."

"Herbalist. Like a doctor?"

"A physician, yes. He has a vast knowledge of plants and uses them for medicines and remedies in conjunction with spell work."

"Ah, so this is a medieval-fantasy setting with magic? Cool. That gives you guys the freedom to make it how you want without getting hung up on the historical details."

Callum's brow arched. "The captain was right. You do speak strangely. The hit to your head may be more severe than it looks. We best get you to Briar as soon as possible."

The nervous pit in my stomach worsened. He didn't seem to be acting.

I took another look around, seeing it with a new set of eyes. Everything was too realistic. Even the most awesome Renaissance festivals lacked this level of accuracy. And if it *was* a festival, where were the patrons? Every person wore full costume and performed tasks like hand-washing clothing and bedding, chopping firewood, and cleaning the barn with no one around to see it, as if they had fully immersed themselves in the role as opposed to putting on a performance.

"Hey, Callum? Be straight with me. You guys are role-players, right? You signed up to experience this type of setting and were given your positions?"

His confusion deepened. "I wasn't given my position as a knight. I earned it through hard work and fortitude."

"Yeah, but really. What do you do when you're not here being a knight? Like in the real world?"

"The real world? This is the only world I know, Evan."

As we entered a courtyard, passing colorful trees and small pools of water surrounded by smooth, white rocks, I pinched my arm hard enough to feel the sting. Definitely not a dream, then. Kidnapping seemed far-fetched, too, considering no one knew who I was.

So, where the hell was I? And *why* was I there?

We neared a door within the courtyard, and Callum knocked once.

"Come in," a man said from the other side.

Callum pushed open the door and nodded for me to go in first before following behind me. Just in case I made a dash for it and ran away? Probably.

Which, with this confusing reality unfolding around me, I might've done it.

Natural light flooded the spacious room, shining through tall windows. Books lined the shelves along the walls, all organized instead of messily thrown in place. I fought the urge to go over and look at them. Potted plants hung from the ceiling, and others sat on shelves closest to the windows. Herbs hung upside down from another shelf, and a cabinet held a collection of glass vials ranging in size from super tiny to large. A small kitchen was on one side, with a double burner stovetop and an oven beside it.

Everything was so neat.

A man with light brown hair and round-framed glasses looked up from the large book he'd been writing in and set the quill aside. "Sir Callum. How may I be of assistance?"

"Sorry to intrude on your work without prior notice," Callum said. "He hit his head."

"Oh, it's no intrusion at all." The man stood from the desk and walked over, his gait smooth. When I thought of a "chief herbalist," I imagined an older dude with wild gray hair and a crooked nose—don't ask me why. He was the complete opposite of what I'd expected. Young, attractive in a scholarly sort of way, and with a gentle voice. A gentleness that showed through his hazel eyes as they shifted to me. "Ah. Quite the bump on your forehead. May I?"

"S-Sure."

His fingers smoothed along my temple and over to where I'd hit my head. I winced at how tender it was. "Apologies." His touch was slightly cool, but I didn't mind. It felt good on my heated skin. "Can you tell me your name?"

"Evan."

Another soft touch. "Nice to meet you, Evan. I'm Briar." He lowered his hand. "Have you experienced any dizziness or confusion?"

Confusion about why I was there? Definitely. But that's not what he meant. "Not really."

"He had trouble getting on the horse," Callum said. "Though, I believe he may just be clumsy."

Briar softly smiled before checking my pupils. "Nausea?"

"No."

He nodded. "Well, I have good news. You'll live."

Something about his gentle nature soothed some of my anxiety. "Thanks, Doc."

"If you do experience any dizziness or nausea, please don't hesitate to let me know. You didn't hit it hard enough to cause internal damage, but if you permit me to do so, I can ease the ache with a light spell."

"A spell?" Surely, all of this was a super-elaborate event I'd somehow gotten dragged into. There was no way he could actually heal me with magic, but I played along. "Okay."

Briar touched my temple again and closed his eyes. The coolness of his fingertips then warmed, and a strange sensation came over me. His eyes opened again, and he smiled. "There. Better?"

The ache was gone. And when I lifted a hand to my head and probed at the spot, it still didn't hurt, even though it had definitely been tender not even five seconds ago. My heart rate accelerated, the beats pounding in my ears. "You... you really..."

"Easy." Callum grabbed my shoulder as I swayed.

"You can actually use magic?" I asked, my voice higher in pitch.

"Yes." Briar frowned at Callum before regarding me again. "You've not met a magic wielder before?"

"Not real magic!" Was I panicking? I felt like I was panicking. "Who are you people? Where the hell am I? Stop with the games and tell me the truth."

"The truth? You're in the kingdom of Bremloc." Briar frowned at my clothes, as though he'd just noticed them for the first time. Typical doctor, I guess. They focused on the injury before anything else. "The better question is who are *you*."

"That's why I brought him to the castle," Callum said. "The captain found him early this morning near the dark wood. He told me to bring him here for questioning."

"The dark wood. I see." Briar studied me. "I sense no dark energy from him. So if he did come from the forest, his soul hasn't been affected."

Dark energy? There was an annoying ringing in my ears. And why was my heart beating so freaking fast?

A light rapping came at the door before it opened and a man stepped inside. A man with fuzzy cat ears jutting from his reddish-brown hair and a long tail that whished behind him.

Now, I'd attended several comic cons in my life. I'd seen countless people dress up as animals, but even the most expensive and realistic costumes paled in comparison to this guy.

"Kuya," Briar said with a welcoming smile. "What can I do for you?"

The man quickly bowed. "Kuya has come to fetch an elixir for Prince Sawyer."

"What are his symptoms?" Briar asked.

"A pounding headache and nausea." The cat boy flashed a nervous smile and rubbed at the back of his hair. "He drank a lot of wine last night. Kuya told him not to, but he didn't listen."

"I have just the thing." Briar stepped over to the cabinet and withdrew a small glass vial. He took it over to a table covered in beakers, various jars filled with an assortment of herbs and ingredients, and mortar and pestles. He ground herbs, added some kind of liquid, and then drained the contents into the vial. Then, he held his hand over it. Light emitted from his palm. The liquid in the vial then glowed a pale blue.

I gaped. *What the hell is going on?*

Briar handed the vial to him. "The best cure for a hangover. Make sure the prince drinks all of it."

"Many thanks to you." The cat boy pocketed the vial and looked at me. His fuzzy ears wiggled as he smiled, flashing a pair of sharp canines. His eyes reminded me of rainbows, a kaleidoscope of colors. They caught the light from the window. "Kuya hasn't seen you before. Who are you?"

"Evan," I said, unable to take my eyes off him. "You… you have a tail."

40

His grin widened. "Kuya *does* have a tail. It's cute, right?" He flicked it back and forth. The way it moved was too natural, not mechanical. He then pointed to his ears. "Kuya has these too. But you can't touch 'em. Only Prince Sawyer can. Kuya loves when he scratches them during naps."

"You're really…" The room spun a little. "You have real ears. And you." I looked at Briar. "You used magic. Twice."

It hadn't been a trick. This Kuya dude's rainbow-colored eyes also lacked the telltale signs of contacts.

The spinning of the room worsened, and the ringing in my ears intensified. Callum said something, but I couldn't make out his words. Briar reached for me. The floor then rose up, coming straight at my face, and everything went dark.

***

"I leave him in your care, and he dies." The deep voice was familiar.

"He's not dead, sir. He only fainted."

"Boy," the deeper voice said before something nudged my leg. Also, familiar. "I know you're awake."

I cracked open my eyelids, relieved to find the lighting in the room bearable. Not too bright, but enough to see the two men standing beside my bed. One with that cinnamon roll face and the other who looked like he wanted to murder me.

"Captain Ice," I said in a scratchy voice. "We meet again." Everything then flooded back to me. The magic. The fuzzy ears. I shot upward.

"Not so fast." Maddox grabbed my shoulders and held me in place. "You're not moving from that spot until I get some answers."

"Yeah, I'd like some too," I told him. "Like what the hell is this place?"

Callum tilted his head to the side. "He keeps asking that question. We've told him which kingdom he's in many times."

"Is this like an *Alice in Wonderland* situation?" I asked. "Have I fallen down a rabbit hole and entered some kind of nether world? Hell, maybe I've gone mad like the Hatter, and this is all happening inside my head. Oh god. Is Kuya the Cheshire cat?" I focused on Maddox. "I'm not sure who you'd be. Someone who's grumpy."

Mr. Grumpy's lips twitched. "I take it you aren't truly Lord of the Muffins, though the title is certainly an interesting one. So, who are you, and where did you come from? You didn't just appear in that field beside the forest."

Actually, me appearing there wasn't t too far-fetched, considering the things I'd recently seen. "I can't remember, okay? Someone must've taken me while I was asleep and dumped me there."

Maddox clenched his jaw. "Stop with the lies. Your innocent act fools no one. Are you one of Onyx's scouts?"

"Who's Onyx?"

"Briar didn't sense dark energy from him," Callum said. The two ignored my question. "Onyx only associates with demons and beasts. Evan is human."

"Of course I'm human! What else would I be?" Maddox sneered at me.

Callum turned to him. "His confusion seems sincere, Captain. I really don't think he has any idea where he is."

Maddox rubbed at his jaw. "Perhaps his memory was erased. Though, that doesn't explain his outlandish way of dress."

"Look, I'm not going to take fashion advice from a dude who looks like he just stepped off the set to *Game of Thrones*. My clothes are comfortable."

The captain's expression didn't waver in the slightest. He must've been awesome at poker.

"Um." I wiggled my feet before sticking one out from the blanket. "Where are my shoes?"

"I was curious," Callum said, dropping his gaze to the floorboards. "I'd never seen craftsmanship such as that."

"You stole my shoes? Wow. Some honorable knight you are."

"Stole? No, not at all." He shook his head. "I only... well... I wanted to see how they'd feel." Maddox glanced at Callum's feet. I did too. Sure enough, there were my missing shoes. The cinnamon roll of a knight smiled. "They are incredibly comfortable."

"Please remove them at once." Maddox pinched the bridge of his nose.

Callum's mouth downturned into a little pout. "Very well."

"Wait," I said. That pout of his was deadly. "You can borrow them. Just don't put a hole in them, okay? They're my best pair of Vans. Cost me like ninety bucks. The skull design was for a limited time only."

In an instant, that beaming smile was aimed at me. "Thank you, Evan. I shall guard them with my life."

"Well, you don't need to go to that extreme. They're awesome but not worth dying over." My stomach rumbled, reminding me I still hadn't eaten. "I'm hungry."

Maddox's eyes narrowed. "Your stomach can wait until I'm finished with my questioning."

"I've told you everything I know." Which wasn't much, but still. "Feed me." Then, because that murderous gleam in his eyes deepened, I added, "Please, sir knight, don't let me starve." I blinked a few times, trying to flutter my eyelashes. If I was in a dating game, Maddox's intimacy meter would be at, like, negative one hundred. Worse than that, I was fairly sure my attempt at being cute missed the mark. Epically.

"Do you have something in your eye?" he asked.

Yep. A total fail. "Only tears. Because I'm about to starve to death."

The muscle in his jaw tightened. He then looked at Callum. "Have the cooks prepare something for him."

"Yes, sir." Callum bowed his head and left the room.

Holy crap. Maybe not a failure after all. Being cute had worked. I did my best to hide my smile.

"A guard will be stationed outside your door," Maddox then said to me. "If you try to escape, it will be your head."

"Is this how you treat all guests of the kingdom?"

"No guest of the kingdom ever journeys that close to the dark wood," he countered. "For all I know, you could've come from one of the warring lands with the intent to bring ruin to our people. Until I'm convinced otherwise, you will go nowhere or do anything without my knowing."

"I want to speak to the person in charge," I said, finally losing my patience. I cringed at my wording. I sounded like a Karen demanding to speak to the manager. But I'd had enough of this shit.

"The person in charge?" Maddox stepped forward, his gaze so intense it gave me shivers. "You're staring at him, boy."

He then left the room, closing the door on his way out.

Blowing out a breath, I shifted to the edge of the bed and stood up. The room was small and kind of cramped, but a decent-sized window let in a nice flood of light. Still sunny. So I hadn't been out for long.

Tap, tap, tap.

I glanced at the window. "Um. Someone there?" The branches on the other side swayed before a hand rose up and pushed up the window pane. I was about to scream before I recognized the head of blond hair. "Lupin?"

He smirked and rested his arm on the sill. "Fancy meeting you again. Have any exciting adventures yet?"

Understanding then slammed into me like a Mack truck. All of this happened right after speaking with him at the mystics shop—a shop I'd almost been convinced I'd dreamed. He'd spoken of wishes and magic. Somehow, this was his fault. *That tricky son of a bitch.*

"You did this to me! Why? How?"

"I did nothing of the sort," Lupin said, expression softening into more of a smile. "All of this is because of you."

"Oh, believe me, I know it's because of me. Me and my curiosity. It led me to a madman. Did you follow me from the festival last night?" I tried to stay calm but failed. Waking up in a strange place with grumpy knights and cat boys would put anyone on edge. "You waited until I fell asleep and then Evan-napped me."

He rolled his eyes. "I did not kidnap you, nor did I follow you. I had no need for it. You're the one who made this possible." Something sparked in his eyes. "Tell me, Evan. Is this world like the one you've seen in your dreams?"

The top of my scalp prickled. "You heard my wish."

"The stone heard your wish. It was spoken from the heart. In that instant, you opened yourself up to the magic. And here you are now."

46

"Well, I take it back!" I said in a harsh whisper. "This whole place is fucking weird. I want to go home."

"No can do. Once a wish is granted, it cannot be undone."

"Undo it anyway."

He clicked his tongue. "You've only just arrived. Why not give it a chance? You may be surprised by how much you come to enjoy being here."

"Oh yeah. Totally a fun time." I motioned around me. "I'm having a blast being a damn prisoner."

"You're not a prisoner. The knight captain will realize you're not a threat soon enough, and you'll be allowed to leave and explore to your heart's content."

"Where is this exactly?" I asked. "I've never heard of Bremloc."

"I suppose you wouldn't have heard of it. Because it doesn't exist in the world you know."

"What does that mean?"

"It's quite simple, really." Lupin traced a design on the windowsill with his finger. "You've been sent to another world."

It took me a moment to respond. The whole thing was absurd. "Another world?"

He nodded. "One with magic and creatures of all types. You'll find demi-humans, demons, mages, and other beings you've only read about in books. You've traveled through the very veil of the mortal realm, passing through time and space and into a realm of fantasy."

If I hadn't seen some of that with my own eyes, I wouldn't have believed him. But I remembered Briar with his glowing hand and Kuya with his ears and tail and knew in my gut Lupin was telling the truth.

"How long will I be here? It may not be much, but I do have a life, you know. I have a job and friends." Well, *friend.* Jonah. Who was more like a friendly coworker as opposed to a close friend. But still. "Take me home."

"Once you made your wish on that stone, powerful magic came into play," he said. "Much greater than any I possess. And the magic used to bring you here has been exhausted. So you see, it's not as simple as me snapping my fingers and taking you back."

"Are you saying I'm stuck here? Forever?"

Lupin's expression softened. "You were guided to the Emporium so you could be here right now, in this kingdom. There are so many lives here your presence will touch for the better. Friends and lovers alike."

"Lovers? Plural?" I plopped back down on the bed. "Now I really know I'm losing my mind. There's no way that's true."

He chuckled. "Being in a fantasy world of magic and non-human beings you can believe but not that more than one person would desire you?"

"You wouldn't believe it either if you were me." I glanced at my hands, my heart sinking a little. "Not many guys give book nerds like me a second glance, especially once they learn I'm not down for randomly hooking up." It was one reason why I'd stopped trying. I was tired of being disappointed. "Now, my friend Jonah? He's a total player and gets all the guys and girls. You should've brought him here instead. He'd probably form his own harem like a cliché, self-insert male protagonist in an anime."

"Your friend Jonah doesn't belong here."

I scoffed. "And I do?"

"Yes. You wished for a place you could call home and feel like you belonged." His voice was softer than before. "That's why you're here. I know everything is confusing right now and you can't see the bigger picture, but the strings of fate connect you to this land. Where your presence here will touch many lives, they will also touch yours."

"You sound like you've glimpsed into my future or something."

"The future cannot be predicted, only estimated. Every decision, no matter how small, can change the course of our lives. It can lead us to people... or take us farther away."

"So cryptic." I scrubbed my hands over my face. An ache started to form behind my eyes. "What do you gain from granting people's wishes or whatever?"

"I don't grant them," Lupin said. "I merely provide the tools. Magic exists in all of us. Each of us has the power to change our lives. One must simply believe."

"Know what I believe? That this is bullshit." Something else occurred to me. "Speaking of bullshit, I'm calling you out on yours. You say the magic used to bring me here is gone, so how are you here? Huh?"

"I'm able to travel between realms at will," he answered. Just as I opened my mouth, he held up a finger. "And before you say anything, I'll have you know that while *I* can travel back and forth, I don't possess the power to bring others along with me. So, I still can't snap my fingers and send you home."

"Well, that's dumb."

Lupin thought for a moment. "You asked why I do this. It's because I know what it's like to be beaten down and close to giving up. On dreams. On life. If the Emporium can help someone, even a little, I find comfort in that."

"What about Saint? What role does he play in all of this?"

His eyes softened. "He is where the strings of fate led me. He's my happily ever after."

Okay, that was sort of sweet. But I wouldn't admit it out loud.

"All right, let's pretend for a moment I'm not hallucinating and all of this is real. What am I supposed to tell everyone? The knight captain thinks I'm a spy. He'll probably tie me up and roast me over the fire if I don't give him answers soon."

"Tell everyone you're a traveler from a distant land who happened upon the field to rest for the night."

"They'll believe that?"

He shrugged. "Only if you say it convincingly enough."

"Gee. That makes me feel all warm and toasty. Toasty… like I'll be when Captain Maddox roasts me and turns me into the centerpiece of their next medieval feast. Apple in my mouth and everything."

"He wouldn't do that," Lupin responded with an amused snort. "He's not a cannibal. The demons, on the other hand…"

I groaned. "You're an evil wizard. I knew not to trust you."

"Evil is a bit of a stretch. It's also subjective." He pushed back from the windowsill. "My advice to you? Have an open mind and take advantage of the opportunity you've been given. All of the happiness you've only ever dreamed of is at your fingertips, Evan."

He then ducked out of sight.

"Lupin? Wait." I rushed to the window and peered out into the courtyard. It was as if he'd vanished into thin air. Irritating wizard. He couldn't just pop up, say he'd sent me to a damn fantasy world, and then disappear, leaving me on my own.

The door swung open, and I flipped around.

Callum entered the room, holding a tray with a plate, a small bowl, and a mug. He frowned. "You're not trying to escape, are you?"

"No," I quickly said. "I was just taking in the view."

"Come eat. I brought eggs, strawberries, oats, and water." Callum placed the tray on the table beside the bed. "I also snuck you some bread fresh from the oven. As thanks for the shoes." He smiled down at said shoes.

"I should be the one thanking you for this awesome food." I plopped back down on the bed and wasted no time before shoving the bread in my mouth. It was still warm, and I groaned. "Carbs. Oh, how I love thee. All that's missing is some coffee."

"Coffee?"

I paused in my chewing. "You don't have coffee here? Say you're joking."

"Oh, we have it," he said. "I was only surprised you have a taste for it. I find it much too bitter. The beans can be purchased in the market. Although, the highest quality is only accessible to nobles."

"I'll take any quality, as long as it's coffee." I was too desperate to be picky. "When can I have a cup?"

"As soon as you're cleared by the captain, you should be able to visit the marketplace. I would bring you some, but we only have tea or water."

"Any idea how long it'll take the captain to get the stick out of his butt? I'm used to at least three cups of coffee per day. Minimum. I'll start going through withdrawals soon. Then, I might cry."

"Please don't cry," Callum said. "I'm not good with tears."

"I find that hard to believe. I don't know you well, but you seem like a genuinely sweet guy. You probably give really big hugs." I nibbled more bread.

He seemed almost shy. "I'll leave you to your meal." He headed for the door but stopped as he reached it. "For what it's worth? I believe you're a sweet person too. While I'm unsure who you are or where you came from, I don't think you're a threat to us. The captain will see that soon. Just give him some time."

The center of my chest warmed. "I appreciate that."

He tipped his head to me before leaving the room.

A positive about the kingdom of Bremloc? The food was amazing. I ate every bit of it and had to force myself not to lick the bowl clean. I placed the dishes back on the tray and walked over to the window.

A warm breeze came through, and I breathed it in, feeling much better than I had earlier. Not only because of my full belly either. After the most bizarre and confusing morning I'd ever had, I finally had some clarity. This wasn't a Renaissance festival filled with actors in costume. This was a legit fantasy world. And although a part of me was nervous about that, my stomach fluttered with excitement.

I had often dreamed of being swept away to the places I'd read about in books. With one chance meeting with a hot wizard in a traveling magic shop, that had become a reality. If I was stuck there for the foreseeable future, I might as well make the most of it.

"Starting with some exploring." I turned from the window and neared the door, yanking it open…

Only to be met with a sneering face.

"Where do you think you're going?" Captain Maddox asked. He was an immovable object in the doorway. Tall and muscled. And oh, so big.

"Nowhere. Just, um…" I tried to peek around him, and he shifted in front of me. I caught a glimpse of a tree though. The room wasn't inside the main part of the castle like I'd assumed and was instead part of its own section of housing. "Am I not allowed to get some fresh air?"

"You can breathe the air fine from your room. There's a window."

"So, this is how it's gonna be, huh?" Sighing, I rocked back on my heels. "I'm like Rapunzel trapped in her tower. No escape apart from the lone window to stare out of and dream of freedom. I even have the blond hair… but mine's shorter. Like, way shorter. Not long enough to use as a rope. I don't mind if it's pulled a little though. But anyway. At least you fed me."

"Who is Rapunzel? And why is she trapped?" His eyes sparked with curiosity… a curiosity that was then swept away. He quietly cleared his throat. "Never mind that. Back inside your room."

"When you said a guard would be stationed outside my door, I didn't expect it to be you. Will you stand out here all night?"

He stared at me, jaw ticking.

"Fine. I'm going." I stepped backward and started to close the door. His eyes didn't leave mine. I paused with the door slightly ajar, staring at him through the crack. "What happens tomorrow?"

"I'll assess whether you're a threat to the kingdom or merely a stumbling fool."

"Stumbling?" I pushed the door a bit more open. "I resent that. I'm graceful. Well, when I want to be."

His cheek twitched.

"What happens if you decide I'm a threat?"

"I suppose you'll learn that answer on the morrow," he said before angling his body forward, resting an arm on the outside of the doorframe. "Sleep well, Muffin Lord."

Before I could respond, he grabbed the handle and pulled the door closed. I laughed at the silly nickname—that I'd given myself—and returned to the window. Orange and dark purple streaked across the sky as the sun inched closer to the horizon.

What tomorrow would bring? Who knew? One thing was certain though: this was bound to be one hell of an adventure.

Chapter Three
Thawing Captain Ice... Kind of

When I woke up the next morning, I expected to be back in my apartment. I lay in bed with my eyes closed, waiting for the clamor of other tenants stomping down the stairs or slamming car doors. I braced myself for the whiffs from the restaurant next door that served the greasiest breakfast on the face of the planet but was cheap, so they got a good amount of business anyway.

Instead, I heard birds chirping and opened my eyes.

Sunlight streamed in through the window, the golden hues creating an almost magical glow as it lit the small room. Blue skies stretched beyond the glass, and the leaves of the tree—the most vibrant shade of green—rustled with the morning breeze.

It was peaceful.

That was until a hard bang came at the door, followed by the deep, grumpy voice I'd come to know so well in the twenty-four hours I'd been there. "Boy. Wake up."

"Good morning to you too," I mumbled, sitting up.

The door swung open, and Maddox entered the room, looking perfectly mouthwatering from head to toe, even with his sneer in place. He filled out his armor *very* well. "Get dressed."

56

"You know? The word 'please' goes a long way." I pulled back the blanket and scooted to the edge of the bed. "You should definitely add it to your vocabulary. Were you out there all night?"

"No," he answered. "Another of my knights took the shift so I could rest. Now, do as I say."

"Yeah, yeah. I'm going." A big stretch then took me over, and I raised my arms above my head with a jaw-popping yawn.

His blue eyes lowered to my bare stomach. The change was minute, but his hard expression wavered a bit.

My face heated. I always slept in my boxers, hating how restricting clothes felt. I regretted it right then. I was what Jonah called a twink. Small and cute—his words. I had minimal muscle definition—not scrawny but definitely no beefcake either. Plain and average described me pretty well.

"Keep staring and you're gonna give me a complex."

"Your undergarments," Maddox said. "They are... peculiar."

"Oh." I glanced at my boxers. He was staring at *them*, not at my body. For some reason, that only made my cheeks hotter. Either from embarrassment or disappointment, who knew? "What's wrong with them?"

"The pattern on the fabric." He took a step closer. "I've not seen anything like it before."

Oh yeah. People in this kingdom wouldn't be familiar with the clothing from my world. The neon green boxers had cartoon hot dogs on them. Some wore sunglasses and had quotes like "want my wiener?" above their heads. I grabbed the blanket and placed it back over my lap. "Yeah, well, tell Callum he's not allowed to steal these. Also, it's not polite to look at a dude's underwear."

Maddox lightly cleared his throat, and his guard went up again, expression hardening. "Make yourself presentable, and join me outside."

"Okay, but I don't have any shoes. Sir Cinnamon Roll is wearing them."

"Cinnamon Roll? You are indeed odd," he said. "I'll find boots for you to wear and set them outside the door."

He pivoted around and exited the room.

I would've killed for a hot shower but had to settle for the basin of water in the corner of the room. At least it wasn't cold—which made no sense. The water, despite sitting out, was warm. I quickly scrubbed my body, dreaming of the hot spring Callum had mentioned the day before. Maybe he'd take me later so I could have a proper full-body soak. If Maddox didn't kill me first.

The fantasy world had Renaissance vibes, but there were modern influences as well. I was happy to find running water when I used the toilet in the connecting closet-type room—thank god—so there seemed to be a plumbing system in place. The toilet flushed; I just had no idea where it went. Not that I really cared *to* know.

Some things were better left to the imagination.

After putting on jeans and a navy blue T-shirt, I opened the bedroom door. A small courtyard greeted me. Other rooms surrounded mine, and people exited them. Probably some of the staff, like

Briar and anyone else who worked around the castle grounds.

Maddox leaned against a tree with that same brooding expression. "Took you long enough. Not many men keep me waiting like you do."

"That's not my fault. I didn't ask you to wait."

He snarled and pushed away from the tree. "Slow, clumsy, *and* mouthy. You are either brave… or incredibly foolish." Stopping in front of me, he bent his head to meet my gaze. "I place my wager on the latter."

"Gambling is in addiction, you know. You should be careful about that."

His lips twitched.

"Is that a smile?"

"No." He nodded to the ground. "Put those on."

A pair of shoes sat beside the door. I plopped down to put them on. "Whoa, these are legit." The leather boots hit me at my ankles, and the shoelaces were made from thin strips of leather. I tied them and stood up, shifting my weight between my feet. "Not as comfy as my Vans, but they'll do, I guess."

"Good." Maddox turned away and motioned with his head for me to follow. I did. "Do you recall anything yet? About where you're from?"

Should I mention the whole "I was sent here from another world" thing? Honesty was the best policy, but being *that* honest might lead to me being thrown in the dungeon or something.

"I come from a land far, far away."

Maddox's brow furrowed. "What is the name of this land?"

"I hail from the kingdom of Arkansas."

59

"I've not heard of this place. Who rules over it?"

"Republicans, mostly." Three men walked past us, nodding their heads to Maddox before continuing on. "Where are you taking me?"

"You're hungry, are you not?" He rested a hand on my lower back to guide me toward the right. Although my shirt acted as a barrier between his hand and my skin, I still tingled where he touched me. "I distinctly recall you mumbling about food as soon as you woke yesterday morning. I thought it best to appease your belly as soon as possible to spare myself more of your whining."

He might've behaved like it was some great chore to do so, but the action was kind.

"Yeah. I could definitely eat."

"Thought so. You will eat morning meal with me." He finally looked at me. "So I can keep an eye on you, of course."

"You haven't eaten yet either?"

"No. I came for you as soon as I dressed for the day."

I had been the first thing on his mind when he woke up. Why did that give me butterflies? Those silly little flutters in my stomach needed to stop. And I needed to get a grip and toss aside any of my romantic ideals.

This might have been a fantasy world with magic, but I was still the same old Evan I'd always been: a dorky bookworm who talked fast when he was nervous and who couldn't flirt to save his life.

"Thank you for thinking of me." My voice dropped in volume.

He was quiet for a few passing beats. "Do not mistake my suspicion of you as me being heartless. I only want what's best for the kingdom."

"Callum said you've dedicated your life to being a knight."

"I have. The knights are my family. I'd gladly give my life for theirs, just as I would for anyone else in Bremloc." There was a short pause. "What of your family?"

"Don't have any."

His blue eyes shifted back to me. "No parents or siblings?"

"Nope and nope," I answered. "I never knew my parents. I grew up in foster care and got shuffled around to different homes." What was the fantasy world equivalent to foster care? An orphanage? Oh well. Maddox seemed to be following my explanation fairly well regardless. "Once old enough, I set off on my own. Been that way ever since."

I'd made it sound a lot easier than it had actually been. Not feeling like I belonged anywhere had been rough. It was lonely and scary navigating the world on my own. The money I made at the café was barely enough to keep a roof over my head and food on my table some months.

"We have that in common," Maddox said, his tone much gentler than usual. "My father was a knight in the Second Order and fell in battle when I was a young boy. I had no mother. She gave her life bringing me into this world. I was then placed in a home with other war orphans and learned early on that the only person I could rely on was myself."

"Look at you now." I tossed him a smile. "Captain of the knights and total badass. I'd say you did well for yourself."

Maddox averted his gaze. And did his cheeks have a bit more color?

Nah. I'm just seeing things.

"Question," I said.

He peered back at me.

"The basin of water in my room was warm. How?"

"How?" Maddox was confused by that. "The rune on the basin keeps the water heated enough for washing comfortably."

Ah. Magic. Should've guessed that much.

"Can you do magic?"

"That's another question." A dash of humor touched his stare before he averted it in front of us. "No, I don't possess that skill. The runes allow those of us without magic to get by."

We passed two women who were knelt beside a garden, digging in the soil and planting seeds. Both snapped their heads toward Maddox before leaning in close and excitedly whispering to each other.

Did they have the hots for him? Not surprising. The man might've been cold as ice, but he was certainly easy on the eyes.

"Are you married?" I asked.

"No."

"Dating anyone? Well, I guess you'd call it courting." Another thought occurred to me. "Oh, maybe knights aren't allowed to date?"

He stopped walking and faced me. Something about his expression was different. He seemed... lighter. Amused, even. "Why do you ask? Interested in filling that role for yourself, Muffin Lord?"

"Um. Of course not." When I laughed, it came out raspy. Nervous. "I'm just trying to get to know you better. That's all. Those ladies are totally checking you out. I'm sure *they'd* love to fill that role."

He looked over at them, confused, before returning his eyes to me. "I haven't the time for courtship. My duty is to my kingdom. Anything else would be an unnecessary distraction."

"A distraction. Right. Like some very suspicious, but harmless, I assure you, stranger appearing out of nowhere and forcing you to play babysitter?"

Maddox's icy expression thawed, and I nearly shit and fell back in it when the very edge of his mouth curved up in the smallest of smiles. "Precisely."

With his raven-black hair and deep blue eyes, he was a knockout. It was hard to make direct eye contact with him, so I looked away. His gaze remained pinned to me though, sending heat rushing through my veins. We continued walking as I tried to make sense of everything.

"I have another question."

"I cannot wait to hear it."

I ignored his obvious sarcasm. "What happens after we eat breakfast? Are you going to grill me some more?"

"Grill you?"

"Yeah. Like question me or whatever."

Maddox stared at me for a moment, face emotionless. A spark then touched his eyes, like embers that still faintly burned among all the ashes. "No."

He then continued walking.

"No?" I hurried after him. "Wow, you walk fast for such a big guy. So, you aren't going to question me anymore? Aren't you worried I'm a spy? Or an evil wizard sent here to bring destruction to your land?"

Maddox's brow shot upward. "I doubt wizards would faint at the sight of magic. Nor would they stumble around like you do." He glanced down. "With your short legs."

"Hey, I don't stumble. And my legs are the perfect length in proportion to my body."

"Mhm."

The man was exasperating. But I kind of liked it. "So, I'm free to wander around on my own?"

"I didn't say that." He nodded to another knight we passed. "I may no longer believe you're a threat, but your arrival in the kingdom still brings forth many questions. Until I have more answers, I'm not letting you out of my sight."

Dammit. That shouldn't have thrilled me as much as it did.

"About that..." I recalled the excuse Lupin had given me. "I remember how I got to the field, so it's not really a mystery anymore."

Maddox halted in step. "Explain."

"I'm a traveler." It wasn't a total lie. I had traveled through time and space, according to

64

Lupin. "I left, uh, the kingdom of Arkansas to explore the world. I was really tired and found the field to sleep in for the night. You found me the next morning, and here we are now."

"What about your confusion upon waking?" he asked. "You had no recollection of your travels."

"Um." I chewed at my bottom lip. "As I said, I was really tired. It was probably a combination of exhaustion, sleep deprivation, being hungry, and too much sun. But after resting, my mind is much clearer."

Maddox carefully watched me. Did he believe the story?

"Evan!" Callum jogged toward us, still wearing my shoes. What he wasn't wearing? A shirt. The dude had a nice body. An athletic build and trim muscle. "Good morning."

"Morning," I responded. He reminded me of an excited puppy greeting his owner. The only thing missing was the wagging tail.

"Captain." He tipped his head to Maddox. "Apologies for my state of undress. I woke late and was rushing around to come and retrieve Evan when the men informed me you'd already done so in my place."

"It's no trouble," the captain responded. "The boy is my responsibility as of now. Return to your quarters and prepare for the day. The scouts should be returning soon, and I expect you to be ready to greet them when they arrive."

"Yes, sir." Callum flashed me another smile before turning on his heels and heading back the way he'd come.

I peered up at Maddox. He must've been around six foot two or three if I had to guess. I stood at a measly five foot seven, and he towered over me. "I'm not a kid, you know, so you can stop referring to me as *boy*."

"Is that so?" He stepped closer, that earlier amusement returning to his mouth.

"Yep. I'm an adult, thank you very much. I just turned twenty-three."

"Could have fooled me. I've seen boys no older than fifteen who are taller than you."

"Hey." I poked his chest. "Don't make fun of my height."

"Or you'll do what exactly?" He snatched hold of my wrist and pulled me in closer to his body.

Any snarky remark I might've had completely vanished from my mind as I stared up into his blue eyes. And fuck, how in the hell did he smell so good? Like leather and warm spice. He was all man, and I was... well, a horny twenty-three-year-old who hadn't gotten laid in going on a year. My pulse quickened.

Lupin had said I'd have a few lovers while in Bremloc. Was Maddox one of them?

Don't be ridiculous. A guy as hot as him wouldn't give me the time of day.

"No response?" he asked, easing his firm hold on my wrist. He didn't release me though. His touch just became more gentle. "Shocking. And here I thought nothing could silence that mouth of yours."

My heart thumped so hard against my ribs I wondered if he could feel it too with his body so close to mine.

"There you are," a smooth voice said from behind us. Briar approached, wearing a white button-down shirt and fitted trousers. The long sleeves of the shirt were pushed to his inner elbows, exposing his pale skin to the morning sun. Behind the round frames of his glasses, his hazel eyes lingered on Maddox before moving to me. "How are you feeling, Evan?"

Apart from all the blood rushing from my head and to my dick? "Fine."

"No headaches?"

"Nope. Not even a little," I responded. Again, with the exception of the ache down south.

"Excellent." The chief herbalist slash physician beamed with a smile. "How did you sleep? When you fainted yesterday, I was worried."

"I slept great. But I appreciate your concern, Doc."

Maddox released my wrist and shifted his body a bit in front of me, placing himself between me and Briar. "We were on our way to eat morning meal. If you'll excuse us."

Briar easily held his gaze. "I'm sure you're quite busy, Captain. Much too busy to deal with something such as this. Allow me to take over from here. It's my field of expertise, after all. Evan should really be in a physician's care considering his memory loss and the fall he took."

"His memory has returned," Maddox coolly said. "He told me where he's from. And you heard him. He is in no pain. I suggest you care for those who actually need your help."

"He may not be in pain, but he should be carefully monitored," Briar countered. "He'd be much safer in my hands."

"Safer?" Maddox said with a slight snarl. "I'm the captain of the Second Order. There are no safer hands for him to be in than mine."

Why did I get the feeling they were… fighting over me? Surely not. I had clearly hit my head harder than I thought if I believed something like that was even possible.

"You suspect him to be a spy, do you not?" Briar asked. "Your concern does not lie in his well-being but rather in whether or not he'll strike against the kingdom. This suspicion will prevent you from caring for him as he needs—"

"Do not presume to tell me my thoughts," Maddox interjected with a growl. "Evan will remain in my charge until I say otherwise. If he happens to hit his pretty little head again, we will pay you a visit. Until then, I suggest you stay out of my way."

Pretty little head?

Briar's smile remained in place, though his eyes narrowed. "But of course. How foolish of me to be concerned about him when you've done such a fine job so far."

"Careful of your tone, physician."

Ignoring the seething knight, Briar regarded me. "Enjoy your morning meal. If you need anything at all, you know where to find me."

"Thanks." My voice trembled. This was all too weird.

Maddox placed his hand on my lower back and guided me away. His stormy expression kept me from saying a word. At first, anyway. My curiosity got the better of me after five whole seconds.

"Do you and Briar not like each other?"

"What?" Maddox looked down at me.

"I sensed hostility between you. Just wondering if there's bad history or something."

"Not at all." He slowed his pace as we approached what I assumed to be the knights' quarters. There was a training field, a stable, and a section of buildings much like the one I'd stayed the night in. "The physician and I have rarely spoken, with the exception of when he's treated my injuries."

"Ah. So you're just that warm and friendly to everyone."

"Warm and friendly?" His stormy expression cleared, like dark clouds dispersing to reveal the sun. A peek of it anyway, like it wasn't ready to fully show its golden rays. "I sense sarcasm."

I tried to hold back my smile but failed. "Just returning the favor. I take your sarcasm and raise you one."

"I feel you'd win that contest. I've only just met you but can already tell that mouth of yours has a mind of its own."

"It's a gift."

"To be completely honest, perhaps I was a bit harsh toward him," Maddox said as he led me toward a firepit where other men were seated. "I don't take kindly to those who challenge my authority."

"Said like a true captain. Oh. I just thought of another question."

He released a drawn-out sigh. "What is it?"

"You're the captain of the Second Order. How many Orders are there? What do you do? You said you can't use magic, but what about magical weapons? Do you slay dragons?"

"That… was much more than one question. Sit." Maddox nodded to a wooden stool. "I'll fetch our food."

"Allow me, Captain," a man I didn't know said before pushing to his feet. "I'll get your breakfast."

"I can manage fine on my own," Maddox told him. "Watch him until I return."

"Yes, sir."

He then left me at the firepit. The six men stared at me between bites of their food. The attention made me nervous. I normally kept to myself, staying inside my little bubble, but that was impossible now. I couldn't hide in that world, not when my very presence sparked so much interest.

I sat down and waved at them. "Hey. I'm Evan."

"My name is Roth," the man closest to me said. "You're the one who was found near the dark wood yesterday morn."

"Yep. That's me." What was so dark about the woods? The forest had appeared pretty normal to me. From the outside, at least. Did demons live inside? Monsters?

Lupin?

The other five then introduced themselves, and the tangle of nerves in my belly started to unravel as the topic shifted from me and back to whatever they'd been discussing prior to my arrival. They mentioned Onyx, the same name I'd heard Briar and Callum say the previous day.

"Bastard is going to get what's coming to him," Roth said. "Goddamn demon. All of his kind needs to be wiped off the map. Same for the beast-men."

"Demi-humans," one of the other knights corrected him. Duke, if I remembered right. "Beast-men is a derogatory term."

"You think I care if it offends them?" Roth dunked his slice of bread into his bowl, sopping up the contents, and shoved it into his mouth. "They're not human. Can't be trusted either. The whole lot of them would tear any of us apart without a second thought if given the chance. Better off dead, if you ask me."

"Don't let Prince Sawyer hear you say that," Duke said, fidgeting with the strap tying back his red hair. "He has a demi-human in his service and is quite fond of him."

Wait. Was he referring to Kuya, the cat boy I'd met at Briar's clinic? He had seemed sweet. Right away, I pegged this Roth guy as a class-A asshole.

"Well, no disrespect to the young *prince*," Roth said, "but the kingdom is fortunate his older brother will eventually take the throne instead of him. He is much too soft."

"What's so wrong about demi-humans?" I asked. "Just because they're not fully human, you think they're beneath you?"

"Of course they're beneath us," Roth responded. "You're not from around here, so maybe you're unfamiliar with how we do things in Bremloc. But the paper we use to wipe our asses has more value than them."

"Enough, Roth," Duke snapped, a hard look in his green eyes. "Demi-humans are citizens of Bremloc, and thus we are sworn to protect them as well. Your views are sorely outdated."

Roth huffed before taking another bite. Good. More food meant he'd shut his big, hateful mouth. He wiped at his lips before standing from the stump. "Watch the boy. I need to take a piss."

"Pay him little mind," Duke told me after Roth was out of earshot. "He isn't nearly as awful as he seems. A demi-human killed his mother when he was a young boy. He's held a grudge against them ever since."

There was so much I wanted—needed—to learn about the world I'd been sent to. Every land had its politics and history. Even fantasy ones like this one.

What I *did* know? They were currently in conflict with a demon named Onyx, but I didn't know who Onyx was, where he lived, or why they fought each other. And then there was the mystery of the dark wood.

"I heard you ask about the Second Order," Duke then said. "There are three in total. The First Order of Knights, or the Royal Order as they're also called, live in the castle and are assigned to the royal household."

"So they're like the elite tier of knights?" I asked.

He nodded. "They rarely see actual battle unless absolutely necessary. They're more like glorified bodyguards; however, they hold a large burden on their shoulders. Protecting the king and his sons is no simple task, what with all the assassination attempts."

"Whoa. Assassination attempts?"

Another nod. "Along with the fight against Onyx, we're also in conflict with the kingdom of Haran. They often send mercenaries, assassins, you name it, to attack King Eidolon and his family."

"Why?"

Duke shrugged. "Why do men do most things? For power. Wealth. To prove they're strongest."

One of the other men looked at me. He had brown hair and a scar on his face. "The king's younger brother worsened the conflict. Or so the stories say."

"What stories?"

"The one about the lost treasure of Haran," he responded.

"Lost treasure?"

The man smirked and leaned in closer. "Stolen."

"Enough questions." Maddox sat to my left. He held two bowls and offered one to me.

"Thanks." I accepted the food. "What's the stolen treasure? And who stole it?"

Maddox sneered at the man with the scar. "Choose your words carefully around him, Quincy. His curiosity and rambling mouth know no bounds." He then regarded me. "There is no lost or stolen treasure. Bremloc has never stolen from the kingdom of Haran. Why would we when our riches far outweigh theirs? It's nothing but a rumor that was spread to tarnish King Eidolon's reputation."

"What about the king's brother?" I nodded to the scarred man—Quincy. "He said the dude pissed off Haran even more."

Maddox shot him another look before turning back to me. "The king's brother died long ago. That's all there is to say on the matter."

"Fine," I said. "One more question. What does the Second Order do?"

"We keep the people of Bremloc safe," Maddox answered, much to my surprise. He had seemed ready to gag me and toss me into the field if it meant escaping my mouth. "Patrols of the kingdom. Combat missions. Fighting in war. Allow me to ask you one in return."

"Go ahead."

"Why are you so curious about the knights?" He side-eyed me. "Do you wish to become one of us?"

"Totally." I scoffed. "Just look at my awesome muscles. I'd be a true force of nature."

"You with a sword is a truly frightening thought." He took a bite of his food, his gaze unwavering on mine. "You'd put your eye out."

"Rude," I said. His tone had been dead serious, but there'd been a spark of amusement in his blue eyes. The jerk. "Do you tease all prisoners of Bremloc like this?"

His amusement deepened, though it never showed on his mouth. "If you were my prisoner, you wouldn't be sitting here with me enjoying breakfast."

Those silly flutters swarmed my belly again. "Speaking of breakfast…" I moved the spoon through the contents. "What is this? Some type of porridge? Is it rice?"

"It's food," he answered before scooping a spoonful into his mouth.

"How kind of you to clear that up," I mumbled. The edge of his lips twitched. I took a bite and groaned a little under my breath. The creamy rice porridge was sweetened with honey and had an assortment of blueberries. "I think my taste buds just had an orgasm."

Maddox coughed. Then coughed again.

"You okay?" I patted his back. "Choke on your food? Don't die on me, Captain. I'm sure you've been in many fights in your life and faced countless enemies. Do you really want porridge to be the thing to take you out?"

"Silence that rambling mouth of yours," he said, his cheeks pinker now than before. He slightly turned his body away from me. "I wish to eat in peace."

"It's because I said orgasm, isn't it? Does it go against the knight's code?"

"Evan, I swear to the gods." He pinched his eyes closed, and as his lips started to twitch, he tightened his jaw and gritted his teeth together. Like he was trying his hardest to refrain from laughing. "Finish your breakfast without another world, or I *will* gag you."

His gaze met mine again. I blinked at him. When I opened my mouth, his brow arched, as if to imply he dared me to say something.

"Gag me with what exactly?" I asked, unable to help myself. "A rope, piece of cloth, or…" My gaze dropped to his pants, and my cheeks heated at the bulge staring back at me. "What would my tombstone say in that case? Death by knightly sausage. The hero of meats."

Maddox made some kind of choking noise before turning his face away from me. He stood and walked away from the firepit, and although I could only see the back of him, his shoulders shook.

He had stepped away to laugh.

That's when I realized Captain Ice wasn't nearly as cold as he led people to believe. Beneath all that snarl? He was a hot-blooded male who laughed at perverted jokes like the rest of us.

After breakfast, Maddox met with the scouts who'd recently returned. I wasn't allowed to listen in, but I could see them from my spot near the fire. The captain's grave expression told me the news they brought wasn't good. He nodded, exchanged a few more words, then dismissed them before approaching me.

"Everything okay?" I asked, standing up.

"I have business elsewhere," he said. "Can I trust you to behave while I'm gone?"

"What business? Where are you going?"

"I need to speak with the king."

"Why? Did the scouts have bad news?"

He stared at me for a few moments. "That's no concern of yours." Slowly, he was reverting back to his icy self. "Before I set out, I need to know what you plan to do. You say you're a traveler. Where is your next destination?"

"Honestly? I have no idea." Lupin had said returning to my world was impossible, which didn't leave me many options. "If it's okay, I'd like to stay in Bremloc. At least for now."

"Very well." He straightened his stance, chin tipping up. Maybe I was mistaken, but he looked pleased by my answer. "In that case, you'll stay here for the day."

"How long will you be gone?"

Maddox called Callum over. "Watch over him until I return."

"Yes, sir," Callum responded.

"You're going to ignore me?" I asked.

Maddox stepped closer. He didn't touch me, but he stood so close I felt the heat of his body. "Ignore you? As if that's possible. You've been a pain in my backside since I found you."

If that was true, why did he look like he was seconds away from smiling?

After looking at me one final time, Maddox left the area. I stared after him, confused by the little flutters in my belly. Was I crushing on him? It had only been a day. Well, two if I counted yesterday.

"Come with me," Callum said, smile bright. "I'll show you around."

***

The tour was brief but informative. The knights slept in barracks, dispersed between several buildings, and the officers had their own rooms. There was also a mess hall where they dined together, played cards, and relaxed. Callum then showed me the stables, the training grounds, and the kitchens.

One thing I noticed? The knights were very well taken care of. The men who risked their lives to protect the kingdom weren't treated like they were disposable. Their quality of life and well-being mattered beyond the battlefield.

That's exactly how it should be.

After the grand tour of the grounds, I spent time hanging out with Callum and the other knights. With the exception of Roth—who I still thought was an asshole—they all seemed to be great guys. By late afternoon, they were joking with me, and that suspicion in their eyes had lessened.

I might've been a stranger in the kingdom, but none of them viewed me as a threat anymore.

I helped them care for the horses and do small tasks around the area. While they trained, I stared in awe. Even though they practiced with dull blades, it was still exciting to watch. Callum was incredible. The cinnamon roll persona flew out the window as he roared, grunted, and took down his opponents, one by one.

"Want to try?" Callum asked, offering me a sword.

"Definitely not. You go ahead. I'll just stand here where it's safe."

He laughed before jumping back in to the duel, facing two men at once and easily holding his own.

Around dinnertime, they led me into the mess hall. The room acted as a sort of gathering place for them. Tables were placed throughout where some took their meals. Others played cards. A large hearth warmed the area, and a smaller one was used to cook whatever was in the large pots hanging over it.

"Rabbit stew," Callum said, reminding me of a puppy again in his excitement. "It's my favorite."

"You'll eat anything," the knight named Quincy said.

Callum blushed. "True." He appeared to be the youngest out of them, but despite that, the men respected him. Their banter was lighthearted. Judging by what I'd witnessed during their training, he more than earned that respect.

I looked out the window, watching the sun inch toward the horizon. The light had shifted, shadowing some areas of the sky.

My second day in this new world had almost come to a close. Would all be like this? I had to admit it wasn't too bad, this life. It was the most social I'd been in a while. Not only that, I had helped earn my keep, which wasn't a bad feeling either.

"Tell us a story from your travels," Quincy said. He had taken a liking to me, for whatever reason. Chocolate-brown hair and eyes that matched, he was handsome in a rugged way— rugged because of the deep scar cutting across the left side of his face. "You come from a far-off land, yes? I'm sure you've seen a few things worthy of mention. Pretty lasses, perhaps?"

"With big jugs?" one named Baden added. "Like the milkmaid I fell in love with in my youth."

"Um." I breathed out a laugh. "Sorry to disappoint, but women with big jugs don't really do it for me." And then, like many times in my life after discovering my sexuality and coming out—because it was never just once—a tingle of fear pierced my chest.

How did they view homosexuality in Bremloc? Was it frowned upon?

Forbidden?

"Tell us stories of pretty lads, then," Quincy casually suggested. He swept a hand over his hair. "I can hardly resist the ones with sharp jawlines and dark eyes."

My heart skipped a beat, and I smiled. "Really?"

"Aye." The scar on his face curved as he returned the expression. "Life is much too short and can be ripped away even faster, especially for us knights. It's why I take pleasure in all that life has to offer. Lasses and lads alike."

"Only lasses for me," Baden said before bumping against Callum. "This one here refuses to tell us his preference."

Callum smiled down at his hands. "Because there's not much to tell. My only love is the Order."

"You sound just like the captain." Duke smiled. His medium-length red hair was pulled back in a low hold, the strands just long enough to be held with the leather strap. "I've never known him to take a lover, male or female."

Because it was a distraction, Maddox had told me.

"So tell us of your travels," Quincy said. "Leave no details out."

"I'd rather hear about why you were so close to the dark wood when the captain found you," Duke said, his green eyes serious. "A damned miracle you weren't mauled in the dead of night."

"Our Evan is small but brave." Quincy slapped me on the back. "The dark wood doesn't frighten him. Instead, he sleeps peacefully beside it, daring the beasts within to come for him."

"I wouldn't go that far," I said, nerves spiking. Fuck. Was the forest really that dangerous? Why in the hell would the wishing stone place me so close to it upon my arrival? I could've died.

Yep. Lupin was an evil wizard, and the Emporium was his house of torture.

"You should join the Order," Baden said. "Put a sword in your hand, and I'm sure you'd be a true terror."

"To himself, mostly," a deep voice said from behind me. A voice that caused little prickles of excitement in my chest.

I turned, ready to spout off at the jerk of a captain for mocking me yet again, but the words caught in my throat as I got an eyeful of him. Pretty sure my damn jaw nearly detached.

Maddox was shirtless, skin damp. His black hair glistened, and droplets of water gathered at the ends of the strands. His trousers hugged his thighs and ass to perfection. The valley of rippling muscle along his abdomen was a land I wanted to explore. With my tongue.

"Why are you wet?" And why was my voice so high? I cleared my throat.

"I washed off the grime of the day," he said, taking a seat beside me. "You're fitting in well. I expected to return and find you gagged and tied up in the shed."

"That would make you happy, wouldn't it?" I nudged his arm. "Too bad for you they like my rambling mouth."

"Aye, we do." Baden nodded.

Maddox's lips did that twitching thing. His attempt to force away a smile. A man brought over a bowl of stew and placed it in front of him. The rest of the knights, seeing that Maddox had his food, then went over to get theirs. I didn't get the impression Maddox had made that rule; it was more like a respectful gesture. His men adored him. That much was evident.

"Here." He slid the bowl to me. "You need to eat."

"But this is yours."

That time, his smile surfaced, albeit briefly. "I'll grab another." Then, as though to ward off any of the budding warm fuzzies attacking my stomach, he added, "I know how much you whine when you're hungry."

Callum choked on his stew as he laughed.

I cut my eyes at the cinnamon roll of a knight before aiming that glare at his captain. Maddox smirked before leaving the table to grab another bowl. My feistiness was forgotten as I took a bite.

The seasoned broth, juicy meat, and chunks of potato were to die for.

"Another mouth orgasm?" Maddox asked, retaking his seat beside me.

I was the one who choked on my stew then.

After dinner, I said goodbye to the knights and found the path Maddox had led me down earlier. Everything looked different in the dark. I stopped and glanced around, unsure if we had come from the left or right side.

"I'll walk you back," Maddox said from behind me. "Last thing I need is you getting lost and stumbling around in the dark."

"I don't need your help." I started forward to prove as much. The toe of my boot chose that moment to bump a rock jutting from the ground, and I tripped.

Maddox grabbed my arm to steady me. "Yes, I can see you're perfectly capable."

I fought the urge to stick my tongue out at him. He enjoyed picking on me. And I... might have enjoyed it too. A little bit. "Fine. You can walk with me. But it's not because I don't know the way."

"It's so you can enjoy my company?" Maddox peered down at me. "Because I'm so warm and friendly?"

I cracked a smile. Damned knight. "Something like that."

We walked in silence for a while, our leisurely pace allowing me to take in the sights of the castle grounds at night. Though dark, the bright moon above us lit the path and guided the way. The main part of the castle was visible above the treetops, the stone turrets stretching toward the sky. Golden light spilled out from a few of the windows, the flickers a sign of a lit hearth. It was close but seemed so far away.

"Will I ever get to go in there?" I asked.

"In the castle?" Maddox glanced at it. "Perhaps someday."

"Did the meeting go well with the king?"

"Still so full of questions," he said. "The meeting went as expected. I relayed the information, received my orders, and then acted upon them." I opened my mouth, but he cut in before I could get a single word out. "And no, I will not discuss those orders with you."

My mouth closed… then opened again. "Will I ever meet the king?"

Maddox slowed in step, and a shadow passed over his face. "You're very curious about the king."

Oh shit. Did he still think I was a spy? An assassin? "Only because I've never met one before. Before you, I'd never met a real knight either."

He appeared to accept that answer. No more was said as we continued toward the courtyard, then over to the door outside my room.

"I suggest you rest well," Maddox said, a touch of humor back in his eyes. "Tomorrow begins early."

"How early are we talking? Do I get coffee first? Callum said I could buy beans from the market. It's been two days since I had a fix. I may die."

That humor spread to his mouth. "If coffee will silence those rambles, I'll see what I can do. But you'll have to earn it."

"Earn it how? Because I'd do some sketchy things for a cup right now. Not even joking."

"You'll find out at first light." He pushed open the door. "Good night, Evan."

I stepped across the threshold and turned back to him. "Good night."

He hesitated before shutting the door. Once it closed, I leaned against it. There were no footsteps. He hadn't moved from the other side. But then, finally, I heard him walk away.

As I crawled into bed that night, I was excited for what awaited me in the morning. Little did I know it wouldn't be anything like I'd expected.

Chapter Four
Evan Gets a Job

"This is bullshit," I said, leaning against the rake. My muscles ached, I was sweaty, and I couldn't remember what it was like to breathe in fresh air. "Well, horse shit, actually."

A horse snorted from the stall beside me.

"Yeah, laugh all you want, Seabiscuit." I used the back of my hand to wipe at my damp forehead. I had taken off my shirt earlier and rolled up the bottom of my jeans but had still managed to get them dirty. "Sweat is in my ass crack. Do you know how that feels? I'll tell ya. It's not good."

The horse made another sound.

I sighed.

Maddox had woken me before the sun even fully rose in the sky, dragged me from bed, and led me to the knights' quarters. My mood had perked up as he'd offered me a steaming mug that wafted an oh-so-familiar scent. Coffee. Had it been the best I'd ever had? Well, no. But beggars couldn't be choosers, and I'd chugged the thing like it was the elixir of life and I was a dying man.

But then, the morning had taken a turn.

"Time to earn your keep," Maddox had said, leading me across the yard.

Which led me to the present. My new life as a stable boy.

"Sorry if I stink," I told Seabiscuit. Not its real name, but he reminded me of the one from the movie. "Do you know Maddox? He's a real pain, isn't he?"

A pain who had dropped me off in the stable and left me. It was about midafternoon now, and my stomach rumbled. I hoped I could eat lunch soon.

"I'm a pain, am I?" a deep voice said from behind me.

My head whirled around, and I inwardly cursed at the way my heart thumped harder at the sight of Maddox. I stepped from the stall and approached him. His eyes followed my every movement. I stopped about two feet away from him. "About time you came back."

Maddox gave me a once-over. "What have you been doing? I told you to clean the stables, not roll around in it."

"Listen here, you." I put my hands on my hips. "I've been working my ass off. And know what I've decided?"

"Oh, do tell me."

"I've decided that the stable-boy life isn't for me. I know it's hard to believe, but I'm not the physical type. Hard labor isn't my forte."

"Hard labor?" His lips did that twitching thing again. "I suppose I'll need to re-evaluate your duties. I'm sure there's a suitable job for you somewhere. Perhaps as the court jester? I believe the position is open."

"That was mean. Besides, if I worked in the castle entertaining the royals, you'd miss my mouth too much. Just admit it."

"I'll do no such thing. Come on." He tipped his head toward the exit. "I'll show you where you can bathe."

"Callum mentioned a hot spring," I said as I rushed to keep pace beside him. "Can I go there? I think I've earned a good soak."

"The spring is a ways up the mountain," he answered. "By the angry growls of your stomach, I fear you'll die of hunger before we reach it."

Insufferable knight. But I inwardly smiled about how in tune he was with me.

He led me to a building beside the barracks. A bath house. There were several deep, steaming tubs. Must've been the same magic that kept the water basin warm. It wasn't as awesome as a hot spring, but the water felt amazing on my sore muscles.

Maddox was the perfect gentleman too, standing outside the door while I washed. He didn't let anyone inside. Hope budded in my chest, and I shoved it back down. There was no way he was interested in me like that. He was just being nice.

Afterward, I changed into clothes that belonged to one of the other knights. The pants were too long, so I had to roll them at the ends, and they were big around the waist. I pulled the belt as tight as it would go before throwing on the tunic—also big.

Maddox smirked as I exited the room, the steam wafting out from behind me. That smirk soon fell.

"Captain!" Baden rode toward us on horseback and pulled the reins to come to a halt in the grass. Blood trickled from his temple, and his armor was tarnished. "My party was on patrol near the dark wood when we were attacked. The knights are holding them off for now, but the beasts keep coming. They're heading for Bremloc."

Maddox instantly sprang into action. He shouted orders to the surrounding knights, and they dropped everything they were doing to obey, gathering weapons and preparing the horses.

I stood in place, heart racing ninety to nothing. Beasts had attacked? How many?

Callum jogged over with two horses in tow, the brown one I'd ridden my first day in the kingdom and the other was the black stallion. Both were saddled.

"Stay here," Maddox told me. "I'll return as soon as I can."

"Be careful." In the two days I'd been there, I'd gotten to know several of the knights. I didn't want anything bad happening to any of them. Especially to the captain whose gaze lingered on mine for several more heartbeats.

Maddox lifted his hand but dropped it before making contact with my cheek. His blue eyes burned with determination... and something a bit tender. He then swung up into the saddle and left with Callum. The other knights rode behind them.

And I watched after them, hoping all made it back safe and sound.

***

Waiting was a special kind of torture. Too restless to sit still, I went inside the mess hall. Bowls and plates had been left on the tables, some still half-full, having been abandoned with the news of the attack.

My heart dropped into my stomach. A stomach that no longer had an appetite.

I gathered the dishes from their lunch, scraped out the food, and placed them in the basin to soak before washing them. An hour passed. Then another. I made the beds in the barracks and tidied up the clothes strewn across the floor, busying my hands to distract my mind. Thoughts rolled around in my head anyway. Worries.

The light shifted as the sun made its journey across the sky. They were still gone.

Still not hungry but knowing I needed to eat, I entered the kitchen area and searched the pantry. Learning my way around a medieval-style kitchen was a challenge at first, but I soon got the hang of it. It helped that there were modern touches to most of it. The stove didn't run on electricity or gas. Instead, logs burned inside that radiated the heat upward. The hearth was also used sometimes, but my clumsy self would probably fall into the fire accidentally, so I'd stick with the stove and oven for now.

Runes powered the oven, allowing it to function just like the ones I knew from my world. I didn't question it. I was just thankful I could experience a bit of normality again.

Baking helped soothe my mind. I found the ingredients I needed for blueberry muffins—and did my best to substitute ones I didn't. As I whipped up the batter, I tried to forget everything apart from the steps. But I'd been baking muffins for so long I could do it in my sleep, so there wasn't much to keep my mind occupied for long. Once the batter was done, I hunted for a muffin pan. Not finding one, I decided to fill skillets with the batter instead and popped them into the oven.

While they baked, I started on dinner.

I chopped carrots, onions, and potatoes before throwing them into a pot and filling it with water. As the vegetables cooked, I seasoned with salt and pepper before smelling some of the other spices in containers and trying a few. I then found leftover rabbit from the night before and added it to the pot. Might as well make enough food for when the others returned.

And they *would* return.

Just hopefully in one piece.

I had just taken the skillets from the oven and the pot off the stove when commotion came from outside. Shouts. I dashed out of the kitchen and ran toward the yard.

The group of knights had diminished in number. Not all had come back. The ones who did were covered in scratches, gashes, and dirt. I swept a gaze amongst them, relief flooding my chest as a certain cinnamon roll came into view.

"What happened?" I asked Callum. "Where are the others?"

"In Briar's clinic," he answered, sliding off his horse. "The horde was larger than we anticipated. We…" He slumped a little, exhaustion weighing him down. Fortunately, I didn't see any injuries apart from a few cuts. "Many of us were wounded."

I observed the group again, my earlier relief fleeing. "Where's Maddox?"

The pain in Callum's eyes made my stomach turn. "The captain… he…"

I was thankful I hadn't eaten anything. Because as the air left my lungs and the turning in my stomach worsened, twisting in knots, I felt like I could puke. "He's dead?"

"No, but he's in critical condition." Callum's eyes glistened. "He jumped in the way to…" He wiped at his face, then said quieter, "To save me."

"Take me to him."

Callum helped me into the saddle and swung up behind me before we rode toward the clinic. The wind on my face caught a tear from the corner of my eye, turning it cold as it rolled down my cheek. How was it possible to care about someone I'd just met?

If Maddox died, I'd kick his ass.

Once at the clinic, Callum helped me down from the horse, and the two of us approached the door. It swung open before we reached it.

"Come in," Briar said as soon as he saw us. Blood stained his hands and the front of his apron. He then went over to wash his hands in the water basin in the corner. "Are you in need of medical assistance as well, Sir Callum?"

"No, I only have minor cuts and bruises," Callum said as we stepped inside. "We came to check on the others."

"They're in the medical wing."

Pained groans sounded from the other room. A set of double doors separated the medical wing from the main part of the clinic. A pressure squeezed my sternum as a man cried out. More tears welled in my eyes.

A guy with shaggy blond hair and a slender frame exited the ward with a pan of bloody rags, his face pale and eyes wide. As he took the pan over to a basin to wash the rags, his hands shook.

"That's Thane," Briar said. "He's my new apprentice."

Emphasis on new. The guy seemed much too shaken compared to Briar, who appeared unaffected by the gruesome scene in the next room.

"Will you fetch more cloth for bandages?" Briar asked him.

"Yes, sir." Thane rushed over to a cabinet and gathered some.

"How's the captain?" I asked. "Can we see him?"

Briar frowned. "I would advise against you entering the medical wing right now. It's not a pleasant sight." He grabbed a tray of medical tools from the table against the wall. "If you'll excuse me, I need to tend to the men."

Despite his warning, Callum and I followed him anyway. Rays of fading sunlight lit the medical wing, shining on rows of cots. Cots that currently held a dozen or so wounded knights. Some lay in the beds, unconscious, and a few sat upright with their heads and torsos bandaged and dazed looks on their faces.

I knew them. Quincy, Duke, and others I had sat and laughed with the previous day. The tears I'd barely held back earlier now fell freely. I hated seeing them like this.

And then I saw Maddox. He lay in a cot at the back of the room. Unmoving.

Briar hurried over to him and carefully removed his armor, using surgical scissors to cut open his tunic. My breath caught at the deep gashes along his ribs. Blood pooled from them.

Callum watched with worried eyes, hand clenching and unclenching at his side. "Will he be all right?"

Briar's brow wrinkled. "I'll do all I can."

"This is my fault." Callum's voice broke. "The horde was retreating, and I let my guard down. I started to help the wounded men and didn't see the Fenrir demon until the thing was lunging at me. The captain jumped between us." He expelled a breath and hung his head. "What if he dies because of me?"

"He's too stubborn to be taken out like this," I told him, trying for a lighter tone and hoping it didn't miss the mark. "He hasn't made fun of me enough yet. That will be his motivation to heal."

That made Callum smile, if only a little.

Maddox stirred on the cot, and his eyes fluttered open. "Callum. Are you… hurt?"

"No. I'm fine," Callum said, kneeling beside him. "All thanks to you."

"G-Good." His eyes closed before he forced them open again. His ragged breaths caused mine to stutter in my chest. "Where's the… boy? Is Evan s-safe?"

Even while gravely injured, he refused to think of me as an adult. The stubborn jerk-wad. And yet, I still went over and sat on the edge of his cot, my chest painfully tight and vision blurring. "Safe and right here to bug you."

"There y-you are," he said. My heart ached as he made a small sound, forehead scrunching.

"When will you stop calling me *boy*?" I brushed aside a strand of his bangs, that ache in my heart growing. "Keep it up and I'll have to beat you up."

Maddox's smile was weak. Shaky. "I'd like to see t-that." His eyes closed again. "You are much too… small."

He lost consciousness.

"Can I do anything?" I asked Briar, eyes burning. "I don't know much about medicine and don't have a magical bone in my body to make special elixirs, but if you tell me what to do, I can help. Like get your supplies or whatever you need."

"Me too," Callum said.

Thane had entered the ward and was tending to a knight in a nearby cot. He and Briar were the only ones in the clinic.

Briar softly smiled despite his tired eyes. "Under normal circumstances, I don't allow those without medical training to assist, but considering the current situation, I don't have the luxury to refuse. Any help would be much appreciated."

"Very much so," Thane said, his voice a bit frail. His nerves were shot. "I've never…"

He didn't need to finish his sentence for me to understand. He was probably fresh out of medical school—or whatever they called it in Bremloc—and hadn't dealt with anything of that magnitude. Even experienced doctors would've been overwhelmed by that many patients at once, some of whom barely clung to life.

Briar didn't allow us to do anything surgery related—for the best, as I would've probably accidently killed someone—but we helped grind herbs for healing salves, fetched more bindings for bandages when he needed them, and helped keep the medical wing clean. We then restocked the medical cabinet.

And I only got queasy by the blood twice, so I was pretty proud of that, considering I covered my eyes anytime blood and gore was shown in movies.

A few hours later, Briar told me and Callum to take a break and eat dinner. I realized I'd never even eaten lunch. The upset over the knights had squashed my appetite, but now that they were resting in their cots, that hunger surfaced again.

I whipped us up something in the small kitchen, making enough for Briar and Thane too. There was an abundance of rice, so I cooked some in a pot and pan-seared fish. What type of fish? Who knew. But it reminded me of cod. I wasn't the best at cooking savory food; my specialty was desserts and pastries. I knew enough for it to be decent though.

"How are you holding up?" I asked Thane, handing him a plate.

"Better," he answered, accepting the food. The panic in his brown eyes had lessened, which was good. "Thank you for the meal."

"Was this your first day at the clinic?"

He shook his head. "My fifth. I graduated from the academy at the top of my class and was stationed here. It's a highly competitive position, and I felt fortunate to earn it. But I didn't expect anything like this."

"This isn't too common," Callum told him. "The attack today took many of us by surprise. Not all days are like this one."

Thane seemed relieved by that.

Briar didn't join us for dinner. After working on the knights and bandaging them, he'd then busied himself by making elixirs. When he finally joined us, the sun had long since set, and moonlight shone through the tall windows.

"You may retire for the night," he told Thane as he washed his hands and dried them off.

Thane nodded before saying good night to me and Callum. As he left, he seemed moments from collapsing. He'd probably be asleep before his head even hit his pillow.

"Thank you both for your help today," Briar said.

"You're welcome," I said before yawning. It had been one hell of a long day. "We make a good team."

Callum stood from his chair. "How's the captain?"

"He will make a full recovery." Briar pulled out three glasses from a cabinet and grabbed a bottle of wine. "I gave him a powerful healing potion that is mending any internal injuries as he sleeps. After a night's rest, he'll be back to his former strength."

"Magic is so awesome," I said, amazed. Briar had stitched their wounds and performed minor surgeries like the doctors from my world, but the magical salves and elixirs had sped up the healing process.

"Yes, but there are limits to it." Briar joined us at the table. He filled the glasses with a bright red wine and gave one to each of us. "Magic is more of a tool that aids in healing. It can be a remedy for many ills, but it's not always an outright cure. At least for me."

"What do you mean?"

"There are some whose powers far surpass mine," he said. "They don't require anything but magic to seal even the deepest wounds. Some can even bring someone back from the brink of death. I can use magic to enhance healing tonics and ease minor pain and aches with a simple spell, but my abilities are moderate at best. It's why I'm always furthering my research into herbology and spells. Always learning. So I can improve my skills and save more lives."

"Many of those men would be dead if not for you," Callum said.

"If not for us." Briar held up his glass. "Thane included."

The three of us clinked them before taking a drink.

"It's sweet," I said, surprised. I had expected it to be bitter and dry like other wines I'd tried, which was why I'd decided long ago I hated the stuff. But this? I could drink the whole glass. I took another sip. "It's a bit tart too. I usually don't like wine, but this might change my mind."

"I'm glad to hear it." Briar dropped his gaze to his glass, and maybe the flickering candlelight was playing tricks on me, but it looked like he was blushing. "It's my own creation. I use a blend of blackberries, blueberries, and raspberries."

I took another—much bigger—drink. "Court physician, skilled herbalist, magic wielder, *and* master winemaker. Impressive."

"You flatter me. I wouldn't say I'm a master by any means." Briar's cheeks darkened even further. Definitely not a trick, then. Why was that so cute? "I merely dabble."

"Careful, Evan." Callum smirked. "Don't drink too much. I doubt it would take much to get you drunk."

He wasn't wrong. I was a total lightweight. The few drinks I'd taken were already having a small effect, causing warmth to spread through my veins. After the day of stressing out and working hard, I welcomed the feeling.

"Can I ask a question?" I set my glass down. "What happened today in the dark wood? And what's so dark about it?" The knights had mentioned beasts dwelling inside it, but I knew very little else.

Callum frowned at his wine.

"You don't have to tell me," I said, inwardly cursing my big mouth. "I'm sure it's the last thing you want to talk about. I'm sorry."

His eyes lifted back to mine, the color like sunlight hitting a glass of bourbon. "Are you sure you want to know? It may give you nightmares."

"Well, now you have to tell me. My curiosity is a force to be reckoned with."

Case in point: how I ended up in Lupin's Emporium, therefore resulting in me being sent to another world. Maybe one day I'd learn my lesson... but it was not this day.

"Okay, but you asked for it." Callum shifted forward. "There be beasts and demons in those dark woods." His voice had taken on an accent, like he was putting on a show. "All of which would love to make you their next meal."

"Tell me more," I said before taking another drink.

"The dark wood separates Bremloc from the borders of Onyx's territory," Briar explained.

"And Onyx is a demon?" I asked.

"Not *a* demon," Callum said. "*The* demon. He's the demon lord. You've really not heard of him during your travels?"

"Nope. Can't say I have." But I was certainly interested in learning about him. I just had to remind myself that this wasn't a book. I wasn't reading about my favorite book boyfriend, Ayden, going on adventures. I couldn't nerd out—or start to simp for the villain like I so often did. These were real people whose lives were at stake. I recalled

Maddox and his pained whimpers, and my chest tightened. "So Onyx is a demon lord with his own kingdom?"

"Kingdom is a slight understatement." Briar took off his glasses and wiped at the lenses before putting them back on. "Onyx lives in a castle within the shadow realm and rules over all the demons and monstrous beings. He sends them to attack Bremloc."

"Typical final boss move, sending his minions to do his dirty work for him. And did you say shadow realm? Is that like the underworld?"

"No," Briar answered. "The underworld is a place for the dead. The beings within the shadow realm are very much alive."

Yeah, I was definitely losing sleep that night.

"Some also call it the realm of monsters." Callum leaned toward me, brows raised and voice exaggerated to add to the suspense. "Filled with creatures from your worst nightmares. Slime beasts that can melt the flesh right off your bones if they touch you. Reptilian demons with venomous fangs and saliva that paralyze their target so they can slither in for the kill, taking their time as they eat you while you're still alive."

"Yep. Totally the shit from nightmares. What else is there?" More wine was consumed. "You mentioned a Fenrir demon?"

"Similar to a wolf, but they're bigger than any wolf you've ever seen and far more lethal," Callum said. "They move lightning fast, and their bite is so strong it can pierce through even the strongest armor."

"Whoa." I sipped more wine, earning a grin from him. He was playing it up to scare me, but I knew what he said was true. Those were the beasts that waited in the dark wood. No wonder Maddox had been so on edge by the thought of me sleeping so close to it. "A Fenrir is what wounded Maddox?"

Callum nodded and became more serious. "He's fortunate it was only a young one. If an adult had gotten hold of him..." He shook his head, letting his sentence hang in the air.

He didn't need to finish it.

The captain wouldn't have come back alive.

Chapter Five
Grim Tales Make For Lousy Bedtime Stories

"Why is Onyx such an evil asshole?" I asked. Every villain had a backstory—a reason for their wickedness. "Does he have a grudge against Bremloc?"

"There are stories as to why, but no one knows for certain." Briar nursed his glass, taking small sips. "Some claim he was born here and cast out long ago, making him bitter. Others say he merely wishes to wage war on humans for no reason other than it amuses him. Whatever the reason, it's resulted in countless deaths over the years."

"Why doesn't anyone storm his castle and kick his ass?"

"Kick his ass?" The physician cocked his head.

Callum snickered. "You get used to the strange things he says."

"I find that hard to believe." Briar looked at me. "But to answer your question, the knights have tried breaching the shadow realm many times but have yet to be successful."

"Because we can't actually locate it," Callum added, rustling the back of his brown hair as he slouched in his seat. "A magical barrier surrounds the realm, hiding it from anyone who tries to find it.

Only those Onyx allows inside can enter. Any attempt to reach him results in us getting lost in the dark wood. Some even go mad if they journey too far in." He took a drink—a small one—before setting his goblet aside. "It's why we mainly focus on keeping the monsters at bay and making sure they don't leave the forest. It's all we *can* do."

"Has Onyx ever allowed anyone beyond the barrier before?" I asked.

Briar shook his head. "Not that I know of."

"There are rumors about one man he allowed through several years ago," Callum countered. "The man was gone for days, no trace of him anywhere, before being found dismembered in the forest. People say Onyx just got bored and wanted to toy with someone."

"That's... unsettling." I finished the last of my wine and wiped at my mouth, making a mental note to never go near the woods again. I had no interest in becoming an Evan kabob or some Fenrir demon's chew toy.

"Well, I think I'm going to turn in for the night," Callum said, stretching as he rose from his chair. "It's been a long day, and I'm exhausted."

"Would you like a calming tonic to help you sleep?" Briar asked.

"No, thank you. Save the supplies for the wounded knights. They need it far more than I do." Callum offered him a smile before turning to me. His expression softened even further. "You know, as we were returning from the mission, the captain spoke of you."

"Really? What did he say?"

104

"That he hoped you hadn't tripped over your own two feet and fallen to your death in our absence. Even while in pain, I'd never seen his eyes look so warm. I could be mistaken, but I believe the thought of returning to you is what gave him the strength to keep going despite the severity of his wound."

Butterflies flooded my stomach. In just the span of three days, a part of me had become attached to the grumpy captain. Much more than I'd realized.

"Good night," Callum then said before leaving the clinic, shutting the door softly behind him.

Briar stood from the table, gathered our glasses, and took them over to the sink. He rinsed them beneath the spout and set them aside to dry. The hour was late, but that didn't stop him from checking his inventory of herbs, jotting down notes, and making another batch of pain-fighting elixirs.

"Were you born with magic? Or can anyone learn how to use it?"

"I learned over the years," he answered after infusing magic into another glass vial. The liquid faintly glowed, swirled, and then calmed. "Although, some *are* born with the gift. They're the ones who are most powerful. Magic exists all around us, and through hard work and self-discipline, even those of us not born with the gift can learn to harness it."

I pushed back from my chair to stand... and immediately grabbed the table as the room spun. "Don't tell Callum, but he was right. I shouldn't have downed the whole glass."

Briar chuckled. "I'll pour you some water. Eat this too." He placed a small loaf of bread in front of me and cut off a slice. "I hope you like fig."

"Never had it, actually." I sat back down, picked up the bread, smelled it, and then took a huge bite. "Oh my god," I said with my mouth full. "This is amazing." I shoved the rest into my mouth before reaching for another piece. "This world is gonna make me fat, and I don't even care."

After pouring me a glass of water from the pitcher, Briar turned back to his workstation and smiled as he mixed more ingredients. "You are unlike anyone I've ever met, Evan."

I paused in my chewing. "Yeah?" I swallowed. "How so?"

"You say what's on your mind, no matter how strange." He placed his hand over the contents of the bowl he'd been stirring, and his palm emitted a soft glow. He then filled six more vials and topped each with a small cork. "You're just... different."

Ever since I was little, people had told me I needed to get my head out of the clouds. And in the instances when I broke out of my shell and tried to socialize, I was too weird or rambled too much about unimportant things. However, when Briar said I was different, I didn't feel like it was a bad thing. The warmth of his voice and twinkle behind his glasses said the opposite.

"Do you need help?" I asked after drinking half the glass of water and stuffing my face with more fig bread. "I feel bad just sitting here watching you work."

"I'm nearly finished." He added another vial to the collection of others. "Though, I could use your help distributing these to the knights, if you don't mind. I already gave them to the ones in greater need, like the captain, but the others could use something to ease their discomfort."

"I don't mind at all." I stood back up, feeling a lot less wobbly now. The bread had soaked up some of the wine and helped clear my head. The magic of carbs.

"These go to the men on the right side of the room," he explained as he placed them in a wooden carrier.

"Got it."

We entered the medical wing, keeping our steps light so we wouldn't disturb their rest. Moonlight created a silvery glow throughout the room as it came through the tall windows. My heart sank at seeing all the knights asleep in their cots, some a lot worse off than others.

One had lost consciousness before being brought to the clinic and had yet to wake. Duke and another one had concussions. The rest were bandaged from bites and claw marks. Quincy's arm had nearly been severed, but Briar had managed to save the limb.

Briar placed the tray on a side table before closing some of the curtains. He then went over to the hearth along the far wall and stoked the logs. He had created a relaxing atmosphere. Certainly more relaxing than the hospital rooms from my own world with their blinding white walls, frigid air, and the strong smell of disinfectant.

I grabbed a vial with blue liquid and knelt beside one of the cots. Duke opened his eyes, and I gave him what I hoped was a kind smile. "Hey there. Brought your medicine."

"Gratitude," he rasped before wincing. "Small but mighty Evan."

What the knights had started calling me. It didn't make me smile like usual. I was too sad.

"Easy." I cradled the back of his head as I helped him sit up to drink the elixir.

It seemed to take effect almost immediately. The pained scrunch of Duke's brow smoothed, and he closed his eyes, relaxing into his pillow. I'd never imagined myself as a nurse or working in the medical field at all, but seeing all of these injured men who'd risked their lives to fight monsters so that other people would be spared made me want to help them too.

Briar and I then distributed the rest of the medicine to the knights.

Maddox lay in his cot at the back of the room, closest to the fire. Briar checked his bandages before nodding to himself and approaching me.

"You should get some rest too," he whispered.

"Yeah. Rest sounds good." My gaze darted back to Maddox.

"Do you wish to see him before you go?" Briar gently asked.

Did I? The knight captain was like a grouchy block of ice. He enjoyed teasing me and bossing me around.

"I'd never seen his eyes look so warm."
Callum's words had caused a similar warmth
smack-dab in the center of my chest.

"Is it okay if I see him?"

"Of course." Briar smiled. Though… it looked
a bit sad for some reason. "I'll be in the other room.
Take your time." He then grabbed the now empty
tray and exited the medical wing.

I suddenly felt nervous as I walked toward
Maddox. My breaths shook, and those silly
butterflies fluttered faster, more chaotic now than
before. Reaching his cot, I rested my hip against the
edge of the mattress and peered down at him.

A sharp, masculine jawline. Long, dark
eyelashes and cupid bow lips. The front of his short
black hair fell over his brow, and I softly moved it
aside with my fingertips. His shirt had been
removed, and even with the bandages around his
torso, I saw the perfectly shaped muscles of his
chest and stomach—the pectorals I wanted to shove
my face into.

What's wrong with me? Drooling over a
sleeping, wounded man. As gently as possible, I
brought the sheet up higher and tucked it in around
him before shifting my gaze back to his face.

His eyes were open.

"Oh. Sorry." I jerked my hands away from the
sheet. Had he seen me checking him out? Lord, I
hoped not. "Didn't mean to wake you. Go back to
sleep."

"Wait," Maddox said as I started to leave. He
grabbed my hand. "Stay."

That one word had been spoken with a quiet vulnerability, as if it was a plea rather than a demand. Surprised, I settled back on the edge of the cot. He didn't release my hand. Instead, he slid his fingers through mine.

"Maybe this is a dumb question, but how are you feeling?"

Firelight flickered across his face, shining on his blue eyes. They looked so much softer than usual. "Much better now that you're here."

Surely, I'd heard him wrong. I could believe many things about this fantasy world, but having the icy—but oh so hot—captain of the knights stare at me with *that* look in his eyes was too much for my brain to process.

"I think you might have a fever," I said. "Or maybe the elixir is making you loopy. The Maddox I know wouldn't say anything like that."

That amused him. "Tell me, Muffin Lord from the kingdom of Arkansas, what is it you think you know about me?"

"Well, you're grumpy and demanding. You don't smile much, unless it's to poke fun at me. And you're stubborn."

"Fair points. Though, I'd say I'm determined rather than stubborn." A ghost of a smile landed on his lips but didn't fully form. "As for poking fun at you... I admit I take much more enjoyment than I probably should in doing so."

"I..." My throat tightened. "I was worried about you."

"You were?"

Not trusting my voice, I nodded.

"When I was attacked by the Fenrir, I thought of you."

"So, you're saying I'm some feral hairy beast? Thanks. You should know, though, that my bark is worse than my bite. Just give me food, and my tail starts wagging."

He chuckled under his breath. "So strange. It is a thing about you that captivates me."

"Yeah, I think the meds are clouding your mind." There was no way someone as boring and average as me could captivate anyone, in this world or in mine.

"My mind is clear." His fingers gently squeezed mine. "Clearer than it's ever been."

I dropped my gaze to our joined hands, unsure how to respond. My breaths shortened, and my heartbeat became erratic. He said his mind was clear, yet mine had never felt more muddled.

"Evan." My name sounded so damn soft on his lips. "Look at me."

Slowly, my gaze returned to his face. His tender expression made my breath freeze in my chest, lungs refusing to work. Or maybe they'd forgotten how.

Maddox rested his hand on the side of my neck before sliding it to my nape. He then gently pulled me down to him, capturing my lips.

A small sound left my throat. For such a strong and seemingly emotionless knight, his kisses were so damn soft.

"Is this all right?" he whispered.

I answered him by easing into the kiss. He dipped his tongue into my mouth, issuing from me another moan. I trembled like it was my first time. That's what it felt like. That nervousness when you realized just how much you were crushing on someone and then having that someone make a move on you. The excited flutters low in your belly as their lips first pressed to yours.

"W-Wait," I said, a bit breathless. "I thought you didn't do this sort of thing."

"I don't."

"I'm confused. You said it was too much of a distraction."

Maddox grabbed hold of my chin. "Oh, you are." He ghosted his lips across mine. "Yet, it is a distraction I welcome in this moment. So silence that mouth, and use it to kiss me instead."

I couldn't argue with that reasoning. The man had been wounded by a damn demonic beast. If I could help him, why not? Kissing him was heroic. For the good of the kingdom.

I'm so full of shit.

Our lips pressed back together, soft and hesitant at first, as though we were both familiarizing ourselves with the shape and feel of the other's lips. He soon deepened the kiss. My skin tingled from where Maddox touched me—my nape that he had in a firm hold and my waist where he'd wrapped an arm around me to draw me in closer.

"Your wound," I said as he pulled me on top of him.

"Doesn't hurt," he said between more kisses. His lips moved from my mouth and trailed down my neck, causing electric pulses in my veins. His strong arms tightened around me as he found the weak spot at the base of my throat and lightly sucked.

"Ah, fuck." I felt so hot, like I would explode any second. My neglected libido was up and running at full speed, desperate for some action that involved more than my hand and the weak orgasms I reached using my tried-but-true collection of spank-bank material.

I cupped the back of his head, digging my fingers in the short strands of his hair. I felt him smile against my neck before he sucked harder. I tried to hold back a moan, and it came out as more of a squeak. Maybe exploding wouldn't have been so bad right then. It would've at least gotten me out of that embarrassing moment where my little squeak was still echoing in my memory. Probably in his too.

"Adorable," Maddox said as he nuzzled my neck. "Let me hear it again."

"I don't squeak on command."

"Is that so?" He lightly grazed his teeth across the same sweet spot on my throat. His big hands moved to my ass and gently squeezed before he yanked me forward, positioning my thighs on each side of him. And when he lifted his hips, grinding his hard bulge against me, he got his wish. The squeaking commenced.

"Stop," I said, fighting a smile. "We aren't the only ones in the room, you inconsiderate ass. I'm sure your men don't want to be woken by our groans as we rut against each other."

"It would be quite the shock for them." Maddox nipped at my jaw. "And did you just call

113

me an ass?" He ground his hips up into me again, harder this time.

But then he winced.

"I told you." I pulled back to look at him. "You hurt yourself, didn't you?"

He stared up at me with a defiant look in his eyes. God. He even made *that* look good.

"Stubborn." I shook my head. "Just like I said you were." The reality of the situation then sunk in. I was straddling Maddox, our lips swollen from sucking face. The same Maddox who bossed me around, made me clean the stables, and who I'd thought hated me. "Why did you kiss me? You wanted a distraction, but why *me*?"

"Because."

"That's not an answer."

"You want to know? Truly?" Maddox slid his hands up my spine. "When I was attacked, you appeared in my mind. I thought of your rambling mouth, sass, and your inability to walk on flat ground without tripping over yourself. I thought of your deep green eyes and the light dusting of freckles on your nose. I'm uncertain as to why I can't get you out of my head, Evan, but those thoughts of you lit a fire in my heart and gave me the strength to make it home."

"We only met three days ago," I whispered.

"Yet, it feels like much longer."

Honestly? It did for me too. Like my mind might not have known him… but my heart did.

I swallowed the sudden tightness in my throat. "You should get some rest. The elixir works better if you're asleep. That's what Briar said."

114

Maddox stared at me for several seconds before giving a small nod of his head. I could practically see the walls lifting again around him, shoving any emotion behind a mask of indifference. "You should rest as well."

I slid off his lap, being careful of his injuries. "Well, um. Good night. I guess."

Why was this so awkward?

He watched me as I took a step back. As I spun around to leave, bumping into the edge of a small table in my haste, I heard him softly laugh. With my cheeks on fire, I quickly walked toward the door and left the medical wing. That's when I noticed I was smiling.

Something had definitely shifted between me and the grumpy captain.

Briar sat at his desk, hunched over a journal as he scribbled notes. He looked up at me as I shut the door, his bangs falling across his glasses. "All done?"

"Yeah."

"Would you like me to walk you to your room?"

"Nah, it's okay." I stepped from the doorway. "You look busy. I can find my way back." Maybe.

Probably.

"It's no trouble at all." He set his quill aside and pushed back from the desk, standing from his chair. He had undone the top few buttons of his shirt, and the casual look went with his somewhat messy hair. "One can easily become lost if you're unfamiliar with the area. I won't be able to sleep unless I know you made it back safe and sound."

Maddox and Briar were total opposites, one snarly and demanding while the other was gentle-natured and kind. Yet, I enjoyed being around both of them.

"Okay," I said. "But only if it won't interrupt your work."

"My studies can wait." Briar walked with me to the door and opened it for me.

"Thanks." My head was still spinning from the hot-as-hell kiss I shared with Maddox. I could still feel the pressure of his lips on mine and taste the warm spice of his skin. The slight scruff of his stubble against my chin. Could still feel the heat in my veins from when our bodies rutted together. The desire had faded some but continued to simmer deep in my core.

"The moon is bright tonight," Briar said, pulling me from my thoughts. His face was angled toward the sky as we moved down the narrow stone path, passing the gardens and an orchard of fruit trees.

I glanced upward and faltered in step—not because I was clumsy. Not at all. The sky was incredible, more stars than I'd ever seen. Brighter too. "The sky doesn't look like this where I come from. You can't see nearly as many stars."

"That seems awfully unpleasant," he responded. "Nights like this make me feel alive. They also make me feel small. Like I'm a mere speck in one massive universe."

"Hey, give yourself more credit. You're a super-talented speck in spectacles who saves lives and makes delicious bread and wine, making all the little specks around you happier."

Briar laughed. "The way your mind works fascinates me." His smile faded—turned sad just like it had earlier in the medical wing. "You fancy the knight captain, don't you?"

"Fancy him? I wouldn't go that far."

"The two of you kissed, did you not?"

"Were you spying on us?"

Briar shook his head. "No. Your lips are a bit swollen, and your cheeks were flushed when you exited the room. It was a simple observation."

"A gentleman doesn't kiss and tell." I sounded just as awkward as I felt.

"I apologize for overstepping," he said. "In all the years I've worked at the castle, I've never known Maddox to show interest in anyone. I suppose it came as a shock."

"Yeah, it shocked me too, if I'm being honest. He's way out of my league."

"Out of your league?" Briar studied me. "The wording is unfamiliar, but I believe I understand the implication." He moved his gaze back to the sky. "Much like how a star cannot see how brightly it shines to those around it, you don't see yourself clearly either, Evan."

"I'm not a star. I'm a speck. Just like you."

He smiled and said nothing more on the subject. He guided me toward a courtyard on the right. A building surrounded it, with multiple doors and windows, reminding me of an apartment complex. Minus the screaming neighbors, junk in the yard, and smell of greasy food like the one I lived in back home. This one was quaint and peaceful.

"Here we are," he said as we stopped in front of my room.

"I appreciate you walking with me." I glanced at the other doors. "Is one of these yours?"

"No," Briar answered. "I have a room above the clinic, so I'm always close if anyone needs me. And with the wounded knights there tonight, I'll more than likely sleep in one of the cots in the ward to watch over them."

"That's very admirable of you, but you gotta remember to take care of yourself too, Doc. You're no good to anyone if you work yourself to death."

"You aren't the first one to say such a thing." He rubbed at the back of his neck. "However, I won't be able to properly rest knowing others need me. As is the life of a physician. My workload is lighter now that Thane is here though."

"Today was rough on him," I said. "But he pulled through."

"He did. There's much more for him to learn, but I'm confident in his abilities. He was born with magic, you see. If properly trained, he can surpass me in no time."

"Well, until the knights get better, I have a once-in-a-lifetime offer for you."

"Oh?" He seemed amused. "Do tell."

"Me." I jabbed a thumb into my chest. "The stable boy life didn't work out for me. Being in the clinic today was hard but rewarding work. So I can come by in the morning to help. Unless I sucked and you don't want me there."

118

"The help would be lovely," Briar said, still amused by something. He lifted a hand and gently brushed the backs of his knuckles across my cheek. "Though I'd be lying if I said I wouldn't enjoy being near you as well."

Heat inched up my neck. Was I imagining that softness in his hazel eyes?

Briar withdrew his hand. "I'll see you in the morning. Sleep well, Evan."

"Y-Yeah. You too."

He waited until I was inside the room before walking away. I rested against the door, heart beating hard in my chest. It squeezed a little too.

Despite being dog-tired, I lay in bed wide awake for what felt like hours, thinking of Maddox. Thinking of Briar. And being confused by my budding attraction toward both of them. I also thought of Jonah.

Did he think I ran away? Got abducted? Was my face flashing across the six o'clock news as a missing person? If so, which picture did they use? Hopefully not my senior photo. I'd started to sneeze right before it was taken, so my eyes were squinted and my mouth was puckered. My plea to retake the photo had been ignored. The asshole photographer had already been pissed off about being underpaid and dismissed my pleas. The picture had haunted me ever since.

I flipped to my side and stared at the tree outside the window. Eventually, my eyelids became too heavy to keep open, and I finally drifted off to sleep.

I'll wake up in the morning to find this was all a dream.

I would be back in my small apartment. Back in my own world.

But when morning came, the same tree I'd stared at before falling asleep greeted me once again. The sun shone through the branches, and birds chirped. Light sounds came from outside as others woke and started their day. Eager to do the same, I hopped out of bed, quickly washed using the water in the basin, dressed, and left the room.

The knights should be waking soon, and I wanted to be there to help Briar and Thane as soon as possible.

Chapter Six
Cat Boys Are Cute When They Pounce

"You have so many books." I glided my fingers across the spines. No dust whatsoever. The books on the other shelves appeared the same. Some had slight wrinkles in the spines and told me they'd been read several times—his favorites.

"Reading is not only the perfect way to unwind after a long day, but it also fuels the mind." Briar gathered supplies and placed them on a tray. "I love learning all I can about the world and the things in it."

"Me too." I turned from the shelf. "Well, I mainly read fiction."

"All stories have their place," he said. "Whether they be to inform the reader or entertain. Feel free to borrow any that catch your eye."

"Thanks." I yawned.

"Would you like for me to make you a cup of tea?" Briar asked. "It's how I start each morning."

"Coffee is how I like to start mine." I smiled at him. Maddox had made some for me yesterday, and while not the best I'd had, it was still good. "I've never developed a taste for tea, but I'm open to trying some of yours."

"I'll put on a pot," he said before walking over to the stove. "If it's not to your liking, I don't have any coffee at the moment, but I can make something similar with dandelion root."

"I've heard of that." Much to my surprise. I'd read an article about it late one night when I should've been sleeping. It was made from dandelions and didn't have any caffeine but still tasted good. Allegedly.

After the water came to a boil, Briar added tea leaves into some kind of device and infused it. He then poured a cup and stirred in some milk and sugar before handing it to me. I sniffed it before taking a sip.

"Do you like it?" he asked.

"Not as amazing as my favorite bean juice, but still damn good." I took a bigger drink.

He smiled. It was a good look on him.

"Sorry I'm late," Thane said as he burst into the clinic, blond hair sticking up in the back and eyes still pink from sleeping hard. "I'll start making healing tonics right away."

"Have a cup of tea first," Briar told him. "I've already brewed the tonics."

Thane's shoulders relaxed, and he nodded. "Some apprentice I am."

"It's a learning process," Briar said. "I have full faith in you."

The younger male beamed and grabbed the cup Briar poured for him.

A while later, the three of us entered the medical wing. My eyes instantly moved to the back of the room where Maddox still slept. Wanting to let him rest as long as possible, I assisted Briar as he checked the other knights' wounds and changed their bandages.

They didn't look like the same bunch I'd seen the night before. Many of them were sitting up in their cots, chatting with us and with each other. Some smiled. The one who had been unconscious was awake and doing a lot better.

Duke and Quincy sat up, speaking about the attack. Quincy's arm was bandaged and in a sling, but he seemed to be in better spirits, considering the pain he'd endured.

"You would've slayed them all," Quincy said to me. "Evan the Small and Mighty."

Duke grinned.

The air felt lighter. The warm sunlight streaming into the room probably helped. It was a new day, and all of them had lived to see it.

"I should make them breakfast," Briar said as we exited the medical wing to discard the soiled bandages. He frowned at his workstation. "I also need to head to the apothecary for more supplies."

"Let me handle breakfast," I told him. "I may not be the best cook in the world, but it's edible, at least."

"More than edible if last night's dinner is any indication," Briar responded with a gentle gleam in his eyes. He nodded to the stove. "If you need anything, let me know. Otherwise, I'll leave you to it."

His confidence in me was reassuring. Made me happy too.

"I can help," Thane offered.

"Nah, it's okay. Go sit down and rest for a bit. I got this."

What meal could I make that would feed a group? Something that could be cooked in a large pot, probably. After checking the small pantry, I found oats and decided on my famous hearty oatmeal. Okay, maybe it wasn't exactly famous, but I loved eating it, so close enough. It was also quick and could feed multiple people. I also found eggs, bell peppers, and cheese and decided to make egg muffins, which were also easy and quick.

I found a large pot and got to work. As the oats cooked, I beat eggs into a bowl, chopped the peppers, combined the mixture, and seasoned with garlic and salt.

"You seem at home in the kitchen," Thane said as he ground herbs.

"You think so?" I focused on the oats. "I guess I am. It's always helped calm my mind." Made me feel a little less alone as I got lost in baking desserts.

Briar returned with a bag of supplies and went over to the workstation, helping Thane with another batch of tonics. I watched, fascinated, as Thane held a vial, closed his eyes, and infused magic into it. The liquid glowed.

"Nice work," Briar said with a nod. He then approached me and looked into the pot on the stovetop. He closed his eyes as he breathed it in. "That smells excellent."

"Thank you." I added a few spoonsful of honey and stirred it in. "If you're good, I'll let you have a bowl."

His nose crinkled with a smile. "I suppose I should be on my best behavior, then."

"There's egg muffins too."

"Egg… muffins?"

"Yep. You haven't heard of them?"

Briar shook his head. "No, but I'm intrigued. I'll gather bowls for the oats."

When he returned with them and touched the small of my back, a tingling warmth trickled through my veins. Not the blazing inferno like I'd felt when Maddox kissed me, but rather a low simmer with a comforting heat. I was kind of crushing on both of them.

Did that make me a bad person?

After dishing out a heaping serving in each bowl, I cut up some apples and added a few slices on top of each one. I then placed the egg muffins on a large plate. Briar helped me situate the bowls on a tray, along with the plate, and helped me pass them out to the knights.

"What is this?" Duke asked, studying the muffin.

Quincy shoved half of it in his mouth and paused in his chewing, eyes falling closed. "Dear gods. That demon must've killed me after all, for this tastes of paradise."

The other knights complimented the food. Seeing their pleased smiles as they ate made me feel good.

Maddox had woken and stood beside his cot, fastening the buttons on his shirt. The sight of him caused little flutters of excitement in my chest. Nerves too. After our kiss, how would he act?

Would he regret it? Treat me coldly and pretend it never happened?

"Hey, you," I said as I approached him with a bowl and a muffin on top. My voice shook a bit. "Should you be up and moving right now?"

He glanced over at me. "Is that your subtle way of telling me to sit back down?"

"Yep."

"I must refuse." Maddox faced me. "Duty calls."

"Duty can wait until you've eaten breakfast," I said, having to tilt my head to meet his gaze. Our height difference thrilled me. He was just so freaking huge. "I cooked it myself."

His blue eyes lowered to the food. "Poison?"

"You asshole."

That earned me one of his rare almost-smiles. He grabbed the spoon, and with his eyes still on me, he took a bite of the oatmeal. Surprise flickered across his handsome features. "It's delicious."

"Don't sound so shocked. I'm not totally useless, you know."

Those deep blue eyes softened. "I never said you were."

My heart fluttered. "Try the muffin too."

"That looks like no muffin I've ever seen." He picked it up and took a bite anyway. "Egg and peppers?"

"Yep." I tried to hide how much it pleased me when he stuffed the rest of it in his mouth and chewed. "Um. So about last night…"

"What of it?" After swallowing the muffin, he lowered the spoon back to the bowl and took a second bite of the oatmeal.

Oh crap. Had it really been the healing tonic that made him act that way toward me? He'd said his mind was clear, but the lust-driven kisses and gropes might've been triggered by the medicine.

"What do you remember?" I cautiously asked. Because if he didn't remember kissing me, I wanted to avoid the mortification of bringing it to his attention.

"Very little." He grabbed his cloak from where it lay draped across the chair beside the cot and clasped it to his armor.

"Oh." I kind of wanted to disappear.

"Evan." Maddox reclosed the small gap between our bodies and rested a hand on the side of my neck. "There is one thing I do recall. You." He angled his head down a bit. "Specifically, your taste as we kissed."

The flutters in my heart? Yeah, they shot straight to my dick. "I'm, uh, glad you remember that."

"I must report to the king about yesterday," he then said. "Behave until I return."

"I always behave."

Maddox didn't kiss me, but he looked like he wanted to as his gaze fell to my mouth. He smoothed his thumb over my bottom lip before pulling away and exiting the medical ward.

I brought a hand to my mouth and smiled. Damn him.

Briar passed him on his way out, and the two exchanged a polite nod. The physician's eyes appeared guarded as he neared me. "Is all well with the captain?"

"Well, he thought my oatmeal was poisoned and didn't want to eat it. But after a bite, he changed his tune. The omelet-turned-muffin sealed the deal. I bet he'll come crawling back for more later."

That seemed to lift Briar's spirits—though I didn't know why they'd been low to begin with. He'd seemed fine earlier. "Are you certain you're not a wizard? Because I do believe you've enchanted us both."

I opened my mouth to respond, but no words came out. Was he flirting with me?

"Anyway, Thane finished with the tonics." Briar dropped his attention to the tray of vials in his hands. His cheeks had some color, the blush noticeable on his pale skin. "Will you help me pass them out?"

"Yeah. Of course."

We distributed the morning medicine, and once the men finished eating, we gathered the empty bowls. The morning was busy but not hectic. Briar discharged a few of the knights but wanted to keep others a bit longer for observation.

"I'm fine," Quincy whined, being one of the ones told to stay.

"Says the one whose arm was nearly ripped off," I said.

He exaggerated a sigh and slumped back to the cot.

A light knock came at the door midafternoon. A petite woman stood in the doorway to the medical wing. Another woman and a guy who looked a bit older than me stood behind her.

"Good afternoon," she said. "We're here to help any way we can."

Briar used his middle finger to push his glasses back up his nose. "You are maids from the main castle?"

"Yes." She bowed her head. "Captain Maddox informed King Eidolon about the emergent situation, and we were instructed to assist you right away. Laundry, supply runs, anything you need."

"Excellent," Briar told her with a smidgeon of relief in his voice. He hid it well, but the exertion was taking a toll on him. "If you wouldn't mind changing the bedding, I'd greatly appreciate it."

"Right away, sir."

Maddox wasn't nearly as grouchy and mean as I'd once thought. He had gone out of his way to request aid for us at the clinic. He had a kind heart beneath all that sneer.

The three of them changed the bedding on the cots and placed the dirty laundry in piles. I returned to the other room to wash out the pot I used to cook breakfast. It felt great to do something productive. Kept my hands busy while my mind wandered.

Thane grabbed a book from one of the shelves and sat it on the table with a light *thump*. The thing was massive. He opened the front and skimmed the text before thumbing through a few pages. I saw illustrations of plants and descriptions. Briar asked him about a few of them, testing his knowledge.

129

He seemed like a strict, but fair, teacher. And definitely easy on the eyes.

Stop simping, I told myself.

While Thane continued his studies, Briar sat at his desk with a stack of documents and read them over.

My lips tingled at the memory of Maddox's thumb tracing them. He had kissed me, but I wasn't sure what he wanted. A fling? Hard sex with no attachments? He didn't seem like the roses and sappy romance type.

I sighed.

"Are you okay?" Briar asked from his desk. As I looked at him, he smiled, and my stomach fluttered.

Yep. I'm crushing on him too.

"Yeah." I placed the last bowl on the rack to dry and stepped over to the counter to devour the last slice of fig bread. "I'm just sad this bread is almost gone."

"I'll make another loaf for you," he said. "I know a wonderful lemon bread recipe as well. I learned it from my father."

"Was he a baker?"

Briar nodded. "He was. My mother was a seamstress."

"I bet they're proud of you," I said between bites. "You grew up to be a damn good physician."

The quill moved across the page as he continued working. His brow crinkled in the center. "Unfortunately, sickness took them before they could see me become one."

I stopped chewing. "Oh, fuck. I'm sorry."

"Don't be." He offered me a weak smile. "That was many years ago. It's also the reason why I chose this profession. I felt powerless when they were sick, wanting to help them but not knowing how. So I learned."

"With tragedy came a new beginning," I said. "You found your purpose."

His hand stilled on the paper, and our eyes met. "There you go again, saying such profound things." His gaze then returned to the paper.

"What'cha working on?" I asked.

"A budget request."

"Oh." I shoved the last of the bread into my mouth. "What's it for?"

"I buy most of the supplies from the local marketplace, but some of the items used in stronger tonics have to be purchased from a higher-grade merchant and are more costly." Briar signed the bottom of a document and folded it. "The royal accounting department gives the clinic a set amount of funds each month, but because of the attack, I'm running low on a few important ingredients. I'll drop it off when I'm finished here."

"I can take it for you," I said. "Thane is busy studying, and you're busy too. I have the time."

"You don't have to. You've done enough already."

"I know I don't have to. I *want* to. Gimme." I stuck out a hand and wiggled my fingers. Amused, he handed over the document. "Very important question incoming. Where's the accounting department?"

Briar rattled off the location and how to get there. "I can ask Thane to do it instead if you prefer," he said after a short pause, cocking his head to the side. Had something in my expression made him change his mind? "I don't want you getting lost."

"Nope. I can do it." I tapped the paper against my hand and stepped toward the door. "Be back in a bit."

"Thank you. I'll await your return."

"I'll try not to keep you waiting too long." I tried to be cute and toss him a wink before spinning toward the door and exiting in a cool way, but I misjudged the distance between my face and the door and smacked right into it.

"Are you all right?" he asked, alarmed. That alarm just horrified me even further.

"I'm okay. I meant to do that." I pushed the door open and got out of there as fast as possible, my cheeks on fire.

Sigh. He was probably laughing at me. Thane too. Hell, I laughed at myself as I strolled through the courtyard. I was just thankful Briar had been the one to see it. Maddox would never have let me live it down.

After leaving the square, I headed toward another set of buildings. The spring morning held a slight chill, but the sun warmed the top of my head as my feet padded down the path. Flowers sprang from the soil, the blooms freshly opened. Tree leaves danced with a light breeze. A light breeze that nearly stole the paper from my hand. I held it tighter and laughed under my breath.

How hard could it be to deliver a simple document?

The answer? Not so simple. It took all of five minutes for me to get lost.

I came to a fork in the path and stopped. "Did he say to take a right or a left here?" I could always just cross my fingers and pick one, hoping it was right.

A rustle came from the bushes.

"Hello?" I asked, voice veering on a squeak.

Silence.

"Just the wind." True or only an attempt to reassure myself? The million-dollar question.

Another rustle sounded, this one much closer.

Okay, maybe not the wind after all. Surely, if it was some wild beast, it wouldn't attack in broad daylight. Probably just a squirrel.

Please let it be a squirrel. Just hopefully not a demonic one with red beady eyes and sharp teeth.

And it was in that moment, as images of a bloodthirsty, monstrous squirrel ran through my head, that something large and furry leapt from the bushes and pounced on me. My high-pitched scream was undoubtedly heard in the next town over. The document flew from my hand, and I landed on my ass in the grass.

The pressure on my chest lightened as whatever evil creature it was pulled back. Rainbow-colored eyes blinked at me before a familiar face came into view. White-tipped cat ears jutted from his reddish-brown hair, and a tail flicked behind him. He wore a purple crop top that showed his tanned belly and loose-fitting pants that fanned out at the bottom.

"Kuya?" I asked.

He grinned, flashing a snaggletooth. "Kuya scared you."

"Scared is an understatement," I said, trying to calm my racing heart. "You almost made me piss myself."

He scurried off me and snatched the document from the grass. "What's this?"

"I need to take it to the accounting department." I slowly pushed to my feet. "It's a budget request for the clinic. But I think I'm lost."

Kuya stuck it in his mouth and started to scamper down the path.

"Hey!" I called after him. "Get back here!"

When I woke up that morning, the last thing I expected was to be pounced on by a cat boy and forced to chase him around the castle grounds. Yet there I was, chasing a cat boy who seemed to be having way too much fun playing "keep-away-from-the-Evan" as he ran with the paper I needed in his mouth.

"Give that back!" My lungs burned, and my legs wobbled as I turned another corner in pursuit of him.

I wasn't a cardio person. Far from it. I was a sit-on-the-couch-and-snack-on-chips-while-reading person. The walks to and from the café was about the extent of my exercise. I'd almost prefer to face off with a demonic squirrel than endure another second of running.

Luckily, the mischievous cat boy put me out of my misery.

Kuya squatted in the grass up ahead, the document still in his mouth. I came to a sharp stop, fighting for my life as I breathed hard. Slowly, I neared him, one hand held up like I'd seen people do in movies when they were approaching a skittish animal.

"I'm not going to hurt you." I took another slow step toward him. "Please don't run away again."

Humor shone in his rainbow eyes, the colors swirling as the sunlight bounced off the irises. His ears wiggled as I inched closer.

"That's it," I said in the same tone used to speak to babies. "Just stay right there."

He grabbed the document from his mouth and leapt back to his feet. "Kuya showed you the way! See?" He nodded to the building behind him. "The accounting department."

"You... you were guiding me?"

With a huge toothy grin, he handed me the paper. "Evan is no longer lost. Kuya helped."

I grabbed it, still trying to catch my breath. "Guess I should thank you. Even if you did almost kill me."

"Kuya?" a man called from a distance. "Where have you gone?"

The cat boy snapped his head in that direction, grin widening. A man then appeared from around the same corner we'd come from. Despite the casualness of his clothes, there was something regal about the way he carried himself. Golden hair fell to the middle of his ears, and he was tall with an athletic build. His expression lit up like the sun as he saw Kuya. "There you are."

"Prince Sawyer." Kuya ran over to him. "You found Kuya."

Wait... *prince*?

"I will always find you," the prince responded, patting the top of Kuya's head. The cat boy closed his eyes and leaned into the touch. Rumbles sounded in his throat—purrs. "Who is your friend?"

"Um," I said, not sure how to act. Should I bow? Get on my hands and knees? Was I even allowed to look at him? I quickly bowed my head. "My name is Evan, Your Majesty. Wait. Isn't that the title used for the king? Your Grace, maybe? No, that's not right either."

"Prince will suffice," he said, lowering his hand from Kuya's head. "You are the traveler I've heard about. The man found beside the dark wood."

"Word really gets around, huh?"

"Very little happens in Bremloc that I don't know about." Prince Sawyer smiled as Kuya nudged his shoulder. "I apologize if he troubled you. He likes to play."

A prince apologizing? Now that's something I certainly didn't expect.

"Oh, no need to apologize. It's totally fine." I waved my hand dismissively. "He actually helped. I couldn't find the accounting department, and he led me here."

"Yes, Kuya helped," the cat boy murmured. He nestled closer and rested his cheek on the prince's chest, his purrs intensifying. "Like a good boy."

136

"The best boy," Prince Sawyer told him before returning his gaze to me. His green eyes were just a shade darker than the grass we stood upon. "Which kingdom are you from?"

Crap. Fooling a knight was one thing, but a prince?

"Not sure you've heard of it," I said, nerves swirling in my stomach. "It's small."

"I've studied many lands. Tell me."

"Arkansas."

His brow furrowed. Silence stretched between us, and my heart thumped painfully. And then, Prince Sawyer laughed. "Well, I suppose I was wrong. There is still much I need to learn. I haven't heard of this kingdom."

I shakily exhaled and forced a smile. "Like I said, it's really small." *And in another world entirely.*

"Well, don't let us keep you from your business," he said. "It was a pleasure finally meeting you."

"It was nice meeting you too, my prince." I tipped my head to him. "Bye, Kuya."

"Kuya will see you again soon," the cat boy said.

The two of them turned and walked down the path. Kuya looked back at me and grinned as he waved. I returned the gesture.

As I continued toward the accounting department, snorting under my breath at the small wet spot on the document from where he'd carried it in his mouth, I couldn't help but think I'd just made a friend.

***

Visiting the hot spring was the best way to end a long day of work. The one problem?

Bathing with other people.

Correction: not just ordinary people, but ones who all looked like they belonged in bodybuilding magazines.

The knights disrobed and walked around with their washboard abs and very well-endowed cocks on display. My thin body with hardly any muscle was laughable in comparison. The area consisted of two small springs and one bigger one. A majority of the men went to the bigger one, while Callum and I chose the smaller one beside a section of rocks.

I walked with my hands over my junk.

"Why do you cover yourself?" Callum asked with a silly grin. He reclined in the steaming water, his brown hair slicked back after he'd dunked his head. He was incredibly sexy. For a cinnamon roll.

"We aren't all built like you, okay?" I eased into the water and sighed as the heat of it touched all my sore muscles. I scrubbed my face and hair before reclining backward. "Now, *this* is the life. I feel almost human again."

"You worked with Briar today, didn't you?"

"Yep," I answered. "I like working in the clinic, but I'm not sure I'm cut out for it."

"You could always return to the knights' quarters. The stew you made was delicious. Not that much was left by the time I got back last night. The men devoured it. They ate the blueberry cake too."

I'd totally forgotten I had cooked while anxiously awaiting their return from the dark wood. "It was supposed to be blueberry muffins, but I couldn't find a muffin tin, so I ended up making a type of skillet cake instead."

"Maybe you can make it again sometime," he said, softly smiling. "It truly lifted the men's spirits."

"Yeah." My throat tightened. "I'd like that."

"And stick around next time, as well. So we can see that cute face of yours." Callum reached over to pinch my cheek, and I swatted him away. He snorted. "No wonder Briar kept you around today."

"He and Thane were swamped and needed help. My face had nothing to do with it."

"Uh-huh. Sure." Callum flashed a dimple.

"What?" I splashed water at him. "Briar is very professional about his work, and he's nice to me, unlike someone else I know."

"Are you referring to the captain?"

"Maybe." I glided my palm over the top of the water, my chest tight all of a sudden. "Speaking of the captain... have you seen him today?"

Because I sure as hell hadn't. He never returned to see me after leaving the medical wing earlier that morning. One whole afternoon and evening without me being blessed by his oh-so-friendly face. I tried not to be upset by it.

"He met with the king earlier," Callum responded. "And then he was sent on a mission."

"Already?" I asked, a cold tinge of worry replacing my earlier disappointment. "But he's still healing from his injury."

"I assure you he's fine. The healing tonics worked their magic."

My worry didn't dissipate though. It turned to lead in my gut. "What was the mission? Hopefully not another patrol in the dark wood."

"He and a few knights left for Exalos. It's a city south of Bremloc. A group of bandits recently blazed through it, plundering goods and wounding several people. They requested aid. The captain should return by tomorrow evening at the latest."

"Why didn't you go with him? Aren't you his second-in-command?"

"I am. As such, it's my responsibility to stay here and take charge in his absence. Besides, he gave me separate orders." A lopsided grin touched Callum's lips. "I'm not at liberty to give exact details, you understand, but let's just say they involved looking after a clumsy traveler."

"For fuck's sake. I'm not clumsy. I'll have you know I walked all over the castle grounds today and didn't fall once. Well, okay. I *did* fall once, but it wasn't my fault. A cat boy pounced on me."

"Kuya?"

"Yep. That would be the culprit."

"He's harmless," Callum said with a laugh. "Mischievous? Yes. Very. But he's sweet. It's no wonder why Prince Sawyer adores him."

"What's their deal anyway? They seemed really close." I leaned back and slowly exhaled, staring up at the bright dusting of stars. The hot

140

spring was a decent walk from the knights' quarters. We'd had to journey up a hill and walk for roughly a mile, but it was worth it.

Callum was quiet as he stared at the sky too. "The prince saved him when they were young boys. Eight or nine, I think. Kuya's family was slaughtered, and he managed to escape. He was found beside a lake outside the kingdom, covered in bruises and severely malnourished. There were reports of a demi-human child stealing from the local butcher, and Kuya was identified as the thief. Prince Cedric, the eldest of the princes, ordered for Kuya to be executed for the crime."

"That's harsh," I said. "He was starving. He shouldn't be killed for stealing a little bit of food."

"Demi-humans are often mistreated that way." Callum's tone took on a serious edge. "Many of them allied with Onyx during the war. The ones who didn't are still seen in a bad light, though, because of it. Prince Cedric despises them and will use any excuse to put them to the sword."

"So Cedric wanted to kill Kuya, but Prince Sawyer intervened?"

"Basically." Callum nodded. "Prince Sawyer begged the king to spare his life. He even said he'd take the punishment in Kuya's place, which King Eidolon of course refused. He did, however, allow Prince Sawyer to take in Kuya with the promise that he keep him out of trouble. Kuya is now his personal manservant. But he's much more like a companion. The prince pampers him."

I recalled the conversation between Roth and Duke. "Some of the knights don't approve of Prince Sawyer."

"You're right. They don't." Callum expelled a breath. "Many believe him to be too sensitive. But I think his kind heart would make him a great king."

"What about Prince Cedric? What's he like?"

"It's not my place to give an opinion on the matter." Callum's brown eyes tightened at the edges. "Perhaps you'll meet him someday and learn that answer for yourself. Though, as your friend, I'd advise you to keep your distance and never get close enough *to* find out."

His warning about the crowned prince was shoved to the back of my head as something else in his statement stuck out.

"We're friends?" I asked, feeling a bit ridiculous by how happy that made me.

Callum scoffed and kicked at me beneath the water. "You better consider me your friend."

"I do."

"Good." He returned to his cinnamon roll self. "I consider you mine as well."

After the much-needed soak in the hot spring, I changed into the clothes Callum had picked up for me. A dark green tunic and black trousers. They fit great.

"They belonged to my younger brother, Gerard," Callum said as we descended the hill back toward the barracks. "He's outgrown them."

"How old is he?"

"Fourteen."

I didn't know whether I should laugh or cry. Curse my small genes. A fourteen-year-old was bigger than me. "Well, tell him thank you for me."

"I will." He beamed with a smile. "Gerard is leaving for the academy soon, where he'll train to become a knight in the Third Order. I'm very proud of him."

"Is the Third Order like the bottom level?" It was the only one Maddox hadn't told me about.

"Yes. All knights begin there and work their way up the ranks."

"Cool. How many siblings do you have?"

"Four," he answered. "Two older sisters, one younger, and Gerard."

"Wow. I bet that was a lively house growing up."

"Very much so."

Given his smile as he spoke of them and his bubbly personality, I got the impression Callum had been shown a lot of love as a child. A close-knit family who probably never missed a meal together. A part of me envied him because of it. Family was an unknown concept for me—something I'd seen from a distance and read about but never experienced for myself.

"Would you like me to walk you home?" he asked.

Home. Not the word I'd use to describe the small room I'd spent the last few nights in. "No, it's okay. I can find my way back on my own."

Callum seemed hesitant at first—more than likely recalling Maddox's orders to watch over me—but he nodded. "Will you be working with Briar again tomorrow?"

"Yeah, I think so. Unless I get promoted to being Kuya's playmate or something, I don't really have many other places I can work." I couldn't swing a sword to save my life, and I fumbled over my words too much to have any kind of job where I had to talk in front of people—which ruled out the *incredibly nice* suggestion from Maddox that I be the court jester.

"If all else fails, you could always return to mucking out the stables," Callum said in a matter-of-fact tone. One that was soon accompanied by a shit-eating grin. "But I must say your skills are better used elsewhere."

"Are you kidding?" I feigned shock. "I'm the best stable boy who ever lived. Just ask Seabiscuit. He saw it all."

Callum laughed. "You're referring to Samson. He rarely sees much action these days. He's older than the other horses. More temperamental too. None of us can ride him. But Captain Maddox refuses to sell him. He has a soft spot for the stallion."

Why did that give *me* a soft spot for a certain captain? Well, an even softer spot. Maddox was very quickly breaking down the barriers around my heart. Even if he *was* stubborn.

"Between us, Callum, I think my skills as a physician's assistant are about as good as my work as a stable boy. Which isn't saying much."

"Fret not, Evan." Callum clapped me on the back. "You'll soon find the place where you belong."

His words ran through my head as I strolled along the path toward my temporary living quarters. The place I belonged. It felt like a sign. A reminder that this was what I'd wished for that night as I'd held the wishing stone, when my heart had been heavy in my chest and the desire for adventure so strong it had been suffocating.

A world like I've only seen in my dreams.

Bremloc was just like those kingdoms I'd escaped to while lost in the pages of a book, but instead of reading about someone else's adventures, I was living my own. The protagonist of my own story.

Movement from my peripheral caused me to look toward a field on the right. A field filled with glowing flowers. And amongst those flowers? A man.

"Briar?" I stepped from the path and approached him.

"Oh. Hello." He stood from his crouched position and greeted me with a warm smile, one of the flowers in his hand.

"Are you stealing flowers?"

"Stealing? No." He laughed and tucked it into the satchel slung across his upper body. "These are called Night Kisses and only bloom beneath the light of a full moon."

"What do they do?" I knelt to look at them. The curved petals shimmered in hues of silver and glowing white.

"They have many uses." Briar dropped down next to me. The excited gleam in his eyes was visible even in the dark. "Depending on what you blend with them, they can ease muscle aches. They also possess calming effects and help relax the mind. I use them for tonics to aid those suffering from insomnia as well."

"You really like this herbology stuff, huh? Not just because you're a physician."

"It fascinates me." His smile became a bit shy. "Much like you do."

My face heated. "There's nothing fascinating about me. I'm kind of boring, actually. If I was a plant, I'd probably be a weed."

"Weeds are resilient," he said. "They adapt to their environment and can survive harsh conditions. A great quality to have. But while I believe you to be resilient, you are not a weed. Far from it." He lifted a hand and lightly smoothed away my bangs. "You are much too beautiful."

Breath snagging in my throat, I tore my gaze from his. "I think you need a new set of glasses, Doc, if you think *I'm* beautiful."

Briar tucked a finger beneath my chin and tipped it up, our eyes meeting again. "You say that, yet you currently have two men under your spell. Captain Maddox and I have very little in common… with the exception of our attraction toward you."

"Then maybe he *needs* glasses while you get yours changed. It's the only explanation."

"My sight is fine," he responded, amusement rich in his voice. That amusement then trickled away, exposing something much more tender underneath. "Since the moment you first walked through my door, you've left me spellbound. Eyes the deepest shade of green, skin as soft as rose petals, and a smile that warms all who see it. Try as I might, I can't get you out of my head."

"Well, I'm constantly in your clinic being a nuisance. That's probably why."

He released a low laugh. "You are far from a nuisance, Evan. I've greatly enjoyed our time together."

"I have too," I whispered, confused and excited at the same time.

After returning from the accounting department earlier, I had spent the afternoon in the clinic. In between tasks, I had looked through more of Briar's books, and he'd allowed me to pick out some to take to my room. He was a lot like me in terms of communication. Long silences often passed, but they weren't awkward with him.

"I find connections with other people difficult," he said. "Many say I'm hard to like. My intelligence is off-putting to many people. Others mistake my quiet nature for egotism, as if I believe myself to be too superior to engage with them."

"I don't think that about you." But I certainly understood the feeling of being judged for being too quiet or too passionate about a subject. "Can't say I'm much better at making connections. I've never really fit in with the people around me."

"Is that why you left your home?" he asked. We were sitting close together in the grass, the patches of Night Kisses glowing around us and the stars bright in the sky. It felt like a dream. Or a scene from a swoony romance novel.

"It's part of it," I admitted, remembering my wish. More so, the deep craving for something *more*. "Do you ever feel like you're going through life in a sort of daze? Like you're existing but not truly living?" I dropped my gaze to one of the silvery flowers. "That's how I felt. Leaving home was kind of impulsive." Aka forced on me by a mysterious magical stone. "But now that I'm here? I don't know. I'm excited to start the day when I wake up in the morning. And I haven't felt like that in a long time."

All thanks to Lupin. As much of a headache as he'd given me, I was grateful in that moment.

"Days had begun to feel that way for me as well." Briar removed his satchel and placed it beside him. "Your arrival in Bremloc changed that. I woke this morning excited by the thought of seeing you."

"Because I'm such an amazing assistant, right?"

He laughed and placed his hand over mine. "Because you make me feel like I never have."

Unsure what to say, I looked at our hands and linked our fingers. His pale skin caught the moonlight, making our contrast even more apparent. In the few days I'd been there, the sun had given my skin a golden shine. It had also brought out more of my freckles.

"May I ask another question?"

"Yeah. Of course. God knows I ask about a million."

"I don't mind your questions." His smile slowly faded. "What are your feelings toward Captain Maddox?"

"My feelings?" Prickles attacked my sternum. "I'm still trying to figure that out. I mean, I hardly know the guy. Why?"

"Because I've never been this captivated by anyone before." Briar's fingertips touched the edge of my brow and trailed down to my cheek. He leaned in closer, his breath tickling my lips. "And I'll be damned if I let another man have you without a fight."

He softly brushed our mouths together but then stilled his advance, as if waiting for permission before continuing. Heat traveled up my neck and to the top of my scalp. This whole situation felt surreal.

The logical side of my brain told me I was incapable of dating two guys at the same time. Did other people play the field a bit before settling with one? Sure. They did it all the time. Until a couple agreed to be exclusive, it wasn't wrong either. But I had always been the type of person who fell hard for one guy and then forgot about everyone else.

Until now.

Where Maddox called to that carnal desire deep in my core, one that made me want to ride him nine ways to Sunday, my attraction to Briar was softer, like moonlight kissing flower petals.

With a small forward push of my head, I kissed him. The boldness of it shocked me. It did him too.

He shakily exhaled through his nostrils as our mouths slid together, once, twice. His hand came to rest at my nape, and he gently brought our bodies closer. His soft kisses and tender touches made me feel... special. Cared for. Like this was more than a lust-driven attraction.

Briar tasted like raspberries, as if he'd had a glass of wine before going flower picking. I dipped my tongue into his mouth, wanting to taste more of him. Notes of berry and fig laced with a flavor that was all him. It was intoxicating.

"Evan," he said under his breath and curled his fingers in the back of my hair, his kisses becoming heavier. A groan rumbled in his throat.

The sound elicited sparks of heat to surge through my bloodstream. I put my arms around his neck and fell backward in the grass, taking him with me. He smiled against my lips as he settled on top of me and cupped my face in one hand.

We kissed surrounded by a field of glowing blossoms. My heart fluttered like hummingbirds' wings with each pass of his mouth on mine. Minutes ticked by as we lost ourselves in the taste of each other. Without a doubt, I knew I could live for a thousand years and never experience anything more romantic than that moment with Briar.

"It's late," he whispered much too soon, pulling back a little. "I'll walk you to your room."

"Already?"

Briar breathed out a laugh before kissing me again, softer than before. He then glided the tip of his nose across mine. "If this continues for much longer, I fear I'll start ripping off your clothes."

My cock twitched. "I mean... I wouldn't mind."

150

"The captain of the Second Order might not have reserves about moving so quickly, yet I prefer to take my time and treat you right."

"Was that a stab at Maddox?" I almost laughed.

Briar only grinned before helping me to my feet.

"I can find my way back on my own," I said. "You need to pick more of these Night Kisses while they're in bloom."

"Are you sure?"

"Yep." Being alone would give my heart a much-needed reprieve. Because it might explode at this point. I took a step back, keeping our gazes locked. "I'll be in your clinic bright and early tomorrow."

"I look forward to it."

So did I.

As I found the path toward the courtyard, my mind raced. I was torn between two men. A dilemma I never thought I'd find myself in. They were complete opposites. Ice and fire. Rough and smooth. But both of them intense in their own way. Those thoughts continued to run through my head long after I crawled into bed.

I tossed and turned, unable to find a comfortable position.

"Trouble sleeping?"

I jumped at the voice and shot upward in bed. A shape stood in front of the open window. "Lupin?"

"At your service." He stepped closer, and as my eyes adjusted, I made out his pale hair, sharp features, and a classy white suit. "You've had quite the eventful few days."

"That's one way of describing it, I guess."

"And tonight ended with a kiss among the flowers. How sweet." He smirked. "I anticipate many more of those during your time here."

"Great. You're a stalker as well? Don't you know it's rude to spy on people?" His statement piqued my curiosity. "How many kisses are we talking about?"

Lupin's smirk widened. "Oh, who can say? You already have two men in your grasp. How many more will fall under your spell, I wonder?"

"You make it sound like I'm the main protagonist from an isekai manga," I said, scrubbing my hands over my face.

"Isekai?"

"A story where someone gets transported to another world," I explained. "Everyone and their brother then wants the main guy's dick. Harem galore. I'm sure my story would have some ridiculously long name too, like 'Reincarnated As An Overpowered Hero In Another World With a Magic Rod All the Men Want to Ride.' And I would come diamonds or something."

"That sense of humor will be the undoing of all your future mates," he said with a laugh. "How could they not fall for you?"

"Future mates?"

"Harem galore," Lupin said with a dramatic flutter of his hand. "One Evan to rule them all."

"No." Then, because I felt it needed repeating, I did so in a firmer tone, "*No*. I refuse to be in some kind of fucked-up dating simulation game."

"I assure you, this is no game, harem king."

"God. Stop," I groaned. "This isn't happening."

"Didn't you once say being in bed with a bunch of hot dudes wouldn't be too bad? You said you wanted to be the heartthrob all the pretty boys drooled over."

"I was joking! At the time, no offense, I thought you were a con artist, and I didn't take you seriously at all."

"Well, surprise. Wish granted. You can have your own harem."

I felt a bit light-headed. "My dating experience is extremely limited. I can barely manage to date one man, let alone two."

"How sweet that you think there will only be two."

I stared at him. "What?"

"The correct number is... well, more than two."

Yep, my brain was about to break. "How many is *more than two*?"

"Five."

"*Five*? Who needs that many?"

"Could be more."

I was overwhelmed just thinking about it. "No. Not gonna happen. I don't want to toy with anyone's feelings, okay? I don't want to juggle multiple men and end up having to choose between them."

"Most people would love this opportunity."

"Yeah, well, I'm not most people."

Sighing, Lupin stepped over to the bed and sat on the edge of it. "I've helped many lost souls over the years. You're the first one who's complained this much."

"Look, I don't mean to seem ungrateful or whatever, but this is *a lot* to process. You can't just drop me into an unknown, magical land, say I'm going to be swimming in dick, and then expect me to accept it with no questions or concerns."

"Swimming in dick. Interesting choice of words."

"I'm being serious."

"As am I," he said. "Well, mostly. The talk of your harem was mainly to tease you, though you can really have one if you so desire."

"This is ridiculous. I just want a simple life."

"You had a simple life. And you were unhappy with it."

"I wasn't unhappy! I was just..." Bored. Unhappy. Borderline depressed. Never feeling like I belonged. My throat clogged up. "Look, it doesn't matter. This has been awesome, but I think you chose the wrong person."

"I didn't choose you. The Emporium did."

"You make it sound like your shop has a mind of its own." I tugged a hand through my hair. What was this, Lupin's Moving Emporium?

He released a breath. "If you truly want to leave, I can help you."

"You can? Really?" I perked up. "What about not having enough magical energy?"

Lupin stood from the bed and walked back over to the window, keeping his back to me. "I should be able to perform the spell on the summer equinox. The moon's energy will boost my mana."

"The summer equinox. That's like a month away," I said, excited by the thought of returning to my own world, away from all this weirdness. Back to my books and games and coffee. Back to electricity and the ability to binge-watch Netflix. "Are you saying I can really go home?"

He glanced back at me, his expression clouded. "If that's what you wish."

"It is!"

"What about the people you've formed attachments to already? Maddox. Briar. Callum. And the demi-human male, Kuya."

My excitement deflated.

"Not so simple now, is it?"

"No," I said, sinking more into the mattress. "I guess it's not."

"There's one more thing you should know." Lupin stared out into the night. "If I send you back, you can never return to this place."

"Never?"

That's when I thought of Maddox. He was brash and icy, but I somehow felt warm when around him. Briar appeared in my head, too, with his gentle smiles and soft kisses. In my time in that world, I'd also made friends. Callum with his silly cinnamon roll grin and shoe-thieving tendencies. Kuya and his habit of referring to himself in the third person—his wiggling ears, snaggletooth, and playfulness. Even Thane, who I didn't know well but who was hardworking and friendly.

I wanted to learn more about all of them. Wanted more time.

"What if I decide to stay past the summer equinox but want to go home someday in the future? Is that an option?"

Lupin shook his head. "The longer you are in this world, the harder it will be to send you back. You must make a choice: stay and allow this land to become your permanent home or leave and never return. You have until the conclusion of the Festival of Lights to make your decision."

"The Festival of Lights?" Wait. Didn't Callum mention something about that?

"It's a festival held every year to welcome summer," Lupin explained. "That's when I'll return for your answer. I suggest you think carefully."

He vanished in the blink of an eye, as if being absorbed by the shadows on the floor.

I plopped to my back and tucked my arms behind my head, staring up at the ceiling as I mulled over what I'd learned. Just one month, and I could leave it all behind. I could return to my own world. But did I want to?

I wasn't so sure anymore.

Chapter Seven
Tale of the Two Men and the Confused Evan

As Briar worked at his desk that afternoon, I sat in an oversized chair beside the window and read a book on the history of Bremloc.

The day had been fairly quiet so far. No dire emergencies apart from a young knight who had caught a shield to the head during a sparring match and needed some tending.

Kuya had popped in once as well, staying long enough to grab a nutritional tonic for Prince Sawyer—the tonic helped rejuvenate the body and gave the drinker a boost of energy. Apparently, the prince had a late night going over documents and working on his studies. Kuya had fluttered around the clinic, touching everything as Thane made the tonic, and then he'd snatched it, nuzzled my arm with his head, and scampered away.

Briar and I hadn't kissed again, but throughout the day, his hand had brushed mine when we were close. We'd shared soft smiles from across the room. For lunch, we'd cooked together in the small kitchen, making a fish dish with baby red roasted potatoes. Both of us were kind of awkward and shy.

I peeked at him over the top of the book. Light brown bangs fell like a curtain over his glasses as he read from an old hardback. He swept them to the side before jotting down notes in a leather-bound journal.

"Find anything interesting?" Briar asked, eyes meeting mine. A smile curved the edge of his mouth. "In the book, I mean."

Yeah, he knew I'd been checking him out. I was about as subtle as a sneeze in church.

"Define interesting. Because, to be honest, this is kind of a snooze fest." Especially by fantasy world standards. "The foundation of the kingdom, the long succession of monarchs and their triumphs, the type of currency… I'm gonna fall asleep."

He chuckled. "Not enough adventure for your liking?"

"Nope." I closed the book. "A swordfight would help. Maybe a love interest or two. But you don't wanna make the plot feel too contrived, ya know?"

"Perhaps you should write your own story."

I am. Sort of anyway. Being sent to this fantasy world had given me a fresh start. The possibilities were endless. I only needed to decide if I wanted to stay and embrace those possibilities.

The clock was ticking.

"You chose that book so you could learn about Bremloc, yes?"

I nodded. "I thought it was a good idea to be informed about the place I call home." Or *might* call home depending on my decision when Lupin returned during the summer festival.

"I have a proposal you may find less tedious." Briar scooted back from his chair and walked to the

158

side of his desk, resting his hip against it. When he crossed his arms, my gaze landed on his biceps. He reminded me of a sexy college professor—one I never would've missed a single day of class if I'd been blessed to have. "Instead of reading about the kingdom, see it for yourself."

"Really? I can go exploring?" I'd been itching to explore since the first morning I woke up there—after all the confusion and dealing with a grumpy captain anyway. But I hadn't yet left the castle grounds.

"You don't need my permission," Briar said, his hazel eyes twinkling with the laugh he didn't release. "However, I'd love to accompany you. If you'll have me."

"Hell yeah." I stood from the chair, stretching my arms over my head. I'd been sitting for too long. "Are you sure? I don't want to take you from your work."

"I can watch over the clinic," Thane said from the workstation, where he was separating different herbs into jars. "But as payment, I'll take something sweet from the market."

Briar smiled. "I'm sure that can be arranged." His hazel eyes shifted back to me. "If you're ready, we can go now before it gets too late—"

Thuds sounded from outside, like something heavy beating against the ground. Horse hooves? The thuds stopped before there came a murmuring of deep voices.

Briar sighed. "Lovely. He's returned."

"Who—"

The front door swung open before Maddox stepped across the threshold. His deep blue eyes instantly found me.

Fuck. Nearly two whole days without seeing him, and I'd forgotten just how strongly I felt his presence. He commandeered every space he was in, like an icy wind sweeping down from the hillside, a chill felt by everyone it touched.

I shivered beneath his hard gaze, but it had nothing to do with being cold. "Hey," I said, my body heating under his scrutiny. "Long time no see."

Without breaking eye contact, Maddox strode toward me, his armor clanking with his steps. His intensity made my knees quiver. Was he mad? Did he change his mind while away on the mission and want to throw me in the dungeon after all?

Hot tingles spread all throughout my body in the short time it took for him to reach me.

"Good." Maddox pulled me into his arms, crushing me to his chest. One of his large hands cupped the back of my head. "You're just as I left you."

He had been... worried about me? As his scent of leather and spice filled my senses, I pressed my face more into his chest.

I'd been worried about him too.

"Like I'd allow anything to happen to Evan," Briar said in a tone I wasn't used to hearing from him. It lacked his usual gentleness. "He was perfectly fine under my care."

"Fortunate for you," Maddox said, still holding me close. "If I'd returned to find even a scratch on him, we'd have words, you and I."

"Oh, like the head wound he received while under *your* care? A wound I healed for him."

"It was just a bump," I said. "I wouldn't call it a head wound. Not exactly."

Both ignored me.

"That was an unfortunate accident that won't be repeated," Maddox snapped.

"See to it that it's not." Briar's voice was just as snippy. "Or you and I will have much more than words exchanged."

"Is that a threat?" Maddox pulled away from me.

"I never make threats. Only promises."

"Bold words coming from a man I could snap in two with my bare hands."

"Um, guys?" I glanced between the two of them. "Can we tone down the murderous impulses for a sec?"

Maddox glared at Briar. The physician glared right back. And I... well, I stood there between them, confused as hell. Guilty too.

It's my fault. I had kissed both of them. My stupid lips had set off a chain reaction of events.

Thane met my gaze with wide eyes. He then turned back to his work, clearly not wanting to get in the middle of their spat.

"Why don't we find something to eat?" I asked, breaking the uncomfortable silence. "It's way too early for dinner, but I never turn down a snack." More silence. "I can make muffins. Any kind you want." And then, because neither of them reacted, I did what I always did when nervous and rambled. "My favorite is banana nut. Not to brag, but baking is one thing I'm really good at it. Well, except for when I burn myself. But still. I've never caught anything on fire, so that's a plus. Do you have bananas here? Bremloc certainly doesn't have a nut shortage. That's for sure."

The two continued to glare at each other for another handful of seconds before Briar averted his gaze to the floor.

Maddox gave a little smirk, as if he'd won some unspoken challenge. He then aimed that smirk at me. It softened around the edges. "What were you rambling about, Muffin Lord?"

I grinned at that. His usage of the silly title I'd thought of on the spot never got old. Especially since Maddox didn't seem like the joking, playful type toward anyone else.

"Evan and I were about to leave for the day," Briar chimed in. My ramble about food had done the trick, cutting through the possessive, high-strung testosterone thick in the air. "He wants to see the kingdom, and I offered to take him. We should be on our way while there's still daylight."

"I'll go with you," Maddox said without missing a beat.

"That won't be necessary. You just returned from a mission. I'm sure you're tired." Briar adjusted his round-framed glasses. "Go report to the king about your travels or whatever you need to do. We can manage without a knight escort."

162

Okay, the daggers were back. If looks could kill, Briar would've been in pieces at the captain's feet. I eyed the sword at his side. He never reached for it, but his hand twitched a little, making me think a part of him wanted to.

"If he leaves these grounds, it will be in my company," Maddox retorted.

"Is that so?" Briar tipped his chin up. "He's not your property, Captain, nor is he your prisoner. Evan can go wherever he chooses, with or without you."

"This is awkward," I mumbled. "I'm, like, right here. Don't I get a say in anything?"

"Very well," Maddox said to me in a less snarly tone. His blue eyes burned with annoyance though. "Who do you wish to escort you? Me or him?"

Briar looked at me. Both waited for an answer.

The decision was... difficult. In more ways than one. Looking at them, remembering their kisses, their soft groans, and the feel of their touch—one calloused from years wielding a sword and the other gentler but no less effective in sending fire through my veins—I couldn't choose between them.

Not yet.

Maybe not ever.

"Well, you know what they say..." I put my hands on my hips, going for a confidence I sorely lacked. "Two is better than one. I mean, I know I can take care of myself. Obviously. But I'd feel safer with both of you beside me."

That was the truth, at least. I felt safer, as well as something… inexplicable. As Maddox had said the night he kissed me, it felt like we'd known each other longer. Our minds were strangers, but our hearts felt familiar. Connected. Mine did strange things when I was around both of them.

"Besides," I added, "you two make a great team. A knight to protect me from evil rogues and creepy things and a super-skilled physician to heal me if I trip over my own two feet and scuff my knee. Or if I run face-first into a knight's armor. Again."

Briar snorted a laugh. Maddox's cheek twitched. The tension between them had mostly dissipated. For now.

"Allow me time to wash up from my travels," Maddox said before walking toward the door. "I'll meet you at the front gate within the hour."

He left the clinic.

Thane breathed a notable sigh of relief. Did the captain intimidate him? Not that I could blame him if so. Maddox was a wall of muscle and snarl that struck fear in the hearts of probably anyone who got on his bad side.

"Before we go, I have something for you." Briar returned to his desk and opened the drawer. He handed me a small bag.

"Money?" I asked after peeking inside. "Why?"

"Payment for your work here in the clinic. Even as a temporary arrangement, surely, you didn't expect to work for free."

"I didn't really think about it, honestly. I was just happy to help you and Thane." The bag held a bunch of copper coins with a few silver ones mixed in. It was one good thing that had come from reading through the dull-as-hell history book: I had a basic understanding of how the currency system worked. "Thank you."

"No, thank *you*." Briar lightly grazed the backs of his knuckles across my cheek. "For everything."

"You're firing me, aren't you? Is it because I ate all your fig bread again?"

Thane chuckled.

"With the emergent situation behind us, I no longer require your assistance." Briar's hand slid to my nape, and his fingers played with the back of my hair just as a smile played at his mouth. "Though, I hope you'll still come to visit me."

"Eh. I'm sure I'll stop by." I grinned up at him. "That fig bread is too good. I can't stay away."

"Ah, so it's the bread that draws you here." He winked. "I should have known."

We shared a smile before he put away the hardback he'd been reading. Something about rare herbs and their medicinal uses. Getting out of the clinic would do him some good as well. He worked way too much.

I pocketed the coins, excited to finally explore the kingdom. What excited me most though? Spending time with the two men who'd, most definitely, taken over my thoughts. And maybe started to worm their way into my heart too.

***

"Took you long enough," Maddox said as we met him at the front gate. He had changed out of his uniform and into an ensemble of black on black—a thin, long-sleeved shirt that hugged his torso almost like body armor, with a shoulder garment that clasped across his chest, a belt with his sword attached, and black pants tucked into boots.

And fuck me. He was wearing black gloves as well, like the kind worn by swordsmen.

"You said within the hour." Briar placed a hand at my lower back and guided me forward. "I believe we're right on time."

Maddox sneered as his gaze dropped to my back—specifically, to the hand resting there. He moved to my opposite side. "You can ride with me."

"Ride?" I asked before seeing the two saddled horses. "Oh."

We would be riding together? Like, in the same saddle? So, so close together. Not sure what made me more nervous: being that high in the air again and possibly falling to my death or having Maddox pressed close behind me.

"One horse is for you," Maddox told Briar. "I hope you know how to ride. If not, you could always walk and meet us there."

"Or we all could walk," I suggested, more to spare myself the humiliation of another horse ride. Callum, bless him, had barely contained his laughter as I'd wobbled in the saddle the last time. "It would be nice to stretch my legs."

"Riding is faster," Maddox said as we reached the black stallion. "We'll do plenty of walking once we're in town. Here. I'll help you up."

I accepted his hand. "I don't know if Callum told you, but I'm not the best at this."

"Oh, he might've mentioned it." Maddox didn't smile, but one showed in his eyes as he helped me into the saddle. He then swung up and settled in behind me. As his chest pressed to my back—and something else pressed against my ass—my body heated. The bulge I'd noticed before was, indeed, massive. He reached past me and grabbed the reins, his lips grazing my nape. "Are you all right?"

I nodded. If I tried to talk, I would've squeaked, and I didn't want to grant him that satisfaction. Again.

Briar seated himself atop the other horse, not as smoothly as Maddox. "We're wasting daylight."

The horses moved at a leisurely pace down the road, their hooves clacking against the cobblestone. Maddox's proximity became a form of comfort; his warmth and how his arms were on each side of me, like a protective wall of muscle. Briar kept pace beside us and smiled at me as our eyes met.

My heart beat faster as I returned his smile.

I stared out across the valley, watching the grass wave with the gentle spring breeze. The sun passed behind a cloud, shading a large area of the land, before coming out on the other side, casting down golden rays. Everything was so vibrant, the fields of flowers, the green grass, and the splash of blue sea to the right.

167

"I didn't realize we were so close to the ocean," I said. The sparkling water stretched for miles and miles, seemingly endless.

"Bremloc is a central trading port," Briar explained. "Merchants travel from all over to trade and sell their wares. Travelers come too, some to visit and others in the hope of starting a new life in the capital."

"Bremloc is the capital kingdom?" I asked, trying to further my geographical understanding. Politics too. Maybe I should've read more of that history book.

"Yes," Maddox answered, his deep voice a pleasant rumble in my ear. Tingles spread down my arms. "The neighboring kingdoms have monarchs as well, but King Eidolon and the two princes are by far the most influential. All other kingdoms must abide by our laws."

Farther in front of us, the tops of buildings came into view with a backdrop of rolling hills. "It's really beautiful here."

"More beautiful than your homeland?" Maddox asked.

"Definitely." Not only was the scenery beautiful in Bremloc, but the people were too. Especially the two with me. "What's Exalos like? That's where you just returned from, right?"

"It is," Maddox responded. "The terrain is rougher in Exalos, with very little grassy plains and located more inland. There are mountain ranges and caves within those mountains that contain valuable minerals and crystals we use here in Bremloc for weapons and spell work. The city is essential to our kingdom."

Minutes later, we neared a section of buildings. The bustle of the marketplace could be heard over the horse hooves on the stone path. Smells reached me too—the familiar scent of baked goods, along with other ones I couldn't place but were still amazing.

Reaching a stable, Maddox spoke to a man, who then allowed us through. He dismounted from the saddle before offering me his hand to help me down.

"Why, thank you, sir knight," I said without thinking.

He paused, expression wavering between amused and perplexed. "Sir knight. I like it." Instead of releasing my hand, he took it firmer in his grasp and pulled me closer. "Does that make you my damsel?"

"If you want a damsel, find a brothel." Briar dropped down beside us and handed the reins to a stable boy, who then led the horse into a stall. "Pay her enough and she'll be anything you want. In fact, that sounds like a lovely idea. You do that while I escort Evan around the market. Take your time."

Okay, I knew I had *no reason* to be jealous, especially considering how I was torn between the two of them, but the thought of Maddox in a brothel caused a twisting in my gut. I grabbed his sleeve on impulse.

Maddox glanced at my hand before his gaze returned to mine. The hardness in his eyes became warm. "I have no interest in brothels. They have nothing I desire." He smoothed his thumb along my jaw. "Stop worrying."

"I'm not worrying," I lied. "You can do whatever you want with whoever you want to do it with. It's not like we're…" My throat tightened, cutting off my words.

"What I want?" Another glide of his thumb. "He's right here in front of me."

Relief flooded my chest.

Briar rested a hand on my side. When he spoke, it was in a soft voice. "The three of us will stay together."

Maddox nodded to him, as if the two had reached some silent understanding. His hand trailed from my jaw to my neck. "We won't leave your side."

Both of them were touching me, their expressions gentle, though Briar's was a bit apologetic. The backs of my eyes burned as emotion swelled in my chest. Did I understand my feelings? Not even a little. But maybe I didn't need to understand them right then.

I just needed to let things unfold naturally, the pieces falling where they may.

"I'll hold you both to that," I said, my voice wobbly. "Can we go shopping now?" I hoped the change of subject would help me get my shit together. "This bag of coins is burning a hole in my pocket. I want to buy all the things."

"Are you searching for anything in particular?" Briar asked, grazing his fingers along my lower back as we left the stable and walked down a short path.

"I'm not sure, but I'll know it when I see it."

The back of Maddox's hand pressed to mine from my left side. "I must insist you refrain from purchasing anything sharp."

I snorted. Being between them caused little tingles of excitement in my belly. We reached the main square of the marketplace. People strolled along, going about their day. Some tipped their heads to Maddox.

"Afternoon, Captain," one woman greeted him with a bright smile.

He gave a subtle nod of his head before continuing on. Behind us, that same woman rushed over to another woman, speaking in excited whispers like the ones from the garden the other morning. The captain was popular with the ladies but paid them little mind. His attention was too focused on me. It thrilled me.

Merchants sold goods from stands along the street and called out like the carnies at carnivals who tried to get you to walk over, spend a fortune, and then leave with little to show for it. I stopped at one of their stands and admired a shiny necklace before moving on. Buildings stood wedged close together, housing a variety of shops. Jewelry, a weapons place, an apothecary, and more beyond that.

"There's so much to see," I said, taking in all the sights and smells. "I don't think we'll make it to everything today."

"We can return another day," Briar responded. "This isn't the only time you'll get to visit."

Little did he know, my time was limited. Only a month left before I needed to make the most important decision of my life. Stay there with them or return to my own world.

I shoved that thought away and approached another stand.

"Fancy a sweetie, dear?" the older woman asked. The *sweetie* in question looked like some type of hard caramel candy, and I needed it in my belly as soon as possible. One copper coin bought me a bag of them. Enough for us to share and take back to Thane too.

"Want one?" I held the bag toward Briar after popping one in my mouth. Smiling, he grabbed a piece. I then turned to Maddox and placed one in his hand. "Here."

"I don't eat sweets." However, that didn't stop him from putting it in his mouth anyway. Something about his grumpy face as he sucked on the candy made me grin. His eyes narrowed at me. "Why do you stare?"

"Because you're kind of adorable," I said, then quickly looked in the other direction to avoid what I was sure would be an unamused sneer. Which brought my focus to Briar.

He sucked on his candy and people-watched, oblivious of my attention on him. His eyes then found mine, and instantly, a smile blossomed on his lips. "Are you having fun?"

"Yeah." My heart thumped harder in my chest. "I really am."

More fun than I'd had in a long time. All thanks to them.

Some of the buildings reminded me of early nineteenth-century England, and others mirrored the establishments from fantasy movies. Bremloc was a melting pot of cultures and people, as well as having both semi-modern and historical architecture and conveniences.

"Make way!" a man exclaimed from behind us.

Maddox and Briar guided me to the edge of the lane as a group of men passed, pulling a rickety wooden cart carrying a massive animal.

"Is that... a boar?" I asked. Though, it didn't look like the ones I knew from my world. It was ginormous. The tusks were probably two feet long, and its brown hide looked thick and leathery with a few patches of fur.

"Yes," Maddox answered, seemingly impressed. "There are always bounties for them."

"Bounties?"

"The adventurers' guild." He pointed to a building at the corner. "People accept jobs, such as hunting beasts, exploring caves, delivering items to another town, or sometimes simply gathering herbs. There are several ranks for an adventurer. The higher your rank, the better bounties you have access to, which means a greater reward if you complete it. Killing a wild boar is a guaranteed way to increase your ranking fast, but many usually die trying."

"Wow." I stared at the men pulling the cart. They stopped in front of the guild headquarters, and one went inside. It was just like every fantasy anime I'd ever watched. "So people can make a living like this? Going on quests and stuff."

"Yes," Briar answered. "Some of my ingredients are difficult to gather, and when I'm swamped with work, I sometimes submit requests to the guild for help."

"Rid yourself of the thought," Maddox said to me, one eyebrow arching. "As amusing as it'd be to see you trying your hand at adventuring, my heart wouldn't be able to handle it."

"I could gather herbs," I told him. "That's not dangerous. I'm just trying to consider my options. Find a way to earn an honest living."

"You could always be my squire," Maddox suggested. "Clean my room, fetch my meals, brush my horse."

"No, thanks."

He chuckled. "Let's continue on."

Briar needed to stop by the apothecary for more supplies, so the three of us popped in so he could browse the shelves. He also purchased a book on advanced alchemy.

"Are you finished?" Maddox asked, gaze sweeping throughout the shop, then flickering toward the windows, where people continued to pass by. He was always on alert. The day out would do him good, maybe get him to loosen up a bit and relax.

"Yes." Briar gathered his purchases, and we left the apothecary. "I've been waiting for that volume to release for what feels like years."

"So, you're an alchemist too?" I asked.

"In a sense." He swept a hand through his bangs to move them out of his eyes. "Infusing magic into the elixirs to enhance the effects is a

174

form of alchemy. Transforming one thing into another. Though, I still have much to learn."

The captain kept his silence during the conversation, his expression hard and cold, but as we passed the blacksmith's shop, I caught a flicker of interest in his eyes. He wouldn't say it, but he clearly wanted to go inside.

"Hold that thought," I said to Briar before bounding toward the door. The two of them called out to me before following. I entered the shop and grinned back at them as they reached the door at the same time.

Maddox allowed Briar to go first and tossed me an exasperated look as he stepped in behind him. I wasn't sure when the change had happened, but those looks didn't make me nervous anymore. I saw beneath them now.

"I thought I said to avoid sharp objects," Maddox said, walking with me down one aisle.

"Afraid I'll cut you?" I put on my most threatening face as I grabbed a dagger from the shelf. A dagger that was, unfortunately, heavier than anticipated. It fumbled from my hand.

Maddox caught it in midair with his lightning-fast reflexes. "Absolutely. You are truly terrifying with a weapon."

Briar pressed his lips together. "I admit, it's a thing we both agree on."

Maddox smirked at him.

"See? You two can get along just fine," I pointed out, pleased. "Our day out was a good idea."

"It hasn't been nearly as headache inducing as I'd assumed it would," the captain muttered before stepping over to a table that had a vast selection of armor and materials. Forearm grips, gauntlets, types of cloth for cloaks and under armor, and a fancy breastplate.

"See anything you like?" I asked.

"Yes." His gaze returned to me. "But the item in question is not for sale."

"What is it?" I scanned the things on the table. "I can go ask about the price."

He reached over to gently bop my chin. "Look who's being adorable now. And so damned oblivious."

My cheeks heated. "Wait. You were talking about me?"

Briar chuckled. "Yes, he's *very* oblivious. What will we do with him?"

"Several things come to mind," Maddox responded, gaze darkening. "Most of which shouldn't be done in public."

I gaped at them, words failing me. I wasn't used to men being so frank in their attraction toward me. Not just Maddox, but Briar too. He was more subtle than the captain, but when he was close, he was always touching me in some way— our arms pressed together or his hand on my back.

"I believe you broke him," Briar said. "Perhaps food will help him recover. It's nearly dinnertime."

"He's always going on about his hungry stomach." Maddox nodded.

"I could go for a burger right about now," I said. "Or a nice big turkey sandwich with juicy tomatoes and crispy bacon. French fries too."

When the two of them exchanged a look, one that almost seemed friendly, I blinked a few times just to make sure I wasn't imagining it. They had gone from rivals who'd nearly brawled in the clinic to civil acquaintances with a shared goal—that goal clearly being who could make me blush the deepest.

"I know a place we can take him," Maddox said.

After leaving the blacksmith's shop, they retook their positions on each side of me, closer now than before. The sky had darkened, though a bit of sunlight could still be seen along the horizon, as though the day wasn't yet ready to end. I felt the same.

I didn't want it to end either.

Maddox took us away from the main square and toward a building. A few men stood outside smoking cigars—or what looked like cigars. Others exited through the front door, stumbling a bit. A sign hung out front with an illustration of a crown and the name The King's Smoker above it.

"A tavern?" I asked. I'd always wanted to go to one. Just like the ones from all the medieval fantasy books I'd inhaled like oxygen.

"You seem awfully excited," Briar said. "Especially for someone who doesn't handle liquor well."

"Why doesn't that surprise me?" Maddox's eyes, a dark cobalt blue in the surrounding dusk, shone with amusement—all at my expense, damn him. "Clumsy *and* a lightweight."

I faltered in step as we reached the door, having misjudged the slight elevation from the ground to the entrance. Such poor timing. It proved him right. Both men grinned but didn't say a word.

Maddox entered first and waited for us to trickle in behind him before retaking his place at my side.

The tavern could've been taken from the set of any fantasy movie. Tables were scattered throughout, some only big enough to seat four men, while the ones in the center of the room were larger, seating up to seven or more.

The group of adventurers from earlier sat at one table, celebrating with huge tankards of ale. Women were there too, some patrons. Others fluttered about, refilling tankards and dishing out heaping plates of food.

"Over here." Maddox guided us over to a round table in the corner and sat in the chair with the wall at his back. Probably so he could have a view of the room. Always on his guard.

I sat beside him, and Briar sat across from me. On a wooden stage, a man strummed a lute and sang in a language I didn't know.

"Evenin'," a woman said after reaching our table. She was plump with strawberry blonde hair braided to one side. The creases around her brown eyes told me she laughed a lot. "What will ya be havin' to drink?"

"Water for me, please," I said. Briar quietly coughed, and I cut my eyes at him. "Unless you want me stripping out of my clothes and dancing naked on the table."

Briar pushed his glasses farther up his nose. "Best we avoid that, so water it is."

Maddox shrugged, one brow lifting, as if to suggest he wouldn't be opposed to me doing it. More than likely so he could add it to his arsenal of things to tease me about. The jerk.

The two of them ordered the house ale, along with three plates of food. I didn't know what kind of food, but I didn't care. I was so hungry I'd even eat that salty-as-hell popcorn from the festival.

The festival. Kind of fitting that attending one had led me to Lupin's shop, resulting in me being sent to Bremloc. And now, with the Festival of Lights approaching, one could possibly send me home.

What the hell am I going to do? My mind spun like the wheel in a game of roulette. Clack, clack, clack. Thoughts moving so fast.

The woman returned with our drinks and said our food would be out shortly before she left again. I wished I would've gotten something stronger than water. Alcohol didn't exactly give a person a clear head, but it would've been nice to block out my muddled thoughts for a while.

"Something on your mind?" Briar asked me as he grabbed his mug. "You're frowning."

He was so perceptive. I looked between the two of them. Maddox was carefully watching me. "Sorry. Just been a long day, I guess. Thank you both for showing me around. It's been fun."

"You've only seen the market. There is much more in Bremloc." Maddox took a drink and wiped his mouth with the back of his hand. "Next time, I can take you to the sea. But you'll have to hold my hand so you don't fall in."

I snorted. "I'm not that clumsy."

Briar pressed his lips together.

The bard strummed his lute one final time, letting the last syllable of the song bleed into the noise of the tavern. Silence hung over our table as we sipped our drinks.

The next performer then took the stage. His voice rang out loud and clear as he introduced himself as Jack, another bard but with a comedic twist. The lyrics of the song told of a busty, blonde tavern wench all the men wanted to *roll around in the hay with*, which got some hoots and hollers from the drinking patrons.

"Busty blonde wenches," I said, amused. "Every man's type."

"Not mine." Briar lightly tapped his finger against his mug, smiling.

"I've recently found an appreciation for blonds," Maddox said, and his blue eyes landed on me. "Though, I wouldn't use the word *busty* to describe him."

I hid my smile behind my mug as I took a drink.

"How long do you plan to stay in Bremloc?" Briar then asked.

Before I could respond, the waitress returned to the table with our food.

"Here you are, my dears." She placed a plate in front of each of us. Some type of meat and vegetable stew inside a bread bowl. "Enjoy."

Despite the amazing smell wafting up from the stew, my once hungry belly now felt kind of unsettled. What should I say? I didn't know how long I'd be there, depending on my decision when Lupin returned.

"Eat." Maddox nodded to my plate, then looked at Briar. "This is your fault. You made him lose his appetite."

"I simply asked him a question." Briar moved a spoon through his stew and let it fall back into the bread bowl with a *slop*. "His loss of appetite is more than likely the result of your poor choice of dining establishments."

"Where would *you* have taken him, then, physician? Back to the apothecary to eat plants?"

Well, their truce was nice while it lasted.

I grabbed my spoon and forced myself to take a bite. The burst of spices on my tongue and the hearty chunks of potatoes, carrots, and beef made me temporarily forget about everything else. A true comfort meal. My hunger returned full force, and I shoveled another spoonful into my mouth.

Maddox didn't smile but seemed pleased nonetheless. He looked at Briar. "See? He likes it."

"That's all that matters," Briar said, his worried gaze lingering on me for a moment longer before dropping to his food. Under the table, he moved his foot forward and rested it against mine. When I gently bumped them together, the tendrils of worry faded, and he smiled.

Until I knew for certain, I wouldn't answer the question. Would they be upset if I left? Seeing the two of them at the table, my heart ached a little. I got the feeling I'd be the one upset.

After we ate, Maddox paid for our meal, and we exited the tavern. Clouds had rolled in, blocking the stars. The smell of rain hung thick in the air, the humidity making my skin sticky. Thunder rumbled in the distance.

"A storm is coming" Briar said, glancing upward. "We should fetch our horses and hurry home."

The storm hit not long after we reached the castle grounds. Rain drummed against the stable roof as Maddox guided the black stallion into its stall. Briar did the same for the horse he'd ridden. A flash of lightning spooked some of the other horses, and they shifted uneasily in their stalls. They weren't the only ones startled.

I hated storms.

Thunder crashed, snapping through the electrified air like a whip. Every one of my muscles seized up, and my hair stood on end. Was my skin clammy? It felt clammy.

"Are you all right?" Briar asked.

Maddox joined us and gave me the same concerned look.

"Yeah. I'm totally fine." But my words proved to be a lie as another loud boom of thunder pierced the air, sounding like a damn bomb going off. I nearly jumped out of my skin. "I'm, uh… not good with storms," I admitted, voice rising in pitch. "A bit of rain I can handle, but—" More lightning flashed, and my words broke off as I squeezed my eyes closed.

How embarrassing. I was twenty-three and scared of thunder.

Arms came around me from behind before a familiar deep voice murmured in my ear, "I've got you."

There was a rustling sound, like a bag being set down, before another set of arms came around me from the front, followed by the calming pressure of a warm body. I opened my eyes to see Briar.

He softly smiled and brought my face to rest against his shoulder. "*We've* got you."

I was sandwiched between the two of them. And I had never felt safer. But I didn't feel like I deserved to feel safe. Didn't feel like I deserved them.

"Why are y'all being so nice to me?" I mumbled into Briar's shoulder, eyes stinging and throat wobbly. The guilt was too much. "You should hate me for how I've strung you along."

Harem king? Yeah, right. I couldn't even kiss two men without suffering nauseating guilt.

"I don't feel that way," Briar responded.

Maddox pressed his face to my nape. "Neither do I."

Another crack of thunder had me freezing up again. The rain pounded harder against the roof, and the wind crashed against the sides of the stable hard enough to make the rafters creak. I whimpered and burrowed more into Briar's chest.

"It's all right," Briar whispered.

Maddox's arms tightened around me, and he kissed the back of my hair. "Let's get him inside."

"The one thing we agree on," Briar responded. "Lead the way."

Chapter Eight
Rainy Nights Make for Warm Cuddles

The closest shelter was the knights' quarters.

Maddox removed the short cloak clasped around his shoulders and draped it over me as the three of us left the stable and rushed toward the cluster of buildings. Flashes filled the air with the echo of thunder not far behind them.

I slipped on the rain-slick grass, but Maddox caught me before I could fall. He then swept me up and carried me the rest of the way. We didn't go into the main gathering hall. Instead, he led us toward the edge of one building and carried me through the doorway. Once inside, he placed me back on my feet.

The room was mostly bare, apart from a shelf holding a few books, a wardrobe, a small round table with two chairs, and a bed in the corner. The stone hearth, unlit, was centered on the back wall.

"Where are we?" I asked.

"My quarters." Maddox knelt in front of me.

"What are you doing?" Heat shot to my nuts. His face was so close.

"Your feet are soaked." He glanced up at me, the gleam in his eyes making me wonder if he'd intentionally thrown my mind straight into the gutter. He undid the laces on my boots. "You need to warm up, or you'll catch a cold."

"He's right," Briar said as he neared the fireplace. He squatted down and added logs before holding out a hand. His lips moved soundlessly and his fingertips sparked. The logs caught fire, and he stood back up. "Bring him closer."

Maddox set aside my wet boots and led me over to the hearth. He treated me so gently. His kindness only deepened my guilt. Made me feel sick. Because he still didn't know that I'd kissed Briar.

"I need to tell you something," I said, throat tight. "Briar and I... well, we—"

"I kissed him last night," Briar interjected as he faced Maddox. "I was fully aware you'd already made an advance on him, yet I refused to let him go without a fight."

It was hard to breathe. Would Maddox punch him? Would he punch *me*? Maybe draw his sword and turn me into Evan sashimi?

"Sit," Maddox told me, nodding to the rug in front of the fire.

"Yes, sir." It just kind of slipped out. Too nervous to look at his expression, I dropped to my knees and shuffled closer to the hearth. The warmth of the crackling flames caused chills to spread along my arms and legs. I stretched out my legs and wiggled my cold toes to warm them.

"I underestimated you, physician." Maddox stared at Briar but rested a hand on the top of my head. "I didn't think you had the grit to make a move on him."

"I may not be a knight, but I'm no coward," Briar countered. "When I truly want something, not many things can stand in my way."

"And you want Evan?"

"Yes. And you?"

"Yes," Maddox said without missing a beat.

"I suppose that makes us rivals."

"Indeed."

I sat on the rug, face hot and not because of the fire. They had a habit of talking about me when I was right in front of them. As for *what* they said? I had trouble believing it was real. I still expected to wake up in my bed, realizing it had all been an incredibly elaborate dream.

"You're not angry?" Briar asked.

"Oh, I wouldn't say that," Maddox said in a cool tone. "I'm seething at the thought of your lips on his. Yet, I'm also impressed. You aren't known for your interest in others."

"Neither are you."

"A thing we have in common."

"Yes." Briar's eyes softened as they fell to me. "We do."

Were they… bonding? Over kissing me, of all things? I moved my gaze back to the fire, confused by their attraction but also enthralled by it. The way they'd held me in the barn as I'd cowered because of the thunder sent a flutter of warmth through my chest. Their confessions deepened that warmth, allowing it to sink into my heart.

For whatever reason, they both wanted me.

I wanted them too. That feeling went beyond their looks. Beyond lust. But it was wrong to want them both.

Right?

"Why do you both like me?" My voice cracked. "I'm not a hot stud with a banging body. I'm average at best. Hell, appearance aside, I'm not even that interesting. Just a dorky bookworm who likes to bake and get lost in books. I don't understand."

"You have a kind heart," Briar softly said. "When you saw the wounded knights in my clinic, you jumped in to help without a second thought. And when you smile, that kind heart shows in your eyes. That's only one of the reasons I'm drawn to you."

"As for me?" Maddox dropped down behind me and pressed his cheek to the side of my head, his deep voice rumbling close to my ear. "I'm fairly sure I fell for you when you smacked face-first into my armor like the graceful muffin lord you are."

I snorted a laugh before a flash of lightning lit up the room. As the loud clap of thunder followed, Maddox wound his arms around me. Briar knelt on my left side and lifted his hand to my temple, brushing aside my bangs.

"I still don't understand," I whispered above the crackle of the flames. "Men don't ever pursue me like this."

"Then they're fools," Briar said. "Because you, Evan, are extraordinary."

"And clumsy," Maddox murmured in my ear. "Yet it only makes you more endearing. Makes me want to wrap you in my arms just like this and protect you from the world."

Briar caressed my cheek. "And your adorableness makes me want to spoil you. Give you anything and everything you desire. All the fig bread you can eat."

"Coffee too," Maddox said. "He loves coffee."

Heart thudding hard in my chest, I placed my hand on Maddox's arm and grabbed Briar with the other. Touching them felt so right, even if my mind struggled to accept that feeling.

"Y'all are making this decision hard for me," I said. Not only with having to choose between them… but also the choice I needed to make on the summer equinox.

"Then don't choose." Maddox trailed his lips down the back of my neck. "At least not for tonight."

"What?" I could barely get that one word out. I felt him smile at my nape. Probably because it sounded like a little squeak.

"I think what he means is…" Briar linked our fingers and leaned toward me, nuzzling the other side of my neck. "Tonight, you can have us both."

Oh, shit.

Delicious tingles spread throughout my body. Briar kissed the base of my throat as Maddox nibbled at my nape, his big hands moving down my abdomen.

Maybe I'm dreaming.

But their lips felt too real. Their hands did too. Maddox slid his beneath my tunic and glided his calloused fingertips across my belly. Briar cupped the other side of my neck, smoothing his thumb along my collarbone.

Along with those tingles of excitement? Nerves. So, of course, that's when my mouth decided to open. "You two said you haven't shown much interest in anyone before." My voice came out rough. "What about sex?"

Right as the question popped out, I regretted it. Just like the pang of jealousy at the thought of Maddox in a brothel, the anticipation of hearing about them being with other people gave me the same dreadful feeling.

"You really wish to know whose been in my bed?" Maddox whispered in my ear.

I swallowed the tightness in my throat. "No."

He breathed out a laugh. "Good. Because I didn't plan on telling you even if you did."

"Why not?"

"Because no one else matters in this moment. Only you do. Anyone that may have come before you is of no importance." He dropped a kiss to the top of my shoulder. His words implied he wasn't a virgin, but neither was I. What it *did* imply? He hadn't loved any of them.

I smiled.

"I will say though… there haven't been many."

I smiled bigger.

"This pleases you?"

"Yep." I rested my head back against his. The other knights had said they'd never seen Maddox show interest in anyone, so he must've done it discreetly.

"Again, I have to agree with the captain." Briar curved a hand around my upper thigh. His hand sat just below my groin, not touching but so close it was teasing. My cock definitely noticed the torturous placement and twitched. "I don't wish to talk about any past lovers. However, I must confess, this will be my first time with a third."

"Mine as well," Maddox said.

"Me too," I responded.

A night that would be a first for all three of us. Special.

Would it go smoothly? Probably not. It wasn't like a romance novel where the dude thrust right in and it was perfect—or a smutty Boys Love manga where the bottom required very little prep before being ridden hard. I was sure things would be a bit awkward as the three of us navigated the unknown waters of a threesome.

Maddox slid my tunic up higher, and I lifted my arms so he could pull it over my head. He tossed it aside before taking me back into his arms, kissing along my shoulder blades. A log in the fireplace popped as Briar settled in front of me, his hazel eyes meeting mine as his hand moved to my trousers. He pulled the string and unfastened them before working them down my hips and thighs. His heated gaze lowered again as he started to pull my boxers down.

And then, he paused, head cocked.

"Evan? What are these?"

"What?" I asked in alarm, worried there was a tick or something on my dick. Or a spider scuttling across the floor. All those things flew through my head at the speed of light. "Is it scary? I'm afraid to look."

"Oh, truly terrifying," Briar responded.

Maddox chuckled low from where he held me from behind. "The strange undergarments. I had the same reaction."

"They're the only ones I have, okay?" I said, cheeks burning hotter. I was relieved though too. No dick rash or insects. "I tried going commando, but I didn't like how my nuts felt. Too vulnerable and exposed. So, I wash these every morning and just rewear them."

"I'll buy more pairs for you," Briar said with a laugh in his voice. I liked seeing a more carefree side to him. In his clinic, he worked so hard. Too hard. When he wasn't making magical elixirs, he was researching herbs and learning how to improve his craft. He touched one of the cartoon hot dogs on my boxers. "I'm afraid there aren't any others quite as amusing or strange as these."

"Fitting for him, then, yes?" Maddox gently nipped at my neck. "A unique set of undergarments for a unique male."

"I wouldn't say I'm unique," I said. "I'm ordinary and blend in with the crowd. Where I come from, most people don't even notice me."

Briar's expression grew softer. "That's their loss."

"And our gain," Maddox said. "Now, rid him of those strange garments."

"I don't take orders from you, Captain," Briar told him.

"You'd rather he keep them on?"

"No." Briar slipped his fingers beneath the waistband of my boxers. "But I'm doing this because I want to. Not because you told me."

"I care little for your reasoning. Just remove them, or I will."

More and more, I was enjoying their banter. Unlike earlier in the clinic when they'd been close to tearing each other's throats out, it seemed less hostile now.

Briar pulled down my boxers, and the heat from the fire jumped right into my body as that same awkwardness that had me covering my junk in the hot spring with Callum returned. I fought the urge to throw my hands over myself just like I'd done then with him.

Yeah, men had seen me naked before, but it was different when the lights were still on, and the other person—persons, in this case—could see every inch of me.

"You're so beautiful." Briar ran his hand over my bare thigh.

"You really are." Maddox flattened his palms against my chest and gently brushed them over my nipples. They beaded under his touch.

"Y'all don't have to flatter me," I said, unsure how else to respond to their compliments. I wasn't used to it. At all. "You already have me naked. It's pretty much a sure deal you're both getting laid tonight."

"Flattery is not the intention." Maddox trailed his hands lower. "We only speak the truth." His fingers moved through my light dusting of pubic hair, coming so close to touching my cock but missing the mark. Instead, he caressed the area on each side of it.

I wiggled on impulse.

"Impatient?" he asked in a somewhat husky voice. "Adorable."

Briar smiled before kissing my chest. I was sandwiched between them again, but neither of them touched me where I wanted—needed—them most. They knew it too, the jerks. I expected this teasing behavior from Maddox but not from my sweet, gentle Briar.

"Not fair." An embarrassing whine sounded in my voice. "Both of you still have your clothes on."

"Ah, he wants fairness," Briar said against my skin before ghosting his lips over my nipple. "Should we oblige?"

"Two against one sounds better to me," Maddox responded, the humor rich in his voice.

"That's not a very knightly thing to say," I muttered.

"With you deliciously naked like this, I'm not feeling too chivalrous. I want you wrecked beneath me."

I hardened at his words and the visual they created. When I tried to form a response, none came.

"Wrecked beneath *you*?" Briar ever so lightly circled his finger around my hip bone, his mouth still hovering by my nipple. "Only after me."

"We'll see about that," Maddox said.

My nipple beaded tighter as Briar's lips did another pass, and the warmth of his breath made me wiggle again. My breaths shortened with the

194

anticipation. When his mouth finally came around it, I cried out.

"Briar," I moaned, spine arching. The sensation of his wet, hot mouth was amazing. Even more so when his tongue joined the mix, flicking against it.

"Does that please you?" Maddox murmured in my ear. "The feel of his mouth?"

"Y-Yes." My cock throbbed between my legs. I tried to press my thighs together, but Briar moved them back apart as he continued that delicious tongue action. "Oh god. You two will be the death of me. I can already feel it."

I was a dead Evan walking—er, sitting. On a rug, buck-ass naked, with one hot-as-hell man holding me from behind while another sucked on my nipple. Both enjoyed teasing me, so who knew how long their torture would last.

I loved it though.

"Have your fun now, physician," Maddox said, his voice even huskier than before. "Because when it's my turn, my name's the one he'll be screaming."

**

Take the best sex I'd ever had, multiply it by ten, and that would only describe the foreplay with Maddox and Briar. Both men took their time with me, transitioning between soft and rough kisses—to my mouth and other parts of my body. Their light touches deepened as they took turns exploring me in front of the warm fire.

The heavy downpour of rain had lightened, the drops no longer beating against the windowpane like bullets. It came down in an easy stream, more relaxing. Lightning still flashed, but the rumbles of thunder sounded more distant. However, each time the thunder boomed louder, they held me a little tighter—kissed me deeper—as if to remind me I was safe.

I needed no reminder.

With them, I'd never felt safer.

Maddox shifted me farther up the rug and lowered himself between my legs, hooking his muscled arms under my raised thighs. I expected him to tease the life out of me like they'd been doing all night. But I was wrong. He took my cock into his mouth. And I... well, I nearly shot my load instantly. It had been too long since anyone had touched me like that. A warm palm was one thing. A hot mouth was completely different.

"That's it," Briar said, holding me against his chest. He pressed kisses into my hair as Maddox worked me with his mouth. "Lose yourself to pleasure."

Maddox's gaze flickered up to meet mine as he took me deeper, then slowly drew back. His lips glistened as they cushioned me, creating a perfect suction as they glided up and down my shaft. The fan of dark lashes hooded over his blue eyes, emanating arousal. Lust. But something tender too.

The physical sensations, the stimulation, was incredible... but so was being wedged between two men I'd come to care for in such a short amount of

196

time. Having them touch and kiss me. It was an intimacy I hadn't expected.

"Let me touch you," I panted, hips quivering. A sheen of sweat covered my body. "Both of you."

Maddox gave my cock another teasing lick before releasing it. I sat forward, took his face in both my hands, and kissed him hard on the mouth. He smiled against my lips.

I fumbled with his shirt, cursing the inventor of the tiny little clasps of his under armor that prevented me from reaching that delectable span of sun-kissed skin.

"Even your fingers are clumsy," he rasped, grabbing my wrist in a gentle hold before helping me.

"Yet, he has us wrapped around them anyway." Briar chuckled and kissed the area between my shoulder blades.

The captain's eyes softened. "That he does."

Finally, with his help, I managed to undo the clasps and tugged the wretched shirt off his broad shoulders and down his arms. Maddox took it the rest of the way off and tossed it aside, and then his mouth was crashing back to mine. But even as we kissed, I sensed Briar behind me—felt the brush of his fingertips down my spine.

They made me feel so cherished with every kiss and every caress. Each one felt so meaningful. Even the little jabs at my obvious gracefulness held an underlying affection.

I palmed Maddox's bare chest, then stilled as my fingers passed over raised areas of his skin along his rib cage. I broke the kiss and looked down at the faint scars. Considering how the attack was only days ago, the wounds should've still been in the healing process. The magic elixirs had sped up the process, leaving nothing but scars behind.

"I'm all right," Maddox whispered, bringing my hand to his mouth. He kissed my fingertips, his blue eyes soft. "Stop frowning."

A lump wedged in my throat and restricted my airway, taking my words along with my oxygen. My eyes stung as I moved my fingers to the sharp line of his jaw, then lower to his Adam's apple. "You're not allowed to get hurt again."

"Are you giving me orders now, Muffin Lord?" Affection thickened his deep voice. "I suppose I can let it slide this once." He brought my face closer to his, his breath on my lips. "I feel as though nothing could keep me from you now."

Briar kissed my upper back. "If the captain does find himself in peril again, know that I'll be there to help him. If only to spare myself the sight of you upset."

My feelings grew for them. Maddox, the protector, and Briar, the nurturer. Both of them made my heart beat faster.

"Enough of this." Maddox touched the place between my eyebrows to smooth away the frown. He kissed me again, softer than before. "Now, take off the physician's clothes." He paused, and I felt his lips twitch. "If you're able."

"Jerk." I exhaled a laugh, and he smirked.

Turning around, I planted my hands on Briar's chest. He smiled and touched my jaw. A flush had crept up his neck, more noticeable against his pale skin. His shirt wasn't nearly as difficult to remove. I popped open the buttons and slid it off him. His muscles were less defined than Maddox's but no less attractive. Both body types appealed to me. More so due to the men they belonged to.

I grazed my teeth along Briar's collarbone, loving his slight intake of air. Where Maddox smelled like warm spice and leather, Briar's scent reminded me of springtime, like magnolia blossoms and morning dew. I couldn't get enough of either of them.

As I found Briar's left nipple and latched on, he sharply exhaled and shuddered beneath me. God. It was hot.

Maddox's big hands came around my hips. I jolted as he smoothed a finger down my crack. He didn't penetrate me at first. He spit and swirled it around before ever so slowly easing the tip of his thumb inside.

I groaned and pressed my face into Briar's chest.

"He likes that," Briar told Maddox, resting his hand on the back of my head. "Keep doing it."

I flicked Briar's nipple with my tongue as Maddox pushed his thumb a little deeper and circled it. More groans, both from me and Briar. The hard line of Briar's erection pushed against mine as he rolled his hips.

I preferred to bottom during sex but had topped a few times. Which way did they like it? I guess I'd find out soon.

"I love the sight of you like this," Maddox said as he fingered me. He reached around with his other hand to stroke my aching cock. "Bare ass in the air and quivering with need."

When he suddenly pulled away, I whined. He left for only a moment to grab something from a drawer, then returned. When his finger eased in again, it did so smoother.

Moaning, I rocked backward against his hand, seeking more. They had lube in Bremloc? Or maybe it was olive oil. I'd read before that's what people used in ancient times. Not that this fantasy world was ancient with its magical conveniences.

Maddox nipped at my ass cheek, a raspy chuckle not far behind. "I feel you squeezing my finger." He then added a second, and I whimpered. When he spoke again, his voice was deeper. "I love how you respond to my touch."

His long, skillful fingers made it impossible to keep quiet. And when he retook hold of my cock? Hoarse, needy groans rumbled in my throat.

As he continued prepping me, I cupped Briar through his trousers. A wet spot had formed in the front of them. Briar's hazel eyes were hooded as he glanced at Maddox over my shoulder, then trailed his gaze down to where the captain had his hand around my shaft, stroking me.

"Touch him," Briar said on a groan, breaths heavy. "I want to watch."

Holy shit. Was the good doctor into voyeurism? And why was the thought of being watched by him so hot?

I had no problem obliging his request... but first? I gently bumped my forehead to Briar's before kissing him. His lips were soft, and he tasted sweet, probably from the piece of candy he'd eaten on our way back from the market.

"You're beautiful too, ya know," I whispered. "And kind."

His eyes misted behind his glasses, and he brought our mouths back together, a bit firmer than before.

I then turned around. Instantly, Maddox's mouth was crashing against mine.

My heart fluttered like a hummingbird's wings, excitement and warmth interweaving in my chest. The two of them might've been okay with sharing me for the night, but I wanted to give them equal attention. I didn't want either to feel left out. Because, as complicated as it was, I cared for both of them. Deeply.

Deeper than I even understood.

As we kissed, Maddox unfastened his trousers and tugged them down his hips. Probably too impatient for me to fumble around with them. I gently bit his bottom lip as the thought crossed my mind. Insufferable knight.

All sass was forgotten as his cock sprang free. The bulge I'd noticed several times before was nothing compared to the reality of seeing it in all its glory. Long, thick, and heavy as my fingers curled around his base.

"You don't even need a sword with a deadly weapon like that in your pants," I said, giving him a slow pull.

Maddox breathed out a laugh. "That mouth of yours never fails to amuse me. But know this..." He grabbed my nape and lowered his face to the area beneath my jaw. "This weapon is only meant for you."

I shuddered. "A threat has never sounded so hot."

Touching wasn't enough; I wanted to taste him. I buried my face against his pecs and licked down his ribs, then lower to the dusting of hair trailing from his navel. I followed that trail with my lips, eager for what awaited me at the end of it. He sat back a bit on the rug, giving me better access.

"God, you're huge." I loved the weighty feel of him in my hand. A drop of precum oozed from his slit, and I wasted no time before lapping it up with my tongue.

"Mmm." Maddox slid his fingers through my hair.

The rustle of clothes reached my ears, and I glanced over to see Briar taking off his pants. A smile curved his lips as our eyes met. He took his cock in his palm and stroked himself as he watched me and Maddox.

I started a slow rhythm, sliding my lips over Maddox's tip and back up before descending again, going farther down each time. Maddox wasn't vocal in his pleasure, but his breathing changed, and his fingers tightened in my blond strands. I took him as deep as I could, eyes stinging, then pulled off with a wet pop before lowering my face to his balls and sucking one into my mouth.

Briar softly groaned from beside us, his hand increasing pace.

The moment was erotic yet intimate, a prelude to what I was certain would be the best night of my life. It already teetered on that edge. What was the final push that propelled me overboard?

Two words: Evan sandwich.

Maddox and Briar exchanged a look, then a subtle nod.

I lifted my head and looked between them, but before I could get a word out, Maddox flipped me to my back on the rug, setting me down gently despite his quick movement. He settled between my legs, a strand of his black hair falling forward as he hovered over me, muscled arms on each side of my head.

"Hi." I nuzzled his nose, earning one of his rare smiles.

That's when I felt another presence. Briar got behind me and propped me up to where my upper body leaned against him while my lower body was left to Maddox's mercy. The captain hooked my legs around his waist and lifted me up a little from the rug, sitting me more in his lap. His hard cock slid against my crack, and I trembled with anticipation.

Not for the first time that night, I was sandwiched between them. My back was pressed to Briar's chest. He enclosed me in his arms and feathered kisses down the side of my neck, his erection poking my lower back.

"So." I swallowed noisily. "Are you both tops?" At Maddox's confusion, I clarified, "You, uh, like to give it rather than take?"

"Yes." He slid his hand to my jaw. His other hand rested under my ass. "Is this okay with you?"

"Yep," I squeaked. "More than okay. I'm the opposite."

Briar placed his mouth beside my ear. "And I like it both ways."

Well, that answered my earlier question.

"What about condoms?" I asked. "Wrapping it before you tap it? Sheathing your sword before plunging into the depths?"

"Most men take a tonic after," Maddox answered. "It rids the body of any sickness that might've been passed during intercourse. But if you're more comfortable with a covering, I can wear one for you."

"Nah, it's okay," I answered. Knowing I could feel him skin on skin risk-free was too tempting to pass up. I'd never gone bareback before. "Magic is so cool."

Briar's chest vibrated with a chuckle. He then kissed my earlobe. "I won't let any harm come to you or your body. I'll prepare us a tonic right after."

Maddox grabbed a glass bottle with a long body and short neck and poured the clear liquid contents into his hand. So, definitely not olive oil. It looked like the lubricant from my world, similar consistency. It felt the same, too, as he used some on my ass, sliding a finger knuckle-deep and circling it.

Briar pressed another kiss to my ear as I groaned.

"Tell me if I hurt you," Maddox said, lifting his other hand to trace my bottom lip with his thumb. "I'll immediately stop."

He could claim all chivalry had flown out the window, that he wanted to wreck me, but the concern in his eyes said the opposite. And damn if it didn't hit the center of my heart like a flaming arrow. Hitting me, then sending fire through my bloodstream.

A fire that blazed hotter as he slicked his cock and guided it into place, slowly easing forward. It stung a bit as his thick cockhead breached me, but the sting faded almost instantly.

Was the lube infused with magic too? Taking away the discomfort? Because fuck, as he moved inside of me, I'd never felt anything more amazing.

Maddox pulled back, then rocked forward. I smoothed my hand down his rippling abs as he found his rhythm, thrusting, withdrawing, and diving in deeper. He filled me completely, the ridges of his thick cock eliciting tingles of pleasure with each thrust. It was mind-altering.

"Does he feel good?" Briar asked, his arms secured around me.

My response came out as a whimpering hum.

"I'll take that as a yes." Briar nuzzled my neck. "Hear how he moans for you, Captain?"

"I do," Maddox said with a soft grunt. Light from the crackling flames flickered across his face, shining on his deep blue eyes. They appeared so damn tender as he regarded me. "Let me hear more of them."

Not like I had much of a choice. As he canted his hips and fucked me deeper, my toes curled, and my whimpers rolled on, one after the other. I reached back and grabbed onto Briar while placing my other hand on Maddox's upper arm. The cords of muscle flexed beneath my palm as he continued his pace.

I turned my head to look at Briar, my body moving with Maddox's thrusts. "I… want you to—" My words broke off into another moan as Maddox nudged my prostate. Electricity zapped through my veins and sent a rush of warmth to pool low in my belly.

"You want me to what?" Briar ran his lips over my cheek.

"To join us," I rasped. "I want you to… feel good… too."

He moved his gaze to Maddox before returning it to me. I hadn't heard them say anything, but like earlier, there must've been a nod or some other gesture they'd exchanged. For two men who bickered a lot, they sure had a way of reading each other. Maybe underneath that snarl and bitterness, they didn't dislike each other as much as they put off.

"Hold on tight, muffin," Maddox said as he gripped my waist.

I laughed at the shortened title—which was undoubtedly now a pet name—and threw my arms around Maddox's neck and went with him as he fell to his back, placing me on top. Our bodies were still connected, except now I straddled him. I gyrated my hips, loving how his fingertips dug deeper into my skin.

He watched me through black lashes, his expression giving very little away. But when I came down harder on him, taking him to the hilt, then

206

gliding back up, his lips parted, releasing the groan I'd been eager to hear.

"You seem pleased with yourself," Maddox said, lids heavy.

"I am." I smiled down at him. "Getting a man like you to moan is no easy feat. I feel victorious. On top of the world, like I can do anything."

"Do anything?" Maddox glanced over my shoulder, a hint of a smile on his mouth. "Even take two cocks?"

"Huh?" I followed his gaze.

Briar stood on his knees behind me, shadows from the fire dancing across his lean body. His light brown hair had been combed back with his fingers, giving him a casual, sexy look. With his round-framed glasses and scholarly vibes, he looked perfectly delicious and oh, so fuckable.

"I don't have to," he said, his tone veering on shy. "If you only want to be with Maddox, I—"

"Get over here." I grabbed his forearm and pulled him closer. Once he was close enough, I turned my face and met him for a kiss. It was a bit sloppy, and our teeth clanked. I was trembling. With nerves. But mostly with excitement.

"Have you ever had two dicks in you at once?"

Jonah's question had seemed ridiculous back then. Never did I imagine that a week later, I'd be in a situation where I'd finally be able to answer him.

If I ever saw him again.

Don't ruin the mood.

I had two sexy men all over me. In that room, in front of the fire, nothing else existed but the three of us—and the double-dicking I was about to receive.

Chapter Nine
Is It Still Pillow Talk If It Happens by the Fire?

This is really happening.

I was already stuffed with the biggest dick I'd ever had the pleasure to know—thanks, Captain Ice. Would another even fit?

Briar drizzled some of the lubricant in his palm and stroked himself. He was smaller than Maddox but still bigger than average. Having both of them inside me might very well kill me.

An honorable death. One I'd have to tell my former e-reader about when I joined him in Bookhalla. Because surely, bookworms destined for paradise wound up there too. Surrounded by books for eternity. Maybe I'd actually be able to tackle my massively long to-be-read pile.

"Evan?" Maddox cupped my cheek. "Are you still alive?"

I blinked at him. "Sorry. The excitement made me spacey. Please proceed."

"Proceed," Briar repeated with a light laugh. "Gods, you are too precious."

Maddox's cock throbbed inside me, and I moved a little, both in an attempt to tease him and also to shift forward so Briar could align our bodies.

He retaliated by pumping his hips up, smirking when I gave a little yelp.

"Such an adorable sound," he said.

"Asshole."

Another smirk. Lord help me. The knight captain had a devilish side I was quickly becoming addicted to.

"I'm nothing if not fair," Maddox said, pulling out of me. I hated the sudden emptiness at the loss of him and wiggled my hips. He glanced at Briar. "I'll let you have a bit of fun before I rejoin you."

"Such a gentleman." Briar slid an arm around my belly. He grazed his fingertips down and gripped my bobbing erection, giving me slow strokes that had my head dropping back against his shoulder and moans escaping my lips. He positioned his cock at my opening but didn't push forward. "May I?"

"Yes," I panted, pushing my ass against him. "God, yes. Do it. Please."

As Briar thrust into me, I arched my back with a breathy sigh. He softly groaned and dropped a kiss to my nape. The hand around my cock lifted before being replaced by a bigger, calloused one. I looked down at Maddox as he stroked me, a determined set to his brow. His erection bobbed against mine, and he then took us both in his hand.

"That's hot," I said, reveling in the glide of his hard cock on mine.

"You feel so good." Briar took hold of my hips and fucked up into me.

The angle was perfect for reaching my sweet spot, and I groaned hard at the tiny explosions of pleasure. That, combined with Maddox's hand working us both simultaneously, sent me hurling toward that edge.

"I'm gonna come," I said, chest heaving and thighs starting to quake. Standing on my knees, I lost strength and slumped more against Maddox, resting my hands on his muscled chest, ass raised.

"So soon?" Maddox lifted up to ghost his mouth over mine, slowing the movement of his hand. "But we've only started with you."

Briar slowed his pace too, but each pump of his hips nudged my prostate. I was about to lose my damn mind.

"Can't…" *Pant.* "Help it." My eyes rolled back as warmth pooled low in my stomach. Tingles sparked in my balls, and they drew up. "Fuck. I'm…"

Maddox squeezed the base of my cock.

"Oh my god," I cried out, hips jolting. He'd denied me release. And I was pretty sure I was about to die because of it. Briar then pulled nearly all the way out, leaving only his tip inside. A frustrated groan tore through my throat. "Please."

"Not yet." Maddox kissed the edge of my mouth. He slowly released me as my body calmed. "When you come, I want it to be with both of us inside you."

I wanted that too.

"Come here," Briar said as his arms came around my middle. He pulled me back up and gently turned my face to his, kissing my cheek. "You are so precious to us, Evan."

Us. I closed my eyes, my sternum aching.

Maddox re-slicked his cock before guiding it into place. His cockhead pressed against Briar's shaft before sliding into me. Briar groaned in my ear and gripped my waist tighter. Maddox's lips parted, and his eyes became hooded.

The three of us were connected. As Maddox pumped his hips up slowly, he and Briar joined in a way too, their cocks sliding together inside of me.

I hooked an arm behind Briar's head and brought his face to mine. His tongue traced the seam of my lips before dipping into my mouth. The sweet taste of him ignited my taste buds, and I groaned, seeking more. His glasses bumped my nose, causing us to break apart with a breathy laugh.

"Sorry," he said before reaching to grab at them.

"Leave them on." I glided the tip of my nose against his chin. "They're sexy."

Maddox shifted beneath me, placing me more in his lap as he rose up and kissed my chest, his strong arms sliding to my back. My heart thudded harder when I realized he was rubbing Briar's abdomen, caressing his skin like a lover.

Briar placed a hand on his forearm, his pale fingers a contrast to Maddox's tanned complexion.

This is exactly how I want it. All of us bringing each other pleasure.

Equal.

It took a little time for them to find a good rhythm, but once they did, I was a goner. Maddox thrust up while Briar drew back and vice versa. Both were hitting me in all the right places. Filling me up. Amplifying every sensation. Each time they rocked into me, my pleasure built, snaking down my spine and gathering down below.

I felt like a bottle rocket on the Fourth of July; my fuse was lit, and the flame was chasing the string to the body that would soon screech as it shot in the air and popped.

I'd never experienced a hands-free orgasm before. When I bottomed, I always had to jerk myself to reach the big O. But not with them. As Maddox slammed against my prostate, quickly followed by Briar, white-hot pleasure shot through me, and I came apart.

Shattered.

"Mmm, there you go," Maddox said with a deep rumble. He licked my nipple before gently biting it. "Squeeze our cocks just like that."

Briar's fingers dug into the tops of my thighs as he started to quake.

"Are you close, physician?" Maddox panted.

Briar's answer came in the form of a drawn-out groan. His hips stilled as his cock pulsed. He burrowed his face in my hair.

As Maddox's breath caught, I rolled my body. His blue eyes flickered up to me, brow scrunched and chest rising and falling quicker. Briar slowly moved back and forth, his cock still half-hard. It pushed the captain over the edge.

Maddox came seconds later, his hips bucking up into me. "Evan! Gods."

I cupped the back of his head and brought him to my chest, holding him as his large body quaked beneath mine. I kissed his temple while Briar's lips grazed my shoulder. The fire popped from beside us, flames crackling along the logs and radiating warmth our way.

Little did I know at the time how that one night would change everything.

***

"The rain's still coming down hard," Briar said as he closed the door behind him. He shrugged off the hooded cloak Maddox had lent him and set it on the back of a chair to dry before removing his muddy boots. A bag was in his hand.

"I appreciate you going," Maddox responded from his place at the small table. A stack of papers sat in front of him. I guess, like Briar being the court physician and always busy, a captain's work was never done either.

"It was no trouble at all."

After we'd held each other in the afterglow, bodies calming, we had cleaned up before Briar went to his clinic for the post-sex tonics. While waiting for him to get back, Maddox had pulled on a pair of black pants—and how the man looked just as hot *in* clothes as he did out of them wasn't fair at all.

Instead of dressing, I had sat in front of the fire and wrapped up in the blanket from Maddox's bed. I pressed my face into it, breathing in his scent of warm spice.

"Drink this." Briar handed a short, round vial to Maddox, who nodded to him, before coming over to me and pulling another from the bag. "You too."

214

"What's it taste like?" I turned the bottle between my fingers. The magenta-colored liquid looked to have the consistency of juice. "Is it gross? Will I puke?"

Maddox uncorked the vial and threw it back in one gulp, then wiped his mouth with the back of his hand. "Imagine walking into a field of flowers, tearing a handful from the soil, then shoving them in your mouth. Much like that."

"Well, the concoction does contain flowers," Briar responded, amused. "Echinacea, to be precise. It naturally boosts the immune system, can reduce inflammation, and has antiviral effects. And when added to an assortment of other plants and infused with the right magic, it becomes a cure against all sexually spread diseases."

"I once ate rose water macarons before." I removed the cork. "I hated them. Flowers don't belong in food." I sipped the tonic and made a face. It was floral and tart, and I immediately wanted to spit it out.

Maddox burst into a laugh. The hearty sound almost made me forget the nasty floral taste in my mouth. "That's why you should drink it in one go."

Briar drank his without reacting whatsoever. His hazel eyes shifted to me. "Evan."

"I know, I know," I said, wiggling a bit on the rug, as though needing to rev up to prepare myself. "I'm drinking it."

"Perhaps this will help entice you." Briar reached into the bag and withdrew something wrapped in a cloth. He unraveled it to reveal a mouthwatering loaf of goodness. "The last of the

215

fig bread from the batch I made this morning. But you can't have it until that vial is empty."

Maddox turned his face away, but I noticed the slight bounce of his stomach as he quietly laughed.

"What's so funny?" I asked.

Humor glinted in his deep blue eyes as he looked at me. "You must be bribed like a child to take your medicine."

Briar laughed before stifling it. He cleared his throat.

"You know… I think I liked it better when you two were fighting. Having you on the same side isn't fair at all."

"Oh, I'm sure by morning, we'll be back to our old, bickering selves," Briar said. But by the softness in his expression, I didn't believe that for a minute.

What happened between the three of us had shifted things. Brought us closer, in more ways than one.

I lifted the vial and chugged it, squirming as I swallowed, then shuddering once it was down. "Okay. The deed is done. Gimme my reward."

"Come and claim it." Briar waved around the slice, taunting me.

Grinning, I crawled over and nipped at his neck. He chuckled and bumped my head with his before kissing my earlobe. Just like how I loved hearing Maddox laugh, I enjoyed this playful side to Briar too.

The two of them had burrowed into my heart. Maybe it was too soon to feel that deeply, but the

216

heart didn't care if one year had passed or one day. And my heart soared when around them.

Maddox glanced over at us before focusing back on the document. His expression hadn't changed, apart from the very slight crease of his brow.

"Get over here, Captain," I said. "That expenses sheet or whatever it is can wait until tomorrow."

"Is that so?" He smirked.

I nodded, hair flopping on my forehead. "I demand cuddles."

"You are in no position to make demands of me." However, Maddox stood from his chair and joined us on the rug anyway.

"Here." I broke the slice into three parts and handed one to them both. "As a thank-you for an amazing day... and night."

"Sharing your treat?" Maddox accepted the bread.

"Well, you two shared *me*. It's only fitting." I nibbled at the fig bread, bouncing a little in place. It was so fucking delicious.

How long would this last? They had agreed to one night. Would they still want me in the morning? Maybe fucking me once was enough to get me out of their system.

I slowed in my chewing.

"Evan?" Briar touched my chin, gently tipping it up to meet his gaze. "Are you feeling all right? Though it's rare, sometimes people can feel nauseated after taking the tonic for the first time."

"I'm okay," I said, not really sure if it was true. I mean, I didn't feel sick, so I wasn't experiencing any side effects of the medicine. But my chest hurt all of a sudden. "Just tired."

"The hour is quite late," Briar said. "Once the rain lets up, we'll walk you home."

The wind howled outside before a gust of heavy rain crashed against the window. Flashes of lightning came before the distant roll of thunder.

"Doesn't sound like it will be letting up anytime soon," Maddox pointed out. "The two of you can sleep here."

"Me as well?" Briar asked. "I don't mind walking back in the rain. I managed fine when retrieving the tonics."

"If you wish to venture back out in the storm, physician, be my guest, but Evan is staying here where it's warm and dry." He paused before adding, in a softer tone, "And yes, the offer does extend to you as well. You can do as you choose."

Briar watched him for a moment, the orange glow of the fire reflecting in his lenses. "I'd like to stay. Thane was still in the clinic, so my absence for one night should be fine."

"Then it's settled. We'll share my bed." Maddox bit off a piece of the bread, and his eyes widened a bit as he chewed. "This is really good."

"I'm pleased you think so." Briar tore off the corner of his. "It was my father's recipe. Though I can't ever seem to make it as good as he did."

"Did you lose him?" Maddox asked, gaze on the burning logs.

"Yes. Him and my mother both."

218

My heart went out to Briar. It was clear how much he'd loved his parents. Their death was what sparked his desire to become a healer.

"I'm sorry for your loss," Maddox said. "My father died in the war with Haran."

Haran. I vaguely remembered Duke talking about the conflict between that kingdom and Bremloc. Haran sent mercenaries and spies in an attempt to overthrow the king. It seemed all worlds, even fantasy ones, couldn't live in peace. War was inevitable as long as there were those hungry for power and willing to do anything to seize it.

"I hate war," I said, burrowing more into the blanket. I'd already finished my bread—sadly.

"As do I." Maddox offered me the rest of his piece, and when I hesitated, he leaned in closer and placed it at my lips. I fought a smile and let him feed me. The hardness in his eyes softened as I chewed. "Yet, war is necessary in order to protect everything we hold dear. Which is why I dedicate my life to the cause."

"I admire both of you," I said after swallowing the bite. "One risks his life on the battlefield, keeping everyone safe, and the other spends his time researching ways to save lives. You both set aside your own needs in the process."

Maddox had said he didn't date anyone because relationships were a distraction. And Briar, based on my own observations, often overworked himself, forgetting to properly rest and eat. All the fig bread he'd made over the past few days had been for me and Thane. He'd barely eaten a slice of it, too busy researching and tending to everyone else's needs.

As the flames started to dim, Maddox added another log and stoked the fire, causing them to flare back up. The wave of heat was nice. I closed my eyes as my skin warmed, from the top of my head and down to my toes.

"What do you want to do, Evan?" Briar asked.

"Do?"

"Your line of work," he clarified. "Bremloc has many different opportunities for people of varying occupations and talents."

"Stable boy is out of the question," Maddox said.

I scoffed. "And what would *you* have me do, sir knight?"

"As I said before, my room could always use a good cleaning," he said, straight-faced. But that amused glint returned to his eyes—an expression he reserved for me. "My knights need their boots scrubbed, weapons sharpened, and their shields polished. The pantry in the main building needs restocking. The floor swept and mopped. I could go on."

"So basically, you want me to be a maid. Is it so you can see me prancing around in a skimpy little outfit and getting all dirty?"

"I like when you're dirty," he said with a degree of devilish charm that nearly had me throwing off the blanket and tackling him for another round. "However, I'd insist you be fully clothed. Too great a temptation for my men for you to *prance around* half-naked."

Briar smiled. "He is quite delectable. With or without clothes."

"Oh my god, stop," I said with a groan. "Teasing me isn't nice. Y'all just like to see me blush."

"It *is* a lovely shade on you." Briar glided his knuckles across my cheek.

The room then lit up with a bright flash of lightning. Instantly, Maddox and Briar reached for me. And as their arms came around me, the following whiplike crack of thunder didn't affect me nearly as much as it normally would've.

"Thanks," I said, my voice muffled by the blanket. I rested my head in the space between their shoulders, leaning on them both. A kiss was pressed into my hair—I wasn't sure which of them it had come from.

"Let's get you into bed." Maddox rubbed small circles on my back.

"Will we all fit?" I asked.

"We'll make it work. If not, I'll take the floor."

"Like hell you will," Briar said, the snap catching me by surprise. "If anyone sleeps on the floor, it will be me. This is your room."

"And you are my guests."

"Back to being a chivalrous knight, I see." I grinned before giving a jaw-cracking yawn. The long day was catching up to me. My body was exhausted, muscles sore from all the walking… and other things. One thing stuck out to me though. A big something. I wiggled a little just to be sure. "Hey. Why doesn't my ass hurt?"

Maddox choked on a laugh.

"I… well." Briar adjusted his glasses, something I'd noticed he did when feeling awkward. "I might've used a bit of magic to ease the… ache… of having both of us… you know. There."

"Can't say the words, physician?"

"Not all of us are as vulgar as you, Captain."

"You used magic?" I asked.

Briar nodded. "I hope that's okay. I should've asked for your permission first." A blush darkened his pale cheeks. "I just wanted to spare you any discomfort."

"Thank you." A warm pressure enclosed my sternum. They were so kind to me. "Can we go to bed now?"

The blanket fell open as I sat up straighter, and their gazes lowered to my exposed chest. It sent a delighted thrill through me. For whatever reason, both of these fine-ass men thought I was beautiful. And clumsy, adorable, and a bunch of other words I'd never used to describe myself.

Okay, maybe clumsy. I couldn't deny that one.

"Yes," Maddox answered. "Morning comes early for all of us." He cleared his throat before rising from the rug and offering me a hand.

Briar did the same.

I stared between their hands before grabbing both at the same time. A choice with a much deeper meaning. I couldn't choose between them. I knew it in my gut—in my heart. Where that would lead us come morning? I didn't know. But I was too sleepy to think more about it right now.

The three of us neared the bed in the corner. It was about the size of a queen. Normally not a problem for two people, but add another to that and make one person a six-foot-two mountain of muscle, and it was sure to be a tight fit.

"You first," Maddox told Briar.

"Why me?"

"Because I sleep on the outside." His hand came to rest on my back. "And Evan will lie between us."

"I suppose that will do." Briar placed his glasses on the nightstand before removing his shirt and crawling into bed. He scooted over until his back pressed to the wall. Light brown hair fell into his eyes as he reached out an arm to me, looking so goddamn enticing. "Your turn."

Don't have to tell me twice.

"Wait." Maddox grabbed my elbow right before I could do a Superman dive into bed. "You can't sleep in that state."

"What state?" I glanced down at my body. My very *naked* body. Still didn't see the problem considering what we'd just done. "Why can't I sleep like this?"

"Because I said so." A tic started in his jaw, and he walked over to the wardrobe, opening it.

Briar tucked one arm behind his head. "I have to agree. You definitely can't come to bed like that."

Had I been mistaken? Did they not find me that attractive despite their statements claiming otherwise? Or maybe the appeal had left now that they'd gotten their rocks off. Suddenly self-conscious, I hugged the blanket closer to my body.

Maddox returned and handed me a shirt. "Put this on."

Confused—and maybe a bit hurt—I turned away from them as I stuck my arms through the shirt and tugged it over my head. It was so baggy on me it fell past my knees.

"Much better," Maddox said, his deep blue eyes roaming my body. "I like you in my clothes."

"Mine would be a better fit," Briar said. "Yours swallow him."

"And that's a problem why?"

"Um." My volume was almost too low to hear, but they stopped talking. One look at me and Briar sat up in bed, as if alarmed, while Maddox placed his hand on my waist.

"What's wrong?" they both asked at the same time.

I dropped my gaze to the floorboards. "Neither of you wanted me naked. Not that it's an issue. I normally feel uncomfortable being naked around guys. I prefer the lights off where they can't see me that well." Or judge me for being too skinny and not toned enough. My eyes stung. "But I was starting to feel kinda comfortable around both of you. You made me feel... I don't know. It doesn't matter. God, I'm rambling. Sorry."

"No," Maddox said, his voice gruff. He yanked me closer and crushed me to his chest, pushing his face into my hair. "I'm the one who needs to apologize. I never thought you'd misunderstand this way."

224

"Misunderstand?" I mumbled, eyes stinging.

He drew back and took my face in both his hands. Pain laced his blue eyes as he wiped away my tears. "Please don't cry. I…" His voice broke. "I can't bear knowing I did this to you. When I said you needed to cover yourself, I meant that no sleep would be had with you looking that appetizing beside me. I assumed you'd laugh at me or roll your eyes like you usually do."

The sheets rustled as Briar got off the bed and wrapped his arms around me from behind. "You silly, beautiful boy. Don't you realize how much we both desire you?" He kissed my hair. "You're so beautiful. Inside and out."

More tears welled in my eyes, but unlike earlier, they didn't come from an aching heart. "Sorry I ruined the moment. I'm not used to this kind of attention. Guess I haven't had the best luck with men in the past. So, insecurity took over, and now we're having a dramatic moment I'll probably cringe about later."

No "probably" about it. This would go into my "relive every embarrassing moment while trying to sleep" file.

Maddox kissed my jaw. "I've never desired anyone the way I desire you."

"I feel the same," Briar said. "And I pray I never meet any of the men who've made you doubt yourself. Because what I'd do to them would go against everything I stand for as a physician."

Maddox breathed out a short laugh. "Another thing we agree on. Though I'd have no qualms about gutting them."

"Perfect. I'll knock them unconscious with a tonic, then you can take them someplace private to deal with them."

"Oh, I'd wait until they awoke first. Wouldn't want them to miss the fun."

How wrong was it to stand between them, hearing them talk about legit murder, and yet feel all warm and toasty on the inside?

"Can we crawl into bed now?" I asked. Not necessarily because I wanted to sleep. I just wanted to be squeezed between them. Surrounded by them. "Make an Evan burrito."

Briar stepped into my field of vision and cocked his head. "An Evan... burrito?"

"Again with that strange way of speech," Maddox said.

"You're strange," I shot back. "With your devilishly good looks, rippling muscles, and huge... heart."

"Heart. Yes. I'm sure that's exactly what you intended to say." Maddox nodded to the bed. "Get in before I throw you."

"Oh, sir knight." I brought a hand to the edge of my mouth and chewed my bottom lip, making my eyes all big and vulnerable. "Please don't be rough with me. I'm just a delicate little thing, you see."

Maddox caught me around the waist, and I squealed as he tossed me onto the mattress. Laughing, Briar joined me on the bed and took position against the wall. Maddox slid in next, a raspy chuckle vibrating in his chest. Soon, I was wedged between them, me on my back and them on their sides facing me.

My cheeks ached from smiling.

"Good night," I said before kissing Maddox. I then turned my head and did the same to Briar. Both of them settled in closer, their arms sliding across my stomach as they held me.

"Good night, muffin," Maddox murmured, nuzzling the side of my hair.

I snickered at the pet name.

"Sleep well, love." Briar rested his head beside mine on the pillow, fingers skating across my belly, soothing me.

That's when I recalled the second part of the wish I'd made on the stone. I'd wished for another life—check—but also that I'd find someone to love me for *me*. Someone who would look at my flaws and quirks and love me all the more for them.

As I lay between Maddox and Briar, the three of us snuggled close together, I wondered if I'd finally found it.

Finally found *them*.

Chapter Ten
The Return of the Cat Boy

I awoke to birds chittering outside the window. Sunlight streamed in, the golden beam a comfort after the stormy night.

Voices sounded from outside the door, men chatting as they passed by, boots heavy on the floorboards. A few laughed.

I stretched my arms above my head, expecting to feel that familiar ache that followed a night of hard sex. It never came. My muscles were a bit sore, but there wasn't even a hint of pain.

Briar. Affection bounced around in my chest, each place it hit becoming warm and tingly. He'd used magic to make sure it wouldn't hurt. Maddox had been so gentle with me too. The tenderness in his blue eyes as our gazes had locked during sex gave me butterflies.

Yep. No doubt about it.

I was crazy about both of them.

The sheet was cold where they should've been lying on each side of me. I pressed my face into the pillow, picking up both of their scents—warm spice and something lightly fruity and sweet.

A light rapping came at the door. "Evan? You awake?" It creaked open before Callum stuck his head into the room, a cinnamon roll grin not far behind. "Good morning."

"Morning," I croaked before sitting up in bed. The tunic Maddox had given me to wear fell off one shoulder, the top having come unfastened overnight. "Do I smell coffee?"

"Good nose." Callum stepped farther into the room and nudged the door closed with his foot. He held a small tray with a steaming mug and food. The golden pastry on the plate definitely got my attention. "Captain Maddox brewed some especially for you. And Briar sent over this." He nodded to the food. "A croissant with blueberry jam and a side of fruit."

My heart was close to bursting. Not only had the two of them taken care of me last night—during and after sex—but they'd gone out of their way that morning to make me breakfast too, despite their busy schedules.

"Thank you for bringing it," I said, making sure the blanket was over my lap. The tunic was long, but I didn't want to risk Callum seeing my dick since I wasn't wearing anything beneath it. "I'm sure you had better things to do."

"It was no trouble. Besides, I'm the only one the captain trusts to enter his quarters when he's gone. Even more so with you here." He placed the tray on the bedside table, his cheeks darkening a shade. "You, uh, have… marks."

"Marks?"

He smiled. "On your neck. Two love bites. Signs of a good night, I take it?"

I adjusted the collar of the tunic to cover them. Freaking possessive men. Which one had given me a hickey? I'd throttle him. Maybe. Possibly. Okay, probably not. A *very* tiny part of me liked the idea of them placing their mark on me.

"Here." Callum handed me the mug.

"You're a lifesaver, Cal." I took a drink and moaned as that first sip of coffee hit my tongue. The brew tasted better than the previous time, less like toxic sludge and richer with a bold flavor, similar to what I was used to. "Maddox made this?"

"He did." Callum's nose wrinkled with another smile. "Don't tell him I told you, but he purchased the beans from the market early this morning so that you'd have it when you woke. He said the coffee we had here wasn't good enough for you."

I glanced at the mug as a pressure filled my chest. "He bought the expensive beans." The ones usually meant for the nobles.

"He wanted you to have the best."

But did I deserve the best? I wasn't so sure. "He didn't need to do that. I don't mind the cheaper coffee."

"You forget he's the captain of the Second Order," Callum said. "Believe me when I say he can easily afford it." His expression shifted to one of admiration—aimed at me. "He's never been like this with anyone, Evan. The physician hasn't either. Not from what I can recall."

My face heated. "I don't know why."

"I think I do. You're funny and kind. You're also the cutest man I've ever seen."

"Stop teasing me. I am not."

"You are. Perhaps you don't see it, but the rest of us do. It's like you have an inner fire that warms everyone around you. That's how I feel anyway."

230

He nodded to the plate. "You should eat before it gets cold."

"Since you were nice enough to bring me breakfast in bed, feel free to have some too."

"Oh no. I couldn't. That's yours." Callum wagged his hand from side to side. "Besides, I've already eaten with the others."

"Will you stay while I eat, then? Please?" I blinked at him, going for pitiful innocence. "I don't want to eat alone."

Callum expelled a sigh and sat on the edge of the bed. "All right, just stop making that face."

When in doubt, be cute. It worked like a charm with these men. Damn if I knew why.

"Yay." I took another drink of coffee—so fucking good—before biting into the jam-filled croissant. Briar had stuffed the pastry with more jam than he'd probably do for anyone else. He knew I liked sweets. And the blueberry jam was to die for; not too sweet and with a slight tartness. "You sure you don't want a bite before I devour it?"

"I'm certain," Callum said with a crinkle-nosed smile. He stood back up and grabbed a bundle he'd brought along with the tray. "I brought you a change of clothes as well."

"More that Gerard outgrew?"

"Yes. He'll be bigger than me at this rate." His smile radiated pride. He unraveled the bundle and placed pants and a tunic on the bed. "My mother made them. She's happy they can still be of use."

"Tell her thank you for me."

"I will." He stepped toward the door, and I smiled when noticing he was still wearing my Vans.

They looked so out of place in that world—a lot like me. "Take your time. We'll meet you outside when you're ready."

Once he left, I finished my breakfast—savoring every drink of coffee—and then explored Maddox's room. Not that there was much *to* explore. The very few books on the shelf were about warfare, the history of weapons, and one was a book of poetry. That one shocked me. The icy, sneering captain of the knights had a love for poetry. Who knew? I slid it back into place and moved on.

A small washroom connected to the room, big enough for a toilet and a large basin of water. Not quite a bathtub but way bigger than the one in my room. I used it to wash off the grime and then dressed for the day.

I was a ball of nervous energy as I approached the door. How would Maddox and Briar behave toward me? The considerate breakfast was a comforting sign, but they could've just done it to be nice. Like a kind gesture to say thanks for the orgasm?

Stop overthinking. Sighing at my overactive mind, I exited the room.

"Morning," Duke greeted me. His red hair fell free, the strands ruffling with the light breeze. "Ready to slay the day, little hero?"

"Hero?" I snorted and joined him in the grass. "I wouldn't go that far. Briar's the one who healed all of you. I just helped pass out the tonics."

"You have my gratitude all the same." He slowed his pace to match mine as we walked through the yard. "I still say we should put a sword in your hand."

Another snort. "I wouldn't even know what to do with a sword." The one in Maddox and Briar's pants was a different story. I handled that type of sword quite well. "Probably poke my eye out, like the captain said."

Duke laughed. "Best stick with kitchen duty, then. The men still speak of the stew and cake you made."

"Really?" I halted in step. "They liked it that much?"

"Aye." He nodded. "Some people are skilled in combat. Others are skilled in medicine and healing. And then there are those like you, I believe, who can heal through food. Soothing the soul. The knights were exhausted and wounded both physically and mentally, yet eating your food lifted even the weariest of spirits. Perhaps a spatula is the type of weapon you should wield."

His words settled over my chest. Helping people with my cooking? I remembered my dream of opening my own café. Back in my world, I'd thought it was impossible. I didn't know if my odds were much better in Bremloc, but that dream stirred to life once again.

Duke patted me on the back before joining Baden near the training field. The two then grabbed swords and began their drills.

Quincy leaned against the fence and watched them, his arm no longer in a sling but still not at its full strength, so he wasn't ready to jump back into training. Briar's magical elixir and surgical work had saved it from being severed at least. Catching my eye, his hard expression lightened a bit, and he nodded. I returned the gesture.

"My men like you."

The sound of that familiar deep voice caused sparks in my heart. I turned to see Maddox as he reached my side, sexy as hell in his black-on-black outfit.

"Does that make you jealous?" I teased. "Who knows. Maybe they'll vote me to be their new captain. I have a badass reputation for being small but mighty, you know. They call me Evan the Brave."

"They do, do they?" Maddox cut his eyes at me, but he couldn't hide the humor dancing in the blue irises.

"Yep. I'm pretty sure I'll have no choice but to steal your position. Sorry."

A throaty chuckle came from him. When he stepped closer, bringing his warm scent with him, my heart knocked in my chest. "How do you feel? Are you sore at all?"

"Never felt better," I answered. "Thanks for the coffee. Callum said you made it for me."

Maddox's eyes softened before he looked away. "I hope it was to your liking."

"It was." I fought a smile. His shyness was too cute. The man could stare death in the face and not bat an eye, but one mention of him doing something sweet and he got all awkward. "Looks like we found your new title."

"New title?"

"Yeah." I bumped his arm with mine and stayed there, leaning against him. "I'm Evan, Lord of the Muffins. And you're Maddox, Captain of the Second Order and Brewer of Coffee."

He scoffed. Pink speckled his cheeks though. "What is Briar's title?"

I thought for a moment. "Briar, Healer of Knights and Master Baker. Not to be confused with mastur*bater*."

Maddox made a choking sound. "Gods. You will be the death of me someday."

"You mentioned Briar without insulting him," I pointed out. "Are you two friends now?"

"We're…" His brow scrunched. "I'm not quite sure. When we woke this morning, we didn't say much before going our separate ways."

"Captain," one of the knights said as he approached, bowing his head. "Your horse is ready."

Maddox nodded to him before returning those blue eyes to me.

"Where are you going?" I asked.

"To a village west of here," he answered. "We received reports of scattered attacks. Not yet known if it's demons or bandits."

"The Third Order can't do it instead? Aren't they like the grunt soldiers who are supposed to deal with this stuff?"

"Knights of the Third Order are joining us," he said. "Most of them are fresh from the academy and need guidance before leading their own expeditions." His face fell a bit. "Their captain was killed in the dark wood."

When all of them were attacked.

"How long will you be gone?"

"Our party should return by sundown."

"You'll…" My heart thrashed around. "You'll be careful, right?"

He grazed his knuckles across my jaw. "Worried about me?"

"No," I lied. "It's just gonna be a pain if you come back injured. I'll have no choice but to return to the clinic and help out again. You're a horrible patient. Stubborn and refuses to stay in bed." I thumped his chest with my closed fist. "You'll need around-the-clock supervision, and I have better things to do than—"

Maddox dipped his head and kissed me, right there in front of all his knights. But I didn't think about them as I locked my arms around his neck and pressed closer. I only thought about him and how, yes, I was worried. He and Briar were… well, I didn't know if I could call them "my men," but that's how I felt.

One night with them, and they'd each laid a claim to me, body and soul.

"Behave while I'm away," he murmured against my lips.

It had become our thing when saying goodbye. He told me to behave, and I rolled my eyes and said I always did. This time, however, I added something.

"Come back to me," I whispered, a shaky pressure enclosing my sternum.

"I will." Maddox traced my bottom lip with his thumb. "You have my word."

I watched as he then joined the group of knights waiting in the yard and swung up into the saddle of the black stallion. He looked every bit a regal knight captain as he led them from the area, horse hooves thudding on the grass, then clacking once reaching the stone path.

Spotting Callum near the stable, I walked toward him.

"Hey again," I said. "Got any chores for me?"

"Chores?" He wiped the sweat from his forehead using the back of his hand. He had just finished defensive drills and was taking a hydration break. He seemed more interested in pouring the water over his head than drinking it though. "You're not helping Briar today?"

"Nope. He fired me." I released an exaggerated sigh. "Probably for the best. It's not good to bone your boss. Or have him bone you."

Callum flashed a lopsided grin. "There aren't any chores for you here, but if you don't mind running an errand, that'd be a lot of help."

"I don't mind at all. What's the errand?" I needed to do *something*. I was kind of just drifting along at the castle, not really fitting in anywhere. It couldn't continue like that forever. I wanted to feel useful.

"Documents need to be taken to the accounting department," he answered. "Details of our expenses for the last month and a budget request for more armor and weapons."

"Well, I have good news. I'm a pro at delivering documents."

"Excellent. You'll find them in the captain's quarters on the table."

"Got it." I started to leave.

"Evan?" he called after me. I stopped and glanced back at him, seeing another smile. Well, more like a shit-eating grin. "Please don't get lost along the way. I like my head right where it is."

Meaning Maddox would kill him. I laughed and continued walking.

The documents were the ones Maddox had worked on last night after our steamy fun by the fire. I exited the room with them tucked under my arm. As I walked down the path beneath the sun, I hummed to myself. I couldn't remember the last time I'd been in such a great mood. In this world or my own.

The warm morning was a sign that spring was nearing its end. Summer was inching closer. A somber reminder that my time was running out. I stopped humming, no longer as elated.

"Evan!" Thane jogged down the path, face bright. Crazy how much lighter he looked without the stress of all the injured knights weighing him down. "Good morning."

"Morning. What are you up to today?"

"I'm on my way to the market." He tapped the paper in his hand. "I have a list of ingredients that need restocking. Briar also wants me to put in an herb-gathering request at the guild. Did you get the croissant? Or did that silly knight eat it?"

"I got it," I responded with a small laugh. "It was delicious."

"Briar made a batch early this morning." Thane shifted his weight to his other foot, fidgeting. Maybe he was like me and didn't make friends easily either. "He was in a really good mood too. Didn't even snap at me when I accidently dropped a vial. I even heard him singing."

I looked down at my boots as my stomach did a little dip.

"But anyway," Thane said, shifting again. "I'll get out of your hair. I just wanted to say hi… and thanks."

"For what?"

He was blushing. "Just for…" He flicked his hand in the air. "Everything. Well. See you." He stepped past me, the tops of his ears red. He then stopped in place but didn't turn around. "Stop by the clinic later today if you have the time. It would be nice to see you. We can have tea and sweets. Okay. Bye."

He took off, faster than before. Smiling at his awkwardness, I continued in the opposite direction. On the way, I made a pit stop at a certain clinic to see a certain sexy physician. Thane mentioning him made me want to see him.

Briar was hunched over an open book at his workstation. A little cauldron bubbled in front of him. He skimmed a page of the book before sprinkling something into the cauldron. Glitter-like purple smoke puffed upward.

"Working on a love potion?" I asked, sidling up next to him. "Because I don't think you need it. You kind of have me mesmerized already."

"Good morning, love." Briar softly smiled and tugged me closer. His fresh scent surrounded me, and I breathed him in, not realizing until then how much I'd missed the smell.

"Morning." Why did my heart almost explode when he called me that? Just like when Maddox called me muffin. "Thanks for the croissant. It was amazing."

"I'm happy you enjoyed it." Briar smoothed his fingertips along my temple, tucking my bangs aside. "Did the captain make your coffee?"

"Yep. Also, amazing."

"Good." Another touch to my temple before he gently brought my face forward and kissed me.

I emitted a small sound and deepened the kiss, winding my arms around his lean waist. The documents in my hand scratched at the back of his shirt.

He kissed me once more before drawing back. "Running an errand for the knights?"

"Yeah. Gotta drop these off at the accounting department, but I wanted to see you first."

A smile broke across his handsome face. "I'm honored."

"I hope I didn't interrupt." I glanced at the cauldron.

"Not at all." He stepped over and touched the book. "It's the one I purchased from the market. I was trying out a spell. It's a bit advanced for me, but I'm confident with practice, I can perfect it."

"What kind of spell?" I peered into the cauldron and crinkled my nose as I got a whiff of something sweet. Maybe it *was* a love potion.

"One to infuse protective energy into an artifact, such as a talisman or charm," he explained. "My healing elixirs can repair injuries from mild to severe, but what if it was possible to prevent the injury from happening in the first place? I'd like to create something the knights can take with them on missions to ward off and repel dark magic. Some demons can cast curses that immobilize their target. The charm would protect the knights from these magical attacks."

I smiled as he spoke.

"I apologize." Briar adjusted his glasses, becoming suddenly awkward. A flush speckled his pale cheeks. "I was rambling."

"I like your rambles. Your brain is really sexy. Smart guys do it for me."

A musical laugh left him, the notes sinking into my heart. "So do the big, protective men as well, I take it." There didn't seem to be any bitterness in his tone. Or in his expression. He looked… happy. "Be careful on your way to the accounting department."

"I will." I nodded to the book. "Good luck with your spell."

Briar pinched my cheek before turning back to his workstation. I left the clinic, and it wasn't long until I started humming again.

I was happy too.

***

"Hello, old friend," I said as I reached the fork in the path that had tripped me up the last time. "We meet again."

Unlike that time though, I wouldn't get lost. I went left, remembering the day I'd chased Kuya around the castle grounds. That little hairball. Even while fighting for my life—wheezing as I ran after him—the way was engraved in my memory.

The people in the accounting department were nice. Two younger men and a woman who looked to be in her fifties. She was the head of the department. I handed over the documents, and the woman scanned the budget request before signing off on it. It was then placed in a separate file and stacked with others. Organized and neat. I thanked them and headed for the door.

"So cute," one of the men whispered from behind me.

"That cute face belongs to Captain Maddox," the other said. "I'd steer clear if I were you."

Smiling, I stepped back outside. I belonged to Captain Maddox, huh? I liked the sound of that. But I also belonged to Briar.

The errand had brought me closer to the main part of the castle, and I stared up at it in awe, imagining lavish balls with handsome men in fancy suits and women in Cinderella-type gowns. I bet the food was incredible. Even the bite-sized hors d'oeuvres.

Lost in my head, I wasn't paying attention to where I was going. My fantasy faded, and I found myself in a courtyard with a huge fountain in the center and flower beds all around it. Tall shrubs had been shaped in uniform ovals. How far had I walked? I was a *lot* closer to the castle.

Probably *too* close.

Two castle guards were walking along the path, wearing green uniforms with black belts around the midsection. They both had swords sheathed at their sides. One stopped as he saw me.

"State your name and purpose," he barked, hand going to his sword's hilt. The other guard followed suit as they approached me.

"Um." Alarmed, I backed away. My back hit one of the shrubs, leaving me nowhere to go. "I'm Evan. I just dropped off a budget request for the knights."

"You are nowhere near the accounting department."

Oh, well, that was awesome. My wandering mind had resulted in wandering legs that obviously had a mind of their own. "I can explain that."

"I suggest you do." Suspicion clouded his eyes. A threat did too.

Remember the Evan sashimi I feared Maddox would make once learning I'd kissed Briar? Well, this guard looked ready to make that a reality. *Farewell, cruel world.*

"Your face is familiar, but I can't place it," the guard said. "How did you get on these grounds?"

"I was brought here by Captain Maddox of the Second Order," I said in a rush, panic rising. Never a good sign. It meant a ramble was coming. "Well, I guess Callum is the one who actually brought me, but Maddox ordered him to because he wanted to question me. Not because I did anything criminal. I was, um, found near the dark wood?"

"That's it," he said with a snap of his fingers. "Sir Callum brought you through the front gates."

"So you're a prisoner?" the other guard asked, his tone gruffer than the other. He drew his sword. "And you escaped."

"No! I didn't escape." I eyed the sharp tip of the blade. "Oh my god. Please don't kill me. I'm too young to die."

"Lower your weapons," a firm voice said from the right. A head of blond hair appeared among the tall shrubs before a man rounded the corner. "He's a friend."

"Prince Sawyer," the guards said in unison, lowering their swords and bowing their heads.

Kuya peeked from around him before smiling wide. "Evan!" He rushed over and latched onto my side. His tail flicked behind him as he nuzzled my shoulder. A fruity scent wafted from his reddish-brown hair. "Kuya missed you."

"Forgive us, Your Highness," one guard said. "We weren't aware he was a friend of the crown."

"You were only doing your duty, and for that, I thank you," the prince responded. "Yet, now that you know who he is, see to it that it doesn't happen again."

The two agreed that it wouldn't, issued another apology, and then bowed before leaving.

"Thank you, um, Your Highness." I tipped my head to him. "I thought I was a goner."

"They wouldn't have killed you," Prince Sawyer said, drawing nearer. "But the trip to the castle dungeon wouldn't have been pleasant by any means, nor would the shackles they would've placed on your wrists."

Kuya returned to the prince's side and squatted beside him. His cat ears wiggled as he ran his palm over a patch of clovers sprouting from the grass. Innocence radiated from him. Remembering the story Callum told me about his past caused an ache in my chest.

Sawyer smiled down at him and placed a hand on top of his head. He then regarded me. "Would you like to take a stroll with us?"

"Oh!" Kuya bounded over to me, tail flicking faster, and grabbed my hand before dragging me closer to the prince. "Yes, Evan will walk with us. Kuya will show him the best napping spot in the garden."

"S-Sure. A walk would be nice." Although, I'd certainly already had a nice walk. Far away from where I was supposed to be. "Sorry for trespassing. I kinda got lost in my head and wasn't paying attention to where I was going."

"Busy daydreaming?" Sawyer asked.

"Yeah." I looked at the castle. "I've never been inside one before. I was thinking about the lavish parties. More specifically, about all the food at them."

Sawyer laughed. "The food is, indeed, the best part." A hardness surfaced in his eyes. "Balls are quite dull. Merely an excuse for the wealthy to strut around showing off said wealth and for fathers to offer up their daughters for marriage arrangements to unite powerful households, making each other even wealthier. As the second prince, I've attended far too many and have been forced to dance with many young noblewomen and princesses from other kingdoms, as our fathers watched from their ornate seats, stuffing their faces as they plotted our futures."

Kuya's ears drooped.

"So arranged marriages are a thing here?" I asked. We had left the courtyard and entered a garden filled with colorful plants, plenty of trees that provided shade from the bright sun, and sitting areas. Water softly rushed from nearby, trickling from a fountain and into a small pond. It was peaceful.

"Among royals, yes." Sawyer stopped beside the pond. Vibrant-colored fish swam beneath the crystal-clear water in a parade of orange, purple, and ocean-blue scales. "I've met with several bride candidates as of late. Not by my choice. My father says if I don't make a decision soon, he will make it for me."

"That sucks," I said. "I can't imagine what that's like. Being forced to marry a stranger. Having my future planned out for me. I'm sorry. You should be allowed to be with who you want."

Prince Sawyer looked at me then, surprise flashing in his green eyes. "No one's ever said that to me before."

Crap. Had I just fucked up? Spoken out of turn?

"Sorry if I offended you. I—"

"No offense taken at all," Sawyer interjected, his voice gentle. Just like his eyes. "Everyone else holds certain expectations for me. There's no sympathy or understanding of what it's truly like to be a royal. Poor, pitiful prince forced to marry a beautiful princess or noblewoman. How tragic." He shook his head. "But not you. You see me as an ordinary person. It's… nice. I see why my Kuya favors you, Evan." He gently rubbed the cat boy's back, causing purrs to vibrate in Kuya's chest. "He's always been a great judge of character."

His Kuya.

How deeply did the prince care for the demi-human? Was that why he'd looked so tormented when mentioning all the potential brides lined up for him? Because his heart already belonged to someone.

"Come with Kuya." The cat boy grabbed my hand and, still holding Prince Sawyer with his other, dragged us over to a weeping willow, the long, thin branches grazing the grass below. Kuya released us and bounded toward it. He touched a strand of the silver-tinged leaves and smiled. "Pretty tree. Will you allow Kuya to nap under your branches?" He rubbed the leaves against his cheek before dashing under the tree and curling up beside the trunk.

Sawyer watched him, his expression hovering somewhere between affectionate and pained.

"He's sweet," I said.

"Yes, he is." Sawyer stared at him for several more seconds before looking at me. "Are you hungry? I can have tea and snacks prepared for us."

"Snacks," Kuya whispered as his fuzzy ears twitched. "Crab… cakes." His eyelids grew heavy, and he closed them before snuggling more into the grass. Soft snores left him moments later.

The prince turned to one of the castle staff nearby—did they follow him around everywhere he went?—and asked them to bring refreshments. He didn't demand it. He even said "please." He wasn't at all how I'd expected a prince to behave.

"Let's let him sleep for a bit." Sawyer motioned to a stone bench beside a trickling fountain. Plushy pillows decorated each side and added a nice cushion as we sat down. "Are you enjoying your stay in Bremloc?"

"Yeah. I am." A lot more than I initially expected. "I visited the market yesterday. That was fun."

"I rarely get the chance to go to the market." Sawyer's green eyes had brown flecks near his pupils, like grass sprouting from rich soil. "Well, unless I'm accompanied by guards. Yet, even then, I still feel so… trapped. Even when I leave these castle walls, I'm still a prisoner within them."

"Being a prince doesn't seem as awesome as people think," I said.

"There are aspects I enjoy, but sometimes I wish for total freedom from my responsibilities. Even if it's only for a single day." He shook his head, as if finding the notion silly. "Ignore me. You must think me pathetic."

"Not at all," I told him, and I meant it. "I'd hate having every aspect of my life controlled too. Sounds suffocating."

"It is."

"Maybe one day you can find a balance between your duties as a prince and the life you crave. Make your own path."

"I'd like that. Forging my own path." He dropped his gaze to his lap. "Although I may complain about being a prince, I do see the benefit of being one. There are so many things I wish to change. Policies to improve the lives of the citizens in Bremloc and strengthen relations with neighboring kingdoms. My position will allow me to work toward those goals."

Spoken like a man who'd be a great king someday. But he wasn't the crown prince, so that day might not ever come.

"I heard there will be a festival soon," I said. "Are you allowed to go?"

"The Festival of Lights." Some of the longing lifted from him. "Yes. I'm allowed to attend. I'm looking forward to it. Merchants sell their wares. There's music and food. Dancing. The atmosphere is almost magical."

Magical enough to grant a wish. Or reverse one. Allowing me to return to my own world.

Three women approached us with trays. Two platters held an assortment of food, and the other had a teapot and three cups, as well as a vessel for sugar and cream. Sawyer and I thanked them, and they bowed their heads before leaving us to enjoy.

"Kuya?" Sawyer called in a lighter tone. He grabbed two round cakes and placed them on a small dish. "I have something for you."

Kuya poked his head from between the long branches of the willow and sniffed the air. "Crab cakes?" He sprung forward, tail whishing behind him. Like before, he wore a crop top that showed a stretch of tanned skin and the trim muscle of his abdomen, the kind formed from an active lifestyle. Probably from all that pouncing.

"This too." Sawyer poured tea into a cup, added a spoonful of sugar and a dash of cream, and then stirred. He handed it to Kuya. "Be careful. It's hot."

Kuya nuzzled Sawyer's cheek before accepting the offerings. He sat on the ground in front of the bench and crisscrossed his legs before tearing into the cakes. He hummed happily as he chewed.

"That's another thing my position allows me to do," Sawyer said, watching Kuya with a tenderness that veered on fragile. "Protect him."

"I don't see how anyone could ever want to hurt him."

Sadness touched his green eyes. "Demi-humans are viewed as lesser beings than us by some in the kingdom. It breaks my heart." He looked at me. "It's one of the things I hope to change someday."

Kuya was oblivious to our conversation as he ate his cakes, sipping tea in between bites. He then stopped chewing and perked his ears up, his gaze pinned to something in the grass. He swallowed the bite, carefully set down his cup, and crouched forward, slowly slinking across the ground. Just like a cat stalking its prey. Even if that prey was a butterfly.

As Kuya reached the butterfly, he pounced. He landed beside it though, clearly not wanting to hurt it. The butterfly flew upward at the commotion, then landed on his nose. He rolled to his back and smiled as its wings slowly moved. He'd just wanted to play.

I helped myself to a sugar cookie. It was a bit crunchier than I liked—I preferred the softer ones without the snap—but it tasted good, especially when dunked in the tea. Kuya returned to his plate and finished off the cakes before crawling over and resting against Sawyer's legs.

"Nap, eat, play, and nap some more," Sawyer fondly said, threading his fingers through Kuya's reddish-brown strands. "Did you save room for dessert?"

Kuya's ears twitched. "Strawberry cake?"

Sawyer grabbed the lone cupcake off the platter and gave it to him. The staff had clearly brought it solely for him. Kuya devoured it in two bites, then settled back against the prince. His rainbow-colored eyes got heavy again, and he closed them.

"He keeps me grounded on the days when all I want is to disappear," Sawyer said.

"Do you love him?" The question slipped out before I could stop it.

His gaze flickered to mine. He didn't answer me, but he didn't have to. The truth showed in his eyes as they returned to the male napping against him. "I apologize for keeping you for so long, Evan."

"Don't be. I've had fun with you and Kuya. I feel like… never mind."

"Tell me," Sawyer pressed. "Leaving me in suspense is cruel."

I laughed at that. It had a nervous shake to it. "Okay. Well. I guess I feel like I've made friends."

His smile softened. "I feel the same. Talking to you is nice."

"Evan is nice," Kuya mumbled, eyes still closed. "Evan is Kuya's friend."

He was too precious for this world. One thousand percent.

After we finished our tea and snacks, a man approached and told Sawyer he was needed for his afternoon lessons. History first, then literature, followed by fencing.

"Duty calls." Sawyer rose from the bench. "I hope we can do this again soon."

"Me too."

Sawyer called over one of the armed men standing nearby. "Sir Noah, please escort Evan back to his quarters and make it known to the rest of the unit and staff that he's permitted on castle grounds by order of the second prince."

"Yes, my prince." Noah bowed to him. He was clean-shaven with a head of silky black hair and eyes like whiskey.

Sawyer and Kuya then left with the older man, who sounded like he was lecturing the young prince about neglecting his studies as they walked toward the castle entrance. Sawyer glanced back at me and did a dramatic roll of his eyes, sticking his tongue from the corner of his mouth.

I laughed. Yeah. I definitely felt like I'd just made another friend.

"Shall we?" Noah motioned to the path.

"We shall," I responded, feeling all proper and shit. Damn. I was in a really good mood. "Sir Noah, is it? Are you a knight of the First Order?"

"I am," he answered.

"But you're so young." Then, I cringed. "I didn't mean that as an insult. I just meant you seem too young to have such a high ranking. Wait. That sounds awful too. Ignore me."

Noah seemed amused. "A pleasure to know the stories are true."

"Stories?"

"Of your rambling mouth."

I suppressed a groan. "That *would* be the thing people talk about, huh? I'm famous for being a motormouth. Did Captain Maddox tell you?"

He only smiled before saying, "We should hurry. I have other obligations."

Saying nothing further, Noah led me to the section of housing I temporarily called home. I thanked him, and he nodded once before leaving. Not wanting to interrupt Briar's work, I slipped into my room and grabbed one of the books he'd lent me. Among his numerous herbology and spell books, he'd had a few fiction novels that had piqued my interest.

With it tucked against my chest, I returned outside and found a cozy spot in the courtyard to read. The spine of the hardback creaked as I opened it and flipped to the first page.

"Long ago, much longer than you or I can recall, there existed a kingdom by the sea…"

The words soon swept me away, and hours passed as I turned the pages, lost in the story about a betrayed hero and his quest to save the land that once cast him out. There was action, angst, and a touch of romance. But for the first time, I realized I wasn't reading to escape from my lonely, boring life.

Because the life I now found myself in?

It wasn't so bad.

Chapter Eleven
The Rise of the Thorn Prince

The mountains in the distance swallowed the last ray of daylight as the sun sank lower in the sky. An end to another day. I walked toward Briar's clinic. I had finished the book and was eager to raid his collection for more. Also eager to see him too.

Okay. Mostly to see him. The book was just an excuse.

"Briar's out right now," Thane said after I'd arrived at the clinic. "But I'm sure he won't mind if you borrow another book. I enjoyed that one as well. He has more from the same author."

"Thanks." I stepped over to the shelf and browsed the books. My mind was elsewhere though. "Any idea where Briar is and when he'll be back?"

"He was summoned to the castle earlier." Thane slathered some of the blueberry jam leftover from breakfast on a slice of bread and shoved it in his mouth. As he chewed, cheeks big and full like a chipmunk, he flipped to the next page of a handwritten journal. He must've been studying Briar's notes. "He came back for a bit but then left again. Not sure where. I apologize for stuffing my face like this. I lost track of time, forgot to eat, and now I'm starving. Do you want some?"

"No, thanks," I said, enjoying this relaxed side of Thane. The complete opposite of the stressed-as-hell apprentice I'd first met. "I'm heading to the knights' quarters after this and will eat something there."

"What business do you have with the knights?"

"Captain Maddox and his party should be returning soon." If they hadn't already. "I thought I'd make them dinner."

"I want to eat your food again," Thane said with a slight pout, unaware of the jam smeared in the crease of his lips. "Fish and potatoes. Mmm. The oats you made that one morning were delicious too. And that egg muffin thing with the peppers."

"I'll bring you a plate later," I promised him before leaving the clinic and continuing down the path.

The winding trails of the castle grounds no longer confused me. The ones leading to the clinic and knights' quarters, at least. I'd walked both several times to see the two men I couldn't get out of my head. And now, out of my heart.

God, I'm a sap. Just a big pile of swoony goo that melted each time one of them tipped up my chin to kiss me or smiled at me.

"Just say what you've come to say, physician," a familiar deep voice grumbled from up ahead. "I've just returned from a mission, and I'm tired."

I halted in step, heart knocking in my chest.

"Very well," Briar said. "The sooner we have this conversation, the better it will be for both of us."

I slowly crept forward and peeked around the corner. Briar and Maddox stood behind the main gathering hall, partially concealed in the canopy of trees. Shadows fell in around them as the evening further welcomed twilight.

"Out with it, then," Maddox demanded, his arms crossed over his wide chest.

Briar stood in front of him. "We need to discuss what happened last night."

"There's very little to discuss." Maddox leaned against the tree. "We fucked and then went to bed. End of story."

"What happened meant much more than fucking," Briar said. "I believe it's safe to assume we're both enamored with Evan, far beyond sexual desire."

My breath snagged in my throat, airway constricting. Eavesdropping was wrong, but my feet were planted in place.

"Enamored." Maddox huffed. "The word seems too small to describe the feelings in my heart when I see him."

"What we call it doesn't matter. The truth remains that we both want him for our own."

"I refuse to step aside," the captain growled. "If that's what you've come to suggest, then—"

"I'm well aware you won't give him up," Briar cut in. "I see the way you look at him. More so, I see the way he looks at you too."

Guilt clawed at my chest.

"I see," Maddox stated, losing some of his bite. "You're the one who is stepping aside."

The following silence seemed to stretch on for hours. Part of me wanted to run far away. A bigger part needed to stay and hear more.

"I don't want to lose him either," Briar said, his voice weaker than before. Brittle. "Evan makes me feel so alive. His warmth. His laugh. The way he fumbles around and blushes. How he rambles when excited or nervous. I…" He raised a hand to his chest and rubbed at the center. "I can't imagine walking away from him. I don't want to."

"I see how he looks at you too," Maddox then said. "Just as we care for him, he cares just as deeply for us." A short pause. "*Both* of us."

"Yes." Briar's gaze lifted back to his. "When we went to the market yesterday, he seemed happiest with us both at his side. It's why I stopped trying to convince you to leave."

"You could never have convinced me to leave him."

"Nor you for me." Briar released a shaky breath. "Where do we go from here? We've both fallen for the same man."

"That we have." Maddox dropped his arms back to his sides, relaxing his defensive stance. He looked exhausted. "As for what we should do about it? I don't know. I've never been in this situation before."

"Neither have I."

The burst of happiness and warmth at knowing they'd fallen for me, just as I had for them, was then swallowed up by a gnawing emptiness.

"I suppose we let him decide," Briar said. "It's all we can do."

"And if he can't choose between us?"

The question hung in the air. Neither man had an answer. Maddox glowered at the ground while Briar cast his gaze upward. The tree branches lightly creaked as a cool wind swept through them.

Tears burned in my eyes as I finally uprooted my feet from the grass and fled the area. I had known this was coming. How silly of me to think they'd be okay with sharing me. It was selfish to even consider it. I ran away from the knights' quarters and toward... I wasn't sure. I didn't really have a destination in mind.

I just needed to get away. To clear my head. To put distance between me and the men whose feelings I'd inadvertently toyed with.

I'm a horrible person. Maybe it would be best if I took Lupin up on his offer, reversed my wish, and returned to my own world. Since I was, clearly, only making people miserable in this one.

A small cry crawled up my throat, and the tears welling in my eyes finally slipped free, one after the other. I hastily wiped at them and kept running. The path widened into a circular courtyard with tall castle walls stretching in front of me.

The front gate?

The guards turned to me, somewhat alarmed. They were there to prevent unauthorized entry into the castle grounds. But what about someone trying to leave them?

"Let him pass," one guard told the other. "Prince Sawyer's orders."

Before I could think twice about it, I passed through the gate and headed down the cobblestone road away from the castle.

Night had fully fallen on Bremloc, and thin clouds wisped in front of the moon, blocking some of its light. In the distance, houses were scattered throughout the kingdom, some closer together and others more secluded, visible only by the lanterns glowing from their windows. The marketplace was beyond the hill, too far to see. I didn't want to go there anyway. The last thing I wanted was to be around people.

For someone who hated running, I was sure doing a lot of it. But my feet refused to stop. My boots thudded against the road before I spotted men on horseback up ahead, probably another unit of knights returning from patrol. I dashed off the road and headed toward a section of woods to the right, not stopping as I burst through the tree line and into the darkness of the forest.

The toe of one boot caught on a fallen branch, and I tripped, crashing to the ground. Hands scraped and stinging from how I'd caught myself during the hard landing, I got back up and wiped them on my pants before continuing on, weaving through the trees.

I ran until I couldn't run anymore.

With my energy waning, I slowed my pace and fought for a breath. My lungs burned, and my limbs felt heavier. Sluggish. Thorn bushes snagged at my tunic, and vines seemed to come alive. Shadows stirred. Nocturnal creatures called amongst the darkness: insects, owls, and god knows what else.

Wait. What the hell am I doing?

As sense slammed back into me, I spun around to leave the woods and return to the castle. Problem was… I couldn't remember which direction I'd come from. Everything looked the same, just an endless stretch of trees and darkness.

The night air held a bit of a chill, and as I inhaled, that chill seeped into my bones. Or maybe it was the sudden awareness of just how alone I was that brought on the chill. Alone and in the woods. At night.

I wiped at my eyes again and tried to retrace my steps. Not that I could see much in the dark. I walked in the direction I thought I had come from, but after what felt like hours and never reaching the tree line, I knew it was the wrong way. Panic set in.

I sprung forward, tearing my way down a different path. More thorns snagged at me, ripping my tunic and cutting my soft flesh beneath.

Stop freaking out and think.

Stopping in place, I surveyed the treetops, as if that would somehow help. Maybe if I was an adventurer from one of my books, I'd know a trick to finding my way out. Unfortunately for me, I wasn't. I was more like the person who got eaten five minutes into the quest.

"Great job, Evan," I muttered. "Way to be dramatic and get yourself lost."

Was I talking to myself to trick my mind into thinking I wasn't alone? Probably. Was it working?

Definitely not.

As a twig snapped not far from me, I squeaked and ducked down, hiding behind the nearest bush.

A horrifying thought then sunk in. The dark wood filled with demons and monsters was farther away from the castle... but how far did it stretch? I could've easily stumbled my way right into it.

Maybe the thing that had snapped the twig was a Fenrir demon. Or one of the reptilian monsters Callum mentioned with venom that paralyzed its target before they ate you alive.

Damn you, Callum. You're an evil cinnamon roll.

What if it was a monstrous wild boar, like the one the adventurers had taken down? My throat clamped shut as more tears pooled in my eyes. I was scared. Hungry and cold too. I wanted Maddox and Briar. Wanted to be squished between them in a warm bed like I'd been last night, feeling so damn safe. Happy.

Not there in that forest, possibly being stalked by some beast that wanted me for dinner.

I curled up on the ground and closed my eyes. Evan the Brave. Yeah, right. Fear had me frozen in place, unable to move. Barely even able to breathe.

Then, I thought of Maddox tossing me one of his almost-smiles and saying something like, "So, you really are a damsel in need of saving." Then, Briar would scoff at him before giving me a gentle, encouraging smile and telling me to get up.

Funny enough, thinking of them helped give me a boost of courage. Dying out there would prevent me from making things right with them.

Steeling my nerves, I grabbed a baseball-sized rock beside me and stood from the ground with it secured in my hand. If something wanted me for dinner, they'd have to fight for the privilege. I was top-shelf meat best enjoyed with a fine glass of wine, and I wouldn't be treated like anything less. I charged forward and ventured through the maze of bushes and trees, continuing my search for a way out of the forest.

I found a clearing instead.

And in the clearing sat a small stone cottage with smoke billowing from the chimney. Warm firelight came from inside, spilling out into the cool late-spring night through various square windows. The smell of something cooking tickled my nose, luring me closer.

Creepy forest? Check.

Random cottage in the middle of said forest enticing a lost soul desperate for some shelter and a warm meal? Check.

Yep. An old witch most definitely lived inside, who would try to throw me into an oven and eat me. But right then, I'd take my chances. I mean, I had a rock. It was a totally legit and deadly weapon when fighting for your life.

"Who are you?" a menacing voice snarled from behind me.

My damn soul nearly exited my body as I jumped. And my amazing, incredibly deadly weapon? Yeah, I dropped it. The rock hit the ground with a depressing *clunk* and rolled away. I spun around and met a pair of glowing purple eyes. I also saw a flash of sharp teeth.

"Don't eat me!" I shrieked. "I'm not top-shelf meat! I'm past my expiration date."

"Who are you?" he repeated with that same snarl, only now it was gruffer. The rest of his face came into view then. Alabaster skin, purple eyes, and medium-length silver hair. And jutting up from that hair? White furry ears.

"E-Evan," I stammered. "My name's Evan."

"Why are you here?" The last word sounded like a growl as it was spoken through clenched teeth. His defenses were sky-high.

"I got lost." Oh no. I sensed a ramble coming on, but I had no control over it. "I didn't mean to. I was upset, you see. I'm kind of in love with two men, and they maybe love me too, and I don't know how to choose between them. They're upset at me. Probably. But not nearly as upset as I am with myself. So, I pulled a Snow White and fled the castle in tears, not really thinking about where I was going. I—"

"The castle?" he interjected, and if I thought he seemed on guard before, he really was now. More than that, he looked pissed. Anger rolled off him. His purple eyes trailed my body once before he stepped toward me. "Golden hair and green eyes. You're one of the princes."

"What? No, I'm not." I waved my hands around. "It's flattering you think so, but believe me, there's not a royal bone in my body. I'm ordinary. A peasant. Or commoner. Whatever y'all call it here. No relation whatsoever to the royal household."

He studied me with cold, untrusting eyes. "You say you aren't a royal, yet you're from the castle."

"Well, I'm not *from* the castle. I live in one of the housing units on the grounds. Still trying to find where I fit, ya know? I was a stable boy for, like, a day. I also helped Briar, er, the court physician for a few days."

More staring. His furry ears twitched. Then, he sharply exhaled. "Leave my sight at once. I'm in no mood for visitors."

"I understand that. Unannounced visitors are the worst." It was my chance to run far away, but I hesitated. Running away was how I'd gotten into this mess in the first place. "But I'm still lost. I was hoping the person who lived here could help me."

"Your hope is misplaced. This is my home." He walked past me, holding a wicker basket in one hand. "You won't find any help here. Leave before I change my mind and decide to kill you after all."

For some reason, I didn't believe he would. And if I was wrong? Well, between him and all the unknown creatures lurking in the forest, I'd take my chances with him.

My gaze fell to his bushy white tail as he continued toward the cottage. Definitely a demi-human like Kuya. But he wasn't a cat. A fox? Maybe a wolf. I trailed after him. "What's your name? Do you live here alone?"

"Boy?" He stopped walking but didn't turn around. "I told you to leave. Don't make me tell you again."

"Okay," I weakly said, staring longingly at the cottage. It looked so cozy and warm. "Can you at least tell me which direction leads back to the castle?"

He released another breath before turning back to me. His purple eyes weren't glowing anymore. Did it only happen when he was angry? "You're bleeding."

I glanced down at my ripped tunic and the scratches on my arms and hands. Thin streaks of blood had dried along my skin, though the deeper cuts still oozed a bit. The knees of my pants were torn too. "I got into a fight with a thorn bush. If you think I look bad, you should see him. His poking days are over."

The demi-human made a rough, throaty sound. A laugh?

"Come inside," he then said. "Supper is cooking on the stove. You can eat and then be on your way."

***

The interior of the cottage lived up to my expectations. Quaint, cozy, and homey with rustic décor in earthy shades of brown, terra-cotta, and splashes of green. Plants were placed throughout the living space, and wooden beams ran along the ceiling. A side table made of a lighter shade of wood stood beside an armchair, topped with a hardback book turned facedown and an unlit candle in a brass holder.

In front of the chair, tucked inside a stone hearth, a fire burned, giving me a nice reprieve from the outside chill. I drifted closer and held out my hands to warm them. "Thank you for letting me come in."

The male—whose name I still didn't know—gave a small nod and advanced toward the kitchen with the wicker basket.

"Not that I'm complaining, but why did you let me in?" Of course I had to ask. Curiosity killed the cat. The same would probably be written on my gravestone too, right above "He pet something he shouldn't."

"Because." He pulled out a zucchini and two bell peppers—one yellow, one red—and set them on the counter. After rinsing them beneath the spout at the sink, he placed the zucchini on a wooden cutting board.

Chop, chop went the knife, creating a slow but steady rhythm.

"Do you need help?" I asked, cautiously approaching him. "I'm kind of handy in the kitchen. Making desserts is my thing, but I can do savory dishes too."

"No." His shoulders tensed, and the knife stilled on the board. "I'd prefer it if you sat down." He then continued chopping the vegetable. "You moving around is making me nervous."

"Why are you nervous?" I slid into a chair at the square table, respecting his wishes. His boundaries too. But seriously. I was like half his size. Definitely not a threat. If I tried to rob or attack him, he could just swat me away like a gnat.

His ears pointed back as he added the chopped zucchini to a bowl and grabbed the yellow bell pepper. "Because you're human."

Demi-humans were citizens of Bremloc but were looked down upon by so many people. I hadn't met many of them, but I hated the thought of them being mistreated. Prince Sawyer did too.

"Is that why you live in the middle of the forest? To get away from humans?"

He didn't answer. He just kept chopping.

"How long have you lived here?"

"Ever since I was a boy." Once both bell peppers were chopped, he added them to the bowl and took it over to the stove. He dumped the vegetables into a cast-iron skillet. "I lived here with my father."

No need to ask if his father was still around. The sudden sadness in his voice answered that question.

"What are you making?" Better to change the subject.

"Chicken and vegetables. The chicken is cooked and resting. I'll slice it and add it to the skillet once these are ready. I'll add broccoli and onion as well."

"Awesome. It smells great." I examined my hands and winced at the tiny cuts and scratches on the heel of my palms. They covered my wrists and went up my forearms too. "Stupid thorns."

The air stirred in front of me, and I jolted as the man knelt in front of my chair. He'd moved so fast and quietly I hadn't even noticed him approaching.

"Allow me," he said, then gently grabbed my hands, turning them palm up. As he studied them, I noted his sharp features. His pale skin looked smooth, no visible flaws, and he smelled like the forest: earthy, like evergreen trees and spring water. Purple eyes lifted to my face, surrounded by a fan of silver lashes. "Minor wounds. That's fortunate. While supper finishes, let's clean these and get you bandaged."

He was beautiful.

"Th-Thanks." I swallowed, confused by my reaction to him. It was a lot like how I'd felt when meeting Maddox and Briar for the first time—when they'd first touched me. I pulled my hands from his. "No need to trouble yourself though. I can clean up on my own."

Touching me had clearly made him uncomfortable. I didn't want to make it worse.

"Very well." He rose from the floor and took a step back. "The washroom is down the hall."

Nodding, I stood and walked that way. Once inside, I shakily exhaled and washed my hands at the sink basin. The water must've come from a nearby well. After scrubbing the dirt from under my nails, I ran the water up both my forearms and used the bar of soap to lather it. My face felt grimy, so I washed it too.

An oval mirror hung in front of the sink, and after patting my face dry, I checked out my reflection. God. I looked like hell. Felt like it too. My dark blond hair was tangled in places, and I picked out some leaves. The skin around my eyes was puffy from crying. That's when I spotted a mark on my neck. Well, two marks.

Hickeys.

I touched them, feeling a quiver in my throat. Had Maddox and Briar noticed me gone yet? Would they come looking for me? Hopefully, they wouldn't worry. After the crap I'd already put them through, I didn't want to add to it. They'd be better off just leaving me to the wolves.

I left the washroom and rejoined the demi-human in the kitchen.

He stood at the stove, stirring the contents of the skillet with a wooden spoon. His bushy tail jutted from the back of his black trousers, slowly moving from side to side, and his furry ears twitched at my approach. Spices filled the air, along with the smell of onion, peppers, and chicken.

"Did you find the bandages?" he asked, setting the spoon aside.

"Nah. But I don't need them. The cuts aren't deep." There were also so many that I'd look like a mummy if I wrapped them all. "My friend is a physician and can help heal them when I get back. He infuses healing tonics with magic."

How weird it was to call Briar my friend when he was so much more. But calling him my lover to a stranger would've been too awkward.

"Is he one of the men you love?" He grabbed two bowls from a cabinet.

So much for not making it awkward. *Thanks, past self, for your rambling mouth.* My cheeks heated. "Uh. Yeah." I tapped a finger on the tabletop. "You sure I can't help you with anything?"

"I'm sure." He scooped food into one bowl, then the other, before carrying them over to the table. "I have water or tea to drink. Which do you prefer?"

"Water, please."

He nodded before filling two glasses. When he placed one in front of me, his hand slightly trembled. I recalled the menacing snarl from when he'd first found me outside—the anger. I understood then it had probably stemmed from fear.

"Thank you," I said, scooting closer to the table. I grabbed my fork but waited for him to sit before digging in.

It wasn't how I'd expected the night to go. I'd planned to cook dinner for the knights and ask Maddox about his mission. Planned to, maybe, have another steamy night with him and Briar. But then those plans had gone to shit.

Now, I was in a fairy-tale cottage in the middle of a dark forest, eating dinner with a demi-human who eyed my hand with the fork, as if afraid I'd try to stab him with it.

Movements slow as not to startle him, I ate a piece of zucchini before shoveling up a bit of everything else, the chicken and the mix of veggies. The spices and juices blended together perfectly, like a celebration on my taste buds. I sighed happily. "You've made me like vegetables. Even broccoli. And I usually hate broccoli."

"I'm pleased you like it. I don't have many opportunities to cook for visitors."

"Would you want to if you did?"

He ate a slice of chicken, not answering.

"Well, you can feed me all you want to." I swallowed another bite. "This is freaking amazing."

He smiled. Or managed something close to a smile. He looked down at his bowl and continued eating.

My gaze wandered the room as we ate in silence. Pots and pans hung from a wrack against one wall, and herbs dried upside down, like the ones in Briar's clinic. Red apples sat in a basket on the counter. Living all the way out there alone, I wondered if he had his own garden. Did he go to the marketplace? Why had he seemed so mad when he thought I was one of the princes?

"Lake," he softly said.

I paused in my chewing and looked at him. "Huh?"

"My name." His purple eyes met mine briefly, before averting back to his food. "My name is Lake."

That feeling from earlier returned, like warmth prickling at my chest. I couldn't explain why. "It's nice to meet you."

His gaze remained on his bowl, but his ears twitched again. "I apologize for my rudeness from before. It's been quite a while since anyone has journeyed this close to my home. It caught me off guard."

"That must get lonely."

"Lonely? Sometimes, I suppose." Lake moved a piece of broccoli around his bowl, a distant look in his eyes. "Keeping to myself is easier."

I breathed out a short laugh, though it wasn't exactly funny. "You sound like me. That's how I was before coming here."

"You aren't from Bremloc?"

"No. I'm from... somewhere else. A kingdom far away from here." I gathered a pepper and a sliver of chicken on my fork. "Connecting to other people has always been hard for me, so I shut out the world. Like you said, it was easier."

"What changed?" he asked.

"Good question. Back home, I was a total wallflower who went unnoticed. And I liked it that way. Here in Bremloc, I'm still awkward and the same old dorky Evan. I guess the difference is I've found people I don't *want* to shut out. People who make me feel like I belong."

The confession stirred in my heart. Then, like the sun breaking through an overcast, stormy sky, the answer became all too clear. A part of me had known it all along.

I didn't want to return to my world. I wanted to stay in this one. With Maddox and Briar. With Callum, Kuya, Thane, and all the knights who had become my friends.

Expression pensive, Lake took another bite. The rest of the meal passed in silence. After we were finished, he carried our dishes to the sink and rinsed them out.

I stood from the table and rested my hands on the back of my chair. "Thanks again for the meal. It was really good." The thought of going back out into the dark forest, alone, made me uneasy, but I didn't want to overstay my welcome. "Do you want me to help you clean up before I go?"

"Go?" He blinked at me before understanding lit his eyes. "Oh. That's right." His gaze returned to the fork. He'd washed it several times. "No. I can clean everything myself."

He was even more awkward than me, which was saying a lot. But where mine came from me being an introverted goofball, his stemmed from something else. Fear. An aversion to people.

"Okay." I stepped away from the chair. "Thanks again. If you ever come to town, maybe I can repay the favor and bake you something. Not to brag, but I make the best muffins."

When he didn't say anything, I started toward the door. There was a soft sloshing of water behind me.

"Evan?" I turned to see Lake staring at me, ears tall and a furrow in his brow. Soap suds covered his hands. "I... I think you should stay. You don't know the way back, and the forest is a dangerous place to wander at night if one doesn't know where to tread."

"But earlier you said I needed to leave after eating."

"Perhaps I changed my mind." His eyes darted away from mine. "You are unlike other humans I've met. You're... kind." He shut off the spout and wiped his hands on a cloth. "I have a spare room. You may sleep here tonight and leave at first light."

My swarming anxiety subsided, and I breathed a sigh of relief. No dark forest for me, thank god. "I appreciate that. Because I totally lied about defeating the thorn bush. He's still alive and probably chomping at the bit to finish what he started."

A smile broke across Lake's face. "I'll show you to your room."

I followed him down the hall and to a staircase that curved up to the second floor. After going up, he turned into the first doorway on the left and lit a lantern, illuminating the room in a soft golden glow. It was small, with a twin-sized bed centered on one wall, a three-shelf bookcase across from it, a nightstand, and blue curtains over the double windows. Doodles of the sun and clouds covered areas of the walls.

"Give me a moment to fetch clean linen," he said before stepping back out into the hall.

I went over to the bookcase and squatted down to check out the few hardbacks, gliding my fingers over the spines. The creases in the spines showed that the books had been well loved, read multiple times.

I pulled one free and flipped through it. A storybook of what looked like children's stories with illustrations on every page. A page in the center was marked, and I opened it to a story about a small red fox.

The illustration showed the fox hunkered down inside a hole in a tree, its ears down and tears in its eyes as it rained.

'Why, oh why, is the fox so sad?
Because, you see, the fox is bad.
But if the fox is bad and has no heart
Then why, oh why, is his breaking apart?'

The next page showed the fox being approached by a rabbit and a squirrel. The two then hugged the fox. Another passage spoke of friendship and looking past appearances. The last page showed the three running through a grassy meadow with the sun shining bright above them. All laughed.

> *'Why, oh why, is the fox so glad?*
> *Because, you see, the fox isn't bad.*
> *All he wanted was a friend to see*
> *That he, the fox, was sweet as could be.'*

Why had this story been marked? Reading it made my heart ache. I slid it back into place and moved on.

A wooden ship sat on the top shelf, looking like a sort of trireme. Another resembled a battleship with canons. Beside the toy ships sat a stuffed brown rabbit with oversized floppy ears and buttons for eyes. I picked it up, touching the loose threads on the nose.

"His name is Mr. Hop," a voice said from the doorway. With a start, I looked back at Lake. A sad smile touched his lips. "At least, that's what I called him when I was a boy."

"Sorry for snooping." I set the rabbit back on the shelf and stood.

"It's all right." Lake walked over to the bed with a bundle in his arms. He tucked a sheet onto the mattress before draping a quilt over it and turning down the top. "This used to be my room. After my father... well, I eventually moved into the bigger room. I rarely come in here, so I apologize for the dust."

"I don't mind. It's better than being out in the woods. Not to be dramatic, but I'm not sure I would've survived out there. You probably saved my life tonight."

Lake's ears wiggled, and his tail flicked once. He fluffed the pillow on the bed before, somewhat awkwardly, stepping away from it. "I'll be in the room down the hall. If you need anything, please let me know."

"Thank you."

He nodded before exiting the room, leaving the door slightly ajar. He must've walked away, but I never heard his steps on the floorboards. He was so quiet.

I sat on the edge of the bed and removed my muddy boots before tugging off my pants and tunic. Well, what was left of the tunic. The thing had been ripped and torn and would need to be mended. I'd have to apologize to Callum once I got back. His mother had made the clothes.

After sliding into bed, I snuggled into the quilt and closed my eyes.

In the morning, I'd return to the castle and talk to Maddox and Briar. Figure things out with them, even if it was upsetting and awkward. Because the time away had made one thing crystal clear. When Lupin returned during the Festival of Lights, I'd tell him my decision.

I wanted to stay in Bremloc.

Even if it meant leaving my other life behind. Forever.

Chapter Twelve
And Then, There Were Three

"The forest doesn't seem so scary now," I said as Lake and I sat on the back veranda that morning with cups of tea and omelets made with egg, red bell pepper, ham, and cheese. My idea. He'd never heard of an omelet before and had seemed fascinated as I'd cooked, tail wagging.

I'd tried not to dwell on how fucking adorable that was.

"Daylight chases away the shadows of night, taking the fear of the unknown with it." Lake took a bite of the omelet, a happy little hum in the back of his throat as he chewed.

Very true. The same trees that had seemed so endless and daunting, the vines that had stretched toward me like long, skeletal fingers, now basked in the morning sunshine. Droplets of dew shone on the leaves and glistened in the grass. A flutter came from a nearby tree before birds flew into the air, chirping as they went.

I sipped my tea, wishing it was coffee. It wasn't bad though. Lake had stirred in honey and added cream. Between him and Briar, I might actually develop a taste for the stuff. "Briar would like this," I said, a knot forming in my chest as I stared at my cup. "He loves tea."

"The physician." Lake nodded. "Tell me of the other male. You mentioned two of them."

"His name is Maddox," I responded. Given how on edge Lake had seemed when believing I was a royal, I wasn't sure if I should tell him about Maddox being the captain of the Second Order. So I decided to keep that bit of info to myself. "Where Briar is softspoken and more of a nurturing type, Maddox can be brash and protective. He likes to poke fun at me, and I pretend to be annoyed by it. But really, I love it."

"And your heart is torn between them?"

"Yeah. I'm gonna talk to them when I get back." I ate the last of my omelet and wiped at my mouth, the gears in my brain turning before squeaking to a halt. It was an impossible choice. "I have no clue what to say. Any advice?"

Lake blinked at me. The sun bounced off his alabaster skin and brought out the silver threads in his purple irises. "I regret to say I can be of no help to you. I have little experience with romance. And by little, I mean none at all." He set his empty cup on the table and stood. "We should leave soon."

"You're coming with me?" I perked up at that. I had thought he was just going to tell me which direction to go and send me off on my own.

"Yes." He stacked our empty plates and placed the silverware on top. "To guide you safely out of the wood."

"Safely?" My gaze darted back to the trees. "So, even in daylight, there are creepy, scary things out for my blood?"

"The thorn bush will not rest until claiming you for its victim," Lake said, tone serious. But one look at him, and I saw the smile glinting in his eyes. "I wouldn't be able to rest at the thought of you facing such wicked beings alone."

"How kind of you," I responded with a snort. Lake was reserved and untrusting of people, but did a playful side exist beneath it all? "At least let me help you clean up from breakfast before we go."

When he agreed, I took it as a small win. Progress. His sky-high walls were lowering bit by bit, giving me a glimpse of the person beyond them. Someone timid but sweet. Together, we cleaned up the kitchen. He washed the dishes, and I dried them before placing them where they belonged.

Afterward, I jogged back up to the room and put on my boots. A creak from the hall snagged my attention.

Lake stood in the doorway with an article of light blue clothing draped over his arm. "Your tunic is ripped. I…" He glanced down, a flush in his cheeks. His tail stilled behind him, hanging low. "I thought this may be a good fit for you. Please don't feel obligated to wear it."

Yep. He was definitely sweet. Generous too. "Thanks. I—"

The sound of hooves beating against the earth came from outside. Horses whinnied, and the shouts of men carried through the open window.

In an instant, Lake went from adorably timid to the aggressive male I'd first encountered last night. The fur on his white tail stood on end as a deep growl churned in his chest. His eyes glowed brighter, and his teeth sharpened.

When I stepped toward him, he snarled at me.

I jerked backward, heartbeats erratic. "L-Lake?"

His growls deepened, and his eyes were wide with panic. I understood then his behavior wasn't geared toward me at all. He was lashing out because he was scared, like a wild animal being cornered. When men's voices sounded again from outside, a shiver passed over his skin. He then turned from the doorway and charged toward the stairs.

I took off after him, not sure what worried me most: him hurting whoever was outside or them hurting him. That worry intensified once I ran out the front door and saw Lake standing in front of a group of men on horseback. Men I knew.

"Evan!" Maddox dismounted from the stallion, a shakiness to his gruff voice. Briar slid off the horse beside his, relief washing across his face.

Callum, Duke, and Baden were there too, as well as a few others. All had come to find me. To bring me home. Emotion balled in my chest and crept up to my throat, tightening it.

"Stay back!" Lake roared, hands at his sides and clawlike fingers gnarled, as if ready to strike. "Leave my land at once."

Maddox unsheathed his sword. "Step aside, wolf." His blue eyes flickered to me before returning to Lake. "Or prepare to be struck down where you stand."

"The only blood that will stain the grass is yours," Lake responded with a snarl. "This is my home, and you're not welcome here."

"He's hurt, Maddox," Briar said, raking his gaze over me.

Maddox clenched his jaw, and his lethal stare burned into Lake. "We aren't leaving without the boy. Hand him over and I may consider letting you keep your head attached. That offer lessens with each passing second, so I suggest you move away from him. *Now.*"

Wait. Did they think Lake kidnapped me? Given the state of my torn clothes and cuts all over my arms and face, they probably thought he'd attacked me too.

"Lake hasn't hurt me." I stepped forward. "He—"

A poor decision on my part. The sudden movement startled Lake, and he turned on me with a growl, knocking me back with the heel of his palm. Losing my footing, I fell backward and hit the ground hard enough for the breath to leave my lungs.

Shock surfaced in Lake's eyes, smoothing the animalistic rage contorting his features. "Evan?" he whispered.

That's when Maddox struck. He lunged toward Lake, sword at the ready. I wanted to scream for them to stop, but I couldn't even breathe. The wind had been knocked out of me. Lake dashed to the side right before the blade made contact, and then he barreled forward, slamming into Maddox with his shoulder.

"N-No," I said through little gasps of air, trying to get up.

Lake disarmed Maddox, flinging his sword aside. That didn't slow the captain's advance. The two then fought hand to hand. Fists blurred as they brawled, each thud of flesh hitting flesh like a punch to my own chest. Maddox then knocked Lake to his knees and pinned his arms back. Callum and the other knights rushed over, weapons drawn.

Before long, they would overpower Lake. Maybe even kill him.

"Stop!" I finally managed to project loud enough for them to hear. Breathing was a bit easier now. "Lake didn't do anything! Please don't hurt him. He's just scared."

Maddox looked at me.

Lake used the distraction to break the hold and put distance between them. As he took a defensive stance in front of me, his gaze darted between the approaching knights. That gaze then settled on me. Regret crumpled his brow. "I'm sorry I pushed you. Are you okay?"

"Yeah. It was my fault anyway." I tried to stand but slumped back to the grass. Not because I was hurt. I was just clumsy, as usual.

"Stay away from him," Maddox growled as Lake stepped toward me. "You've done enough, wolf."

When Briar tried to approach, Lake growled. Maddox stuck out his hand to stop Briar from getting any closer. Tension hung thick in the air.

What cut through it?

"Kuya helped find you, Evan!" The cat boy scampered forward, having ridden on the back of Callum's horse. He stopped in the grass not far from Lake and put his arms behind his back, rising up and down on the balls of his bare feet. "Kuya went to Briar for medicine, but Briar was gone. Thane said you were missing, and Kuya got worried. So Kuya came with Briar and Captain Maddox to find you."

Lake cocked his head at Kuya, still on his guard but more levelheaded now. "A demi-human? Why do you associate with these men?"

"Because Kuya trusts them."

"But they hate our kind," Lake countered. "They'd kill you without a second thought."

"No." Kuya shook his head. "They're nice humans. Evan is a nice human too."

"He is." Lake looked at me with a wave of regret crashing over him. More of his anger faded. Seeing Kuya had helped calm him even more.

"Of course, I came too," Callum said, wearing a smile, even if it wobbled a bit. "You're one of my closest friends."

"I knew you'd be fine," Duke stated in a nonchalant tone, sheathing his sword before sweeping his hand through the back of his red hair. "But I came just to make these worrywarts feel better."

Baden grinned. "Do not be fooled by his lies. He kept saying, 'Evan is too small and cute to be lost in the woods. What if something eats him?'"

Duke shoved him, and Baden shoved him back.

My vision blurred. "I'm sorry for worrying everyone."

"Your names are Briar and Maddox?" Lake then asked, looking between them. "Evan mentioned the two of you. Please know that I never hurt him."

Maddox tensed, and the hand resting on his now sheathed sword tightened, the knuckles turning white. "Yet, you attacked us."

"Because you were trespassing," Lake snapped. "You and your men rode up on my home armed with weapons and shouting. I had every right to defend my territory. How was I to know you were no threat to me or Evan?"

"After I ran away from the castle last night, I got lost in the woods, and Lake found me," I explained, hoping to ease the new wave of building tension. "Well, I found his cottage first, and then he invited me inside. He fed me and gave me a place to stay for the night. He was actually about to lead me back to the castle before you showed up."

"He helped you?" Maddox asked with suspicion ringing in his tone.

"Is that so hard to believe?" Lake shot back. "Demi-humans aren't the beasts you make us out to be."

"Says the wolf," Baden chimed in, no longer easygoing like before. "All wolves joined Onyx years ago."

"Clearly not all of them." Lake sneered. "I've never allied with the demon lord and have no intention of doing so. My father felt the same, which is why he built this home away from all of you."

"And where is your father now?" Baden's gaze shifted to the cottage.

"Your king killed him!" Lake snapped. "Or, I should say, the king's men. His only crime was existing in a world that cast him out for no reason other than their own blind hatred. He went to the marketplace one morning and never returned. I learned later that you *honorable* knights wrongly mistook him for one of Onyx's subjects and executed him in the square for everyone to see. I heard that the spectators cheered as his decapitated head rolled across the dais. You call us beasts, yet you're the true monsters."

So that's why Lake had become angry at the possibility of me being one of the princes. He was angry at the king for doing nothing to stop the execution. Angry at every human who'd cheered as his father died. Hearing his story? I couldn't blame him.

"Lake," I said, tears stinging my eyes.

His hard stare instantly softened when meeting mine. His sorrow was clear as day. Sorrow about his father… and maybe something else too. He then looked toward Maddox and Briar. "You may approach. *Only* you." He cut his eyes at Baden. "The rest of you stay where you are."

Briar rushed forward first and dropped down at my side. "Thank the gods you're all right." He pulled me into his arms and pushed his face into my hair, shuddering. "We were so worried about you, silly, beautiful boy. Let me have a look at you." He drew back, his eyes glistening behind his glasses as he skimmed his fingers down my cheek. "Nothing I can't heal."

Warmth radiated from his palm as he used a basic healing spell, the same one he'd used the first day I had met him. And as his fresh scent surrounded me, I choked on a small sob and burrowed into him.

"It's okay," he whispered, petting the back of my hair. "You're okay. You're safe."

Another scent hit me then. Spice and leather. Arms came around me from behind before something soft pressed to my nape. "Do not *ever* run away from us again. Do you hear me?" Maddox held me tighter. "Gods. My heart stopped when I learned you were missing. I've never been so terrified."

"I'm sorry," I said again. I couldn't say it enough. "About everything. Running away and making everyone worry. Upsetting both of you because I'm a horrible person."

"Horrible person?" Maddox asked.

As more tears welled in my eyes, I hastily wiped at them, annoyed at myself. "I heard you talking last night. You were upset about me choosing between you. That's why—" *Hiccup.* God, I was a sobbing mess now. How embarrassing. "That's why I ran. I thought it'd be better if I just went away."

"Shh." Briar wiped at my wet cheeks. "Enough of that. We'll talk more once we get you home."

I was then lifted from the ground as Maddox picked me up. He cradled me to his chest and walked toward his horse. Briar kept pace beside us, his hand finding mine and our fingers threading together. The rocking motion of Maddox's body, along with the relief of being with both of them again, relaxed the anxious pit of nerves that had twisted in my gut during the earlier commotion. Crying had helped me some too, releasing endorphins or whatever.

"Wait," Lake said, stepping after us. He then halted in place, hesitating as his purple eyes fell to me. "Will I see you again?"

"No," Maddox told him. "You won't."

"I wasn't speaking to you, knight."

"That's Captain. Not knight."

"You are no captain of mine," Lake responded.

"Don't fight," I said, surprised by how weak my voice sounded. Exhaustion had crept up on me. I felt like I could zonk out for the rest of the day.

Briar gently squeezed my fingers. "Let's take him home so he can rest."

Maddox nodded and continued forward. They were getting along fairly well, so there didn't seem to be animosity between them. For now, anyway. Would that change once I was safely back at the castle?

"We've both fallen for the same man," Briar had said.

And god. I'd fallen for them too. All I wanted in that moment was to return with them and feel their arms around me.

However, as Maddox seated me on the stallion and swung up into the saddle behind me, I looked at Lake. He stared back at me, expression shadowed. I couldn't explain why, but the thought of never seeing him again caused an ache to tear through my chest.

And as Maddox guided the horse toward the trees and I saw Lake's face crumple, I thought of that story about the red fox. People thought the fox was bad, so they had cast him out. When really, he was sweet and loved to laugh and play. He'd only wanted a friend who would see the truth.

Had Lake reread that story over and over because he felt like that too? Misunderstood and lonely.

The cottage faded from sight as we traveled deeper into the forest. I rested against Maddox and let my eyes fall shut. He had one arm wrapped around my middle and occasionally pressed kisses into my hair.

I didn't stay awake long. During the journey, sleep closed in around me, much like the shroud of the forest, and I dreamed of a hollow inside the base of a tree. Rain came down hard, some of the drops catching on the leaves of the branches. But instead of a small fox, I saw a white wolf pup. He trembled as lightning flashed and thunder boomed. Tears shone in his purple eyes.

Sometime later, I awoke in Maddox's bed. Neither he nor Briar was in the room, but I heard them speaking softly outside the door.

I tried to sit up, but my limbs weighed heavily. I felt groggy and a bit out of it. A small glass vial on the bedside table caught my eye, empty. It looked like the ones Briar used for his elixirs. Had he given me one to help me rest?

The thoughtfulness burrowed into my chest.

The door creaked open before Briar stepped through. Maddox trailed behind him.

"You're awake." Briar approached the bed and sat on the edge of it. He smoothed a hand over my hair. "How do you feel?"

"Tired." My voice sounded croaky, and my throat was dry.

Maddox stepped closer and looked down at me, gaze hard. Guarded. "You should get more rest."

"So should you," I said, noting the dark circles under his blue eyes. I would've bet my entire collection of mint-condition, out-of-print BL manga that he hadn't slept a wink last night.

"It's late afternoon now. You've been sleeping for hours." Briar soothingly combed his fingers through my hair. "Are you hungry?"

"A ridiculous question," Maddox said with a scoff. "He is always hungry."

"I don't recall asking for your input, Captain."

"I don't require your permission for anything, physician. This is my goddamned room."

I smiled at their bantering. "Food sounds nice, but if it's okay, I'd like to just stay like this for a while. With both of you."

Briar rested his hand on my cheek. "We're right here."

I leaned into his touch before peering up at Maddox. He hadn't made a move to touch me. I couldn't blame him for being pissed. I'd caused them unnecessary worry. Or maybe his irritation stemmed from the conversation I'd overheard. His patience with me was thinning.

Even so, I slid my hand across the mattress, reaching for him.

He eyed my hand as a tic started in his jaw. Yeah... he was pissed. Just as I started to pull my hand back, he grabbed it, his hold loose at first but quickly tightening. A tremble went through his large body before he joined Briar on the bed.

"Don't ever scare us like that again," Maddox whispered, lifting my hand to his lips before kissing my knuckles. "I can survive many things in this life, Evan, but losing you is not one of them."

Us. As if he viewed Briar and himself as a pair. The medicine must've still been messing with my head because there was no way that was true.

"I won't," I responded, voice shaking.

"You said you heard our conversation from last night." Briar traced my jawline and trailed his hand up to my temple, like he was mapping my face with his fingertips. "That's why you ran?"

I nodded.

Maddox huffed, yet his hold on me tightened. "Foolish boy. It's fortunate we found you in one piece. And in the company of a wolf no less."

"His name is Lake," I said. Images from my dream stirred in my head—the sad wolf with purple eyes. "He's untrusting of people, but he's really kind."

Just then, a monstrous sound filled the room... coming from my stomach.

Briar breathed out a laugh. "I'll make you something to eat." He stood from the bed and walked toward the door.

Maddox brushed our thumbs together once before standing as well.

"Wait." I tried to sit up but slumped back down, my muscles still not wanting to cooperate. I needed to make things right with them. As right as I could anyway. "We need to talk."

"Later," Maddox said. "Focus on resting for now."

***

"Feel better?" Callum asked, his brown hair damp and his skin slightly pink from the hot water. "A dip in the hot spring can cure any ailment."

He had taken me to the spring shortly after I'd cooked dinner for the knights—knights who had complained that I shouldn't have been on my feet working after my "attack" in the forest. I reassured them that the only thing that had attacked me was a thorn bush and that I was fine. When Duke started calling me Evan the Thorn Prince, the other knights had laughed and relaxed. I had too.

Well, mostly relaxed.

Briar and Maddox had been preoccupied with work since visiting me earlier but said we would "talk later." The anticipation was killing me. I wanted to get it over with, like ripping off a Band-Aid. The sooner, the better.

"I feel like a new man." I tugged the shirt over my head and smoothed it down. It was the one I'd worn when coming to Bremloc. "I'm sorry about ruining the clothes you let me borrow. I'll pay you back for them."

292

I still had money left from the bag of coins Briar had given me for my clinic work.

"Pay it no mind," Callum said as we walked along the path leading back to the knights' housing. He had put on trousers but kept his shirt off. "All that matters is you're safe. But I hope you'll think twice about venturing into the forest by yourself again."

"No worries about that. Lesson learned." A shiver passed through me at the thought. "I can add 'explorer' to my list of things I suck at."

Instead of smiling like usual when I poked fun at myself, Callum's expression turned solemn. "Captain Maddox and Briar weren't the only ones worried about you. When the guards at the front gate said you fled the castle grounds and disappeared into the night, every knight in our unit had been ready to go after you. Many of us didn't even sleep last night. You've become dear to us all, Evan. Remember that the next time you think we'll be better off without you."

Callum's sunshine personality and goofy grins made him easygoing and carefree, which only made the moments like this when he lost the cinnamon roll persona and became serious that much more impactful.

"Sorry, Cal. Seriously." Emotion clogged my throat. "I wasn't thinking."

"You're forgiven." He offered me a tight smile and patted the top of my head. "The others are expecting us. Let's hurry back."

The sun had fully set, taking the light with it but not the warmth. Humidity hung in the evening air, further proof that summer was nearly upon us. Stars began to appear in the sky as we walked, but I didn't recognize any of the constellations. No Big Dipper or Orion's Belt. I was in a different realm within the vast expanse of the universe.

Wanting to stay in Bremloc didn't mean I wouldn't miss the world I once knew. Of course there were things I'd miss about my old life, but I was excited about learning about this one. Learning the constellations and mythologies surrounding them. Excited about fully embracing the opportunity I'd been given.

"Thorn Prince!" Duke exclaimed as we entered the courtyard outside the gathering hall. He raised his mug, the contents sloshing over the rim.

I struck a little pose, placing one hand on my cocked hip and flinging my head back, tucking the other beneath my chin. The knights sitting with him around the firepit laughed. I'd never felt that comfortable with people before where I could be silly and not suffer horrible embarrassment afterward. Well, while sober anyway.

As I came out of the pose, my gaze landed on Maddox. He leaned against the post of the mess hall, a smirk in place. Okay, he was the exception. I was mortified.

"Oh, please don't stop on my account," he said. "Do continue."

Cheeks burning hot, I crossed my arms over my chest. "Sorry. It was a onetime performance."

"Pity." He pushed away from the post and tipped his head for me to follow him. "Come with me. It's time for our talk."

Oh shit.

"Go easy on him, Captain," Baden said from the circle of men around the fire. "It would be a shame to never eat his cooking again. I'll be dreaming about that chocolate cake he made tonight for dessert."

I smiled. It had been my first time baking it for them. Hopefully not the last.

"Aye to that." Quincy clinked his mug to Baden's. "And along with the food, the view has also greatly improved since he's come here."

Huh? The view?

"Admire the view to your heart's content, Q," Maddox told him, still amused. "But if you touch, I'll do what the demon in the dark wood failed to do and remove the offensive limb from your body."

"Oh!" Several knights exclaimed at once before bursting into laughs. Quincy joined in too.

Still confused, I was only half paying attention when Maddox placed his hand on my lower back and guided me from the courtyard. I'd assumed he would take me to his quarters, but several paces later, I realized we were heading in the opposite direction.

"Where are we going?" We moved along a narrow path, passing the orchard of trees he and Briar had met beneath last night. The clouds drifting across the moon made it darker. "Are you taking me out here to dispose of me?"

"An interesting thought, but no."

"Interesting?" I bumped against his side. "Jerk."

His lips curved into a smile. It was soft. "I heard you have a new title. Thorn Prince suits you quite well. Though, I must say, Clumsy Prince would suit you much better."

"That's it." I stopped walking. "I'm going home."

A laugh rumbled in his chest. "So the men can tease you, but I can't?"

I fought a grin and returned to his side. "You seem happier tonight." A huge difference from earlier in his room.

"Do I?" Maddox linked our fingers as we moved at a leisurely pace. "Perhaps I am."

"Any reason why?" I loved the feel of his big hand in mine and lightly swung our arms between us.

"You'll know soon enough."

"Patience isn't one of my virtues."

"Oh, I'm well aware of that. But unfortunately for you, I don't mind making you suffer a little."

"Sadist."

He laughed again, this time harder, as if it had taken him more off guard.

"The clinic?" I asked a bit later as we neared the building. A curtain was over the window, but light showed on the other side of it. "I see now. Briar has been mastering his magic skills, and y'all came to a solution. You're going to clone me."

"Clone you?" Maddox frowned.

Ah, he was unfamiliar with the word. "Like take my DNA—er, I guess you don't know that term either. Okay. Take my blood and bodily tissue to create two of me."

"Two of you?" His smirk returned. "A frightening thought. I can barely handle one."

I was the one who laughed that time. "You're so mean to me."

Maddox let go of my hand and stopped in front of the clinic door. And then he pressed me against it, his mouth crashing to mine.

Surprised, I groaned and linked my fingers behind his neck. His taste exploded on my tongue, a bit like honey and liquor, as though he'd drank honey mead with the other knights while Callum and I had been at the hot spring. Tingles spread through my body in that familiar way, like every fiber of my being wanted to feel him. Wanted to taste him.

"I've never allowed myself to feel this way about anyone," he said with a pant against my lips. "I tried to fight it, but it's a battle I know I can't win. It's one no amount of training could've ever prepared me for." He kissed me again. It was softer than before, shakier. "I love you, Evan. So much it scares me."

His confession draped over my heart and wrapped around it, just like his arms around my waist. I rose up on my tiptoes and rested my head against his, sliding my fingers through the silky black strands of his hair. "I love you too." My voice shook. "I think I have since the night you first kissed me."

"I feel like I've been waiting for you my entire life." His nose bumped mine. He traced the seam of my lips with his tongue before dipping it inside my mouth. It was the kind of all-consuming kiss I felt down to my toes.

A kiss that ended abruptly as the door opened behind me.

"Oh," Briar said from the other side. "Apologies for the interruption."

"I'm sure you're very remorseful about it," Maddox muttered.

Briar's cheek twitched before he opened the door wider. "Please come in."

This is it. The talk I had been anticipating all freaking day. Nerves jostled in my belly as I stepped through the doorway, wondering, not for the first time, what the hell I'd gotten myself into.

Chapter Thirteen
Pinch Me, I Must Be Dreaming

"Awesome weather we're having tonight," I said, hands on my hips as I looked at the window. The window that was covered by a curtain. "All humid and stuff."

Maddox coughed.

"You sound thirsty," I told him. "I'll go get you a glass of water. Not from here though. I'll get it from the spring on the other side of the castle grounds."

"No, you will stop pacing, stop delaying, and face us like the fearsome muffin lord you are." Maddox relaxed against the counter and tipped his head to a barstool at the island in front of him. "Sit. We need to talk."

"We need to talk," I repeated with a groan. "Those are the worst four words ever. Right above 'we have no coffee.'"

"Well, I'm taking care of the latter. Coffee is on the way." Briar heated water at the stove. Another smell lingered in the air too, like something baking. He met my stare with a knowing smile. "You'll only get a slice if you sit down."

I was too antsy to sit still, but the promise of sweets and coffee trumped that feeling. The knights had devoured the chocolate cake earlier before I could get a piece, and I needed a sweet fix stat. I slid onto the barstool. "Okay. I'm sitting."

"Good boy," Maddox said.

My heart rate accelerated. "You know? I've never been into praise kinks or anything, but when you say that in your deep, sexy voice, I kind of like it."

"Your attempt to change the subject is admirable."

"Thanks," I said. "It's a gift."

His lips twitched.

Briar used a device that reminded me of a french press and poured hot water over ground coffee beans. The same ones Maddox had purchased for me from the market. The smell alone was to die for. But there would be no dying until I had a cup—or eight—and several slices of dessert.

"So." I drummed my fingers against the top of the island counter. "How are we supposed to do this? Big, important talks freak me out. I don't know where to start."

"Then allow me to begin." Briar filled a cup with the fresh brew and doctored it just how I liked, adding sugar and the perfect amount of cream. He set it in front of me. "As you overheard last night, we've both fallen for you."

"That's still hard for me to believe." I curved my hands around the cup and breathed in the familiar smell, finding comfort in that familiarity. I took a much-needed sip and hummed a little at the bold flavor. Him knowing just how I liked my coffee showed how much he cared. Which didn't help my nerves any because I knew what was coming.

When I took another drink, my hands shook so bad I nearly spilled some of it.

"You doubt us?" Briar filled a second cup and handed it to Maddox.

"No." And it was true. I believed them, even if I didn't think I was worthy of those feelings. "I don't doubt you at all."

Maddox stared down at his cup. Silent.

"But we need to know how *you* feel," Briar said.

"How I feel?"

"Well, I suppose the question is more so aimed at your feelings for me." Briar adjusted his round-framed glasses and met my gaze only briefly before averting it. That one second of eye contact was enough for me to see the tinges of worry in his hazel eyes. "I heard your confession for the captain outside the door. You love him."

Maddox smiled… but that smile faltered when he looked at Briar.

"I won't assume you share those same feelings for me," Briar said, pouring a cup for himself. He stirred in some sugar but didn't take a drink. He just stared at the swirling liquid. "And if that's the case, then this discussion will be brief and easily resolved."

As the worry deepened in his eyes, my heart fucking ached, like someone was using my heartstrings to play a fiddle—badly. Just yanking and pulling and scraping a bow across them. Or whatever the fuck you used to play a fiddle.

"There's nothing easy about this," I finally said, voice unsteady. My heart lifted into my throat. "Because while I love Maddox… I love you too, Briar."

Relief smoothed the worried crease of his brow, though a smidgeon of disbelief lingered in his eyes. "You do?"

Nodding, I slid off the barstool and closed the gap between us, winding my arms around Briar's lean waist. His heart thrummed wildly beneath my ear as I snuggled into his chest. "You're just like those moonlight flowers. Rare and beautiful. Not everyone gets to see the blossoms, but the ones who do never forget. That's how I feel about you."

Briar returned my embrace, hiding his face in my hair.

Maddox cleared his throat. "If he's a flower, what am I?"

"A sword." I nuzzled Briar's chest before turning to look over at my knight. "Deadly and a true work of art. Forged to perfection. I mean, just look at those muscles. Rawr."

He lightly snorted. "I will accept that answer." He took a drink of coffee before setting the cup aside.

The lighthearted moment couldn't last forever. Much like this dance we were doing.

Throat tight, I stepped back from Briar so I could see both of them. "Last night when I heard you talking, you asked what would happen if I couldn't choose between you. That's what's stressing me out. Because I don't know *how* to choose. I didn't intend to fall for both of you, but it happened anyway."

One way or another, however this night ended, someone would get hurt. Either me losing both of them or choosing one over the other. Both options royally sucked.

Maddox and Briar exchanged a look. Neither said a word, but like the few instances before, they seemed to understand each other regardless.

Briar took my left hand in his. "You running away worried us sick, but one positive came from it. We set our differences aside and worked together to find you. Your safety, your happiness, is all that matters." He glanced at Maddox before returning his gaze to me. "A decision was reached in those dreadful hours of wondering where you were and if you were okay. The captain is actually the one who suggested it, much to my surprise. Although, I'd be lying if I said I wasn't already considering it."

"Suggested what?" I asked.

Maddox grabbed my right hand. "That you don't need to choose."

"Wait." There was a loud ringing in my ears. "I... don't understand."

Both men stepped close enough that I felt the heat of their bodies. They then placed my hands on each of their chests—over their hearts.

"Neither of us can let you go," Maddox said, his big hand curling around my wrist.

"So we decided not to," Briar added, softly kissing my fingertips.

I had to be misunderstanding. They couldn't seriously be suggesting what I thought they were.

"He's speechless." Maddox looked at Briar. "You broke him."

"*I* broke him?" Briar threaded his fingers with mine and tossed him a smile. "You're the one he compared to a sword. I'm the beautiful flower, remember?"

"A flower, my ass. Unless it's the thorn on the stem of a rose, you prickly bastard."

"Um. Guys?" I gently pulled from their hold. "I'm oblivious as fuck sometimes, and I overthink everything. Are you suggesting I be with both of you? Like as a couple? Wait, throuple? I don't know the right label."

"We're not suggesting anything." Maddox snatched my hand back and gave me an expression that implied how dare I pull away in the first place. "We love you, and you feel the same for us. That's all there is to it. What we call it doesn't matter."

Hope built in my chest. "But won't you be upset having to share me?"

"Not at all." Briar's smile softened. "I quite enjoy the sight of him touching you."

Maddox smirked at him. "There may be times when I touch you too."

Oh my fuck, that's so hot.

A little whimper crawled up my throat. "I'm one hundred percent okay with that."

"I'm pleased you think so." Maddox drew me closer to his muscled body. "But know that you're the one my hands crave to touch the most." He skimmed his lips along my jaw, giving me shivers. "And who I yearn to kiss."

Briar dipped his face to my neck. "The one we adore."

The ball of emotion in my throat tingled—a tingle I also felt behind my eyes. "So, this is real? I can really have you both? I'm not dreaming?"

"It's not a dream, love," Briar said, locking his arms around my waist. He placed one hand on Maddox's forearm, holding him too.

"I…" My heart banged against my ribs. My breaths quickened. "I don't know what to say."

"Say yes." Briar kissed my earlobe.

"To what?"

"Such a silly, clumsy, oblivious muffin." Maddox glided his fingers down my neck, his deep blue eyes like an ocean I wanted to dive into, get in lost in. A smile shone in them. Something tender did too. "Let me phrase it in a way you'll understand. We are yours, Evan, in body and in heart. Will you be ours?"

"Yes." Heat sparked in my veins as I felt both of them against me.

My men.

No relationship was the same. The only rules we needed to follow were the ones we set between us, not what society dictated—the one in Bremloc or the one from my old world. We would eventually need to work out all those details, but communication was key. Being open and honest with each other was the most important thing.

"This is cause for some celebratory dessert." With a smile still in place, Briar stepped over to the wood-burning oven and used a mitt to pull out some type of bread. The cause of the delicious baking smell.

"Is that blueberry?" I asked, sniffing the air. I inched closer.

"Blueberry and lemon." Briar set it on the counter. "I said I'd make it for you someday."

"What a beautiful day it is. Or night. Whatever. I need it in my belly."

Maddox chuckled. "And with the sight of food, we are all but forgotten, physician."

"Nuh-uh." I turned back to them. "I can stuff my face with this goodness and cuddle you both at the same time. It's called multitasking."

"Says the one who can't walk on flat ground without tripping."

"Would you want him any other way?" Briar asked.

"No." When Maddox smiled at me, it was genuine and soft, smoothing his normally brooding features. "I wouldn't change a single thing about him."

"Neither would I," Briar said, the edges of his eyes crinkling.

The way they were staring at me? My heart sputtered before kicking back into gear. I'd never felt so special to anyone before. "If y'all don't stop, I'm gonna cry again."

"Sap." Maddox tugged me closer and feathered light kisses across my brow. "Yet, you're our sap."

I smiled into his chest.

Once the bread cooled a bit, Briar cut off a thick piece and handed me the plate. My mouth was salivating before I even got the first bite into my mouth. And when I did finally get it in my mouth? Dear lord. It was incredible. Perfectly soft, still warm on the inside, and not too sweet. It didn't even need glaze or icing to go with it.

They talked to each other as I gobbled up the lemon-blueberry amazingness, and when I looked at them, their gazes were on me, humor in their eyes.

"Aren't y'all gonna eat some?" I asked with my mouth full.

"Watching you is much more enjoyable," Briar said.

"Your loss." I shoveled the last of it in my mouth and then dabbed at the crumbs on the plate, the only remnants left of the amazingness.

"He's pouting now," Maddox stated, taking me back into his arms. He brushed the edge of my lips. "We should add messy to your long list of titles."

I nuzzled his hand, earning a soft smile as my reward. Funny how I used to call him Captain Ice. Because right then, Maddox was so fucking warm.

"Why don't we take this upstairs?" Briar asked, drawing our attention. An unmistakable lust blazed through his hazel eyes, darkening them.

"You read my mind," Maddox responded before picking me up and throwing me over his shoulder.

"Hey! I'm not a sack of potatoes you can just carry and throw around as you see fit."

"Shh." Maddox slapped my ass. "Sack of potatoes do not speak."

I laughed as the three of us moved toward the medical wing and passed through it. No patients slept in the cots. The wing was empty. Because of the powerful healing tonics, no one stayed there for long. Briar led us through a doorway at the back of the room and up a set of wooden stairs.

"I've never seen your room before," I said, wiggling on Maddox's shoulder. He swatted my ass again.

"That's right. You haven't," Briar said, as if it had just occurred to him too. "Well. No time like the present."

Did I get the chance to actually have a look around his living space? That would be a hard no. Right as we stepped inside, Maddox carried me over to the bed and tossed me on top of it. He lifted the bottom of my shirt and kissed my belly, sliding his hands along my ribs as he worked the shirt the rest of the way off.

The mattress dipped beside me as Briar joined us. He lightly grazed his teeth across my shoulder before licking down my chest. As his tongue flicked my nipple, I arched up into him and groaned.

"I love how needy you are," Maddox rasped, palming my thighs before forcing my legs apart. "How you moan." He looked at Briar with a slight smirk. "Lick him until he squirms."

"An order I have no trouble following." Briar ever so slowly—softly—took my nipple back into his mouth, his warm breath causing it to bead tighter. He didn't fully close his lips around it. He exhaled, letting his breath tickle and tease at the same time. Mostly tease.

While Briar tormented my upper body in the best way, Maddox popped the button on my jeans and slid them down my legs. He laughed under his breath, and I didn't need to look to know the reason. After the bath earlier, I had changed into the clothes I'd been wearing when arriving in Bremloc—a T-shirt, my jeans, and the boxers with the animated hot dogs printed across them.

Boxers that didn't stay on long.

He tugged them down my hips and discarded them with the rest of my clothes. Despite it not being the first time they'd seen me naked, a bit of insecurity still washed over me as I lay on the bed, fully exposed.

"So beautiful," Maddox murmured from between my legs, rubbing his cheek against my inner thigh.

My insecurity was then forgotten as the two of them kissed, licked, and nipped at my skin. Briar closed his lips around my nipple and sucked. The sound that left me was rough and needy. He had me squirming in no time at all, alternating between flicking his tongue and suckling. When my legs tried to close of their own accord, Maddox kept them open. His hand gripped the base of my cock and gave me a slow pull from root to tip.

And when he took me into his mouth, the explosion of wet heat had me crying out, voice cracking.

Chills danced across my naked flesh as they focused on my stimulation points, Briar flicking his tongue against my nipple and tweaking the other between two fingers, while Maddox moved up and down my shaft, taking me all the way to the back of his throat.

"Oh my god." I panted, chest heaving and muscles tightening. Maddox fucked me with his mouth, increasing his pace. Briar increased his too, his tongue flicking at an inhuman speed. I was about to lose my damn mind. "I—"

My orgasm slammed into me without warning, tearing from me a raspy groan. Maddox swallowed every drop, his blue eyes heated as he looked up at me, watching me shudder and writhe. Briar then grabbed me by the jaw and melded his mouth to mine, kissing me. My body jolted once more before Maddox pulled off my cock.

"You turned me into an Evan blob," I told them as the waves of my release receded, leaving my body like a heap of jelly.

"The most precious blob." Briar lightly bumped our noses together, and I grinned.

Maddox crawled up my body and settled on top of me, sliding his hand to my nape.

"Hey, you," I said.

Eyelids heavy, he stared down at me through his long, dark lashes before dipping his head and kissing me. I tasted myself on his lips. Lips that pressed firmly to mine in a demanding kiss, making my toes curl. Something else was firm too. His hard bulge pressed into me, the material of his pants probably stretched to its limit.

Yeah, sword described him pretty well. But not any sword. He would be one of those huge ones you had to wield with two hands.

Briar kissed Maddox's shoulder before tucking a finger beneath his chin and bringing their mouths together. Watching them kiss was hot as hell. It also made me happy in other ways. Especially when the kiss broke and they smiled at each other.

The night was far from over. They had taken care of me, and I had every intention of repaying that kindness in full.

As they kissed again, I reached down and palmed both of their cocks through their pants. I was still in recovery mode, but they were revved up and ready to go. Briar trembled as Maddox moved from his lips and sucked beneath his jaw.

Was it smooth as we fumbled around on the bed to undress each other? Not even a little. My fingers got caught in the strings while trying to unfasten Briar's trousers, and his glasses were knocked off at one point.

Maddox laughed as Briar and I struggled to pry off his much-too-complicated upper armor—two thin leather pieces laced across his chest in a style similar to a corset. But the soft, breathy chuckles in between hard, sloppy kisses were a million times better. Because it was real.

Once we were all naked, I moved between Maddox's legs and took his weighty cock in hand. My lips stretched around his thick shaft as I sunk down as far as I could, then pulled back up with a wet pop. I couldn't take him too far without triggering my gag reflex, but his quickening breaths told me he liked what I was doing.

Briar gave himself lazy strokes as he watched me suck Maddox. I loved that he got turned on by it. I definitely understood the appeal; I'd thought it was hot watching them together too.

"Come here," Maddox told him in a gruff tone.

As Briar obeyed, Maddox grabbed him by the nape and kissed him hard. Their tongues fought for dominance as I returned my lips to Maddox's cock. But it wasn't enough. I wanted to touch both of them. I then shifted up a bit and grabbed Briar's base. The two of them moved closer on the bed and turned inward, allowing me to take one into my mouth, then go to the other, sucking them both.

They let me have my fun for a few more minutes before I was grabbed and tossed to my back, putting me at their mercy once again. Maddox used a vial of oil he'd found in the nightstand and eased the tip of one slicked finger inside me. I grinned down at him, and he nipped at my fleshy inner thigh, causing me to yelp.

Briar lay on his side facing me, trailing his fingertips up and down my rib cage as Maddox prepared me. His other arm was beneath my head like a pillow.

"Ah, fuck," I said on a whimper as Maddox curled two fingers inside me, pressing against my prostate.

Briar dropped a kiss to my chest before unwinding from me and scooting lower on the bed. He had taken off his glasses, giving me a perfect view of his hazel eyes as they flickered up to me. And as Maddox fingered me, Briar wrapped his fingers around my shaft and teasingly brushed his lips across my cockhead.

"This is where you kill me, isn't it?" I asked, bracing myself for the sweet torture I was about to endure.

"Kill you?" Maddox smirked. "Never."

"You're smirking. That's never a good sign." I looked at Briar, who was stroking me slowly. "You're the nice one."

"Am I though?" Briar eased my tip into his mouth in the same way he'd done with my nipple earlier. The evil tease.

Maddox circled his fingers inside me before pulling nearly all the way out. His hand then stayed there like that. That smirk surfaced again. "Hearing you whine is nearly as pleasing as your moans."

Briar chuckled before taking me deep into his mouth, creating toe-curling suction.

Fortunately for me, they were too worked up to torture me for too long. Briar dragged me on top of him, and I straddled his waist, resting my hands on his lean chest. He gripped my hips as I positioned his tip at my entrance and lowered my body, taking him inside me.

"Gods, Evan," Briar moaned, rolling his hips up into me.

"That's it," Maddox murmured from behind me, grabbing my neck in a loose hold. He nuzzled beneath my ear. "Keep riding him."

There was something incredibly hot about Maddox telling me what to do, encouraging me, while I fucked another man. He nipped at my shoulder, then grazed his teeth along the curve of my neck as I rode Briar's cock.

"Aren't you going to join us, Captain?" Briar breathily asked, so fucking handsome with his light brown bangs lying mussed across his brow and a smile lingering at the edge of his mouth.

I reached back with one arm to grab Maddox. "Please?"

I needed both of them. Needed all three of us to be joined.

Maddox softly kissed my cheek before reaching for the oil. With his cock slick, he guided it into place. But he didn't penetrate right away. "Briar?"

"Give me a moment," Briar said before sliding his hands to the globes of my ass. Warmth emitted from his palms. He was using magic to make sure it didn't hurt me, just like last time. "All right. He's ready."

Even while high on lust, the two of them were focused on me, making sure I was comfortable. It caused a lump in my throat.

Maddox feathered kisses across my nape as he slowly eased forward. Like before, it took a little time for them to find the right rhythm, but once they did, none of us lasted long. Maybe it was the rush of serotonin that came from confessing your feelings to someone and having them return that affection, but I was on cloud nine long before they sent me soaring.

Briar came first, his hips bucking up into me as his cock pulsed. Ripples of pleasure shot down my spine before I cried out, following him. Maddox locked an arm around my waist and buried his face in the back of my hair as he softly groaned.

Afterward, I collapsed on Briar's chest, and he wound his arms around me. Maddox settled in beside us and pulled us both against him, nuzzling Briar's temple before kissing mine.

314

"So this is how it will be now?" I asked, emotion thick in my voice. The pessimistic side of my brain had trouble believing it was real, that I was allowed to have them both.

"Well, sometimes we'll be in my bed," Maddox said. "This one is too small."

"You're just too big," Briar responded, making circles on my lower back with his fingertips. His eyes shut, and his breaths started to even out.

"It's past your bedtime, physician."

"I sleep when it suits me."

"Both of you need to sleep," I said. "By the sound of it, neither of you got much of it last night." *Because of me.* Tendrils of guilt remained in my gut.

"Is that an order, Muffin Lord?"

I cracked a smile at the silly nickname, but my response was interrupted by a jaw-cracking yawn. I cuddled more into Briar's chest and tucked my head under his chin, closing my eyes. Maddox shifted on the bed before I felt the blanket being tucked in around us.

"Don't leave," I said, peering at him through lids I could barely keep open.

"I wouldn't dream of it." Maddox settled back in place and slid his arm beneath Briar's head. Briar turned his face toward him, and Maddox softly kissed him.

My heart fucking soared at the sight.

As we lay in each other's arms, bodies tangled in the sheet and love bites covering our sweat-damp skin, I remembered the night I had clutched the wishing stone to my chest, lonely, depressed, and desperate for a change. Desperate for something to fill the emptiness in my heart and make me feel alive.

I found it with them.

***

The next morning, I woke in Maddox's arms. He slept like a rock beside me, the only movement being his chest as he breathed. Briar was gone, probably having woken earlier and decided to let us sleep in.

Sunlight spilled into the room, catching on the particles in the air. The bed was in the corner, away from the window, so the flood of light wasn't shining directly on us. I estimated it was midmorning, perhaps closer to noon. It wasn't like Maddox to still be asleep that late in the day. He usually woke with the sun.

I lightly traced the edge of his jaw before ghosting my fingers over his lips. They softly parted beneath my touch. His exhaustion was my fault. My presence in Bremloc had shaken up his routine, knocked everything off-balance.

Wanting him to sleep for as long as possible—because fuck knows he clearly needed it—I carefully unwound from his arms and slid out of bed. He didn't even stir, further evidence that he was right where he needed to be: in bed, asleep. I moved the sheet up his body to cover him and then pressed a kiss to his forehead.

After gathering my clothes that were strewn across the floor, I quickly dressed and left the room, shutting the door softly behind me. I descended the stairs and turned the corner that led down a short hallway and to the medical wing.

When I reached the main part of the clinic, Briar was at his workstation, tinkering with something silver. He was so focused on his work he didn't notice I entered the room. He read a passage in the spell book, then returned to the trinket and muttered what sounded like an incantation. One that wasn't successful if him cursing under his breath was any indication.

Sighing, he set the silver trinket aside and sat back in his chair, taking off his glasses before scrubbing his hands over his face.

"No luck?" I asked.

His head snapped in my direction, the lines of frustration instantly smoothing as our eyes met. He put his glasses back on before walking over and pulling me into his arms. "Good morning, love. Sleep well?"

"Mhm." I returned his hold, breathing in his fresh, slightly floral scent, like champagne and magnolia blossoms. "Did you?"

"Yes. It was the best night of sleep I've had in quite a while."

"Me too." I gave him a quick kiss on the lips before glancing at the workstation. "Still trying to infuse an object with protective energy?"

"I've had a bit of success, but only with very basic protective charms. They're strong enough to ward off minor spells, yet are worthless when faced with more powerful magic."

"I believe in you," I said before kissing him again, letting my mouth linger on his.

The door opened behind me as Thane came in, his arms full of supplies—more herbs, some vials, and wrapped meat purchased from the butcher in the market. "Morning, Evan!"

"Morning," I greeted him. "Need help?"

"No, thank you." Thane placed the items on the counter. "I wouldn't mind if you cooked us lunch soon though."

"Thane," Briar said with a snap, similar to a father scolding his mouthy kid.

"What?" The apprentice shrugged. "It was worth a try. Besides, you complain when *I* cook."

"Because you burn it," Briar responded. "Then there was the time you managed to burn the chicken *and* undercook it at the same time. How you did that is beyond my comprehension."

"It's why I'm a physician's apprentice and not a chef."

"I can cook," I told them, fighting a grin. "I don't mind at all."

Feeding people was the one time I felt useful. And if I planned to stay in that world forever, I would eventually need to find work. Maybe the castle was looking for a pastry chef. Something to ask Prince Sawyer the next time I saw him. Then again, working in the castle might be too intimidating. Deadly too. Knowing my luck, I'd accidentally spill something on one of the princes, or god forbid, the king himself, and then end up with my head on the chopping block.

Yep. Avoid the castle at all costs. I made a mental note to go to the market instead. The King's Smoker might be a good place to start. There was another tavern called The Drunken Toad too.

Briar kissed me on the forehead before stepping away. "I have something for you."

"Oh no," I said, recalling the previous night. The three of us had fallen asleep shortly after having sex… which meant we hadn't taken a certain post-lovemaking tonic. "The flower juice. I'm gonna throw up."

He chuckled and went over to the kitchen counter, grabbing the leftover bread. "Breakfast, actually. Thane tried to eat it all this morning, but I was sure to save you a big slice."

Thane grinned.

I blinked, confused. Afraid to hope. "No nasty tonic? Really?"

Briar nodded. "The tonic rids the body of disease. Since the three of us have only been with each other since then, we don't need to take it again."

"That's literally the best news I've heard all day," I said, then beamed at the blueberry and lemon bread. "Well, second best. Come to daddy, you amazing goodness."

"How unfortunate," a deep voice came from the door to the medical wing. Maddox stepped through looking sinfully sexy, his black hair tousled and pink marks on his muscled torso from how hard he'd slept. Other marks were on him too. Those I'd made myself. A bit of possessiveness stirred in me. Yeah, I saw the appeal of giving a lover bite marks.

"Unfortunate?" I asked him. "You wanted to drink that nasty stuff?"

"No." Maddox strode over and wrapped me in his arms, placing his mouth to my ear. "It's unfortunate I don't get to hear you whine as you take your medicine."

"I could always whip one up for him as a precaution," Briar suggested.

"I like the way your mind works, physician."

"Both of you are so mean to me." I tried to weasel out of Maddox's hold, but he kept me in place. Not that I tried *that* hard. Having his arms around me felt too damn good. Even if he was a jerk who lived for my pain.

Maddox barked out a laugh.

"Here you are, love," Briar said, handing me a plate with a massive slice of the bread. "I'll make your coffee."

"Do I get coffee and bread too?" Maddox asked.

Briar's eyes gleamed from behind his lenses. "Perhaps. If you behave."

Maddox shoulder-checked him before resting his hand on Briar's waist. My heart warmed as Briar leaned against him a little, a hint of a smile on his lips.

"All of the happiness you've only ever dreamed of is at your fingertips, Evan," Lupin had said shortly after I'd come to Bremloc.

And as I watched the two men I loved playfully nudge each other and start to bicker, I realized he'd been right all along.

320

Chapter Fourteen

Royal Luncheon Ruined by a Royal Pain in the Ass

"I mean this in the most respectful way possible, but you look like shit."

Maybe not the politest thing to say to a prince who was kind enough to invite you to an awesome lunch in the palace garden, but this prince was quickly becoming a friend. Talking to him was easy. And he was seriously looking rough—tired eyes and a smile that didn't quite reach them.

Prince Sawyer exhaled, a light chuckle blending with the sigh. "It appears I haven't been dealing with the stress as well as I'd hoped."

We sat at a table beneath the shade of a gazebo, and a warm wind swept through. The days were only getting hotter. The approaching of summer still made me anxious. I had decided to stay in Bremloc, but it didn't make saying goodbye to my old world any easier.

"Wanna talk about it?" I asked.

"Since we last spoke, I've met with several bride candidates," Sawyer said, petting the top of Kuya's head, who sat on the ground, resting against his legs. He had been offered a chair but declined it, preferring to be as close to Sawyer as possible.

"Any winners?" I asked, though given his expression, I could guess the answer.

"One admired herself in every reflective surface she passed, uninterested in actual conversation. The closest she managed was to ask whether the emerald or sapphire necklace looked best with her dress before deciding neither was good enough and choosing one far more extravagant. Another lashed out at one of the castle servants for daring to bring her a pastry to enjoy with our afternoon tea."

I frowned. "Why would she get mad about a pastry? Sounds like heaven to me."

"She said the servant did it in a malicious scheme to make her fat." Sawyer expelled another sigh. "Then there was the princess who was not only unsatisfied with the accommodations of her room during her stay in the castle but offended by them. Not enough frills on the gown given to her as a welcoming gift and too many windows. Because don't we realize too much sunlight is bad for the skin?"

"Kuya loves the sun," the cat boy said before snatching a jelly tart from the platter in front of us. He scampered away to curl up in the blanket of green grass beside the gazebo, his rainbow-colored eyes catching the sunlight as he devoured the treat.

"He didn't like any of the women," Sawyer said, his attention on Kuya.

"Sounds like you didn't either."

"What I like or don't like means little to my father," he said, voice strained. "Marriages are for political gain, not love." He shook his head. "But enough about me. How are you? I heard about your incident in the forest, and of course, Kuya shared with me what happened when they found you. I wished to check in on you sooner, but…"

"But you've had your hands full of women?"

He cringed. "A dream for many men, I'm sure. For me, not so much."

"I've been well," I said, taking pity on the poor guy and changing the subject.

Better than well, actually. Over a week had passed since Briar, Maddox, and I'd made things official between us. Their duties kept them busy for most of the day, but our nights were rarely spent apart. Whether it was in Maddox's bed or Briar's, I fell asleep with both of them wrapped around me.

With the exception of last night. Briar had left yesterday for the magical academy to be a guest lecturer for the students and would be gone for another day.

"I'm glad to hear it." Sawyer ate a grape from his plate. Our lunch had consisted of turkey and tomato sandwiches on a flaky, buttery croissant, a side of mixed fruit, and strawberry jelly tarts for dessert. The day was too warm for hot tea, so we drank water from a pitcher kept cold by a magical rune. "Kuya also mentioned a demi-human who helped you."

"His name is Lake." I had kept quiet about him to anyone not part of the rescue-Evan party because of how poorly demi-humans—especially wolves—were viewed, but Sawyer didn't share those negative views. I trusted him. "Did Kuya tell you what kind of demi-human he is?"

"A wolf." His voice had dipped in volume. So the castle attendants standing not too far away wouldn't hear? "His father was ruthlessly murdered." Murdered, not killed. The distinction mattered. It showed how seriously Sawyer took the matter and that he, too, believed it to have been wrong. He then glanced around us and forced a smile, tipping his head to one of the attendants who had stepped a bit closer. Still with that fake smile, he told me under his breath, "We shouldn't discuss it any further. Not here."

Understood.

"How about this weather we're having today?" I said loudly, fanning my face. "Summer's right around the corner. I'd love to go for a swim."

When the prince smiled again, it was more relaxed. "The sea is still much too frigid to swim in, but perhaps we can journey down to the shore and dip our feet in the water."

I was excited by the thought. "I'll have to ask for permission. The last time I left the castle walls, as you're well aware, didn't exactly go well. And let's just say that two men have been keeping a super-close eye on me since then."

More than two, actually. Callum, Duke, and Quincy were never far from my sight when I wandered the grounds. Baden was less noticeable, but I'd caught him watching me too, especially when Maddox was busy. They were basically my babysitters now.

"Ah, so like the Royal Guard following me everywhere, you have your own personal force of guards." Sawyer grabbed a tart from the platter and handed it to Kuya as the cat boy rushed back over. Kuya gently head-butted the prince's arm, purrs rumbling in his chest, before dashing back out into the sunlight. "Rumors are circulating the castle. I'm ashamed to say I've been greatly intrigued by them."

"What rumors?"

"About you, Captain Maddox of the Second Order, and the chief physician. The three of you are romantically involved, yes?"

"Oh. That." My heart hammered in my chest. "Yeah, we are."

Sawyer laughed at whatever expression had crossed my face. Given my suddenly hot cheeks and spiked heart rate, I could only imagine what he saw. "No reason to be alarmed. People are merely curious. Before your arrival in Bremloc, Captain Maddox had quite a frosty reputation. And Briar, while polite, seemed distant and detached from those around him. Both look much happier now, as do all who are fortunate enough to meet you. Me included."

"Because of my dashing good looks, right?" I fluttered my eyelashes at him.

He nearly choked on the second grape he'd popped into his mouth.

"Please don't die, Prince Sawyer. Kuya would be sad. I would too. And out of all the heroic and awesome ways to die, do you really want 'choked on a grape' written on your tombstone?"

He laughed harder.

Kuya's ears twitched before he turned to us with a wide grin. Jelly was smeared at the corner of his lips. His grin then vanished as his gaze fell on something behind us.

"How sweet," an unfamiliar voice said before a guy who looked just like Sawyer but with slightly bigger muscles and shorter hair joined us beneath the gazebo. He wore an elaborate, deep crimson outfit with golden sigils on the chest and shoulder that marked him as someone of high rank. "My baby brother has made a new friend."

Baby brother? Oh shit. So this must be—

"Cedric," Sawyer greeted him, voice taut. "I didn't know you were back in the capital."

"I returned this morning." Cedric helped himself to fruit from the platter. By Sawyer's sudden shift in mood, his shoulders tense, I knew right away he didn't care much for his brother. "Did you miss me while I was gone?"

Sawyer didn't answer.

"Oh, how you wound me." Cedric placed his hands on the back of Sawyer's chair, causing my friend to tense a bit more. "Here I am working hard to deepen our relationship with the neighboring kingdoms, forging strong alliances and ensuring the ones we already have do not falter, and you treat me so coldly." He then leaned down, his mouth close to Sawyer's ear. "You're fortunate I'm in a good mood, little brother, or I would have you punished for this insolence."

The accompanying smirk to his words was chilling. My first impression of Prince Cedric was he enjoyed intimidating those around him—got off on it. Callum had said he'd tried to kill Kuya years ago. Knowing someone like him was first in line to rule was a truly frightening notion.

That smirk then transitioned to something far more threatening as Cedric's green eyes landed on me. "How dare you look at me so directly. Lower your eyes before I have them plucked from your skull."

Stomach in knots, I looked at my now empty plate.

"Evan is my guest," Sawyer said. "Please do not speak to him so cruelly."

"Cruel?" Cedric snorted. "I was only joking." I kept my gaze lowered but watched him move from the corner of my eye—move closer to *me*. He stood across from me and rested both hands on the table between us, leaning in. "You. Eyes up."

I obeyed, doing all I could to keep my chin from shaking. I had been afraid when first meeting Lake in the forest, but the fear I felt while staring into Cedric's green eyes was on another level.

"Your name is Evan, yes?"

"Yes, sir," I responded, inwardly cringing. That wasn't the correct way to address him, but it was too late to take it back now. I'd just found true happiness for the first time in my life. I didn't want it ripped away so fast. And this dude screamed impulsive, murderous bastard. He'd probably slit my throat just for shits and giggles.

"Sir," he repeated, that cold smirk returning to his mouth. "How adorable. I take it you are unfamiliar with addressing those of royal blood." His gaze shifted to Sawyer before returning to me. "Or perhaps my darling brother has given you too much freedom in his presence. You will address me as Your Highness. Understood?"

"Yes, Your Highness."

"Excellent. I'm thrilled some commoners can be taught so easily." He leaned closer and grabbed my jaw. I forced myself not to jerk away. "Unless I'm somehow mistaken and you aren't a mere commoner? Do you have a title I'm unaware of?"

I pressed my lips together. *Do not say Lord of the Muffins.* This wasn't Maddox. Even when my captain had shot ice daggers at me in the beginning, I had never felt any real threat from him. Which was why I'd rambled and said silly shit. Cedric would most definitely kill me for the "endearing" qualities Lupin claimed made my men fall for me.

"No, Your Highness," I responded, though challengingly, seeing as to how he still had hold of my face, fingertips digging into my skin. "No rank or title. Just Evan."

"Well, *just* Evan…" Cedric released my jaw and straightened back up. "You should feel honored to have met and spoken to the future king of Bremloc. Perhaps it will be a story to share with your commoner friends when drinking yourselves into a stupor or whatever it is you commoners do with your spare time."

Was that really how he viewed the people he'd someday rule over? Disgusting.

"Not only my friends, Your Highness," I said before I could bite my tongue. "I'm sure I'll tell my grandkids about it someday. I even want it written on my grave. A lowly commoner such as myself will never know a greater honor."

Cedric stepped around the table and turned my chair to face him, the legs scraping against the floor. He rested his hand on the back of it and bent down to my eye level. His expression caused the knots to tighten in my gut. "Is that sarcasm I detect?"

"Please, Cedric," Sawyer said, standing from his chair. "Evan didn't—"

"Why so worried, little brother? It's not as though I plan to rip out his tongue for it." Cedric didn't take his eyes off me as he answered Sawyer, and that hard gleam in his eyes? Yeah, it said that's exactly what he wanted to do. He palmed my cheek before pinching it between two fingers. "This close, I see you are quite the beauty. For a male. Adorably flushed soft skin and plump lips." He smoothed his thumb across them. "But you should learn when to keep them closed."

When I didn't respond, his amusement grew.

"Look at that. You *are* a quick learner." He patted my cheek—hard—and pulled away. His gaze flickered to Kuya, and disgust clouded his expression. "Still keeping that beast around, I see. You'll regret it one day when it kills you in your sleep."

"Kuya wouldn't," the cat boy said, shaking his head. "Kuya loves Prince Sawyer."

"How dare you speak to me," Cedric snapped at him. "Being my brother's attendant grants you certain freedoms, such as keeping your head, but it will only shield you for so long, beast."

"Your Royal Highness?" an auburn-haired man asked from the gazebo steps. His uniform was fancier than that of the castle guards, all black with a splash of red at his collar. The hilt of his sword shone with gold, and the wrists of his uniform had gold cufflinks. A flash of silver lingered beneath his sleeves. Under armor, maybe? "The king requests your presence in the throne room."

"Duty calls," Cedric said with a sigh, his eyes returning to me. "I suspect we will meet again, Evan. I trust you'll remember the lessons you learned today for when that time comes."

Cedric left the gazebo, not paying any of the attendants or guards a bit of attention. It was clear he believed them to be beneath him.

"Prince Sawyer," the uniformed man said with a tip of his head before following the royal douche-canoe.

"That was Sir Keegan of the First Order," Sawyer told me. "He's assigned to watch over Cedric."

"Poor guy," I said on impulse, then freaked a little. Cedric might've been an asshole, but that didn't give me the right to basically insult him. He was the crown prince. "Um. I didn't—"

"Don't fret. Between you and me, I share the sentiment." Sawyer stood from his chair and held out his hand to Kuya. The cat boy dashed over and grabbed it with both his hands, his reddish-brown tail swishing behind him. The prince appeared to calm with Kuya's presence—and his touch. He looked at me. "I apologize for Cedric's behavior. He wasn't always so... mean-spirited. At one time, we were close. But then his power went to his head."

"Why doesn't he like demi-humans?"

"Our upbringing." Sawyer grabbed a napkin off the table and wiped at Kuya's mouth. Kuya playfully nipped at his fingers, causing the prince to smile tenderly. "The war with Onyx started before my birth, but Cedric was a toddler when the conflict heightened. He witnessed the knights marching for battle. He felt the fear as our father armored up to join the fight."

"The king fought too?" I asked.

He nodded. "My father is loyal to his people. He cares deeply for this kingdom and would lay down his life if necessary to protect it. Many demi-humans sided with Onyx during the war. One of them was a wolf who served at my father's side as his loyal advisor. He betrayed my father to ally with the demon lord, nearly resulting in the king's death when he led the men into a trap. So I think my brother views all of them as traitors."

Okay, it made sense. But it didn't excuse Cedric's shitty behavior and attitude.

A different man in uniform approached. Brown hair was swept back from his face, and his amber eyes stuck out against his dark skin. "Prince Sawyer? The king has requested your presence as well."

"Thank you, Sir Anton," Sawyer responded. He then looked at me. "With Cedric back, my father more than likely wishes to have a family meeting. Our trip to the sea will have to be postponed for another day."

"That's okay. It'd be best to wait for it to warm up anyway so we can fully enjoy it. Unless there are, like, monstrous sea creatures that will try to eat us. Then I'll just admire the water from a safe distance."

He smiled. "The sea monsters never journey this close to the kingdom, though they stir quite the trouble for the merchant ships during their travels."

Kuya clapped a hand on my shoulder, his rainbow eyes twinkling. "Kuya will bite the monsters to protect Evan."

"My fierce kitten," Sawyer murmured as he touched Kuya's jaw, his voice dipping. He then withdrew his hand and quietly cleared his throat. "I look forward to our next visit, Evan. Take care of yourself, and do try not to get lost in the woods again."

"Can't make any promises," I said with a grin. "They don't call me the Thorn Prince for nothing." A name that had most definitely stuck within Maddox's unit of knights, thanks to Duke.

Sawyer gently squeezed Kuya's hand before releasing it. "Do you mind walking Evan home while I go see the king?"

"Kuya doesn't mind." He bounded closer to me, grabbing me by the wrist. "Come, come."

After saying goodbye to Sawyer, Kuya and I found the path leading from the palace garden and walked at a leisurely pace, neither of us in any sort of hurry. He skipped down the trail and hummed, stopping every so often to admire a flower or chase a bumblebee.

"Evan?" Kuya rose from the grass, where he'd pounced toward a butterfly. He dusted off his pants and fidgeted with the strings connecting the front of his crop top. His sudden seriousness took me off guard.

"Is everything okay?"

When his gaze lifted, his eyes glistened. "Kuya tries to be happy but can't."

Damn if that didn't make my heart hurt. "What's wrong?"

"Prince Sawyer has to find a wife," he said weakly, returning to my side. He had plucked a dandelion from the grass and slowly rolled the stem between two fingers. "Kuya has no right to be sad about it."

"Of course you have a right to be upset." That ache in my chest spread. "You love him."

"Love isn't enough." Kuya knelt down and placed the flower on the grass. Then, he stayed there like that, just staring at it. "He's a prince. We can never be together."

He didn't sound like himself. The bubbly, playful cat boy was gone. Heartbreak would do that. Seeing someone so sweet broken down like this felt so wrong.

"What do you say about getting out of here?" I asked.

He peered up at me, head tilting to the side. "Where would we go?"

"Anywhere you want." Maybe getting away for a while would help cheer him up or at least get his mind off the things upsetting him.

"Your men will worry if you're away from home for too long."

I shook my head. "Maddox is away on another mission and won't be back until tonight, and Briar traveled to the academy early yesterday morning to speak to the students studying the healing arts. He probably won't be back until tomorrow afternoon. Truth be told, I could use the distraction too."

"Evan misses them?" Kuya stood back up.

"Yeah." Embarrassingly so. I hadn't seen Briar in a full day, and it had only been a few hours since I kissed Maddox goodbye, but I missed them both so much it hurt. I was a hopeless romantic who definitely got attached too fast.

Deeper than me missing them, I worried about them too. Maddox's profession put him in harm's way every single time he left, and with reports coming in of the group of bandits still attacking the neighboring lands, I got nervous at the thought of Briar traveling too.

"Then Kuya will go with Evan." He grabbed my hand and pulled me in the opposite direction. I could tell he was forcing a lighter tone. In an attempt to make me feel better? "We will not be sad and instead have fun."

"Doing what?"

"Exploring," he said, flashing his canines as he gave me a toothy grin. "The kingdom of Bremloc awaits."

Chapter Fifteen
Did We Just Become Besties?

The market was less crowded than it'd been the previous time I'd visited. Which I didn't mind. Fewer people meant less anxiety.

Kuya bought a bag of roasted almonds from a vendor, and we munched on it as we walked the lanes. One woman was selling wind chimes made with colorful stones, and Kuya's eyes sparkled as he watched them move with the breeze.

Spotting a bookstore, I asked if we could take a look. As I stepped inside and browsed the shelves of books, I was hit with that familiar comfort I used to feel when being in bookstores in my old world. The smell of the books. All the stories waiting to be read. I found the latest book in the series I'd borrowed from Briar and bought it, along with a cool bookmark with a wolf engraving and a leather journal I thought my handsome physician would like.

Things would never be the same as they were in my old life, but the bookstore had given me some of those same feelings.

"Good. Evan found a present." Kuya's ears flicked. "Now Kuya wants one."

"Anything specific?" I asked as we exited the bookstore.

"Cake."

I laughed. "I think there's a bakery around here somewhere."

"This way." He looped his arm through mine and steered me around a corner and past a line of shops.

Finding the bakery, we ducked into it. My mouth watered as the scent of freshly baked bread wafted around me.

"We have both savory and sweet," the baker told us. "If you want anything other than bread, we also have a selection of pastries and cakes."

"Do you have anything with strawberry?" Kuya asked.

The baker's eyes narrowed. "No."

I skimmed the items and stopped at one in particular. "Is that not a strawberry pastry right there?" It looked similar to a Danish, made of multilayered, flaky dough and topped with jam and cream. Sliced strawberries were also on top.

"Oh," the baker said. "That's not for sale. Apologies." He didn't sound—or look—sorry at all though. Annoyed would be a better description.

"Why not? That's not good business practice to offer something and then claim it's not available." I then realized where his annoyance had come from. Suspected, at least. It was because Kuya was a demi-human. "One would almost think you're discriminating against your customers."

He glared at Kuya again before looking back at me. "I suppose I can make an exception this once. Shall I bag it for you?"

"No," I said. "You can stick it up your ass though. I'm sure it tastes like shit anyway."

I then looped mine and Kuya's arms back together and left the shop. He offered me a small smile and gently bumped me.

"Does that happen often?" I asked once we were back outside.

"Yes. It's why Prince Sawyer doesn't like for Kuya to go anywhere without him." He led us over to a fountain in the center of the square and sat on the ledge around it, bringing his knees up. His tail curved in around him, the tip slowly moving across the stone slab. "When he's with Kuya, humans aren't mean."

"Fuck that guy. If you want strawberry cake, I'll make one for you."

"Evan bakes?"

I sat beside him. "Yep. I haven't gotten the chance to do much of it since coming here, with the exception of baking a few things for the knights. I miss it." My job at the café was one of the main things I missed about my world. Baking and making coffee had relaxed my mind and made me happy.

"Then you should bake a cake," he said, nodding. "And allow Kuya to eat it."

"I'd like that." The fountain trickled behind us, the sound soothing. "You know… I had a dream of opening my own book café."

"Book café?"

"A place people could go to enjoy a nice cup of coffee and read. I'd serve baked goods too, like muffins, cakes, cookies, and pies. Maybe even sandwiches. Hearty soup during the winter."

"Kuya wishes to go to this place." He scooted closer to me, tail flicking.

A sad pang went through my chest. "It's just a silly dream."

He stared at me for a moment. When he finally spoke, it lacked his usual lightheartedness. "Don't call your dreams silly, Evan. Words hold power."

"You're right. It's just hard to imagine it becoming a reality." Here in Bremloc or in my own world.

"When Kuya was a young boy, his parents were killed by humans." His gaze became distant. "They tried to kill Kuya too, but he ran and ran until he couldn't run anymore. Kuya had no money. No place to call home. People threw things when Kuya passed through villages, calling him a beast. Kuya remembers being hungry and cold a lot. Sometimes, when the pain in his belly became too great, Kuya's ashamed to say he stole food."

My sternum tightened.

"Don't be sad for Kuya," he then said, resting his hand over one of mine. "You said the book café is your dream. Well, Kuya had a dream, too, back then. He wished to find a home. Wished to find someone who'd chase away the bad memories and make Kuya feel safe."

"Then you met Prince Sawyer?"

Warmth swept through his rainbow eyes. "He saved Kuya. But before he came along, Kuya met someone else."

"Who?"

"A sorcerer," he answered. "Kuya had just stolen meat from the butcher and was running from

338

the men pursuing him when a shop appeared. Kuya dashed inside to hide."

Wait. A shop that just appeared?

"Shiny objects were inside the shop," he continued. "Pretty rocks and crystals. Glowing orbs. And yes, Kuya touched them all." I tried to smile at that, but I could barely even breathe through the pressure building in my chest. "A man with brown hair offered to cook the meat Kuya stole and offered tea and cookies until it was ready. As Kuya ate, another man approached. Kuya was scared of him at first, but he said not to be afraid. That the shop had chosen Kuya."

The Emporium.

"What happened next?" I couldn't stop the shakes from passing through my body. Until that moment, I had refrained from telling anyone about Lupin and his shop, mainly because I feared they'd call me crazy or, even worse, believe me and then think I was a threat once learning I came from a different world.

But Kuya had met him too.

"Lupin, that was his name, he gave Kuya a paper lantern and said to light it once the sun went to sleep. He said it would lead Kuya to where he belonged. So Kuya did this. The lantern floated into the air, and Kuya followed it but became tired after a while and found a bed of flowers beside a lake and curled up to sleep. That's when Prince Sawyer found Kuya. He was out hunting with Prince Cedric and their royal attendant. Kuya was wanted for thieving, you see. Bad Kuya. But Prince Sawyer wouldn't let anyone hurt Kuya. He wrapped his cloak around Kuya and let Kuya ride his horse back to the castle." His expression softened even further. "Kuya fell in love with him as days turned to weeks. He's Kuya's most treasured person."

"What about Lupin?" I asked. "Did you ever see him again?"

"No. But the lantern? As Prince Sawyer helped Kuya onto his horse, Kuya saw it on the grassy bank of the lake, no longer lit. It had guided Kuya just as Lupin said." He turned around on the ledge and glided his hand over the surface of the fountain pool. "The lantern helped Kuya find his prince."

It was the perfect opening to tell him about my own meeting with Lupin and the shop that seemed to have a mind of its own, but the words stuck in my throat.

"There's something Evan wants to say?" He returned his attention to the water, gently tapping at it with the tip of his fingers.

I exhaled a shaky laugh. "You're observant." I grabbed a roasted almond from the bag and nibbled on it. And then, before I could talk myself out of it, I said, "I've met him too. Lupin."

Kuya whipped his head back around, eyes wide.

"The shop appeared to me like it did with you. I went inside, browsed a little. Other people came in too, each of them sad or run-down in some way, but when they left the shop with the items Lupin helped them find, they seemed lighter." I was rambling, but now that the words were coming out, I couldn't stop them. "It was my birthday. I was depressed because

I was once again spending it alone. Lupin then showed me a wishing stone."

"Did Evan make a wish on the stone?"

I slowly nodded. My heart constricted. "It's how I ended up in Bremloc."

"Evan wished to come to the kingdom?"

"No, I hadn't even heard of Bremloc before then. My wish was to find the place I belonged, somewhere I'd be happy. I guess a lot like you did with the lantern. After making the wish, I woke up here."

He wrapped his arms around his knees. "And does Evan feel like he belongs here in Bremloc?"

Faces appeared in my mind. Maddox and his deep blue eyes. Briar and his soft smiles. Callum, Duke, and Baden. Kuya. I may not understand everything, but I really did feel like I belonged there with them.

"More and more each day," I answered. "This kingdom is somewhere I can really call home. It's… special."

"Then the stone worked." He smiled. "Kuya is happy Evan made the wish."

"Me too."

We sat in a comfortable silence after that. My friendship with him felt stronger now. Lupin and Saint had come into both of our lives when we were at our lowest and helped lift us back up. Helped us find happiness.

People strolled through the square, some dressed in fancy attire. Nobles, probably. Some of the women carried decorative parasols to block the sun, the bottom of their big gowns rustling as they walked arm in arm with their husbands. Mischievous boys with holes in the knees of their trousers poked fun at each other and ran through the square, dodging other people. A little girl rode on a man's shoulders and excitedly pointed to the park beyond the fountain.

"Magnolia blossoms," Kuya said, looking where she pointed. "Pretty pink and white flowers. Kuya likes them too."

"Do you wanna go sit beneath them?"

He perked up, ears doing that cute little twitching thing. "Can we?"

"Let's go." I hopped off the stone fountain and grabbed his hand.

He beamed as we made our way over to the park. Once there, Kuya cupped one of the low-hanging star-shaped blossoms in his palm and asked it for permission to sit beneath its shade. He rubbed it against his cheek before leading me to the trunk of the tree and sitting down.

"Does Evan feel less sad now?" Kuya laid his head on my shoulder. His reddish-brown ears tickled my cheek, but I didn't mind it.

"Yeah. Spending the day with you cheered me up."

"It cheered up Kuya too."

As we enjoyed the shade and the gentle late-spring breeze, I closed my eyes. I thought of Lupin and his traveling Emporium. I was sure he was out there right now, helping someone at the edge of their rope, someone desperate for another life.

Just like he'd helped me.

***

My rumbling belly woke me from the nap I hadn't meant to take beneath the shade of the magnolia blossoms.

"Evan sounds like a monster," Kuya mumbled as the grumble woke him too. He stretched out his arms and yawned, exposing his sharper teeth. "Evan needs food."

As we left the park and veered toward the marketplace—specifically, toward the amazing smells coming *from* the market—I figured we had probably slept for a good hour or more. The sun's position in the sky had changed, though it was difficult to see it through the clouds that had rolled in. Was it supposed to storm?

God, I hoped not.

Beyond the town square, we stopped at a food stand. The old man smiled at Kuya and offered him a sample of meat. That right there was enough to make me want to buy from him—him being nice to Kuya.

"We'll take two servings," I said before paying for our food. The man handed each of us a skewer of herb-crusted chicken. I bit into it and hummed in appreciation as the juices hit my tongue.

As we ate, we journeyed deeper into town. I didn't have much money left but wanted to find a gift for Maddox. I had bought the journal for Briar, which he'd get a lot of use out of, considering all of his research.

What would Maddox like? A dagger? Not sure I had enough to afford one of those.

After eating the last chunk of chicken from the skewer, I pulled the bag from my pocket and dumped the coins into my palm. One silver and two copper. I was still learning the value of the currency, but after doing a bit of calculating and estimating based on my previous purchases, I wagered I probably had the modern-day equivalent of sixteen bucks left, give or take a few dollars. Definitely not enough for a dagger, unless it was super tiny.

"Oh!" Kuya rushed over to one of the booths. He grinned back at me before admiring whatever had snagged his attention. "It's so shiny."

I walked over to see a selection of necklaces, rings, and decorative hair pins. One ring in particular caught my eye. It was the least extravagant of the lot, with a silver flat band and a dark green stone in the center.

"See anything that strikes your fancy?" the woman asked.

"How much is this?" I pointed to it.

"One silver," she said.

"I'll take it." I handed her a coin, and she gave me the ring. The band was big enough to fit one of Maddox's fingers. He didn't really seem like the jewelry type, but something about it made me think he'd like it. Hopefully.

With both of their gifts secured and my belly full, I smiled as we continued down the street.

"Is Evan ready to return home?"

"Not yet. Is it okay if we stay out a bit longer? I want to see more of the kingdom."

"Then Kuya will be your guide."

And what an adorable guide he was. He led me through town, explaining the different establishments and the best places to play and nap. He showed me the school, a brick-type building with a scenic courtyard where kids played. The whole medieval-fantasy atmosphere literally felt like stepping into the pages of one of my favorite books.

More clouds rolled in, blocking more of the sun. The cloud cover was nice at first, but the air soon changed, thickened. Darker clouds approached from the west, quickly filling the sky.

"Rain is coming," Kuya said, studying the sky. "We should go home."

"Good idea," I said, hating the thought of being stuck out in the rain.

But as we changed direction and began making our way back toward the castle, a raindrop hit the top of my head. That one raindrop soon turned into a damn torrential downpour. Kuya was very much like his animal counterpart and scrambled to find somewhere dry. He grabbed my arm and fled from the street and down a narrow dirt path lined with trees.

As we ran, I did my best to cover the bag with my book and Briar's journal. The thick canopy of trees helped protect us from the rain too, thankfully.

A two-story cottage sat up ahead, some of the windows busted and the paint on the door chipping off. No light—or life, for that matter—came from inside. It didn't look like anyone had stepped foot inside in months, maybe years. As the rain came down harder, we sprinted toward it and jiggled the door handle. It was unlocked, so we rushed inside and closed it behind us.

"Kuya doesn't like the rain!" He flung water from his hair, tail flicking in agitation.

"Sorry. If I hadn't wanted to go sightseeing, we would've been home by the time it hit."

"Don't be sorry," he said, batting at his hair again. "Kuya had a nice time in town, and the food was yummy." He wrapped his arms around his torso, shivering a little. "Abandoned little cottage in the woods saved us from the rain. Wonder why it's all alone."

I surveyed the room. Apart from a lone chair and a broken table turned on its side, there was very little furniture. The air was musty, and I sneezed at the dust stirred up by us moving around. The rain didn't sound like it was letting up anytime soon, so I ventured farther into the cottage, passing from one room to another.

Kuya followed behind me and grabbed the back of my shirt as thunder rumbled. Normally, I would've been scared too, but his fear canceled out mine. Funny how things worked out that way sometimes.

"It's okay," I said, putting on a brave face and letting him cling to me. When another boom of thunder hit, so close and loud it rumbled the walls, I squeezed my eyes shut and did my best to calm my racing heart. "We're safe."

To distract my mind, I continued my walkthrough of the cottage. After passing beneath an arched doorway, we came to a bigger room. A bar ran along one wall, and more tables littered the floor, the wood of the legs cracked and some rotting.

"Maybe this used to be a tavern?" I asked, seeing a tankard with a broken handle lying beside one of the overturned tables. "Or some type of restaurant?"

Suddenly, Kuya released my shirt and jogged over to the bar. Exploring had distracted his mind, too, by the look of it. He glided a hand across the top before turning toward a doorway on the left and dashing through it.

"Hidden little room," he said with a hum. "What treasures will Kuya find?"

I heard rustling sounds, like he was digging through something. And then, he stopped.

I waited a few seconds, not hearing anything more. "Kuya?"

"Evan!"

"What's wrong?" I dropped my bag on the floor and rushed over, worry cinching in my chest. Had he hurt himself? Cut himself on a broken board or glass bottle? Rounding the edge of the bar, I ran through the doorway into the other room. I found him standing in the middle of the room and did a quick scan of his body. "Are you hurt?"

He shook his head. "Look what Kuya found!" He bounced over to the counter and hopped on top of it, holding out both arms. "A kitchen for Evan to bake his cakes."

Now that I knew he was okay and the nauseous pit in my stomach had eased, I finally took in the room. There was a large counter and an oval island across from it, two stoves, and a wall of cabinets.

Run-down? Sure. I doubted any of it worked and would need a butt-load of repairs before being of much use.

But the set of wide windows on one wall would let in a flood of natural light during bright sunny days. The oval island was big enough for serving platters filled with desserts, sandwiches, and anything else I wanted to make. I imagined whipping up muffin batter at the counter and popping it into the oven. Imagined the scent of brewing coffee and baked treats filling the air. And with me, the men who owned my heart.

"My café," I whispered, my sternum tightening.

Kuya slipped his arms around my waist and laid his head on my shoulder. "Evan's dream isn't silly."

A bright flash then lit up the room, a loud boom less than a second behind it. Kuya jolted and buried his face against my shirt, little whimpers leaving him. I returned his hold and repeated that everything was okay, that he was safe.

Eventually, the storm passed. The heavy rain transitioned to a light sprinkle before stopping altogether. Rumbles of thunder still echoed in the distance, but the worst was behind us.

As we exited the cottage, I turned back to look at it, longing heavy in my chest. Exploring Bremloc had kept us out later in the day, causing us to be caught in the storm that then forced us to take shelter in the cottage. A cottage with a dining area slash bar, a large kitchen, and several other sitting rooms that were covered in dust now but would be perfect for rows of bookshelves and comfy chairs.

It felt like fate. Like we'd been meant to find it.

The late afternoon had rolled into the evening, leaving the sky dark as we walked back toward town. The clouds blocked the stars, and only a peek of the moon managed to break through them before vanishing once again.

"Um," I said as we reached the end of the path and stepped out into a section of town. Lampposts were lit, allowing light to bleed into the dark night. Not that the light helped me much. Buildings stretched on both sides of us, and the street curved in different directions. Nothing looked familiar. "Do you know where we are?"

Kuya crinkled his nose. "Evan would get lost without Kuya."

"I can't argue with that." So much for my very brief idea to become an adventurer back when I'd visited the market with Maddox and Briar and learned about the guild. I'd get lost just doing something simple like picking flowers from the hillside. With my luck, I'd end up slipping and rolling down said hill too.

"Kuya will show Evan the way." He grabbed my shirt and pulled me with him to the left. I was glad he seemed to be back to his old self again, humming and flicking his tail. I didn't like seeing him scared or upset.

"Evening, gentlemen," a silky, feminine voice called out to us. A woman stood in the front doorway of a building, leaning against the frame. Dark, curly hair spilled over one shoulder. Her corseted gown emphasized her huge boobs, and the slit down the side showed the bare skin of her upper thigh. Well, almost bare. She wore a lacy garter. "In need of some company?"

Oh my fucking god. It was a brothel.

"No, thanks," I quickly said, my face on fire.

She smiled. "You're a virgin? No reason to be shy. My girls will more than take care of you. And with a face like yours, they may even give you a discount."

How was it possible for me to have been fucked to within an inch of my life the morning before—a steamy goodbye before Briar left— taking two dicks at the same time, and still come across as a bashful little virgin? Curse my cute genes and nervousness.

"Evan is no virgin," Kuya told her, ears perked up. "He has two men who give him a lot of loving and even more who wish to do so."

"Kuya," I hissed. And where in the hell had he gotten the notion that more men wanted me? Who?

"Men, you say?" Her smile didn't falter. "This establishment caters to all desires. We have the most beautiful women in Bremloc, as well as the most beautiful men. Come inside and see for yourself."

"Is there cake?" Kuya asked.

I bumped his side, and he returned the gesture.

"Run along home, boys," she said, her seductive smile slipping into something kinder. More genuine. "As for you, my blushing non-virgin, if you really do have two men waiting for you, treat them well, but ensure they treat you just as well. Love is rare in this world. Hold on to it."

She then greeted the three men approaching the door, amping up her seductiveness once again to lure them closer. Not that they needed the extra enticing. One looked ready to blow his load just from getting an eyeful of her boobs—which she ever so skillfully slid her hand across to draw more attention to them.

I had never looked down on sex workers. They did what they had to in order to put food on their table. Some even enjoyed it. And that was okay too. As we continued the journey home, I thought over her advice. Maddox and Briar treated me amazingly. I only hoped they felt just as cherished as I did.

Kuya hopped over a puddle of water, then bounced over to one of the shop windows to peek inside. Just as fast, he dashed away from it and scampered forward, tail whishing. He was full of energy, whereas I felt ready to collapse.

I couldn't wait to crawl into bed. Even better if that bed also held two warm bodies for me to snuggle against and kiss. My heart sank when I remembered Briar wouldn't be back until the following day. Not having him in bed with me and Maddox last night had felt so weird. I'd tossed and turned all night.

Was Briar eating enough? When he got busy with work, he often forgot to eat and take care of himself.

Lost in my thoughts, I hadn't noticed Kuya had stopped walking and slammed right into him.

"Sorry," I said, rubbing at my aching nose. The back of his head was hard as a rock. "Why are you—"

Kuya suddenly grabbed my arm and sprinted forward, dragging me with him as he left the street and cut down an alleyway between two buildings. We ran all the way down it, then turned the corner and ran down another.

"Where are we going?" I asked, my boots skidding against the cobblestone as we ran. "And do we have to run to get there? I don't think I—"

"Shh." Kuya pressed me against the side of a building before going still. His ears twitched as he scanned the shadows.

I tried to quiet my breathing, to no avail. Not that I'd had any doubts, but I was one hundred percent sure I'd never survive in a horror movie. I'd be the person who tripped over their own two feet while being chased, getting stabbed or eaten. Or the one who breathed way too loud while trying to hide from the killer.

My anxiety spiked as seconds ticked by. "What's going on?" I whispered, my heavy breaths making my voice louder than intended.

"Kuya needs Evan to stay quiet." He stared down the alley before looking at me. "We're being followed."

Chapter Sixteen
Stalked and… Kissed?

"Followed?" I asked, panic rising. "By who?"

"If Kuya knew that, Kuya would bite them." He slid his arm through mine and guided us toward the end of the alleyway, his ears twitching every which way. His nostrils wiggled as he sniffed. "Their scent is… familiar somehow."

"One of the knights, maybe?" Hopefully.

I wouldn't put it past them to have followed us on the outing, staying out of sight. Maddox had given Callum orders to watch over me in his absence, but even without those orders, I knew Callum—as well as many of the others—would've done so on their own.

"No." Kuya shook his head. "The scent isn't human. Come."

He dashed from the alley and kept close to the wall of the building, staying in the shadows. I didn't move nearly as stealthily, clutching my shopping bag to my chest to try to prevent it from crinkling too loud.

Good thing he knew which direction to go because I sure as hell didn't. After several heart-pounding minutes of maneuvering down the side streets, I began to recognize some of our surroundings.

The headquarters of the adventurers' guild stood at the corner, light coming from inside. Two women leaned against the outside wall. They wore chest armor and had daggers sheathed in holsters around their thighs.

"Those idiots," one muttered to the other. "They'll never find the shadow realm. It is but a fool's quest. The knights can't even locate it."

"But can you imagine the reward for capturing the demon lord?" the other asked. Her blonde hair was shaved on the sides and pulled back in a braided ponytail. "We'd be set for life, never again having to worry about money."

Some adventurers were going after the demon lord? As in, they had willingly journeyed into the dark wood, where all the demonic beasts and creepy things lived? Fuck that. No amount of money was worth that risk.

Kuya and I passed the guild, the women's voices fading behind us as we headed down another road. In the distance, the castle could be seen atop a hill, the towers stretching toward the night sky.

Almost home.

Were we still being followed? Kuya stayed alert, his rainbow eyes constantly shifting among our surroundings. Thankfully, he didn't make me run the whole way. Once on the main castle road, we slowed our pace. My legs wobbled from exertion, and my throat was dry.

"Give me a sec," I said, stopping in place and resting my hands on my knees, trying to catch my breath. "About to die."

Trees lined one side of the road, the forest beyond them thick. The same forest I'd gotten lost in about two weeks ago. Branches moved as I stared, and leaves rustled. Tingles of fear spread through me, but it could've just been my eyes playing tricks on me.

A dark shape flitted from one tree to another.

Kuya hissed, his ears going back as he bared his teeth. "We need to leave. Now."

Our pursuer had other ideas.

Someone darted from the tree line, moving so fast my mind didn't even have time to process what was happening before they slammed into my chest, knocking the bag from my hand and sending me off-balance. But I didn't fall. Someone had hold of me. And they were carrying me in their arms back toward the forest.

"No!" Kuya exclaimed. Steps sounded from behind me, little, fretful growls mixed in. "Evan!"

Fear had me frozen. I couldn't move or speak. I was being carried off into the woods to be eaten. But just as my anxiety was about to send me into a full-blown panic attack, a scent tickled my nose, like warm earth and spring water.

"Lake?" I rasped, trying to focus on his face.

Purple eyes lowered to mine, softly glowing in the dark. His silver hair rustled with the speed at which we were moving. Bushes and tree trunks blurred as we passed them. He didn't say anything. He only cupped the back of my head and held me closer, protecting me from any outstretched branches or vines.

Kuya's calls grew distant. Not even he was quick enough to keep up with the wolf.

Questions swam through my head. Why had Lake captured me? And why was he so close to town to begin with? Humans made him uneasy.

"You need to put me down." The shaking of my voice made the demand sound feeble. "Please, Lake."

He stopped running but didn't release me. His gaze darted around us before settling on my face. The moon cut through the overhead clouds and filtered through the branches, the beams shining on his pale skin and silver hair.

"Can you put me down?"

His hold tightened on me instead, and the softest of whimpers climbed up his throat.

"Lake?"

"I…" Gently, he placed me on the ground feet-first but didn't fully let go. Worry wound through his eyes, visible even in the moonlit forest. "I don't know why I…" He then jerked away, that worry twisting into fright. "I'm sorry, Evan. I'm not sure what came over me."

"Hey, it's okay." I stepped forward and came to a sudden stop as the movement startled him. "I'm not mad. Just, um, confused."

"I'm confused as well," he said, voice taut. His tall ears slumped a bit, and his poofy tail lowered. "Since you left, I've been… lonely."

Like the little red fox from his storybook. Misunderstood and craving companionship. Lake stood at over six feet and had broad shoulders and a muscled, athletic build. His eyes held a quiet intensity. At first glance, he could be intimidating. But deep down, I knew he had a gentle heart.

"I busied myself with gardening," he continued. "I read books, whittled, painted, and crafted a new chair and table for the back patio. But nothing I did helped. I was restless and couldn't get you off my mind."

"So you came to see me?"

"Yes." Lake slowly stepped back. "I didn't mean to frighten you. I followed you and the cat for a while. Before I knew it, I was snatching you from the road and carrying you here."

"Not to eat me, I hope," I teased, trying to lighten the mood.

It worked. A ghost of a smile landed on his lips. "Never to eat you."

"I'm sorry, too, by the way."

"What for?" His ears perked back up, and god, it was cute.

"For what happened the morning after I stayed with you. I never got the chance to apologize." Guilt pressed down on me. "The knights thought you were holding me hostage and were in full-on defense mode. You didn't deserve it."

"Didn't I?" Lake asked softly. "I was mean to you when we first met. Or have you forgotten my threat to kill you?"

"You weren't serious. You were just trying to scare me off. But unfortunately for you, facing the dark forest was way scarier than being around you, so you got stuck with me anyway."

"How unfortunate, indeed," he said with a small smile. "You came into my quiet, bleak world and showed me how colorful life can be. Now I can't forget it. Or you."

Flutters danced along my heartstrings.

"I'm sure your friend will alert the others, and they'll come for you soon." Lake swept his gaze around us. "I should leave."

"Wait." I shuffled forward and felt a jolt of satisfaction when he didn't react. He let me approach him. I had no idea what to say. Stopping him had been impulsive. I just hated the thought of him returning to an empty house. "Come back with me."

"I can't," he said with a firm shake of his head. "I'm... not good around other people. I don't trust humans."

"I'm human, and you still came all the way here to see *me*."

Lake gripped his opposite bicep, taking an awkward stance. "You're different."

A skittering of leaves sounded behind him as something quickly approached. I caught a glimpse of reddish-brown hair and a long tail before arms came around Lake's neck and legs around his torso.

"Kuya will save Evan!" He started nipping at Lake's throat. "Kuya kill."

Kill Lake with cuteness, maybe.

Lake could've easily thrown Kuya off him. I'd witnessed how quickly he could move. And with his muscles, he had strength on top of that stealth and swiftness. But he allowed Kuya to gnaw at his neck, not even lifting his arms to try to stop him when a bead of blood trickled down.

"It's okay!" I rushed forward, closing the small space between us. "No killing for Kuya. Stop biting him. Lake is my friend."

"*Kuya* is Evan's friend." He lifted his head. "Lake is a bad wolf who stole Evan away."

At the word "bad," Lake's ears drooped.

"He's not bad," I said, my heart constricting. Surprise flashed across Lake's face as he looked at me. "He just wanted to talk to me."

"Okay, he can live for now." Kuya hopped down from Lake's back and stepped around him, grabbing me. He hid his face against my shoulder. "Kuya was so scared."

"I'm sorry for scaring you," Lake told him. He slowly wiped at his neck, then glanced at the small streaks of blood on his fingers. "I should head home."

"There's a festival soon," I blurted out. "Food, music, and games to celebrate the beginning of summer. This will be my first year going, but I heard it's fun. You should come."

"The Festival of Lights," Lake said with a bit of wistfulness. "Each year, I see the lanterns as they float up to the sky but never dared venture closer. I've always thought they were beautiful."

"I'm excited to see them for the first time. We can experience it together."

"I can't. The humans will take one look at me and…" He shook his head. "It wouldn't be wise for me to attend."

Kuya nuzzled me once before hopping over to a hollowed-out log jutting from the grass. He dropped down and tried to look beneath it. What a brave soul. I would've bet my left nut a snake was under there, just waiting to strike. He sneezed at something before crawling inside the log.

"He's going to get bit," I said with a sigh. "And then Sawyer will have my head."

Lake offered me a thin smile. "I assure you he's the deadliest thing over there. His teeth are like tiny needles." He rubbed at his neck again.

"Sorry about that. Does it hurt too bad? I can grab a healing tonic from the clinic and bring it back to you."

"I'm fine," Lake said. "Demi-humans heal faster."

"Really? Wow. That's cool." There was still so much about this world I didn't know—about the customs, forms of magic, and the different beings who inhabited the land.

"It's late," he then said. "Your men will be worried about you."

Briar was still at the academy and didn't know I wasn't in bed, safe and sound. But Maddox? If he had returned from his mission to find me gone, he'd send a search party soon. If he hadn't already.

"We should hang out again soon," I said.

"Hang out?"

"Visit with each other," I clarified, then grinned. "But maybe don't abduct me next time. I almost pissed my pants."

"Understood." Lake exhaled through his nostrils and lifted a hand to the back of his hair, scratching. He looked so awkward and shy. "I suppose this is farewell, then. For now."

"Yeah." Neither of us moved. "Oh!" I looked over at the log. "Kuya, did you bring my bag by chance?"

"Evan's bag of presents," came his reply, his voice echoing a bit in the hollow wood. "Kuya dropped it in the grass before pouncing on Lake."

"Wait just a second," I told Lake before going over and searching the ground for the bag. Finding it, I rifled through it for the book I bought and opened to the first page where I'd placed a bookmark. I then jogged back over to him. "Here."

Carefully, he grabbed it, head tilting. "A strip of leather?"

"A bookmark. It has a wolf on it. See?" I pointed to the etching. "I bought it earlier. But I want you to have it."

"Why?"

"You like to read," I said, recalling all of his books. "So now when you sit down with a book, you'll have this, and maybe you'll think of me and won't feel so alone." I cringed. "Okay. Saying that out loud sounds cheesy. You don't have to keep it. I—"

"No," Lake softly interjected, clutching the bookmark to his chest. "I'll treasure it. Thank you."

"You're welcome." Thank god it was dark because my face got hot. Lake called to a part of me, like he'd already wormed his way into my chest. Not as deeply as the two men I loved but deep enough that I was sad at having to say goodbye to him.

"Blushing beneath the moonlight," Lake whispered, closing the gap between our bodies with one step forward. Hesitantly, he reached for my cheek and grazed his fingertips across my heated skin. "You're so beautiful you make my chest ache."

He thought I was beautiful?

Lake dipped his head and leaned in, slow and unsure. His breath fanned against my lips. My scalp and the tips of my ears tingled as a weightlessness came over me, like I was being drawn into his gravitational orbit.

And then, Lake kissed me.

My brain stopped working as our lips met; the gears jammed, and the machine malfunctioned. The heat from my cheeks radiated to my chest and shot outward, sizzling as it blazed through my veins. One pressing of his mouth on mine was all it had taken to ignite a powerful force in my core, an intensity I knew couldn't be bottled back up.

Several guys had kissed me in my life, but only three of them had ever made me feel like this. Briar, Maddox, and now… him.

I hadn't even kissed him back yet. I was too stunned and confused. Through the confusion and jammed clogs in my brain, a bit of sense returned.

"W-Wait," I stammered, drawing back from his lips. I slapped a shaking hand over my mouth. "I can't do this."

Lake touched his lips, the shock I felt washing across his face too. "I've never done that before. I… I'm sorry. I shouldn't have…"

Then, he took off running toward the shadows, dashing between the trees.

"Lake!" I started to go after him, but of course, my boot caught between two rocks, and I stumbled forward, catching myself on my hands and knees. Rocks and fallen thorns dug into my palms and pierced through the material of my pants, and my ankle twisted at an odd angle.

I was too focused on finding Lake to register any pain. But he was gone, already out of sight. No sound reached my ears.

Kuya rushed over and dropped down beside me, alarm in his eyes as they roamed over me. He whimpered and grabbed my hands. "Evan's bleeding."

"I'm okay." I winced at the sharp sting. Well, so much for not registering the pain. I definitely felt it now. "My gracefulness holds no equal."

"Kuya will take Evan home." He helped me to my feet.

He allowed me to lean on him as we started a slow walk out of the forest and back toward the main road. When I put weight on my ankle a while later, it didn't hurt nearly as much. That's where the good news ended.

The beating of hooves against the lane came from ahead of us before men appeared on horseback. They had just left the castle gates.

"Oh no," I mumbled, recognizing the one in front riding the black stallion. "I'm a dead Evan walking."

"Kuya is dead too," he said as a white horse galloped forward. The blond-haired man atop it was unmistakable. "So, so dead."

"Kuya!" Prince Sawyer pulled on the reins to halt the horse and dismounted. As he rushed toward us, his personal knight, Noah, followed close behind. Sawyer pulled Kuya into his arms. "Thank the gods you're safe."

It seemed my men weren't the only ones who overreacted. Then again, neither of us had told anyone about our day out, and we'd been gone all afternoon and late into the evening.

My gaze shifted to Maddox. A very grumpy Maddox, who, if looks could kill, would have me rotating on a spit over a fire and then serve me on a silver platter as the main course, a muffin in my mouth instead of an apple.

I'm so dead.

Chapter Seventeen
Cuteness is the Ultimate Power
(I Hope)

Maddox hopped off his horse and strode toward me, his expression hard.

"Hey, handsome," I said, going for cute and flirty. It had worked in the past. "Damn, look at you. Dressed in all black and looking like a snack."

"Why is it every time you venture off on your own, you return to me injured?" he growled, giving me the up-down. His voice was just as hard as his expression, but beneath the growly irritation, I heard the worry he couldn't fully hide. Saw it in his eyes, too, as they fell to my hurt ankle. "You're limping."

"It's nothing. I'm fi—"

Maddox pulled me into a crushing hug. That's when I felt the ever-so-subtle tremble in his large body. "You worried me. Coming home and not knowing where you were?" He pressed kisses into my hair as another quake went through him. "If anything happened to you…"

"I promise I'm okay," I managed to say through the lump in my throat. "I didn't mean to worry you. Kuya and I had some free time and thought it would be fun to visit the market. Then we got caught in the storm and found a place to lay low until it passed."

His arms tightened around me. "Were you scared during the storm?"

"Are you kidding? I'm Evan, Prince of Thorns and Lord of the Muffins. Storms don't scare me one bit."

"That's my boy," Duke said from atop his horse.

"Your boy?" Callum retorted. "Say that again and you may find your throat slit."

"The captain wouldn't dare." Duke winked at Maddox. "He'd miss me too much."

Maddox gave a slight shake of his head before examining me, his eyes gleaming with that same worry from earlier. "How did you hurt yourself? Or did someone else hurt you? Tell me their name, and I'll hunt them down."

"I fell," I said, expelling a nervous laugh—that most definitely amped up his suspicion.

"You falling? I can believe." He grabbed my chin and forced my face up. "But there's something you're hiding behind those green eyes."

I didn't want to mention Lake in front of everyone. Certainly didn't want anyone else to hear that he'd snatched me and carried me into the woods. And kissed me—which I fully intended to disclose to Maddox and Briar. Honesty was the key to a healthy relationship. Plus, the guilt would eat me alive otherwise.

But for now?

I snuggled into Maddox's chest, my stomach fluttering at his familiar scent. "I'll tell you everything once we get home."

"I'll hold you to that." Maddox placed me on his stallion and swung up into the saddle behind me, arms coming around me to grab the reins.

"Evan, your presents!" Kuya was on the back of Sawyer's horse and held up my bag.

"Presents?" Maddox asked me.

"For you and Briar."

A soft smile crossed his face before he moved the horse in that direction, coming up beside Prince Sawyer's white steed. Kuya handed over the bag, and I thanked him as I brought it to my chest.

Maddox allowed Prince Sawyer and Sir Noah to lead the way before guiding the horse toward the castle gates. Callum, Duke, and Baden followed behind us.

"Where's Quincy?" I asked.

Baden snorted. "In the medical ward. The fool got hit with an arrow."

"What? Is he okay?"

"Yes," Duke answered, mirroring Baden's amusement. "Though, I'm not sure the same can be said for his pride."

I blinked.

"The arrow caught him in the backside," Callum explained. "He was getting on his horse when it struck the left side of his rear."

"The padding saved him." Baden coughed to cover a laugh. "Your cooking is more than likely to thank for that. It's all of those extra helpings."

"Poor Quincy," I said. "I'm glad it wasn't too serious. But who attacked you?"

"We had a run-in with a group of bandits on our way back to Bremloc," Maddox answered. "They had an archer hiding in the trees along the king's road who managed to let loose an arrow before I took her down."

"I'm sorry." Shame flared in my belly. "The last thing you need after returning from a dangerous mission is to come after me. Again."

Would I always be so useless? All I did was cause trouble and worry everyone around me. The backs of my eyes burned.

"Don't be sorry," Maddox murmured in my ear, one arm tightening around my waist. "You leaving the castle grounds shouldn't worry me as much as it does. Gathering a search party was perhaps a bit of an overreaction on my part. I'm not too proud to admit I can be stubborn and overprotective."

"With good reason, apparently. Look at me. I can't even have a nice day out with a friend without finding something to trip over. More times than not, it's my own feet."

"And what precious feet they are."

"Do you have a foot fetish, sir knight?" I angled my head to look back at him. "If you ask nicely, I'll let you kiss them."

He laughed. "I'll leave the foot kissing to the other male who shares our bed."

The mention of Briar caused warmth to swarm my chest. Made it ache some too. "I hope he's doing okay."

"You miss him?"

More burning in my eyes. I nodded.

Maddox nuzzled my ear. "Me too."

I smiled at that. As the knights' quarters came into view, I expected him to veer toward the stable. He kept to the narrow path instead, the stallion's hooves clacking against the stone.

"I'm taking you to the clinic," Maddox said, picking up on my confusion. He had learned to read me so well.

"Why? I said I'm fine."

"Because I said so."

As we arrived at the clinic, Maddox dismounted first before lifting me off the horse. He didn't allow me to walk even a step. My ankle was semi back to normal, but I knew better than to argue with him. The front door opened before we reached it, and my heart nearly burst at seeing the man on the other side.

"Briar!" I wiggled against Maddox in my excitement. "I didn't think you'd be home until tomorrow."

"Gods, the joy on your face right now made the long day of travel worth every second," Briar said. "I finished business sooner than expected and left right away." His smile fell as he took in the sight of me. Maddox stopped in front of him, and he did a quick examination of my palms. "Blood and dirt on your hands and knees. Come in. Let me have a better look at you."

"He sprained his ankle too."

"I did not." I rolled my eyes. "My ankle is fine."

"I'll take a look anyway," Briar said.

Maddox carried me over to the comfy chair by the fireplace before kneeling in front of me and untying my boots. He didn't seem surprised at all by Briar's presence, which told me he'd known our physician had come home early. So much for missing him as he'd claimed. The sneaky knight.

As he carefully removed my boots, I brushed my fingers over the top of his black hair, earning me one of his rare, soft smiles.

Briar knelt beside Maddox and gently inspected my ankle, the coolness of his fingertips nice against my skin. "Not a sprain. No swelling either. Good."

"Told you."

"I'll whip up something for those cuts." Briar kissed my knee before rising from the floor and walking over to his workstation.

Thane walked through the door from the medical wing, a bundle of sheets in his arms. One look at me and the smooth line of his brow crinkled with worry. "Evan? Are you hurt?"

"Nah, I'm okay. These two are just worrywarts. How's Quincy?"

"Better," Thane answered. "I gave him a healing tonic, and he's sleeping now."

"Thank you for caring for him," Maddox said.

The apprentice grew shy. "You're welcome." He then rushed from the room. Poor guy. The captain's dark blue eyes, and the intensity often found in them, had the power to turn all of us to mush. Or stone, depending on Maddox's mood at the time.

370

Briar returned with a wooden bowl filled with something green and paste-like. "Quincy will be well enough to leave in the morning and return to his duties."

Maddox's face softened just a tad. "You have my thanks as well."

"It's my pleasure." Briar's expression was a bit softer now too.

"Are you putting that goo on me?" I asked. "Will it hurt?"

"Goo?" Briar snorted. "You never fail to amuse me, love. No, it won't hurt at all. It will soothe the ache." He rolled up my pants legs and applied it to my scraped knees.

My skin tingled, and the slight sting of them faded. "Magical goo, I thank you for your service."

"The herb used for the salve is found on the outskirts of Bremloc," Briar said. "With the right dose of magical energy, it's highly effective for treating skin irritations of any kind, as well as healing minor nicks and scratches."

"Don't the healing tonics help with that too?"

"They do." He grabbed my hands and turned them palm up before applying the salve to the scrapes there too. "But it's always wise to know several methods, for you never know when one will be unavailable to you."

"How was the trip to the academy?" I asked. "Did the students fawn over you and your amazing good looks?"

Briar pushed his glasses back with one finger, a shyness coming over him. "The students were eager to learn from me, yes, but my appearance had nothing to do with it. They were awed by my title."

"Yes, your title as the chief physician helped with their eagerness, I'm sure," Maddox said. "You hold the highest position in the kingdom for those in the healing arts. Yet it's your endless hard work and dedication to Bremloc that I find most admirable."

"You flatter me, knight."

Maddox huffed and turned his face away. "I flatter no one. I merely speak the truth."

They had grown closer during our time together, and I couldn't have been happier. I only hoped what I was about to say wouldn't pop that balloon of warm fuzzy happiness.

"So, um." I rested my hands on the arms of the chair and tapped my index finger against it. "I have a confession. I didn't fall on the main road coming back from town. I…uh, fell in the forest."

"What were you doing in the forest?" Maddox asked with a tic in his jaw.

I imagined a huge pin nearing the balloon, the sharp point gleaming. His sharp jawline could pop it too. *Okay, stop drooling over him and just spit it out.*

"Well, you see… I might've been snatched from the road and carried to the forest."

"You were abducted?" Briar asked, his hard expression matching Maddox's. And here I thought he'd be the more understanding of the two. But I guess when it came to me, both of them had the potential for sweet murder.

"Yes and no," I answered. "Lake took me."

"The wolf?" Maddox asked. "Did he hurt you? I swear to the gods I will drag him from his cottage and rip off his arms."

"Easy, killer," I said. "He only wanted to talk. He was lonely." I brought my hands together on my lap and picked at my nail. "We talked for a few minutes, and I said he should come to the festival in a few days. He didn't think that'd be a good idea. Kuya then pounced on him and tried to chomp him to death."

"I knew I liked that cat," Briar said.

Maddox nodded.

"*Anyway*." I cleared my throat, heat spreading up my neck and to the top of my scalp. "After we said goodbye, he sort of... kissed me."

"What?" they exclaimed simultaneously, their expressions and voices scarily similar.

"For full transparency, you should know I didn't kiss him back, but I also didn't pull away. Not at first." My face burned hot. "Once I came to my senses, I broke the kiss and told him we couldn't do that. That's when Lake said he was sorry and ran away. I tried to run after him, and, well..." I motioned to my ankle and scrapes—that had healed now because of the magical green goo. "Here we are now."

"I see." Briar gave a slow nod. "It seems you've collected another."

"Another what?" I asked.

"Another poor soul who's fallen under your spell." Maddox grabbed my left hand, and when I chanced a peek at him, the worried tangles in the pit of my stomach unwound. He was smiling. "For full transparency, *you* should know I didn't need to ask the other knights if they'd help search for you tonight. They learned you weren't on the castle grounds and worried nearly as much as I did. You have all of us wrapped around your precious little finger." He lifted my hand to his lips and kissed each of my fingertips. "And we would lay down our lives to protect yours."

"I don't want you to though." Tightness compressed my chest cavity, pressing against my heart. "I don't want any of you getting hurt because of me. Ever."

"That's not up to you." Briar took my other hand, his soulful eyes a warmer hazel than usual, like sunlight bouncing off soft green leaves and sinking into tree bark. "You mean the world to me, Evan."

"To us," Maddox added.

Briar offered him a small smile.

"So you're not mad at me?" I asked. "Even though I kind of, sort of kissed someone else?"

"No," Maddox answered. "I suspected the wolf cared for you the morning I met him. The way he looked at you as I took you away is burned into my memory. I felt his desperation."

"As did I." Briar kissed my middle knuckle. "I believe we'll see him again."

"What makes you so sure?"

"Because of you." Briar poked my nose, and I wiggled it, causing him to smile. "Wolves have long memories and form deep bonds. Bonds not easily broken. Him coming for you tonight is proof he's already bound himself to you. He may not even realize it yet."

"Excellent," Maddox muttered. "If the wolf does come back around, I refuse to share my bed with him. He can sleep on the rug like a good pup."

The casual way they spoke of potentially sharing me with yet another male left me dumbfounded. But then I recalled what Lupin said about me having multiple lovers while in Bremloc. Maybe the strings of fate not only attached me to them but bound them to each other too.

Only time would tell.

"What's in the bag?" Briar asked, glancing at it beside my chair.

"Oh. That." I grabbed it off the floor. "When Kuya and I were in town today, I kind of got you two something." I felt nervous now. What if they hated the gifts? "Don't get too excited or expect much. It's nothing big."

"If it's from you, I already adore it," Briar said.

"Open the bag," Maddox said, cheek twitching as I narrowed my eyes at him. "Please, oh Muffin Lord."

Grinning, I pulled out the book. "That's for me, but you can read it too, Briar. It's the newest release in the series you let me borrow."

"Excellent." Briar smiled as he looked it over. "One of the few fiction series I enjoy."

Maddox eyed the book before returning his gaze to the bag. He reminded me of a little kid waiting for their turn to open a present on Christmas morning. Told to be patient, or they wouldn't get anything. It was a level of cuteness I hadn't expected.

So, of course, I made him wait a bit longer.

"I got this for you." I handed the journal to Briar. "I thought you could use it for jotting down research notes or making ingredient lists for potions and spells."

With a tender smile on his handsome face, Briar rubbed the top of the journal before flipping through it. He then sat up more and grabbed me by the nape, bringing our lips together for a short but sweet kiss. "It's the perfect gift. I'll think of you each time I write in it. Thanks, love."

"You're welcome." I kissed him once more. He smiled again. Maybe he hadn't stopped. I knew I hadn't. Having both of them with me felt too amazing.

"Do I get one too?" Maddox asked, his deep blue eyes on the journal before returning to me.

"Nope." I reached into the bag and grabbed the ring. The merchant had wrapped it in a silky cloth, so when I withdrew it, he cocked his head. "Close your eyes."

He snarled his upper lip. "I'm not a child."

"I guess you won't be getting this awesome gift, then." I closed it in my fist.

After shooting me a glare that lacked any actual annoyance, Maddox shut his eyes.

"Hold out your hand."

The edge of his mouth hitched up, and he obeyed, lifting his left hand.

I placed the cloth on his palm. "Okay. You can look now."

Maddox opened his eyes and observed the small bundle. "The muffin lord has given the knight a lucky favor in the form of a handkerchief."

I laughed. "*Open* it."

He unraveled the corners and pulled away the cloth to reveal the ring. His brow dipped in the center as he grabbed the silver band and examined it closer. He was quiet.

"Um." I fidgeted in my chair as his silence drew on. "I wasn't sure if you liked jewelry, but... I mean, it's okay if you don't wanna wear it. It may be difficult to wield a sword while wearing a ring anyway. I probably should've gotten you a necklace instead or saved enough money to get you something useful, like a dagger or—"

"Evan?"

During my nervous ramble, I had lowered my gaze to my lap. When I looked back at him, the softness in his eyes cushioned the aching places in my chest.

"The stone matches your eyes," Maddox whispered, grazing the pad of his thumb over it. He then rose from the floor and took me in his arms, dropping his face to my neck. "I'll wear it with pride. And every time I see it, no matter how far apart we are, I'll feel like I'm home."

"That's not fair," I said, voice shaking. "You're not allowed to make me cry."

He exhaled a rough laugh before kissing my collarbone. "Let's get you to bed."

"I'm not tired yet," I mumbled into his dark hair.

"Good, because I have no intention of letting you sleep anytime soon." Maddox drew back from my neck and smirked over at Briar before aiming that heart-stopping look at me. "We need to give our physician a proper welcome home."

My insufferable—and insatiable—captain then threw me over his shoulder and stepped into the medical ward. Quincy lay in the first cot, on his side to not put pressure on his wounded ass cheek, and snored. Briar quickly checked on the sleeping knight before continuing behind us.

Once upstairs, the "proper welcome home" consisted of stripping me down and tossing me around like a rag doll, kissing, licking, and nibbling every inch of me. It felt more like *my* welcome home than Briar's. The two of them worshiped my body in ways they hadn't before, their mouths, tongues, and hands roaming, stimulating all my sensitive spots.

They took their time, neither rushing as they prepared me for the toe-curling pounding they had planned for me. Once I was ready, Maddox slid between my legs and took me first, bracing himself on the wall behind my head as he railed me into oblivion.

"Don't stop," Briar said, caressing Maddox's muscled bicep as he watched him fuck me. "I wish to hear more of his moans."

He certainly got his wish. Maddox angled his hips and plunged deeper, issuing from me a chorus of breathy moans I couldn't hold back even if I'd wanted to.

"So beautiful." Briar kissed my jaw and combed his fingers through my hair. I reached over and took hold of his cock, stroking him as Maddox rocked into me. He softly groaned and rested our heads together.

Maddox slipped one arm behind me and leaned forward. His lips grazed mine before landing a kiss. He then moved from my mouth to Briar's, kissing him too.

In a few days, the Festival of Lights would mark the beginning of summer. But for me?

It would mark the official start of an amazing life with the men I loved.

***

"I know it's not much to look at right now, but with a touch of love, it can be something special."

Maddox and Briar swept their gazes around the cottage Kuya and I had taken shelter in during the storm the previous day. I had told them about it that morning—as well as my dream of opening a café—and they'd wanted to see it for themselves. In the light of day, with a clear blue sky bringing warmth and sunlight into the dusty confines of the run-down kitchen, the charm was even more apparent. I saw all the possibilities.

"You'd serve coffee here?" Briar asked, touching the counter before brushing the dust off on his pants. He continued studying the room.

"Yep." I was about to burst with nervous energy. Talking about my dream made me feel so exposed. Vulnerable. "Coffee, as well as baked goods and some savory things too, like sandwiches and soups."

"Similar to a tavern, then," Maddox said. "But instead of an establishment to drink and be rowdy, it would be one to unwind and relax."

"Exactly." I smiled so big my cheeks ached.

The more I thought about it, the more it made sense. Bremloc had a few restaurants, a bakery, and taverns but no cafés. There wasn't a single place in the kingdom where you could walk in, order a coffee, and sit and enjoy it with a pastry. In fact, coffee wasn't served anywhere at all. Commoners brewed a sludge-like concoction that could hardly be called coffee. Only nobles could afford quality beans, and even they had to have someone make it for them—because lord forbid they lift a finger to make it themselves.

"Everyone would be welcome in my café," I said, excitement building. "Quality food and drink at an affordable price. I mean, that's the goal, at least. I'd need to research where to obtain my ingredients and all of that stuff, maybe even grow my own crops. I also need to actually, you know, get permission. Probably need to get a business license, too, and fill out a ton of paperwork to buy this place and fix it up. But all of that aside—" I chewed my bottom lip. "—what do you think?"

"That was a lot of words," Maddox said, amused.

"Sorry. It's probably a silly idea. I don't have money to purchase the building and no plan on how to go about starting a business here. I just…" My throat got tight. "Never mind. I'm sorry I dragged you guys all the way here for nothing."

Briar and Maddox exchanged a look before both stepped toward me, one on each side.

"It's not silly." Briar rubbed the small of my back. "I think it's a wonderful idea."

"If this is what you want, we'll help you make it a reality." Maddox slid his arm around my waist. His fingers grazed Briar's hip. "We support you."

"Stop it." I turned my face into his chest. "You're making my eyes leak again, damn you."

Briar softly laughed and held me closer. "You and Prince Sawyer have become friends. I'm sure you can speak with him about your café, and he'll tell you what you'd need to do. One step at a time."

"Maybe you could bake some things too," I told him, switching from Maddox's chest to his. God, I loved them both so much. When they held me in their arms, I felt like nothing could hurt me. "That fig bread would be a best seller. The lemon blueberry too."

Briar smiled into my hair. "Perhaps. But the first slice would always go to you, love."

"The knights would enjoy coming here," Maddox said, his hand finding mine. My heart thumped harder when I felt the band of his ring. "A place for us to relax after a long day. They'd be all too eager to devour your cooking too."

"You'd need to ban Sir Callum." Briar chuckled. "He would eat you out of house and home."

"Quincy too," Maddox said. "All of them, really. Perhaps none of them should be allowed a foot inside the door."

I relaxed more against them, my heart swelling. "Speaking of home, the cottage has a second story. If I'm able to buy this place, I thought I could move here, too, and live upstairs."

"You'd move from the castle grounds?" Maddox asked. "Why? You don't need to. You fit perfectly in my bed."

"As much as I love hopping between your beds, I can't do that forever," I responded. "And my room at the castle is only temporary." A room I hadn't used in about two weeks because of said bed hopping. "I need to lay down roots in Bremloc and build a real life here, and this is a way for me to do it."

"I'll miss you being so close, but I understand," Briar said. "My one condition is you having a big bed for me and the captain when we visit."

"Of course." I grinned.

"You wish to lay down roots here." Maddox pressed his face into my hair. "Does that mean you're no longer interested in traveling the world, my muffin lord?"

"I don't need to travel anywhere else," I said, the truth settling over my heart. "I'm right where I want to be."

With them.

In this kingdom that was better than anything I had ever dreamed.

Chapter Eighteen
The Festival of Lights

The first day of summer was perfect, not too hot or humid, just blue skies, a warm breeze, and excitement buzzing in the air as the citizens of Bremloc gathered for the festival.

More merchants had set up booths and tents in the market, some selling trinkets and others a variety of food. My mouth watered as we walked down the lane.

"Uh-oh," Maddox said from my right. "I know that look well. We must feed him before he starts to whine."

"We wouldn't want that," Briar responded, walking to my left. He stopped at one of the food stalls and purchased three servings of pork meatballs with a sticky glaze over them. He handed one to Maddox, who thanked him, and instead of handing one to me, he held it to my lips. "Fancy a bite?"

I took a little nibble and groaned. The sticky glaze on the pork was mildly sweet but smokey too. Similar to the barbeque from my old world. Not that I could tell them that. They still didn't know I had been isekai'd to their kingdom.

I planned to tell them someday. When the time was right.

"He can feed himself, physician," Maddox said with a snarl on his lips but no bite in his tone.

"Are you jealous?" Briar smirked. "I can feed you too, Captain. You only need to ask."

Maddox glowered at him before shoving an entire meatball into his mouth and looking away. His other hand rested on my side, and it thrilled me that he felt comfortable enough to touch me in public. Briar was the same. He leaned in and wiped sauce from the corner of my lip before softly kissing me.

"Delicious," Briar murmured against my lips before kissing them again.

Maddox then grabbed my jaw, angled my face the way he wanted it, and kissed me. "Very delicious."

The two of them would be the death of me someday. They did crazy things to my heart.

People in Bremloc didn't even bat an eye seeing us hold hands and kiss. Heterosexuality wasn't the standard here. As we walked, I noticed a few other same-sex couples.

Two women sat beside the large fountain in the square, feeding each other pieces of candy before one kissed the other.

A man waited beside a lamppost, dressed in a nicely tailored suit and holding blue flowers. Another man then approached, slightly younger in appearance and wearing a knight's uniform. The patch on his shoulder told me he was from the Third Order. The dashing gentleman beamed with a smile before pulling the knight into his arms. The two held each other like that for so long I suspected it had been a while since they'd been able to do so.

"Evan?" Briar asked. "What's the matter?"

Maddox looked at me, frowning.

"Nothing," I responded.

"The shakiness in your voice isn't very convincing," Maddox said.

"I promise nothing's wrong." I linked mine and Maddox's fingers before reaching for Briar's hand. "I'm just happy. You're both so busy but made time to spend the day with me."

"I'll always make time for you." Briar brought our joined hands up and kissed my knuckle.

"As will I." Maddox tugged me closer and, after tossing a look at Briar, kissed me on the lips. One-upping him.

Briar rolled his eyes.

"Who's the jealous one now, physician?"

"I liked you better when you glared at everyone and didn't speak much," Briar countered. But I caught the curve of his mouth before he looked in the other direction.

"Step right up, ladies and gents!" an exuberant voice called out. A man in a flashy red-and-gold costume stood on a small wooden stage that had been set up at the edge of the square. "For what you are about to see is an extraordinary feat of courage!"

Entertainers had traveled to the kingdom for the festival as well. Among the merchant booths, there were a few tents where patrons could play games to win prizes, like hitting a metal plate with a rounded hammer in a test of strength or guessing the location of a hidden gem in a sleight-of-hand trick.

"A feat of courage?" Maddox stared at the stage.

"Do you wanna watch?" I asked.

"No. I'm sure it's uninteresting." Maddox cleared his throat and looked toward the other side of the square. "Where do you want to go next?"

Briar and I looked at each other before each grabbing one of Maddox's arms and walking over to the stage. It was clear our captain wanted to watch the show; he just tried to hide that interest. As we stood in the crowd near the front of the stage, he watched with fascination as a man with a bushy beard and bald head lifted a massive ball of iron above his head.

A woman then came out and withdrew three long daggers. She threw them into a wooden target to emphasize how sharp they were before lighting them on fire. As she tossed them in the air and juggled, a younger guy stepped out from backstage and lit the blade of a fourth dagger. And then, he threw it at her head.

A gasp went through the crowd as the woman caught the dagger inches from her face. Cheers erupted as she started to juggle it too.

Maddox couldn't take his eyes off the stage... and I couldn't take my eyes off him. He appeared so much younger as he allowed himself a moment to enjoy the show. The hard lines of his face smoothed and a spark of wonder shone in his deep blue eyes. Afterward, he tossed a few coins into the hat the performers passed around.

"My favorite part was the knife juggler," I said, holding his arm. "She was badass."

"Badass?" Briar asked from my other side. "Another of your strange words."

"Thank you both," Maddox softly said, his gaze on the ground. "I enjoyed the performance."

"I knew you would," Briar said. "Stubborn captain." Warmth filled his voice though. A warmth that reflected in the small smile Maddox gave him in response.

I pressed closer, resting my cheek on Maddox's bicep. He smoothed his hand down the back of my hair while Briar threaded our fingers together.

We continued through the market, stopping every so often to browse a booth or watch a street performer. Bards strummed lutes and sang about distant lands and the beautiful women they had to leave behind. Others sang of adventure.

"Kuya likes this song!"

I snapped my head in the direction the voice had come from, a smile instantly blooming across my face. Through the crowd, I spotted a familiar pair of reddish-brown cat ears and a swishing tail. Prince Sawyer walked by Kuya's side, with Sir Noah and three guards keeping a close distance behind them.

Maddox steered us that way and bowed his head once we reached them. "Prince Sawyer."

"Captain Maddox," Sawyer greeted him, then nodded to Briar. His green eyes then fell to me, a smile not far behind. "It's good to see you again, my friend."

"You too." I tipped my head to him.

"Evan!" Kuya lunged forward, arms coming around my torso. Purrs rumbled in his throat as he nuzzled my shoulder. "Kuya missed you."

"I missed you too," I said, although it had only been two days since I'd last seen him. I had met with him and Sawyer again for lunch in the palace garden, where I'd also mentioned my interest in the abandoned cottage. The prince had seemed excited by the thought of the café and said he'd speak to his father about it on my behalf.

Kuya pulled away and scampered back to Sawyer's side. Sir Noah glanced at him, expression serious apart from the slight twitching of his lips. The adorable cat boy charmed everyone.

Well, almost everyone.

"Make way!" a man roared above the noise, and the crowd of people moved aside.

Prince Cedric strolled down the lane with a force of guards at his back. I counted six of them, but more probably followed from a distance. "Baby brother," he said once at Sawyer's side. His gaze then moved along the rest of us.

"Your Highness." Briar bowed his head. His tone was polite but lacked his usual warmth.

Maddox didn't speak, but he bowed as well.

Cedric, however, was too intently focused on me to pay them any mind. "Evan. Rumor has it you plan to open some sort of dining establishment here in the kingdom."

"The rumor is correct, Your Highness," I said, choosing not to expand upon my answer. The less this dickwad knew, the better. I didn't trust him one bit.

"Interesting." Cedric's gaze roamed my body in a way that made me uncomfortable. "Well, I do hope it works in your favor."

"Thank you, Your Highness."

His smile turned cunning. "I see our lessons didn't go to waste. Your uncouth mouth learned to behave. If only the same could be said about that indignant stare. Progress is progress, I suppose. Though, for your sake, you should improve upon this and soon. I may not always be in such a forgiving mood."

Maddox tensed at my side. Briar did too. Neither of them liked how the crown prince spoke to me but couldn't say a word without risking being thrown into shackles or, worse, beheaded. Because this sleazy, cocky prick wouldn't think twice before executing someone for simply looking at him in the wrong way.

Cedric turned to Sawyer. "Enjoy the rest of the festival, baby brother." His gaze hardened when landing on Kuya. "And do try to keep that beast under control. We don't need it biting anyone or thieving."

Kuya's ears went all the way back. One of his hands curled, his nails digging into his palm so hard it drew blood.

"He is no harm to anyone." Sawyer placed a hand on Kuya's shoulder, and he instantly relaxed.

"See to it that it stays that way." The royal pain in the ass then continued forward, his guards falling into step behind him.

"Let me see," Sawyer gently said, holding out his hand. Kuya uncurled his fist and displayed his palm. "You're bleeding."

"Allow me, Your Highness," Briar said and waited for Sawyer to nod before approaching. He took Kuya's hand in his, and a soft white light filled the gaps between them.

"Your magic is impressive, physician," Sawyer said, examining Kuya's palm afterward. "You don't even require the use of tonics now."

"You are much too kind, Your Highness," Briar responded. "I can only use basic healing spells for minor wounds. Tonics are still needed for more severe injuries."

"For now." Sawyer smiled at him. "When we first met, you couldn't perform even the basic healing spells. Yet you worked day and night to find a cure for me when no other physician was able."

"You were sick?" I asked, shocked. It never occurred to me to ask how Briar became the court physician at such a young age. He was only thirty-two. I had assumed he'd been at the top of his class and had been given the position because of his academics.

"Yes," Sawyer answered. "I was a sickly child, often having to spend my days in bed while other kids were allowed to go outside and play. When I was seven, I nearly died. Healers from all over the lands came to Bremloc to try to cure me, to no avail. But Briar refused to give up on me. He managed to brew an elixir that restored my health and earned my father's respect and eternal gratitude. He was soon assigned as the court physician and has faithfully served my family and our knights ever since."

A flush crept to Briar's cheeks. Maddox smirked and gently bumped against him.

"He's kind of amazing like that," I said, smiling at my sexy physician, whose blush deepened, so apparent on his pale skin.

"He is," Sawyer agreed, then reached for Kuya's hand. "I met Kuya two years later."

Sawyer didn't need to clarify his meaning. If he'd died, he wouldn't have been with Cedric when Kuya was found. Kuya would've undoubtedly been executed as a result. Briar, in a way, had saved both of their lives.

"What about you?" I asked Maddox. "Any big heroic deed that made you the captain of the Second Order?"

"Only my strength and fortitude," he responded.

"Permission to speak, Your Highness?" Noah asked from behind Sawyer.

"Of course, Sir Noah."

Noah stepped forward. His black hair reminded me of raven's wings in sunlight, hints of blue throughout the strands. "Before he earned his position, Captain Maddox saved many lives in the dark wood. Several units had been dispersed to ward off a demon hoard heading for the kingdom, and the captain of the Second Order was slain by an upper-level demon, leaving the unit without a leader. Those of us in the First Order had been ordered to ride out and aid them. When we arrived, knights were dropping one by one, the death toll only climbing as panic ensued even with reinforcements. But I was present in those woods when Captain Maddox shouted for everyone to listen. He then took charge and led us into victory. If not for him, I wouldn't be standing here today. Neither would many other knights."

"Why am I just now learning this?" I glanced between the two men who had stolen my heart. "You two are freaking heroes."

"You never asked." Maddox shrugged.

"I wouldn't say I'm a hero," Briar said.

They were both too modest. The handsome dorks.

"Kuya is hungry." The cat boy rubbed his tanned belly, wearing another of his crop tops, this one a dark green with brown leather straps fastening together the front.

Sawyer's eyes crinkled at the edges as he placed a hand on Kuya's back. "Anything sound good?"

"Cake!" Kuya flashed a toothy grin that showed off his sharp canines.

I laughed under my breath. No surprise there.

"Oh, on the subject of cake," Sawyer said, glancing at me. "I spoke to my father, and he believes an establishment like the one you intend to open would be beneficial to Bremloc's growth and prosperity."

"Really?" My voice rose in pitch, like it always did when I was excited.

"Yes. He will grant you an audience soon to discuss the matter further."

Yeah, my excitement dropped right into my gut. "Your father... the *king*... wants to speak to *me*. Like one-on-one?"

Sawyer laughed. "Don't look so frightened, my friend. It will be all right, I promise. But for now?" He grabbed Kuya's hand. "Let's enjoy the festival."

***

The setting sun inched closer to the mountain in the distance, replacing sections of blue sky with shades of orange and gold. The lampposts lining the street flickered on, and other lights blinked on among the rows of tents and market stands, some using oil and others magic.

"It's nearly time for the lanterns," Briar said.

"Someone looks excited," Maddox said, eyes on me. "Do you have a specific wish you hope will be granted?"

"A wish?"

"Yes." Briar guided us through the square and toward the park filled with magnolia trees, the blossoms vibrant even in the fading daylight. "You write your wishes down and send them with the lantern when it lifts into the air. It's believed that by sending it away, you're also ridding yourself of negativity and ensuring good luck for the coming months."

"That's a nice thought," I said. "We had something similar in my old worl—er, kingdom. We did it at the end of the year though."

"The space of time between one season and another holds magic powerful enough to grant wishes," Briar then said. "Or so many believe."

Wishes. Like the one I spoke when clutching the stone. The one that sent me to Bremloc.

Lupin.

I searched the crowd for him. He had said he'd meet me during the festival, to either reverse my wish and send me back to my old life or to make it official and allow me to stay in this world forever. That's when I caught a glimmer of pale blond hair.

Lupin met my gaze from between the magnolia trees and tipped his head to me. He then turned and walked toward the edge of the park, disappearing among the thick greenery.

He wanted me to follow him.

Sneaking away from Maddox and Briar unnoticed was impossible. Even amidst their current banter session—something about which snack I'd prefer between chocolate-covered pecans and caramel candy—their gazes occasionally darted to me. Always aware of me. I could invite them along, but that would require a ton of explaining. An explanation they may or may not believe. Or accept.

"Um." I wrung my hands together. "Will you guys be okay if I step away for a few minutes?"

"Where are you going?" Maddox asked.

"Over there." I nodded to the denser section of trees.

"Why?"

"Just… because."

Briar frowned. "If there's somewhere you wish to go, we'll accompany you."

"No, it's okay. I can go by myself. But I won't be gone long, and I promise I won't fall or hurt myself in any way. Or, you know, get kidnapped."

"I'm going with you," Maddox said without hesitation.

Briar watched me for a second before looking at Maddox. "We can't smother him. He's not a child."

"You say smothering, and I say protecting. Or have you forgotten all the times he's returned from a trip to the woods covered in scrapes and cuts?"

"Please," I said, voice breaking a bit. "I... I need to do this alone."

What Maddox saw in my expression right then? I didn't know. But he accepted whatever it was and gave a curt nod. "We'll be waiting here for you. Be careful."

"I will." I kissed both of them on the lips before turning away. I felt their gazes on me as I walked in the direction Lupin had gone.

The path through the trees was short and led to a small pond. Lily pads floated on top of the gleaming surface, reflecting the glow of lightning bugs. Trees with long branches touched the edge of the water, and thick vines with small white flowers grew between them.

"Good evening," Lupin greeted me from where he stood on the grassy bank, one hand behind his back and the other at his side. "I take it you have an answer for me?"

"Yeah." I joined him on the bank and stared across the water. "But first, I want to apologize."

"For what?"

"I was so freaked-out when I first got here that I never got the chance to thank you." I looked at him. "So, thank you, Lupin. For everything. This has been the best month of my life."

"Does this mean you want to stay?"

"I think you already know the answer."

He smiled. "There are no certainties, only probabilities. I hoped you'd come to see this land as your home. Your presence will better the lives of many people here, just as they will better yours."

My chin wobbled as I focused back on the pond. A tiny frog leapt off a lily pad, causing a little *bloop* in the water. "I do see this as my home."

"Even if it means saying goodbye to your old life for good?"

"Yeah. I mean, this is a big decision. Knowing I can't ever return, the finality of it, is kinda scary. But what scares me more? Never seeing Briar's smile again or hearing Maddox laugh. Never holding them again. But it's more than that too." I forced words past the burning in my throat. "I'd miss Callum and the knights. I'd miss playing with Kuya and having tea with Sawyer. I've come to care about so many people here and would be devastated to leave them."

I thought of Lake, too, with his sad purple eyes. I barely knew him but felt tied to him as well. Just as I was tied to all the other people who'd come into my life.

"I'm exactly where I want to be," I said. "Can I ask a question though?"

"Of course," he said.

"What will happen in my old world? Am I a missing person? I don't have many friends, but I don't want Jonah worrying about me."

Lupin's smile turned a bit sad. "Your decision to stay here set things into motion. Anyone who's ever met you will soon forget you existed. Every memory of you will be erased."

"Wow. That's kind of depressing." But it was for the best. If no one remembered I existed, they couldn't miss me.

"Does this change your mind?" he asked.

"No." I touched the center of my chest. "This is where I wanna be."

"My work here is done, then." Lupin offered me a kind smile. "Enjoy this life to the fullest, Evan. Don't let a single moment go to waste."

"I won't." I watched as he pulled out a silver pocket watch. "Is that how you travel between realms?"

"Perhaps." He cocked his head at me. "Is there something else you wish to ask me before I go?"

Damn, he was good. Or maybe I was just obvious.

"You mentioned once that I'd have multiple lovers here." Saying those words aloud sounded so freaking weird.

"Five," he said. "Briar, Maddox, and three others."

"Is Lake one of them?" I asked.

"Do you wish for him to be?"

"I don't know." And I really didn't. "I'm happy with Briar and Maddox."

When Lupin smiled again, there was a touch of mystery to it. "As I said earlier, there are no certainties. Every choice you make will lead you down one path or cause you to veer away from it. Allow me to give you a word of caution though. One of the three other males meant to love you also has an alternate, less favorable path with which you are bound."

"What do you mean?"

Lupin's expression shadowed. "He will either love you… or be the cause of your death."

"Wait. What?" I squeaked. "My death? One of them is going to kill me? Which one? When will I know? What the hell, Lupin?"

"Calm down," he said.

"You want me to calm down? You just said one of my potential future lovers is *going to kill me*."

"No, I said, he *might* kill you."

"Oh, thanks. That's so much more reassuring." My stomach was in knots.

"Does this knowledge change your decision to stay?"

"No," I answered without a second's thought. "I mean, I could just as easily be hit by a truck crossing the road in my old world. It still doesn't make me feel all warm and toasty though."

"There's a chance you may not even meet him. As I said—"

"Yeah, yeah, no certainties, blah, blah." I inhaled and sharply released the breath. Then did it again to try to calm my racing heart.

There was a one out of three chance it could be Lake. But beneath his distrust of others and bouts of defensiveness, he had a gentle soul. I felt it. That left two others. Maybe my wish for the lantern should be to never meet my maybe-murderer.

"Try not to dwell on it," Lupin said, pulling me from my whirling thoughts. He glanced at the pocket watch again. "Go enjoy the festival with those you love. You have two men eagerly awaiting your return."

Okay, now *that* thought made me all warm and toasty. And as Lupin said, I might not even meet the dude who may or may not turn me into worm food.

It was a worry for another day.

I walked toward the path but turned back as I reached the trees. Lupin was already gone. Had the watch zapped him to a different realm? Or maybe it had taken him back to Saint, where they'd spend the night wrapped in each other's arms.

Just like I planned to do with the men *I* loved.

I continued down the short pathway, not surprised in the least to find two familiar faces on the other side. Maddox leaned against a magnolia tree, his arms crossed over his wide chest, and Briar fiddled with a lantern.

"Good to see you in one piece," Maddox muttered.

"He's salty you wouldn't let us come with you," Briar said. "I told him you'd be fine."

"Yet you kept looking at the trees and fiddling with—" Maddox motioned to the lantern. More were at Briar's feet. "—all of those."

"They needed to be set up so we can write our messages and light them." Briar pushed his glasses up his nose. "You could've made yourself useful and helped, Captain."

"My very presence is useful."

"Okay, you two," I said with a laugh. "Let's go light these babies up."

Briar reached for me, and I slipped my hand inside his. "I know the perfect place." He distributed the paper lanterns, handing one to each of us.

"What's it made of?" I asked, petting the crinkly outside.

"Rice paper with a bamboo frame," Briar said, leading us from the park and toward a small hill. As we went up it, my shoe slipped on the grass.

Maddox barked out a laugh as he grabbed me. He then pulled me closer and put his mouth at my ear. "My clumsy muffin."

"Half of that muffin is mine." Briar rested a hand on my waist.

"But a bigger half is mine," Maddox whispered.

Briar scoffed. "It's unwise to anger me, Captain. I'm incredibly knowledgeable of poisons and deadly plants. It would be a shame if one happened to find its way into your breakfast."

"You'd miss me too much," Maddox said, letting go of me with one arm and placing it around Briar instead. "Just admit it."

Briar swallowed hard, his eyes dropping to Maddox's lips. "You wish."

I smiled and snuggled between the two of them. "Speaking of wishes, what will you guys wish for tonight?"

"You're not supposed to tell." Briar winked at me. "Or else it won't come true."

We reached the top of the hill just as the first lantern lifted into the sky. An orange glow radiated from inside the cream-colored material.

"Kuya found you!" a voice exclaimed from behind me. I barely had time to turn before Kuya pounced on me, not knocking me over, but almost. The huge muscled knight at my side steadied my balance. Kuya grinned. "Are you ready to send your sky lantern to the stars? Be sure to whisper your wishes so it can tell the gods."

Sawyer crested the hill, a smile breaking across his face. "May we join you?"

"Of course, Your Highness," Briar said. "It would be an honor."

"The honor is mine." Sawyer handed a lantern to Kuya, who instantly tried to bite it. His smile softened as he petted Kuya's hair.

"Do you want to write a message first?" Briar asked me. "I have a quill if you do."

"No," I said, so happy I could burst. "I don't need to make a wish. I have everything I want right here."

"As do I." He caressed my cheek.

Maddox caught me around the waist and pecked kisses down my nape, making me giggle.

"Bring Kuya cake," the cat boy told his lantern in a loud whisper before waiting for Sawyer to light it for him. His rainbow eyes widened as the lantern floated upward.

The rest of us then lit the candle wicks and released our lanterns into the air. Maddox held me on one side, and Briar was on my other. I felt them touch each other too, their arms behind my back, connecting the three of us.

Something silver caught my eye from the trees on the other side of the hill. Lake stood against one, his face tilted to the sky as he watched the floating lanterns. In the dark, his purple eyes softly glowed.

"I told you he'd return," Briar whispered in my ear.

"He can stay there." Maddox lightly huffed. He then nuzzled my neck. "Is it wrong to fight to the death over a muffin?"

"Oh, stop," I said, then giggled again as he pecked more kisses against my skin.

As the two of them held me, I watched two lanterns gently bump each other and drift apart. When I looked back at the trees, Lake was gone. But somehow, I knew he was still nearby. Still watching the lanterns he thought were so beautiful.

Where would life take me next? I didn't know. But for once, I was having my own adventures instead of just reading about them.

And I couldn't wait to see where this new life would take me next, with the men I cherished by my side.

The End... For Now

About the Author

When not writing, Jaclyn can be found drinking a ridiculous amount of coffee, binging anime, and inhaling manga like oxygen. The men in her head never leave her alone, but she doesn't want them to. Writing is her passion and she's thankful for each day she's able to live her dream.

All types of genres interest her. She has written contemporary, urban fantasy, paranormal, and historical.

Other Books by Jaclyn Osborn

Standalone
Brighter Shades of Light (college professor/student)
Frost (MM Jack Frost retelling)
Perfectly Us
Cheater and the Saint
Tangled Up In You

Sons of the Fallen Series
Galen
Castor
Daman
Gray
Bellamy
Raiden
Alastair
Beyond the Storm (A Companion Novel)

Tales of Fate Series
Found at Sea
The Nymph Prince
A Warrior's Heart

Historical
Axios: A Spartan Tale
Eryx: A Spartan Tale

Ivy Grove Series
The Ghost of Ellwood
The Curse of Redwood

A Blue Harbor Romance Series
Topping the Jock
Dating the Boss

Unexpected Love Series
His Temptation
His Surrender
His Courage

Christmas
Hensley Manor
A Gift of Time

Love in Addersfield Series
Declan
Royal

Port Haven Series (YA)
Noah's Song
Reaching Avery

Printed in Great Britain
by Amazon